BOOK PEOPLE

ALSO BY PAIGE NICK

Unpresidented (2017)
Dutch Courage (2016)
Death by Carbs (2015)
Pens Behaving Badly (2015)
This Way Up (2011)
A Million Miles from Normal (2010)

Co-authored with Sarah Lotz and Helen Moffett
A Girl Walks into a Bar
A Girl Walks into a Wedding
A Girl Walks into a Blind Date

BOOK PEOPLE

A Novel by Paige Nick

MACMILLAN

First published in 2025
by Pan Macmillan South Africa
Private Bag X19
Northlands
Johannesburg
2116

www.panmacmillan.co.za

ISBN 978-1-77010-906-3
e-ISBN 978-1-77010-907-0

© 2025 Paige Nick

All rights reserved. No part of this publication may be reproduced, stored in or introduced into a retrieval system, or transmitted, in any form or by any means (electronic, mechanical, photocopying, recording or otherwise), without the prior written permission of the publisher. Any person who does any unauthorised act in relation to this publication may be liable to criminal prosecution and civil claims for damages.

This book is a work of fiction. Names, characters, businesses, organisations, places and events are either the product of the author's imagination, used with permission, or are used fictitiously. Any resemblance to actual persons, living or dead, events or locales is entirely coincidental.

Editing by Helen Moffett
Proofreading by Jane Bowman
Design and typesetting by Nyx Design
Cover design by CTB Design
Author photo by Luca Pace

Printed by novus print, a division of Novus Holdings

For all the members of the actual, real-life
Good Book Appreciation Society on Facebook.
Who are a trillion times nicer than the
members of this entirely (mostly) fictional group.

PROLOGUE

WEST MERCIA POLICE INTERVIEW TRANSCRIPT

NORMA JACOBS: I never wanted to run a book club. Or any club. I think you should know that from the start.

DS SNOPES: And yet, you ended up running one with over ninety thousand members?

NORMA JACOBS: I honestly don't know how I got here. I'm not very sociable, I don't even drink wine. And Isn't wine nine-tenths of the point of a book club?

DS SNOPES: I wouldn't know, I've never belonged to one.

NORMA JACOBS: I know a woman who just cuts to the chase and calls hers a 'book pub'.

DS SNOPES: So, you don't like book clubs?

NORMA JACOBS: A book club of one might be fun.

DS SNOPES: I suspect that might defeat the object.

NORMA JACOBS: The nice thing about reading, if you ask me, is that it's not a spectator sport.

DS SNOPES: So, let me get this straight: you don't like book clubs, and never wanted to run one, and don't particularly like people, and yet, here you are, running a large, and recently quite controversial one?

NORMA JACOBS: It was an accident.

DS SNOPES: You'd better tell me about that.

NORMA JACOBS: Oh, not the same kind of accident Edna Molton had. Nothing criminal like that.

DS SNOPES: No?

NORMA JACOBS: God, no! In the beginning, there were just three of us, a perfectly reasonable amount of people for a book club. We met at work – Megan, Priya and me. A miracle already, since I barely talk to anyone at work. But none of us are so great with people and all of us really like books, so we gravitated towards each other. When Priya left to go to another firm, I started the group on Facebook so we could still talk about what we were reading. Megan came up with the name, The Good Book Appreciation Society. Then, because Facebook is exponential, other people started joining, which was when Megan and Priya left the group, because why would two introverts stay when there are all these people there? And nine years and one controversy later, here we are.

DS SNOPES: And you run the club alone?

NORMA JACOBS: Honestly, it's less stressful to just do it myself than it is to work with other people.

BOOK PEOPLE

DS SNOPES: Sounds like a lot of work.

NORMA JACOBS: That's what Steve always said.

DS SNOPES: Steve Watson, your boyfriend?

NORMA JACOBS: Ex-boyfriend! Not because he's dead or anything, we just broke up. He has this thing about the club needing to make money. He doesn't get it. Money's not what it's about, it's about books and reading ... sorry, I'm rambling.

DS SNOPES: Yes, let's get back on track. I asked if running the club is a big job?

NORMA JACOBS: Not so bad, a bit time-consuming. The members are pretty well behaved.

DS SNOPES: Nobody argues on the page?

NORMA JACOBS: Well, no, of course they argue. Everyone has an opinion on everything. But, isn't that the point of a book club? Some people love a particular book or author, others hate it, then things get heated, because everyone always thinks their opinion is right. Especially online.

DS SNOPES: I thought you said they were 'pretty well behaved'?

NORMA JACOBS: They are, on the whole. The page tends to be informally community-managed. The members like to tell tales, report each other. If someone posts something that goes against the group guidelines, or something bullying or what they consider rude or racist or politically incorrect or out of line, or sometimes even just an opinion opposed to their own, then I'll get a dozen members reporting the post or comment.

DS SNOPES: And then what happens?

NORMA JACOBS: I have a couple of options. I can close the comments or delete anything that goes against our community standards.

DS SNOPES: Which are?

NORMA JACOBS: The kinds of things you'd expect. We're opposed to racism, violence, hate speech, posting spam, that kind of thing. My most extreme recourse is to remove an offender from the group and block them from ever rejoining if they do something really wrong. But in the case of an argument between members, or if someone feels particularly outraged, they usually leave a stinking comment and then remove themselves from the group. They want the last word. Essentially, they stomp out of the virtual room in a huff and slam the virtual door behind them.

DS SNOPES: And is this virtual stomping and slamming of doors what Harry Shields chose to do?

NORMA JACOBS: ... Um ...

DS SNOPES: Ms Jacobs?

NORMA JACOBS: (Sighs) If it was, you wouldn't be here questioning me about a crime, would you?

THREE WEEKS EARLIER

THE GOOD BOOK APPRECIATION SOCIETY

MEMBERS: 12 994

Harry Shields: Book Review – *The Dangerous Path*, by Anthony P. Harker

© Harry Shields

The Dangerous Path is Anthony P. Harker's debut novel. The hero of this sprawling drama is Marcus, a Wall Street banker, living the American dream. Until late one night in 2007, when he's faced with the opportunity to either prevent the global financial crisis **OR** further his career and make a fortune. But here's the catch; he can only pick one. And so the tension builds.

The Dangerous Path has a compelling plot, with vivid characters and themes that feel more like current events than fiction. This debut is that rare thing; a great sprawling American novel. The kind that only pops up every decade or so.

If you've already read *The Dangerous Path* and are looking for something similar, but with a British twist, I think you'll love my second novel, *Once on a Tuesday*, published by Victory Books. Both share ambitious writing and a compelling page-turning plot. If you liked the one, you should love the other. And you don't have to take my word for it, the *Sunday Times* gave *Once on a Tuesday* two thumbs up, and called it 'a post-political story for our times, told with empathy, truth and guts.'

I'd say read 'em both!

COMMENTS:

Chris Colt: I loved The Dangerous Path. Thanks for the heads up, will look out for your novel @Harry Shields.

Ruth Burstein: It was a bit too testosterone-filled for me, but if you like that kind of thing, more power to you.

Chris Colt: @Ruth Burstein, are you one of those feminist types? Gotta say, I'm a fan of a bit of testosterone. I'm looking forward to the read.

Ruth Burstein: @Chris Colt, are you even serious? I'm not going to waste my breath on you.

Geneva Fulverton: @Harry Shields, it feels like you wrote that entire review of 'a great American novel' just so you could punt your own book as 'a great British novel'. Oh, to have the confidence of a middle-aged white male author. And you, @Chris Colt, I don't even know where to start.

Shanti Khumar: Has the world not moved on from this echo-chamber-aspiration to write the Great American Novel? How dull and muscular. Honestly, I'm way more interested in a great Serbian novel, or a great, African, Indian or Middle Eastern one.

Chris Colt: But then you would say that @Shanti Khumar.

[Freda Kruger has reported this comment.]

Sylvia Strain: Even if you say so yourself @Harry Shields.

Felicitas Gonzalez: Self-promo alert.

Shireen Worcestershire-Watts: Is it fiction or non-fiction?

Harry

Feeling smug about his deftly camouflaged book punt, Harry refreshed his inbox. Nothing. He stared at the screen for a moment, then refreshed again, in case an email from his agent had arrived between refreshes. Technology was getting faster all the time.

Still nothing.

He checked his phone. Myra had last been on WhatsApp three minutes earlier. And he had last WhatsApped her three days earlier. But there was still no blue tick on his message. His query 'Hi Myra, did you get it?' was suspended in purgatory.

If a WhatsApp lands in a mobile phone, and nobody reads it, did it ever even arrive?

Perhaps she'd deactivated her blue ticks. For all he knew, she was drafting an email to him that second. Even better, drafting one to the slew of publishers who would get into a rabid bidding war the minute they discovered Harry Shields had delivered the manuscript of his third novel.

He just-in-case-refreshed again. And there it was, one new email downloading ... slowly.

Of course, when it came through an agonising three seconds later, it wasn't from Myra Berelowitz, agent to the writing stars. It was spam from a big book chain, trying to flog him a copy of Anthony P. Harker's novel, *The Dangerous Path*. His friend Phyllis might be a rampant conspiracy theorist, but she was right about one thing: the internet was always watching and listening to everything you said or typed. Like a drunken uncle, picking up a few words, but never the whole context.

Harry trashed the spam, then refreshed his inbox again. When nothing else materialised, he clicked over to Microsoft Word and the manuscript for his latest novel, *The Wednesday Protocol*. He scrolled to the end – page 528 – and re-read the last chapter.

He wasn't wrong, he thought, as he scrolled over the last few lines, this was good writing. As good, if not better, than anything he'd ever written. So why hadn't he heard back from Myra yet? Insecurity pricked at him. What if she was losing interest in him?

But perhaps he was just being unreasonable? After all, globally respected agents were busy people. They didn't read manuscripts in five days, even ones by award-nominated authors. There was likely a queue of manuscripts on her desk. As well as launches and lunches to attend, deals to make, publishers to schmooze, other authors to manage. Although the thought of Myra having other authors hurt Harry's feelings. He preferred to imagine a world where he was Myra's main focus. But the reality was that one marginally successful, award-nominated, soon-to-be award-winning author in the barn did not a stable make.

Harry closed the manuscript document and tried to put it out of his mind. He had plenty to distract himself with while waiting for feedback from Myra. The Golden Page Awards were coming up, and he needed to get going on his acceptance speech. Sales may have been skittish on his second novel, but the awards judges would see through that to his raw talent, he was sure of it. And once he'd won, imagine how his sales would soar.

Harry shook out his hands, opened a new document, then cricked his neck on both sides as he considered the blank page and flashing cursor.

He had to make sure he thanked all the right people when he won his award. Those Oscar speeches often went viral when the actor thanked the great lord above or their agent, bull terrier, giant koi, Zen master, astral reader, personal trainer, mother and co-stars, but then forgot to thank their spouse. It was practically legal grounds for divorce in LA. Harry wouldn't let that happen. His speech would be powerful but funny, charming and endearing, but also self-deprecating – nobody liked a winner who took themselves too seriously. Striking the right note wasn't going to be easy.

People never expected a dental hygienist or interior designer to deliver a ground-breaking speech, but when you were a writer, even something as simple as writing a note in the communal office birthday card was loaded with expectations. You couldn't just say 'Have a good one, mate.' People wanted witticisms and originality. And then there were his future archives to consider. One day he would donate his work, including his notebooks, journals, correspondence and of course speeches and greeting cards, to a museum or library – the British Library, if they played their cards right. So the quality and heft of every word was crucial. His awards speech needed to be worthy of an award in its own right.

Harry steepled his fingers and leaned back in his Herman Miller Sayl, arguably the most ergonomic writer's chair in the world. His study was lined with books, and he scanned the shelves for inspiration. He'd run out of space years ago, and now books had to be jammed in sideways on top of other books, which had thrown out his alphabetical system. There were also chaotic sub-stacked book piles next to his bed, on every table and ledge, and up against the walls in the lounge of their townhouse in Ealing, lending it, he thought, an academic air.

His wife, Victoria, was also a reader, although not as voracious as he was, mostly because as a surgeon, she didn't have the time. Her tastes leant to non-fiction. An additional problem, as they couldn't share books, stacks or shelves, which further aggravated their shelf-shortage situation.

The Unveiling by Aaqel Abus caught Harry's eye. Now there was a classic. Astonishingly good, vivid, sharp, the stuff of publishing legend.

Harry recalled watching a panel with the author at a literary festival years earlier. During the Q&A at the end of the panel, a man in the audience said he'd been a leader in a political group calling to have Abus's book banned and burned when it first came out. Standing there, more than a decade later, the man apologised to Abus, saying he'd since read the book, and thought it excellent. He said that looking back, he didn't know what all the fuss had been about.

Harry agreed. Abus's book was exceptional. The author made it seem easy. But then isn't that how it was with all good writing? Seemingly effortless. Like Olympic-level ice skating. You watched the pros, then put on skates and imagined you'd also glide – only to wind up in a moon boot for six to eight weeks.

Abus's book had changed the world. At the very least, it had changed the world's view of the challenges women living in the Middle East faced. A book any author could only dream of writing. It was almost annoying how good it was.

He decided to review it on The Good Book Appreciation Society page. That would distract him from the Myra drought. Plus it would make an excellent writing exercise to get him in the mood to tackle his award acceptance speech.

Harry clicked back to Chrome to check how many likes and comments his earlier review-slash-book punt had received on The Good Book Appreciation Society. Scanning them, he mumbled at the haters, preened at the fans, appreciated Chris Colt's great taste in books (despite his questionable social skills), then logged out of his Facebook account and logged straight back in as one of his online alter egos, Gaill A.

THE GOOD BOOK APPRECIATION SOCIETY

MEMBERS: 12 995

Gaill A: This is not a new book, but I've been so busy working on my MBA, I'm ashamed to admit that I only just got around to reading *The Unveiling* by Aaqel Abus.

This book has won dozens of awards, has been lauded by critics and praised by readers the world over, and is regularly referred to as one of the greatest classics of our time.

It came out in 1992 and was subsequently banned in several countries. And the author received numerous death threats that forced him out of public life for over two decades.

Honestly, I can see why the author went into hiding. If I'd written a load of rubbish like this, I also wouldn't want to show my face around the literary water cooler.

Perhaps we were so starved of political and social insight then that we overlooked the technicalities of good writing? Today we certainly expect more from our pacing. This was sluggish and stylistically flawed.

I get what an important topic this is; however, this feels like a case of the

Emperor's new clothes. A few big names said it was great, and the rest of the world just nodded their heads in time to the music. But I believe a critical reader should be able to put subject matter aside, stand up and be objective. The writing was poor, and I struggled to make it to the end of this plodding, bloated, boring, over-hyped piece of schlock.

COMMENTS:

Ruth Burstein: I haven't read the book, but I applaud your honesty, @Gaill A. So often people are scared to be truthful about a book that's won an award, or a book that's had critical acclaim, or a lot of press. We need more honest reviewers out there, like yourself.

Avukile Chingwita: Precisely, we aren't sheep, we are readers.

Shireen Worcestershire-Watts: What a weird comparison. Sheep can't even read.

Shanti Khumar: What is wrong with you all? When this book was banned Abus was scared for his life. He and his family had to leave their home and go into hiding for years. Dozens of people went to jail just for reading it. Many lost their livelihoods, some their lives, trying to defend the right to freedom of speech over this book. It might just be one of the most important works of our time, highlighting the plight of people forced to live under the brutal rule of dictators and tyrants. @Gaill A, your review is more of an indictment of you than it is of this author.

Harry Shields: Having a book banned and getting death threats can't be easy, but I bet the PR does wonders for book sales.

Geneva Fulverton: You wish you had death threats, @Harry Shields? You wouldn't be so keen on them if you got a few and had people coming after you.

Shanti Khumar: @Harry Shields, your comment minimises the trauma thousands of courageous people are still forced to endure to this day. Those brave souls whose lives are threatened for whistle-blowing, taking a brave political stance while under violent regimes or protecting those more vulnerable than themselves. I don't think it's something to take so lightly.

Harry Shields: Shoot me down if you want, but as an author myself, I would rather people were offended by my book, talked about it, burnt it, even threatened me over it, as opposed to ignoring it.

Shanti Khumar: Oh you're an author are you? None of us would have known, since you haven't told us here already a thousand times! Congratulations again for being *an author*.

Geneva Fulverton: If @Harry Shields carries on like this, @Shanti Khumar, he might just get the death threats he's always dreamed of. 'Shoot me down' indeed.

Norma

Norma hummed a few notes of '9 to 5' by Dolly Parton, as she tidied her desk and packed her laptop bag.

'Night, Mac, don't work too late,' she said as she passed her colleague's desk on her way out. They were the only ones left in the office. The rest of the chairs were practically still spinning from the five pm stampede.

'Cheers Nora,' he said, raising a hand.

'It's NORMA, you prat,' she mumbled to herself as she stabbed the lift button. 'We've only been working together for seven years.'

Fifteen minutes later, on the standing-room-only Tube, Norma scrolled The Good Book Appreciation Society Facebook Page. She usually checked in on the group several times a day; first thing in the morning before doing the *Guardian* crossword, then on the Tube on her way to work, mid-morning while she was making a cup of tea, then during her lunch break and again on the Tube going home, and a few more times in the evening. It was more like having a baby than a hobby.

The page was busy, with four or five new posts a day, ranging from book reviews to comments about the reading life, chatter about anticipated new releases, book recommendations, book queries, or members crowd-sourcing what to read or listen to next. Each of these posts resulting in anything from two to a hundred and two comments. Sometimes fun, sometimes serious, often interesting, every now and then argumentative. And then there were the direct messages which filtered through to her inbox, from members wanting all sorts of things from Norma as the page's admin.

In general, Norma thought Facebook was a toxic sinkhole of bad behaviour, political and religious overkill, propaganda, questionable opinions, and unsolicited pet and kid overshares. She only stuck around to manage the group. She had no interest in making new friends or following people, commenting and liking. Anyway, who was there to follow? Since she'd emigrated to London fifteen years ago, she'd gradually lost touch with most of her old South African friends, and her mum wasn't online at all. Her best friend, Marina, wasn't on social media, and the rest of Norma's family circle was covered by a few WhatsApp group configurations. So that just left the people she worked with, or had been at school with a zillion years earlier, and she sincerely hoped she'd never run into any of them again, virtually or in real life.

Norma scanned the new reviews that had popped up on the page; they were mostly of mid-range women's fiction titles, one self-help title, and a review from an author on the group. Harry was one of those guys who regularly punted his own work on the page. He just couldn't self-help himself. And this latest post was his most brazen, blatant self-promo yet, barely disguised as a book review.

An author telling you how good their book is? How original. It's like a mother telling you how talented her child is. Of course she would, and of course the child wouldn't be.

Norma couldn't understand why the authors on the group didn't step back and let the readers do the heavy lifting for them. Surely it was obvious, even to a narcissistic writer, that unsolicited word of mouth praise, from an honest fan, with no ulterior motives other than a great recommendation from the heart, had to be more effective than over-baked self-promotion?

Norma scanned another new review on the page which was also getting attention. A member had eviscerated that famous novel by

Aaqel Abus, and was taking some heat over it. Norma had only ever read rave reviews of this novel and had thought it excellent when she'd first read it. It was a modern classic.

People were so strange, she thought, as she clicked through to her direct messages and eyed the girl wearing a onesie and Mickey Mouse ears sitting in the next seat.

Her first new direct message was from a member, @Marco Remo.

> hi
> i wud like to pblish a book how do i go abt doing tht?

Norma laughed, gave her spectacles a nudge, then scanned the next new DM, from an @Anne Merring.

> Hello GBAS Admin,
> I'm attaching my space opera to this mail for you to read. It is 250 000 words and is the first in a trilogy. As you love books so much, I am sure you will want to help me find a publisher and am hoping you'll agree to edit it in exchange for a share (say 1%) of my future royalties. I know for a fact that this book will be a bestseller. This little nugget will make you an instant millionaire. Offers like this don't land in your inbox every day.

'Really? You'd be surprised,' Norma said aloud, and the woman with the Mickey Mouse ears, who was shamelessly reading over her shoulder, tutted her agreement, as Norma moved on to her last unread message.

> Hello Norma, you don't know me but I'm a member of your book club, The Good Book Appreciation Society. My new novel is a heartbreaking saga about a war widow caught in a time warp, who falls in love with a horse, who is actually

the trapped soul of her dead husband. Please can I send you a copy of the novel, so you can review it on The Good Book Appreciation Society page? I can offer you a bottle of wine (colour of your choice) as payment.

Running the club had been an education for Norma in books, publishing, people and their weirdnesses. She was regularly approached by people (with varying degrees of literacy) who had (or hadn't quite yet) written books, as well as people flogging everything from ball-point pens to bookmarks, writing workshops and laptop stands. Everybody seemed to confuse her with someone who had some influence in the publishing industry, rather than an accountant who liked to escape into books, and had accidentally started a book club because she felt lonely, unfulfilled and uninspired by her day job.

Thinking about her job, Norma allowed herself a small smile as she lugged her groceries and laptop to the flat she shared with her boyfriend, Steve. All she had to do was work up the courage to tell him the Big News. She'd been putting it off for weeks, despite the fact that her procrastination wasn't going to stop it happening. That Tube had left the station months earlier. Poor Steve. He didn't know what was coming, and she was certain he wasn't going to like it – as certain as she was that she would never enjoy a book about a dead husband's soul trapped in a horse.

Harry

Harry logged out of his Gaill A account and went to make coffee. Of course he didn't feel that way about the Abus book – it was a work of genius, but he found the freedom of anonymity cathartic. There was something deeply satisfying about being able to insult without repercussions. Slagging off the Abus had also made him feel better about not hearing back from Myra. Plus, he thought that line he'd written about the water cooler was golden.

Freshly brewed coffee by his side, writing muscles warmed, Harry felt ready to conquer his acceptance speech. Just as soon as he'd logged back into Facebook under another alias, to agree with his previous alias about the Abus, and then logged back in as himself, to post his own outrage at the post.

He might even start a thread on X or Threads about that perfectly disgusting Gaill A post, from his paid-for blue-ticked X profile, tagging the author and the publisher and including a trending hashtag, to see if he could get the whole shebang to go viral. Then they would all see how woke and #MeToo Harry Shields really was.

Harry's mobile rang, and when he saw Myra's name flash on the screen, he lurched for it, bumping his coffee cup, so that the boiling liquid sloshed into his keyboard and down his sleeve.

'Myra, I'm glad you called,' he said as he hopped around mopping up the coffee with the pages of an earlier draft of his manuscript, trying to sound casual, his voice an octave too high, his scalded arm stinging.

'You called me twelve times, Harold, I could hardly not,' Myra said.

Harry choked out an awkward laugh.

'I'm not joking, Harold. I count three missed calls on my mobile, two messages left with my PA, four emails, and seven WhatsApps in three days.'

Myra was the only person in the world who called him by his full name, other than his late mother, and Victoria when infuriated.

'Have you been arrested? Did you lose a foot? Are you terminal, Harold?'

'It's just ...' Harry stuttered, 'I sent you my manuscript, I wanted to make sure it's not stuck in your spam filter, and see what you thought of it?'

'You sent it three days ago, Harold.'

'Actually, it was five,' Harry interjected.

He could hear her taking a drag of her vape, and it brought on a sense memory of the smell of cloves that always hung about her.

'You can't possibly have thought I'd already read it?'

'Of course not,' Harry said with a fake chuckle, as he dabbed less intently at his keyboard.

'It's somewhere in the region of a hundred and twenty-seven thousand words, Harold.'

Harry felt like she had now said his name too many times.

'Anyway,' she sighed, 'well done on getting your magnum opus finished. I'm looking forward to scanning it at my earliest convenience.'

'I think you'll love it, Myra. Honestly, I believe this to be my finest work.'

'It's all lined up on my desk and I'll read it as soon as I get a gap, yes?'

'I look forward to hearing what you think, Myra.'

'But no more phone calls, alright Harold?' Myra said, a warning note in her voice. 'Otherwise I'll never have time to read it. Yes?'

'Yes Myra, thank you Myra,' Harry said, glad she couldn't see him flushing.

'Got to dash, I'm having dinner with Muriel Barbery ...'

And the line went dead.

Harry did a more focused coffee spill clean-up, applied an expired burn shield to his arm from their near-empty household first-aid kit, and thought about how the cobbler's children never had any shoes, and the surgeon's husband never had any ibuprofen.

Then he logged out of his Facebook profile and logged directly back in. This time as Bernard Phillips: retired octogenarian orthodontist from Bridgeport, Connecticut. With three ex-wives, four children, seven grandchildren and a vast Rolex collection. As well as a public penchant for literary fiction, and a more private side-interest in Wilbur Smith, Jeffrey Archer and John le Carré. Let nobody ever accuse Harold Shields of not fleshing out his characters thoroughly.

His acceptance speech would have to wait.

THE GOOD BOOK APPRECIATION SOCIETY

MEMBERS: 13 005

Bernard Phillips: I agree with that club member who reviewed the Abus earlier, I couldn't get through it either. But you know what I *have* been able to get through? Well, let me tell you, I'm three-quarters of the way through *Monday Never Comes*, the debut novel by our very own Harry Shields. And, dear reader, I cannot put it down.

Intriguing, thought-provoking, even thrilling. Effortlessly brilliant and brimming with big ideas, plot twists and intrigue. I would bill it as a contemporary literary thriller. I'm trying to read it slowly to make it last longer, but with a plot that whips along like wildfire, it's a difficult task. This has kept me up way past my bedtime. What a novel, what an author. Perfect weekend read. Highly recommend. Seven stars out of five. Back to it.

COMMENTS:

Michelle Zanders: Never heard of it. Will look it up.

Ruth Burstein: I generally don't like this kind of book. Middle-aged white guys trying to be edgy and current, but, as always, taking up too much space in the world.

Harry Shields: Have you read it yet, @Ruth Burstein? You might find you enjoy it.

Ruth Burstein: You're the author though, aren't you? So of course you would say that.

Geneva Fulverton: You're right @Ruth Burstein; fancies blowing his own horn, this one.

Norma

'Any chance of a hand with these bags?' Norma called out.

'You can fuck right off!' Steve yelled from the other room.

Norma screwed up her nose to stop her spectacles sliding down, and hummed 'I Can't Get No Satisfaction' by the Rolling Stones, as she lugged her groceries, handbag and laptop through the living room into the kitchen. Steve was on the couch, as to be expected, leaning into his laptop. He was wearing his big headphones, the ones with the microphone that made him look like a pilot for the national carrier of an Eastern European country.

Flecks of saliva flew out of his mouth as he swore and bashed at the keyboard. He didn't take his eyes off *Overwatch* as she walked past him. She could have been a naked burglar on a unicycle, juggling flaming chainsaws, and he still wouldn't have given her a glance.

'Oi-oi, when did you get home?' Steve asked, when he looked up ten minutes later.

'Good game?' Norma asked.

'Oh, you know …' Steve murmured as he took off his headphones, cruised into the kitchen and grabbed an apple as she was packing them into the fruit bowl.

'How'd the writing go today?' Norma asked.

'Excellent, just brilliant,' he said, taking a bite and chewing with his mouth open.

'Sarcastic much?' Norma said.

'Yeah, well, writing's not like that, Norma. You don't just sit down and bash out a couple of thousand words in a day.'

'I thought that was exactly what writing was like,' Norma said. 'You know, made up of time spent writing.'

'You're not a writer, you wouldn't understand,' Steve said, taking another bite, his mouth still full from the last bite.

'I think you'd be surprised what I understand,' Norma said. Like basic manners, she thought, but didn't say. 'What about job hunting? What's that like? Wait, let me guess, you don't just sit down and bash out a couple of job applications in a day?'

'Now you're catching on,' Steve said.

'So an unsuccessful writing and job-hunting day. Now what?'

'Curry takeout?' Steve suggested.

'You buying?' she asked.

'You're crabby. Did somebody's spreadsheets not add up at work today?'

'Oh, you know, you're not a worker, you wouldn't understand,' Norma said, shooting him a glare.

Later, as they ate their curries and watched some rubbish Steve was streaming, Norma considered opening her mouth and letting her Big News tumble out. She imagined how liberating it would feel to have it all out in the open. She glanced at Steve: he'd put on a stone since he'd stopped working, and his eyes were circled by the dark rings of gaming, vaping, insomnia and poor dietary decisions. She needed to tell him, but he was already in such a miserable mood, it seemed cruel to tell him something that would make him even more unhappy.

Norma pushed her takeaway container away. What did he have to be so cheerless about, anyway? It wasn't like he had a stressful job. He didn't spend fifteen hours a day in a sweatshop, there was always food in the fridge, a strong wifi signal, and batteries in the remote. Throw a pile of novels into the mix, and she would have been happily tucked up in their little flat in her pyjamas for years.

As she reached for her mobile to check in on The Good Book Appreciation Society, a WhatsApp pinged in from Marina.

> Tell him yet?

> Not yet.

> Chicken shit!

Marina always hit the nail hard and perfectly on the head.

> You're his twin sister and you know the news. Can't you use twin telepathy and transplant it straight from your head into his?

> We're not identical twins, so it doesn't work like that. Tell him already ffs!

Norma glanced at Steve, still at one with the couch. Neither of them had said a word in over forty-five minutes. She cleared her throat and quietly hummed a couple of notes of 'Breathe' by Faith Hill. 'Steve, I need to tell you something,' she finally said.

'Yeah?' he said, not taking his eyes off the screen.

Norma paused, wondering how to word it. Should she just blurt the news out or go in with an explanation first? Instead she took a detour: 'You won't believe what happened on the group today.'

'Let me guess, someone used "your" instead of "you're" and brought the reading world to its knees? Or should I say, "it's knees"?'

'No. Not that. It's ... we hit thirteen thousand members.'

'Impressive,' Steve said, making eye contact for a moment. 'I don't get it, though. What do you lot go on about on that page all day and all night? Don't you have anything better to do?'

Norma eyed his PlayStation console, with the worn buttons, and the headphones he used to scream down the internet into *Overwatch*, all day and all night. 'Booky stuff mostly,' she said. 'It can get quite interesting. Earlier today there was a discussion about Enid Blyton and whether it's okay to still read and promote her books, since it's been revealed how racist and xenophobic she was.'

'Bet that got heated,' Steve said.

'They're book people, so it was mostly polite, but through gritted teeth and with big words. It's wild how angry people get when it comes to the books they've grown up loving. "Five get outraged on social media."'

'Did you have to shut the conversation down?' Steve asked.

'Not yet, but I'm keeping an eye on it.'

'Hell hath no fury like a reader scorned,' Steve said.

'Pretty much.'

'Do your members buy a lot of books?' Steve asked.

'I think so. Book people, you know? We buy books even when we already have a dozen on our to-read pile, we can't help ourselves. We're essentially addicts, only our drug of choice is legal. Expensive, but legal.'

'So they're wealthy,' Steve commented, then considered her for a moment. 'I don't know why you don't charge them a membership fee to belong to the group. You could be coining it.'

Norma nodded, only half listening as her phone buzzed with another WhatsApp from Marina.

> Still procrastinating?

> It's not so easy.

> Christ, Norma, you need to tell him already, ffs.

> I'm trying. But SOMEBODY keeps texting me.

I swear, this is like back when I
taught sky-diving.

I was always having to kick
those fuckers out of the plane.

Marina was right, but then she was always right – it was her superpower. Everything about Marina was super. She was so perfectly interesting. She and Steve were the same age, that's how it worked with twins, but you'd never guess it to look at them. While Steve was about as regular a bloke as you could get, Marina had an elegant, timeless quality. Somehow retro, vintage and modern all at the same time. She could look anywhere from 29 to 59, depending on the time of day, the weather, the angle, location and lighting.

Norma knew she had to tell Steve her news though, for no other reason than she couldn't face waking up to another day having to tell her best friend that one more night had gone by without her putting on her big-girl pants.

'Steve ...' she said, clearing her throat again.

'Yeah?' He said, turning to his laptop and firing up *Overwatch* again.

Norma took a deep breath, 'I've ... I've ...'

'What, Norma? I've, I've, I've ... Have you got Tourette's or something? I swear sometimes I think you're a bit special. Spit it out,' Steve snapped.

'I've got a long day tomorrow, think I'll head to bed,' Norma said, chicken shit that she was. She could picture Marina's eye-roll emojis already.

'See you,' Steve said, turning back to his screen.

THE GOOD BOOK APPRECIATION SOCIETY

MEMBERS: 13 022

Edna Molton: Hello reading friends. I have fourteen hours of flying coming up. Please can you recommend a great read? Preferably something entertaining and absorbing.

COMMENTS:

Lucille Cooper: Do you read paper books or e-books, @Edna Molton? I usually load a few different titles onto my Kindle for a flight – that way, if one doesn't grab me, I have others to choose from. There's no fate worse than running out of something to read on a long-haul flight. And added bonus, e-books don't take up any space in your luggage and you don't have to lug them across an airport.

Dax Goby: I think you'll find that the plane crashing and everyone on board dying a bloody death might be a worse fate than running out of reading material on a flight @Lucille Cooper. #JustSaying

Lucille Cooper: Thanks for pointing that out @Dax Goby. Yes, I wouldn't want anyone else to get hurt, of course. But me personally, I'd rather go down in flames than have nothing to read on a long-haul flight. Book lover forever!

Dax Goby: @Lucille Cooper, a woman after my own heart.

Harry Shields: @Edna Molton, why not try my second novel, *Once on a Tuesday* (Victory Books), it's guaranteed to enthrall, and make that fourteen-hour flight feel like four hours. In fact, I'm willing to wager that when the wheels come down, you'll wish the flight had been longer, so you could carry on reading.

Geneva Fulverton: Oh no, here we go again! Mr Self-promo graces us with his presence once more. Aren't we lucky?

Shireen Worcestershire-Watts: We are lucky, the actual author right here in our little club. Wow! Star-struck.

Geneva Fulverton: I was being sarcastic, dear. He's here all the time, punting his own work.

Harry Shields: Punting my own work, or offering valuable insights on great publishing gems and adding value in this literary community? I like to think it's the latter.

Bernard Phillips: I reckon that's a pretty good suggestion from @Harry Shields for you, @Edna Molton. As I mentioned in a post on this page earlier, I loved *Monday Never Comes*. In fact, I'd go as far as to say that it was my book of the year. I couldn't put it down.

Edna Molton: Thank you for your suggestion. I think they may have a copy in my library. I'll take a look.

Harry Shields: You'll love it, @Edna Molton, guaranteed. And thank you @Bernard Phillips, I'm so pleased you enjoyed it. @Geneva Fulverton, don't knock it till you try it.

Harry

Harry's knees creaked as he crouched to peer at the shelf closest to the floor. Authors weren't as flexible as some – tight hip flexors, from all that sitting.

When it came to bookshops, alphabetical order was another in a long line of unfair crap shoots for authors. Where your book was shelved in each store depended on an algorithm, based on shelf capacity and the number of books stocked. It was a lottery. You were lucky if you got eyeline. 'S' was a popular first letter for author surnames, so at least he was in good company, alongside Shakespeare, Salinger, Steinbeck, and more currently, Shriver, Stroud and Shteyngart.

Harry finally spotted his books before his knees gave in. They had four copies of his first novel, and only two of his most recent one. Would he have preferred it if there were fifty of them in a pyramid on the table as you walked in the door? Sure. Would he have wanted a life-size cardboard cut-out of himself beside that? Sure. Although if they were going that far, maybe they could make it a little taller than life-sized. But the world was the world, book sales were book sales, and so instead he got a grand total of six copies, one of them already looking a little worse for wear, on the shelf closest to the floor. He soothed himself with the hopeful logic that perhaps they had already sold two copies of his latest, that is, if they had originally stocked an equal amount of both books.

The truth was, sales hadn't been quite as buoyant on his second novel as they had been on his debut. Although 'buoyant' wasn't the exact word his publisher had used. Theirs had been rather more dramatic.

And that was why he was now kneeling on the floor of the shop. What was the point of floor-level shelves in bookshops anyway? It was wasted space. Nobody ever browsed down there, not even people with good knees. And how was he supposed to sell books if nobody could see them? If he wanted a good deal from publishers on his next novel, he needed to sell as many copies of his last book as possible. Selling books these days felt a lot like pushing a square wheel up a round hill. In the snow. In the Ukraine. While missiles whizzed past your ears. Was he being overly dramatic about it? Sure. But was it also a life and death situation for him? Yes, definitely.

Harry looked over both shoulders to make sure security wasn't looking, then pulled all six copies off the floor-level shelf and swapped them with the latest Stephen King release, which had been sitting in prime position at eye level. The King wasn't short of sales, so Harry reckoned he wasn't doing too much damage with the swap. And anyway, Harry had heard he was one of those gracious authors.

Once he'd moved his books to eye-level, Harry turned each one so their covers were facing forward.

'Where are you, Harry?'

He started at the sound of Victoria's voice, and dropped one of his books on the floor with an embarrassingly loud clatter.

'There you are. What are you doing? You're going to make us late for brunch with Neil and Clive,' Victoria called, as he scrambled to pick up his book, desperate not to draw attention to himself.

'I'm coming, it's just ... this display ... it was all wrong,' Harry stuttered.

'Not this again, Harry. Didn't you almost get arrested for shoplifting last time we were in this bookshop?' Victoria said in carrying tones.

'Like I told them, I wasn't shoplifting, I was droplifting,' Harry whispered.

'Same difference,' Victoria said.

'No, it's completely different. I told you, Victoria. When I called, they said they'd sold out of my books, and the manager said they weren't planning on reordering. So I was just leaving a couple of my own copies on the shelf in case any of my die-hard fans came into the store looking for me. I wasn't stealing, I was giving back. They wouldn't even have had to pay me for those books. It was an act of goodwill, community service even. I should have been given a medal, not a warning.'

'If you carry on like this, they're going to stop letting you in this shop altogether, darling. They'll put a little picture of your face up at the till with a sign that says, "Do not serve this man". Like they do at petrol stations, after people drive off without paying. And anyway, you do know that they just go around at the end of the day and put all the books back in the right place, don't you?'

Harry strode past her out of the shop. 'We all do what we have to do, Victoria. It's not easy being an author.'

'I know love, unlike being a surgeon,' he heard Victoria say as she followed him out.

THE GOOD BOOK APPRECIATION SOCIETY

MEMBERS: 13 027

Michelle Zanders: Please can we talk about bad reviews for a moment? Or perhaps, more accurately, honest reviews that lean towards the negative, because is that really a bad review? Surely by its definition, a 'bad review' is one that has been badly written, i.e., full of errors?

I recently read a book that was not for me. At. All. These things happen. It's a title that has been well-reviewed here, but I ended up putting it down after 147 pages, which is unheard of for me. Usually, once I'm that far in, I persevere. Call it misplaced loyalty.

Ever since I put it down, I've been wondering whether to post a review about it here or not. You see, I would never lie about my experience as a reader. So, if I were to post about it, I would have to say negative things. And the author is on this page too, so that adds a double layer of restraint and caution for the reviewer. Because there's this move now globally to keep these kinds of honest, or as many call them, 'bad' reviews to ourselves, and only post 'good reviews'. We don't want to hurt anyone's feelings, they say. There's enough negativity in the world already, they say. Everyone should get a trophy just for entering, they say, blah, blah, blah.

But surely, not posting honest impressions of a book does a disservice to this community? And ultimately to the author and publisher too? Why are we holding back in order to spare an author's feelings? Of course it takes work to write a book, but it takes work to run a hotel or restaurant too, and that doesn't stop us jumping onto Tripadvisor with a thousand opinions.

I even believe an honest negative review benefits the publisher. In terms of the technical, if they know the book is riddled with errors, or the typesetting in the Kindle version has a glitch, they can fix the tech, or solve it in the next print run. And in terms of the content, by censoring ourselves, do we not underestimate our fellow club members' ability to look past one reader's personal tastes and find an element of the story that interests them? To make an educated decision for themselves?Just because I didn't like a book, doesn't mean it's bad, it just means I didn't like it. In the same way that just because I don't like pineapple on pizza, doesn't mean it's disgusting (even though it clearly is).

COMMENTS:

Mikaela Pace: Name and shame. What was the book that you DNF?

Michelle Zanders: It was by an author who happens to be on this page (often promoting his books), so I'm not sure I want to reveal that info, for all the reasons I mentioned in my review.

Felicity Mauberger: As my mother always used to say, honesty is the best policy.

Sylvia Strain: I'm sure your mother also always used to say, if you've got nothing nice to say, don't say anything at all.

Felicity Mauberger: Maybe you should take her advice sometime @Sylvia Strain.

[Sylvia Strain has left the group.]

Linda Petal Dabb: Oh no you guys, Sylvia left the group. Let's try and remember to always be kind. I'll DM her to make sure she's okay. Peace and understanding. 🌸🌀

Michelle Zanders: But surely not saying what you honestly think undermines the whole point of a book club, @Linda Petal Dabb?

Ruth Burstein: I agree. I've spent my money, I've given up my time. I don't see the point of not sharing my honest thoughts, just to protect an author I've never met.

Harry Shields: As an author myself (*Monday Never Comes*, and *Once on a Tuesday*), the truth is that often inexperienced reviewers don't understand the anatomy or architecture of a great novel, or what it takes to write one, let alone what it takes to write an effective review. Reviewing is an art form, remember. And writing critical reviews in particular, take skill. Honestly, as an award-nominated author, I generally only consider negative reviews when they've been written by an experienced professional reviewer. In my experience (vast), an ignorant negative review, from a clueless reviewer, is about as useful as an umbrella in a hurricane.

Brian Wilder: Oh you're a published author, are you? You don't say. We wouldn't have known. Why don't you tell us again!

Harry Shields: It's a fact: I am. I've written two novels, both of which have been published to great acclaim, the most recent nominated for and soon to win a Golden Page award. And my third manuscript is currently with my agent. Why does that make you so cross @Brian Wilder? Jealous, perhaps?

Brian Wilder: Of what? Your shitty attempts at literature, or your constant need to self-promote? Nothing to be that proud of, mate. Just because you wrote something and managed to get it published, you think you can tell the reading public they're not smart enough to review books. Classic narcissist.

Harry Shields: Share your obtuse, ignorant, negative views, if you must, @Brian Wilder. But please know that when an idiot (such as yourself) writes a bad review, it reflects more poorly on you than it does on the book or author you're skewering with your embarrassing inexperience.

Brian Wilder: @Harry Shields, let me make sure I'm getting this right, you're saying that if one hasn't been published, one is an 'idiot' and one's literary opinions hold no value? Talk about reductive! Not to mention insulting. You do know you're on a book club review page, don't you?

Harry Shields: Let me guess @Brian Wilder, you're working on a manuscript, so you think that instantly makes you a writer. More than half the people on the planet want to or are in the process of writing a book, but that doesn't make them authors. It barely makes them writers. And just because someone wants to write a book, it certainly doesn't mean that they should. You are a very obvious case in point.

Brian Wilder: You're argument is limited by the construct of time. Just because someone hasn't been published yet, doesn't mean they aren't a writer. Not to mention the fact that you have insultingly disregarded the experience the members of this club have garnered through a lifetime of reading.

Harry Shields: @Brian Wilder, with that kind of grammar, frankly we're lucky you haven't been published.

Michelle Zanders: Ahem, sometimes people can be a bit too honest.

Avukile Chingwita: And this, people, is why we can't have nice things!

Mikaela Pace: *Grabs popcorn*

Linda Petal Dabb: Play nicely boys. Love and light. 🌸🌈

Norma

Urgh, Norma thought as she lay in bed, scrolling through the comments on the new post. All she wanted to do was read a couple of chapters, then turn out the light and be done for the day. But now there was this post about bad reviews, which had made that silly Sylvia Strain leave the group, and was racking up a ton of furious comments and angry exclamation marks.

Someone had picked the most ridiculous argument with that annoying author who always punted his own work, and now they were having a proper go at each other.

Why did people have to behave like this online? If any of them had met at a cocktail party or art exhibition, or even in the queue at the dry cleaners, they'd probably get on, or at the very least just politely disagree with each other, move on to the next conversation and remark later to their partner that they didn't much care for that person. But online they were instant enemies, ready to fight to the death. And over what? An opposing view? It made no sense.

Norma clicked through to the profile of the member arguing with Harry Shields. With group admin access, she could see that Brian Wilder had joined the club a month earlier, and this was his first interaction on the page. Members usually lurked for a while before commenting or posting, let alone leaping into full-blown arguments like this one.

The Wilder guy had no profile picture, just the app-supplied icon for those who didn't want to be visually represented and his profile was set to 'private', so she had no other info to go on.

Possibly a troll. Or could it be a bot? She wondered if AI had developed so far as to be capable of intelligent thought? Although this wasn't a very intelligent argument.

Norma went back to the post and scrolled through some of their new back and forths. It wasn't anything she felt she needed to intervene in yet. They were both seemingly grown men, perfectly capable of taking a few hits, and they were both giving as good as they got. A right pair of clowns. She would check in on them again in the morning in case she needed to close down the comments section. Nobody ever warned you that running a book page would be a lot like being a kindergarten teacher.

Harry

That Wilder bloke had riled Harry up. Who did he think he was? And what kind of name was Wilder anyway? He was clearly a troll. And Harry wouldn't engage with him further – he would get back to work on his acceptance speech. A far more important use of his time.

Harry clicked over to the empty page in Microsoft Word, and typed, 'People like that are 100% what's wrong with this world.'

It wasn't much of an opening line for an awards acceptance speech, but Harry couldn't write when he was agitated. The annoyance took up too much space in his brain. All constructive thought got replaced with perfect comebacks, which always arrived too late. He thought of them as staircase revelations, popping into his head while he was on the toilet the next morning, or waking him up in the middle of the night; even now, as he was trying to write his award-winning acceptance speech for his future-award-winning book.

The world was full of wannabe writers. Sometimes they even called themselves 'authors' without ever having been published. The outrageous cheek of it. Cultural appropriation at its worst. That Wilder con was obviously one of those. You couldn't as much as lift your knife and fork at a dinner party, or get into a conversation with someone in the waiting room at the proctologists, before it came out that they had a novel or a partial novel or an idea for a novel. It was so undignified. The world needed more readers, not more writers.

And then there were those self-published, self-proclaimed 'authors' on Amazon, who were just as bad. Harry felt the urge to complain to someone about it, but Victoria wouldn't let him talk to her about it anymore; while this subject drove him into a fury, it drove her into the off-licence.

Harry checked the time in Baltimore, then called Phyllis.

They'd met at a literary festival in Ho Chi Minh City, as debut authors on their first international panel. Bonding over nerves and later using Google Translate to catch a train to a Michelin-starred restaurant he'd read about.

Writers needed other writers when it came to conversations about the writing life. It was like going to war or to boarding school. Unless you'd been there, you couldn't possibly understand what it was really like. That, and you often ended up having your head dunked in the toilet.

Harry thought Phyllis Johnstone was a fairly talented crime writer. She was also a major conspiracy theorist, which he'd discovered that first night at the restaurant. Before they'd even ordered the wine, she'd said she thought the translator on their panel had not been translating what they were actually saying. She suspected the woman had been offering her own version of their answers, with added political propaganda. A hunch she was basing on the length of the translated Vietnamese answers not seeming to match up with the length of either her or Harry's answers in English.

That was fair enough, but then over starters, she'd gone on to tell him that she'd seen proof that Elvis and Bigfoot were both being held, cryogenically frozen, in a secret underground bunker in Nevada. And over dessert, she'd shared that it wasn't drug overdoses that had killed both Heath Ledger and Amy Winehouse – it had been the Freemasons. Harry liked her instantly, despite – or perhaps because of – her crazy streak.

They emailed and spoke a lot, comparing word counts, contract notes, to-read lists, and the flotsam and jetsam of writerly life.

'Buddy,' Phyllis said when his call connected.

'Hey, Phyl.'

'Did you hear back from Myra yet?'

'She received my MS, but she's taking her time getting to it.'

'How long has she had it?'

'A week,' Harry said.

'Maybe she's anti-Semitic?' Phyllis said.

'Myra Berelowitz? I don't know about that,' Harry said. 'Are you all set for the London Festival of Books?'

'My passport is valid and stamped, so I guess if *they* want to track me now, they've got easy access,' Phyllis said. 'I'm looking forward to our panel, it will be great to catch up.'

'Phyl, did you see that wanna-be writer being an idiot on The Good Book Appreciation Society on Facebook?'

'I hardly ever go on there. What happened?' Phyllis asked.

'This guy, Phyl, you won't believe it! He openly attacked me in the comments section of some pathetic thread on bad reviews.'

'Is he a literary critic?'

'No, just some troll.' Harry said.

'I'd walk away, Harry. Haters are gonna hate, as the kids today say.'

'You're probably right,' Harry said.

They pencilled in dinner after their panel before hanging up, then Harry refreshed his inbox. Still nothing from Myra, so he logged back into Facebook to scan the feed for new comments before bed. Phyllis was right, he was better off not responding.

THE GOOD BOOK APPRECIATION SOCIETY

MEMBERS: 13 027

(CONT.)

Linda Petal Dabb: Play nicely, boys. Love and light. 🌸🌈

Michelle Zanders: I certainly didn't mean to start an argument with my post, I was simply questioning why we're so averse to honest, negative reviews? And I guess fragile masculinity is the answer. Case in point.

Chris Colt: Oh here we go, what's the feminist version of the race card called? Let's blame everything on the men, shall we.

[Freda Kruger has reported this comment.]

Avukile Chingwita: Honesty is always the best policy, in my view. But is it really helpful to be so unnecessarily rude? (ahem @Harry Shields, @Brian Wilder @Chris Colt). By the same token, I agree with your post, @Michelle Zanders – sugar-coating a review is equally dangerous.

Karen Granger: I won't ever write about a book here if I didn't like it. I'm scared I'll tread on toes. What if the author sees it? This one time, I decided not to review a book I didn't like; it was very badly edited. But tons of other people here loved it and didn't even mention the mistakes. Were they lying? Or just unobservant? Or does spelling and grammar no longer matter in this world? And don't even get me started on the world's endemic apostrophe abuse. Sigh. #WordNerd #GrammarMatters

Brian Wilder: I see your latest novel has a lousy three stars on Goodreads @Harry Shields, and only 63 reviews. And If those reviews are anything to go by, you're barely a published author yourself.

Harry Shields: I wasn't going to respond to you any further, you pathetic troll! But to set the record straight, it's actually three point six stars, which is almost a four. And the book was only launched recently, so people are still reading it. A concept you wouldn't understand, since you are borderline illiterate.

[Freda Kruger has reported this comment.]

Norma

Norma stood with her key an inch from the keyhole. She was ready. She was resolved. She was going to tell Steve the news the second she walked over the threshold. She wouldn't even put her handbag down, or give herself half a chance to change her mind.

'Steve, we need to tal—' Norma started.

'Don't even ask, I've had a shocker of a day,' Steve said, holding up his palm.

Norma exhaled and sunk onto the couch. 'What happened?' she asked, wondering, yet again, how hanging out in your pyjamas on a comfortable, stained, saggy couch, with no deadlines and no commitments, could consistently produce a shocker of a day?

'I thought I said: don't even ask!'

Norma felt deflated. How was she going to face more WhatsApp-tennis shame with Marina? Plus, if Steve ever found out that she'd told his twin her news before she'd told him, he'd be even angrier about that than the thing she'd been too chicken to tell him about.

'Steve, we need to talk,' she tried again.

'You're not going to nag me about job hunting again, are you? We've talked about this a thousand times, and we agreed, I need to put as much energy into writing my book as I would into a day job, so I can get it finished and sold. You do want me to finish it, don't you?'

'That's not what I need to talk to you about,' Norma said.

'Listen Norma, I've had a particularly shite day. I can't deal with your negativity right now.'

'This is hard for me to say,' Norma said, shifting her spectacles on her nose, and humming a bar of 'Bridge Over Troubled Waters'.

'Oh, shit, you're humming. It IS bad! What?' Steve said, putting down the remote.

'I wrote a book,' Norma stammered.

'You what now?' Steve said with a laugh.

'A book ... you know, with pages, and words ... I wrote one.'

'Like a novel?' Steve asked.

'Yes, quite like a novel. In fact, exactly like a novel.'

'No you didn't.' Steve laughed again.

'Is it that hard to believe?' Norma asked, hurt.

'But you're a reader, not a writer,' Steve said.

'I didn't know the two were mutually exclusive ...' Norma started.

'And anyway, you're a chartered accountant,' he cut in.

'So now neither readers nor chartered accountants can be writers? Yes, that makes perfect sense, Steve.'

'Well, also ... you're not very creative, are you? I'm the creative one in the relationship, innit? You're the one who's good with numbers and spreadsheets and shit like that. I do the writing.'

'If you say so.'

'What's it even about?' Steve asked.

'It's hard to explain,' Norma said.

'What's it called?'

'*Train Smash*,' Norma said, feeling exposed. Saying it out loud was nothing like thinking it in her head. The title suddenly felt childish. 'I might still change that,' she added.

'Can I see it?' He had a shocked, drawn look on his face. It felt like the longest he'd maintained eye contact with her in months.

'I don't know if it's any good. I don't even know if it's actually a book, and not just a bunch of words all in a row. I was hoping you'd take a look. You have more experience than I do.'

'Experience, eh? Because I've been writing mine for so long?' Steve said.

'Obviously that's not what I meant. I meant it as a compliment, actually.'

'We've been together for …' Norma noted his pause. 'A few years,' he continued, 'and I had no idea you even wanted to write a book.'

'Still got some surprises up my sleeve!' Norma tried for jokey, but it didn't land.

'When did you write it, though?'

'I found gaps. During my lunch hour at work, an hour or two before bed, while you were down here gaming … somehow over time, the words racked up,' Norma said, instantly regretting the comment, aware of how mean it sounded, especially since he'd been struggling to get words down since the day she'd met him. She knew it was unreasonable, but she felt guilty – almost as if she'd stolen his flow.

Steve stared at her, nodding slowly. 'Where is it?' he asked, his voice strangled.

Norma pulled a stack of printed pages from her laptop bag.

'Wow, you had that at the ready.'

'I printed it at the office earlier. I thought I may as well use their paper and toner instead of ours,' Norma lied. She'd printed it out weeks earlier when she'd first planned on telling him, and she'd been lugging it around with her ever since. No wonder writers had bad backs.

Steve weighed it in his hands. 'You actually wrote a book.'

'Are you upset?' Norma asked.

Steve shook his head.

'Angry?'

'More surprised,' he said.

But Norma could tell he was trying to hide his feelings. 'I'm sorry I didn't tell you before, love, but I was playing around at first. I didn't know if it was even going to be a thing. So I didn't tell anyone. Mostly because it never felt real, and I worried that if I talked about it before it was finished, I'd just become one of those annoying people who only ever talk about writing a book. And then, suddenly, there it was ... finished.' She felt another pang of guilt as she watched her words settle on him.

'Just like that, finished. As easy as writing a shopping list. All good. No, I get it. You're a proper writer! The words just flowed ...' Steve said, his voice low, sandpaper-coarse.

'I understand how this must make you feel, Steve. I think that's another reason why I haven't been able to tell you. I didn't know how to do it without hurting you. I know how long you've been working on your manuscript and how much has gone into it ...' Norma trailed off.

'I'm fine,' Steve said, his voice the opposite of fine. 'There's room for more than one author in the world.'

They sat in silence.

'Perhaps you'd be willing to have a read?' Norma eventually said.

Steve gave a slight nod, and then silence descended again, thick and stifling. Norma felt the urge to evaporate. 'Want to grab some dinner?' she asked faux lightly. 'A kebab or something?'

'Not hungry,' he said.

'I might pop out.'

'You do you,' he said, dropping her manuscript on the coffee table like it was on fire. Then he reached for his pouch, and started rolling a joint. 'Hey, Margaret Atwood,' he called out as she got to the door, his voice cold, 'do we have any crisps?'

'Kitchen cupboard, top shelf on the left,' Norma answered. 'Won't be long.'

Steve didn't respond.

Her relief at being out of the flat hit as she stepped into the street. Closely followed by annoyance as she realised she'd left her coat, phone and keys in the living room. But there was no way she was going back for them. There wasn't enough room in there for all three of them: him, her and his mood.

THE GOOD BOOK APPRECIATION SOCIETY

MEMBERS: 13 999

Edna Molton: Once on a Tuesday is the second novel by Harry Shields. And as you've probably seen here numerous times, it comes highly recommended by the author himself no less.

What a load of twaddle. Absolute rubbish! Abhorrent! Useless! Who's publishing this nonsense? I feel like my dog could have written a better book, and he doesn't even have opposable thumbs, or a laptop. And he likes licking his own balls.

It was the most pretentious attempt at a novel I've ever read. And I've read Jack Kerouac's entire stream of consciousness.

And let's not even talk about the errors. This couldn't possibly have been edited professionally. And then there's the cover — amateur hour. I googled to see if this book had been self-published. It hadn't, which surprised me, as it smacks of it.

Ever since I gave up on it, fifty pages from the end (I couldn't be bothered to finish it, too thin on plot), I've wondered who the author slept with to get this utter dross published? And this is Shields's second novel! So, assuming that the author would have gotten better at his craft since his

BOOK PEOPLE

first book, I can only imagine how awful that first one is.

This novel is a big fat no for me, and if you're a discerning reader, it should be a big, fat no for you too. In the incapable hands of this so-called 'author', it goes to seed after twelve pages.

In fact, I feel embarrassed for him having punted this book everywhere, clearly not realising how awful it is.

I saw another reader on this page bill it as a contemporary literary thriller (it may have even been the author tooting his own horn again, as he's been known to do). I, however, would bill it as contemporary literary drivel. So, thanks for the recommendation, but here's a recommendation of my own: don't waste your time on this car crash of a novel.

Give up your day job, Shields. The world needs trees more than it needs your writing.

COMMENTS:

Thomas Dooley: That's rough. As much as I'm a fan of an honest review, I'm glad I'm not that author.

Chris Colt: Oh my, Mrs Molton!

Linda Petal Dabb: Why can't we all just get along? Kindness and love.

Avukile Chingwita: Saucer of milk at table two.

Shireen Worcestershire-Watts: Huh? Milk?

Lucille Cooper: I'm sorry you didn't enjoy this one. How was your long-haul flight and your trip @Edna Molton? And did you take my advice and load other books on your Kindle too, so you had more to choose from? Let us know if you found anything good.

Dax Goby: @Lucille Cooper, I'm a Kindle fan, too and I came across a big Kindle books sale. If you don't mind the liberty, I thought I might drop you some suggestions via DM of a few I liked? I see we've had similar taste in the past, and it's always nice to talk about books with a like-minded reader.

Lucille Cooper: OOOooh exciting. Thank you for letting me know, @Dax Goby, and I'd love to hear your recommendations.

Shanti Khumar: I think this review hits below the belt. There are ways of saying you didn't enjoy a book without being this rude. Where are your manners, reader-reviewer?

Michelle Zanders: Yes, but as per my post the other day, don't we owe it to our fellow members to be honest about a book?

Shanti Khumar: Yes, of course we do, but there's honest and then there's cruel. This feels like a hatchet job.

Ruth Burstein: I for one salute you, dear Edna. I'd rather read a harsh honest review, than a puffy dishonest one.

Shanti Khumar: I'm all for honesty and truth, @Ruth Burstein, but in a community there has to be some peer-review ethics.

Ruth Burstein: That's because your politics are clearly overly, overtly and exaggeratedly intersectional.

Chris Colt: Oooh cat fight!

BOOK PEOPLE

Avukile Chingwita: You're getting off topic, ladies!

Karen Granger: I'm sorry, but the term 'ladies' is now often considered demeaning. #WordsMatter

Shanti Khumar: Oh why bother!

Geneva Fulverton: Ultimately, we're The Good Gook Appreciation Society, not The Let's Pretend it's a Good Book Appreciation Society, or The Let Me Promote My Own Book Society. So I also appreciate the honesty of this reviewer. It's saved me the time and money wasted on this book.

Mikaela Pace: *Grabs popcorn*

Felicitas Gonzalez: Following.

Shireen Worcestershire-Watts: Following.

Sunar Pandor: Ooh I've seen this author punting his own books on this group before, I don't want to be here when he sees this post!

Mikaela Pace: I do.

[Freda Kruger has reported this post.]

Norma

Norma hovered outside the front door for the second time that day, trying to decide whether to ring the bell or knock, feeling ridiculous for having to ask for access to her own home. She went with a quiet knock in the end. It felt less intrusive. She didn't want to disturb Steve if he was reading her manuscript. When she didn't hear anything she knocked louder; and after a few more moments, she rang the doorbell, humming 'Don't Speak' by No Doubt while she waited.

Steve pulled the door open, then returned to the lounge without a word, shoulders slumped.

'I brought you a kebab,' she said, dropping the foil-wrapped parcel on the coffee table. 'Extra garlic sauce.'

'Not hungry,' he said, without looking up.

In the dimness of the room, she saw her phone light up. If it was Marina, Norma could finally tell her she'd done it. She'd gotten out one truth, and now there was only one more to go. Not even Marina knew her other secret, yet. When she picked up her mobile she had a dozen direct message notifications, which struck her as odd; she hadn't been away from her mobile for more than an hour.

I'M WARNING YOU!

The first message she saw had been typed in angry all caps. Norma hummed the first few lines of 'Under Pressure' by Bowie and Queen. Steve glared at her. She flushed and sidled out of the room so she could hum in peace.

Perched on the edge of her bed, Norma scrolled to the beginning of the unread messages. The first one also shouted at her in all caps.

AN IMPORTANT MESSAGE FOR THE ADMIN OF
THE GOOD BOOK APPRECIATION SOCIETY!

My name is Harry Shields, I am an author
and a member of your club. There is a post
on your page which is utterly unacceptable.
You need to do something about it IMMEDIATELY!

Harry Shields. She recognised the name. He was that annoying novelist who always punted his own work on the page and had gotten in that stupid spat with that other member. One of those types who never let anyone forget he was an author.

She scrolled through the rest of his messages:

My first novel is called *Monday Never Comes*.
My second award-nominated novel is titled *Once on a Tuesday*.
Both published by Victory Books, London's twenty-seventh
largest publisher.
Edna Molton, a member of your group has written
a defamatory post reviewing my second novel
in what clearly amounts to hate speech.

Norma tugged at the neck of her sweater.

This matter had better be dealt with urgently!!!

I'M WARNING YOU!

This was one part of running the club that she did not like. She hummed, scratched at her neck, then started typing.

> Hi Harry. Thank you for bringing this post to my attention. As the only admin on the page I count on our members to help me keep an eye on things. I've been out for a few hours and sometimes posts slip through. I'll take a look.

Norma toggled over to the page and grimaced. At first glance, he wasn't wrong – Edna Molton's review was downright vicious. But this was where things got complicated. It was a book review page, so there were always going to be negative reviews, as well as those authors, publishers or publicists who would be mortally wounded by them.

Norma returned to Messenger and tapped out another careful response.

> I'm sorry you've been on the receiving end of this negative review. As an author, it can't be easy to read something like this about your work. However, I can't see anything in the post that contravenes group rules or community standards. After all, we do encourage honest reviews. So, while I admit this particular review does seem more personal and to be frank, unpleasant than most, it's simply an honest reader review, which is exactly what the platform has been created to encourage. So, I'm not sure there's much I can do about it.

Three dots bounced along the screen, indicating that the author was typing at the other end of the internet. Norma felt a dull headache forming behind her eyes as she hummed the refrain from 'It's a Hard Knock Life' by Jay-Z, until Harry's response pinged into her inbox.

>   I don't think you understand.
>   This is easily the most slanderous,
>   libellous review I've ever read.
>   You have to remove it!

Norma adjusted her spectacles and typed another response:

>   Of course, I understand why this has upset you. But all I can do at this stage is keep a close eye on the page to make sure things don't get out of hand.

>   Are you insane? This is out of hand already,
>   that review is a hatchet job.
>   It's defamatory, it's sickening, it's disgusting.
>   You have to do something about it.

>   Don't they say in publishing that all publicity is good publicity? Wouldn't you rather this than the alternative?

>   What's the alternative? A good review?
>   Because yes, that's definitely what I'd prefer.

>   I meant wouldn't you rather have people reading your book and saying bad things they honestly feel about it, and starting open conversations about your writing, rather than never being read?

No!!! As it happens, I would REALLY
rather just get a GOOD,
non-slandering, non-attack of a review!!!!

> I'm sure I read somewhere that negative
> reviews can lead to increased sales, because
> they attract attention. And people become
> curious as to whether the book is as bad as
> the reviewer claims. So, while it's not ideal,
> I don't think this situation is as bad as you
> think it is.

You're wrong! This situation is way-way
worse than I think it is. You have no idea
what this feels like.

> Surely if you put something out in the world,
> there's bound to be someone or some-ten
> who don't like it. Law of averages and all that.
> Doesn't it come with the territory?

You wouldn't understand. You're not a writer.

Norma winced. That was what Steve had said.

That review amounts to hate speech.
Probably even manslaughter.
You need to do something
about it IMMEDIATELY.

> I don't think that's what manslaughter means.

If you don't do something you'll leave
me no choice but to report it to Facebook!

It's called Meta now.

I'll report it to both of them.
And sue the lot of you.

Feel free, but I suspect you won't get much
help from the Meta-verse, they're too busy
trying to buy other planets.

FINE!

Norma could sense that he wasn't really 'FINE' and that she was losing him to his fury.

Harry, if I can give you one piece of advice.
As the founder of this group, I've seen this
happen before. Whatever you do, I urge you
not to respond to that review. Feel free to
disagree with me, sue me if you must, but trust
me on this one thing: you do NOT want book
people turning on you.

There was no response and the 'just-typing' dots had stopped bouncing.

Harry ...? Are you still there?

Norma rubbed the bridge of her nose and hummed 'Bad Moon Rising' by Creedence Clearwater Revival. There was no reasoning with some people.

Harry

This was outrageous. How could this be happening to him? And the person who ran that group, Norma somebody or other, didn't seem to give a damn that he was under attack.

He clicked on the post and reported it to Facebook, or Meta or whatever it was called. Prompted with a multiple-choice selection for the reason he was reporting the post, he hovered over 'Harassment' for a moment, but then went with 'Hate Speech'.

But ultimately, the interaction sent him on a digital loop that didn't lead to a real human being at any point. The bot or the algorithm or the alien or whatever humanity-free entity ran these things, promised to look into his issue.

Who was this Edna Molton anyway? And who did she think she was? Did she not know that he was an internationally published, award-nominated author? Harry clicked on Edna's profile. She'd joined The Good Book Appreciation Society eight years earlier. So she was a long-standing member, and it looked like in all those years, his only interaction with her on the page had been the week before, when she'd asked members for something to read on a long-haul flight, and he'd suggested his book. Harry felt bile rise in his throat as some of the more choice words from the review swam in front of his eyes: 'drivel, useless, abhorrent'. These were downright violent terms.

Next, he clicked through to Edna's personal profile on Facebook. He would send her a strongly worded message. An official-sounding cease and desist. There were legal characters in two of his novels – after all that research, he was practically a lawyer himself.

But Edna Molton's profile had the highest possible privacy settings, and they didn't have any mutual friends or groups in common, other than The Good Book Appreciation Society, so none of her content or information was visible to him. There wasn't even an option to send her a friend request or direct message – she lived in a social media cul-de-sac. All he could see was her name and generic old-lady profile picture, taken somewhere outdoors, a pair of binoculars slung around her neck.

'Bloody birder,' Harry hissed, as he turned to Google and searched for 'Edna Molton', which returned 'About 836 000 results in 0,55 seconds'. Why the computer always bragged about how long it took to generate these results niggled. It was an algorithm, a fancy calculator, not some impressive champion human feat, where someone deserved a medal for doing their job at supersonic speed.

Harry scrolled through the results, but they all looked like different kinds of Edna Moltons. Younger, or living in a different country; a twenty-five-year-old marine biologist in the Bahamas or a civil rights activist in a southern American state. None appeared anything like this unacceptable British old-lady Edna Molton.

How was he supposed to just let this go? The world always told authors not to respond to reviews; even that negligent idiot who ran the group had warned him against it. But surely in this case they were all wrong? That Molton woman clearly hadn't understood the nuances of his novel. He wondered if she'd even read it. He reread the review, noting that the details she'd included in her review seemed vague enough that they could have simply come from a close reading of the blurb.

Harry *had* to comment. He just had to. He needed to defend his work, set the record straight. He settled into his Herman Miller Sayl, clicked to create a new post and got to work, crafting his response.

'I hear a lot of typing,' Victoria said, slipping into the study twenty minutes later, finding him hunched over his laptop in his pyjamas, his face inches from the screen as he smashed at the keyboard.

'*Once on a Tuesday* got a review.'

'That's fantastic, congratulations darling,' Victoria said. 'But why aren't you dressed? We're going to be late.'

'No, you don't understand, Vicks, it's a stinker. And not just a regular stinker, it's a personal attack, a hideous hatchet job.'

'Oh Harry, it can't be that bad,' Victoria said, 'and more importantly, you're going to make us late. You still have to get ready and the car will be here innnn …' Victoria consulted her watch '… four minutes ago.'

'Don't gaslight me. If I say it's bad, it's bad!' Harry yelled.

'No need to shout, darling. I didn't write the review. And anyway, there's no such thing as bad publicity. Now will you please go get ready. You can tell me all about it in the car. If we miss the curtain, they won't let us in.'

'Why does everyone keep saying there's no such thing as bad publicity? It's really annoying.'

'Because Harry, despite how it makes you feel, it's true. We really have to go now, these tickets cost the GDP of a small island country, and I'm not missing this show because you're having some kind of existential bad-review crisis.'

'I mean it, Vicks, this is serious, even potentially libellous. We should sue.'

'No Harry, the cholecystectomy I have to do at eleven tomorrow is serious. This is just some kind of mania. Please, I'm begging you, can we talk about it at drinks after the show? Remember the show? The one we bought tickets to see a year ago, because it's so popular that the entire run sold out on the first day, so they had to add a second performance every night for the rest of the season?'

'I don't think I can go to a show in light of what's happening here, Victoria. I should probably stay here and manage this review.'

Victoria shook her head in disbelief. 'Harold Shields, I swear, if you do not log out of social media, pull yourself off that outrageously expensive Herman Miller Sayl right this second, put on a clean pair of pants, and come with your wife to this show, not only will you be out of a marriage, but you will also be out of a home, and out of a lifestyle to which you've become very accustomed, faster than you can say "standing ovation". I'll be waiting in the car, which is now most definitely already here,' Victoria snapped as she marched out of the study.

Seconds later, Harry heard the front door slam.

He quickly scanned the post he'd angry-typed in response to that bloody awful review, then pressed enter to publish it, slammed his laptop shut and raced into the bedroom to change. As he picked up his mobile on the way out the door, he cursed as he noticed that he'd forgotten to charge it, and the battery was minutes away from dying.

Norma

'That stupid author, that stupid, stupid, stupid fucking author!' Norma shouted.

He'd only gone and responded to the review, and not graciously either. She'd had a feeling he wouldn't be able to contain his ego or his rage. And he hadn't just left a comment on that woman's review, he'd created a whole new post on the page. And it was pretty inflammatory.

'This is not going to end well,' she muttered.

Norma wondered if she should delete Harry's furious response post before too many people saw it, to save him getting slaughtered?

But there was no rule against being an egotistical fool, and posting a rude, ungracious response to a review of your own book, although (and she made a mental note for future reference), there probably should be.

Another option would be to close commenting on the thread, which meant people could read his post, but they couldn't comment on it. Then ultimately, as people posted new reviews and commented on other posts, his post would sink lower down the page, until it hit full algorithm obscurity. But how would that look? It wasn't Norma's place to censor members, even if it was for their own good. She wished he'd taken her advice.

Authors made the worst club members. Generally massive narcissists, they joined the group to lurk and scroll, waiting for the right moment to dive-bomb the page and promote their own books. Or they used the search function to see if anyone had reviewed their books, and then took great offence if they either didn't find any reviews, or found any that were vaguely uncomplimentary. Never happy. Just like that Harry chap. Miserable without reviews, and miserable with them.

Sure, Edna Molton's review had been a scathing hatchet job, but Harry's response was hardly any better. Nobody had levelled up here to be the bigger person. Surely, Norma thought, as a published author, public opinion was an expected outcome?

She'd seen it time and time again. A reader made a vaguely negative comment or criticism of a book, and the author immediately got defensive, commenting with passive-aggressive good humour, or, as in Harry's case, just plain aggressive-aggressive bad humour.

After that, there was never much Norma could do, other than sit back and watch as the members turned on the once revered author and tore them limb from inky limb. The readers on the group might not be writers themselves, but they had all read enough books to be able to string together angry sentences of their own. It could be quite enjoyable to watch from the schadenfreude side-lines, in a grab-the-popcorn and watch-the-car-crash kind of way. But no fun if you were on the receiving end.

Considering how brutal the publishing industry was, Norma was always surprised at how thin-skinned authors were. If she ever managed to get her manuscript published, she vowed she would step away the second it hit the shelves.

Harry was on his own now, Norma thought, as she set her phone to silent and reached for the novel she was reading. Fiction was just about always preferable to real life.

Harry

'She called it "drivel",' Harry hissed.

Victoria ignored him and continued staring straight ahead at the stage.

'She said it was thin on plot. Thin on plot! It's supposed to be thin on plot, it's literary fiction. And anyway, it's not thin on plot, if anything it has too much plot, everyone's said that.'

Victoria still didn't respond. The lady on the other side of Harry cleared her throat loudly for the third time. Harry hoped she didn't have a cold; the last thing he needed was her filthy germs.

'Why aren't you more outraged, Victoria?'

'I am outraged, Harry. I'm outraged that you made us late for the theatre. I'm outraged that I can't enjoy this play I've been waiting to see for nine months, because my selfish husband is obsessing about some faceless reader who didn't fawn all over him in an online book club that means absolutely nothing in the big literary scheme of things. So yes, I'm outraged about a lot of things,' Victoria hissed back.

'She's not faceless, her profile picture is clearly of her with binoculars, in a field. I think it's somewhere in Devon. I should add to my response that she should forget about writing reviews and stick to birdwatching!'

'Oh god, please tell me you didn't respond to that review, Harry?'

'I had to, Vicks, I had to defend myself,' Harry squeaked.

Victoria dropped her head back against her seat and closed her eyes. 'Please can we just watch the show?' she pleaded.

'Yes, please can we just watch the show,' the woman sitting next to them said.

'Can I borrow your mobile? My battery died,' Harry whispered to his wife.

'We're at the theatre,' Victoria said, with a glare that bored through his skull.

Harry turned to ask the woman next to him if he could use her mobile, but she gave him such a dirty look that he shut his mouth, sat on his hands and stared directly ahead. But he didn't catch a moment of the play, starring the recently knighted actor and Hollywood's latest ingénue, and instead spent the next one hundred and twenty minutes obsessing over Edna Molton and her ten-paragraph-long hatchet-job of a review.

THE GOOD BOOK APPRECIATION SOCIETY

MEMBERS: 14 002

Harry Shields:

To @Edna Molton.

As the author of the novel you took it upon yourself to eviscerate, I wanted to respond to your review. If we could call it that. To be honest, it was in fact a violent hatchet job.

I know everyone says authors shouldn't respond to reviews of their books, but that doesn't seem fair. Politicians get whole debates in which to respond to their opponents and detractors, comedians get to respond to hecklers, so why shouldn't a review also be an opportunity for open discussion, as opposed to a one-way-street of abusive, ignorant opinion?

Firstly, I suspect that you've never actually read my book, *Once on a Tuesda*y (Victory Books). If you had, your review might have been more positive, more balanced, more reflective, and more tempered and nuanced. I say this as my novel has garnered dozens of previous reviews, and none have ever had anything quite so dramatically negative to say.

I can't speak to the motivation behind your attack, which feels pointed and personal, and smacks of more than simple opinion, and is more of a simpleton's opinion.

Please don't take this the wrong way – I am not ageist – however, I don't believe you're the audience for this book, my dear. It's a younger person's take on modern London and the politics of the day, and your profile appears to be that of an old reader. To my mind, it simply isn't the kind of book you should be reading or reviewing. I'm sure there are plenty of cosy murder mysteries that would better appeal to your sensibilities.

Lastly, a question to the other reviewers here, do we really believe ugly reviews like this help anyone? How would you feel if you put your heart on a page, and a person who had never so much as written a pamphlet had a million idiotic, egregious, untruthful and inelegant opinions on it? I think you should all call her out on it. This reviewer deserves to be cancelled.

By all means tell us what you're reading, but perhaps leave the critical thinking and critical reviewing to professionals (such as published authors) who are clearly better equipped for the job.

COMMENTS:

[Freda Kruger has reported this post.]

Geneva Fulverton: What gives you the right to decide who gets to review a book?

Michelle Zanders: If we aren't professional reviewers and our opinions don't count, why are you so bothered by what we think of your books?

Shanti Khumar: That IS ageist. Shame on you.

Lucille Cooper: If I had ever been even vaguely tempted to pick up one of your books and settle down with a packet of Jaffa Cakes to read it, I am certainly not tempted now. Talk about an instant turn-off. And I'll usually go with any excuse to eat Jaffa Cakes.

Dax Goby: I LOVE a Jaffa Cake!

Thomas Dooley: Hi Harry, I am a writer too. (Internationally published, five novels, you'll find them on Amazon.) Listen, buddy, it's clear that this has upset you. And of course, I know as well as the next author how much it hurts to read a negative review of one's blood, sweat and tears. But this is not the way to go, my friend. Don't get caught up in this fray. It does not become you. The best thing you can do now is delete your post, ignore the review and get on with your life.

Geneva Fulverton: Another shameless self-promoting author! God help us.

[Freda Kruger has reported this comment.]

Edna Molton: Typical! @Harry Shields, you beg us to review your book, until you don't like what we have to say, then you change your mind and you want us to shut up. That's not how it works. In addition, your response is almost as poorly crafted as your book. Which, spoiler alert, I hated.

Ruth Burstein: As I recall, you've been nagging people to read your books. You should be careful what you wish for.

Geneva Fulverton: @Harry Shields, you once said on this page, when people were commenting on the death threats that Aaqel Abus received over his novel, and I quote … 'Shoot me down if you want, but as an author myself, I would rather people were offended by my book, talked about it, burnt it, even threatened me over it, as opposed to ignoring it.' End quote. I guess that's not the case when it actually comes down to it.

Edna Molton: Harry Shields is an author who thinks readers don't have the right to their own opinions on the books they're reading if they aren't professional reviewers. And he didn't appreciate my honest review. Just wait till we all, all of us non-professional 'idiot' reviewers, go over to Goodreads and flood it with 1-star reviews! Who's with me?

Avukile Chingwita: I'm with you, @Edna Molton. The book is out. The author had plenty of time to use his words while he was writing it and make sure they were up to scratch. Once the book is published he doesn't get to bully reviewers into liking it. It's not our fault he wrote a turd. I'm heading over to Goodreads now to leave my own one-star review too.

Zach Davis: I've never even read this book, but I'm logging into Goodreads right now, to give it one-star. Epic fail, author, epic fail.

Thomas Dooley: @Harry Shields, don't say I didn't warn you.

Felicity Mauberger: Don't listen to the sensitive little baby, Edna, love. What a prat. None of us will ever buy his books again. Poor tantrummy toddler doesn't know how to deal with a bad review.

Dax Goby: Authors like this make me sick. What you do is not rocket science or brain surgery, mate. It's just writing, making up shit. Get over yourself. Good book, bad book, it's not that big a deal. Reading is all that's important.

Lucille Cooper: I couldn't agree more.

Chris Colt: Maybe @Harry Shields has a point, the women should leave the professional reviewing to the men.

[Freda Kruger has reported this comment.]

Harry

Harry may have blacked out for a second. He heard a high-pitched sound. Part wail, part keening, which he realised was coming from inside the room. And inside him.

'What's the matter? What happened?' Victoria came skidding barefoot into his study, still in the dress she'd worn to the theatre.

Harry covered his mouth with his hand as he stared wide-eyed at his screen.

'What is it, Harry?' Victoria said, leaning over his shoulder to look at the screen.

'My life is over,' Harry whispered.

'Oh don't be so dram—' Victoria started. 'Oh Harry!' She laid a hand on his arm as she ran her eye down the reams of abusive comments on Harry's post. 'Why on earth did you respond?'

'My career is over.'

'No, it isn't. These things happen all the time. In a few days some politician or pope or actor will sleep with the help, and everyone will fixate on that next, these things always blow over, you'll see,' Victoria said.

'You don't understand,' Harry said. 'There's no coming back from this.'

'There's no point torturing yourself over this, Harry. And at least it's Facebook and not X. It's a war zone over there. Come to bed, take a

Zopiclone, and by tomorrow it will have blown over.'

'Are you mad? I can't just leave it. I have to do something, say something, phone someone, make it stop.'

'Darling, it's after midnight, there's very little we can do now. You'll only make things worse. And who would you call anyway? Things will look better in the morning, they always do.'

'Go on up, I'll be there in a minute,' Harry said, staring at his screen.

Victoria sighed as she left.

Harry scrolled back through the comments on his post, reported as many of them as he could to Meta or whoever, then clicked over to his direct message inbox, which was overflowing with hate mail. He was going to have to respond on the page again to sort this whole mess out.

Norma

'What are you still doing up?' Steve asked, looking up from his laptop as Norma padded through the lounge to the kitchen.

'Thought I'd make some tea. You won't believe what's happening on the group.'

'Let me guess, someone dog-eared a page?'

'One of the authors in the group got a shockingly bad review.' Norma said.

'Did they deserve it?' Steve asked.

'I don't know. He is a bit of a twat, but I don't think anyone deserves to be completely eviscerated online. I warned him not to respond, but he couldn't help himself. And now the group is ripping him to shreds.'

'What will you do?' Steve asked

'Maybe shut the whole thread down. It's turned super-ugly, super-fast. People turn into monsters on social media.'

'You wouldn't catch me dead on there, Facebook is a septic abscess.'

'Trust me, I wouldn't be on there either if I wasn't running the club. Poor, dumb Harry.'

'Let this be a warning to you, Norma, publishing isn't always as fun and glamorous as it appears.'

'I didn't write a book because I thought it would be fun and glamorous, Steve. I wrote a book because ... I don't know why ... because I had to, because work was crushing my soul. But also, because it was in me, and I needed to get it out. And like I said earlier, it was a fun exercise, but I probably won't take it any further. Let's see what you think of it first.'

Steve shrugged.

'I appreciate you agreeing to read it with an open mind. I know this must be tough.'

Steve just stared at her, his eyes flat.

'I'm going to go check on the page again, then try get some sleep. You coming to bed?'

'Not tired. Going to hang out here a bit longer,' Steve said, returning to his laptop.

THE GOOD BOOK APPRECIATION SOCIETY

MEMBERS: 14 004

(CONT.)

Gerry Rawson: So, book club friends, how do we feel about writers who comment on reviews of their own books?

Geneva Fulverton: We are not a fan, @Gerry Rawson.

Felicity Mauberger: I think if you can't handle criticism, you should consider NOT becoming an author.

Harry Shields: And I think, if you can't handle writing a competent review, you shouldn't attempt one.

Geneva Fulverton: This author needs to learn that when you're writing a book, the ball is entirely in your court. You get to make all the decisions and have full ownership of it. But once it's out in the world, the power and responsibility shift and you no longer have any control over what people think of it.

Harry Shields: I don't want control. But I would settle for some common decency, which, alongside manners, you seem to be severely lacking @Geneva Fulverton.

[Freda Kruger has reported this comment.]

Felicity Mauberger: So first you recommended that Edna read your book, then slam her when she does, but doesn't enjoy it. You're an arsehole!

[Freda Kruger has reported this comment.]

Harry Shields: It takes one to know one @Felicity Mauberger.

[Freda Kruger has reported this comment.]

Linda Petal Dabb: Come on friends, is this really necessary? Joy and kindness. 🌸🌈

Thomas Dooley: Still commenting, Harry? Perhaps you'll never learn.

Harry Shields: Nobody asked you, @Thomas Dooley.

Thomas Dooley: Sheesh bud, I was on your side! And if you scroll up you'll see @Gerry Rawson did actually ask.

Gerry Rawson: He's right, I did.

Avukile Chingwita: Harry, I don't know you, but in my opinion, you can't tell readers how to feel about your words. And anyway, they're not really your words anymore, they're the reader's words to experience and understand however they choose. Essentially what I'm saying is maybe you should STFU and move on.

[Freda Kruger has reported this comment.]

Harry Shields: You're right @Avukile Chingwita, you don't know me. Maybe you should mind your own business, take your own advice, STFU and move on yourself!

[Freda Kruger has reported this comment.]

Michelle Zanders: And this was the same author who was begging us to read his book just a couple of days ago! Be careful what you wish for.

Harry Shields: @Michelle Zanders, I wish for the type of readers who are smart enough to understand how to review books properly.

Prince Princeton: Follow me to get thousands of followers.

[Freda Kruger has reported this comment.]

Tammi Kentridge: This book was actually on my list for our next book club, but I think I'm going to give it a miss, this is all toxic AF.

Harry Shields: No, wait. you're making a big mistake, @Tammi Kentridge, your book club will love it. Look, this is what other book clubs have had to say about it:
    'The Sister's Book Club: We loved this book. Completely and wholly.'
    'Wine-Lover's Book Club, Essex, UK: We were spellbound.'

Tammi Kentridge: Everyone knows those shouts are paid for by the publishers. And have you learnt nothing from this whole ordeal about not responding?

Harry Shields: You tell me not to respond, and in the same sentence ask a question which by its nature requires a response. You're ridiculous, @Tammi Kentridge.

Ruth Burstein: Yet another fragile white male author who thinks the world owes him a good review. And then throws his toys out the cot if they don't love his work as much as he loves his own work. Boo hoo. What a baby!

Harry Shields: @Ruth Burstein, call me a baby. But YOU have your hard work, integrity and personality violently slandered out of sheer spite, and see how that makes you feel!

Gaill A: You all know that I'm a very critical reviewer, but this review of Harry Shields's book hits below the belt. This author does not deserve this kind of vicious attack. I've read both his books and I think he's an exceptional writer.

Harry Shields: Thank you @Gaill A. Too kind.

Bernard Phillips: Like @Gaill A, I too love this author's work. If he wrote an address on an envelope, I'd want to read it. I think he was right to respond. If everyone else gets the opportunity to say what they think, what kind of double standard says he can't respond? @Harry Shields, ignore all these haters and go write another book. And to the group, it's easy to gang up on an author from behind the safety and anonymity of a computer screen. Let's not be bullies!

Harry Shields: Thank you @Bernard Phillips. You sound like my kind of reader. Smart, erudite, and clearly able to write a decent review.

Brian Wilder: This is typical of a Badly Behaved Author. This author needs a few more one-star reviews on Goodreads to chop him down to size!

Harry Shields: Admin – @Norma Jacobs please remove this last comment from @Brian Wilder. It's irrelevant and unacceptable hate speech.

Finn Andersohn: Ding ding ding, Author Behaving Badly alert! Everybody, let's go to Goodreads. You know what to do.

Harry

The second Harry's phone was charged enough for him to turn it on, he rang Phyllis.

'Harry, we're about to sit down for lunch, can I call you straight back aft—'

'Something bad happened, Phyllis.'

'What?' Phyllis sounded worried.

'I can't look! This is hell, I am literally in hell, my career is over,' Harry whimpered.

'Slow down, what happened?'

'It all started with that disgusting review that old bat left of *Once on a Tuesday*, on that Facebook book club I told you about.'

'I thought you said you weren't going to engage with them. Please Harry, tell me you didn't respond?'

'I responded,' Harry responded.

'Oh shit. Harry, that's not good, buddy.'

'No, it's really not good.'

'How not good is it?' Phyllis asked.

'I don't know, I can't look. I need you to look for me, Phyl.'

'Aren't you supposed to be working on your speech for the awards? Why are you wasting time and energy on this trash?'

'Don't shout at me, okay? I'm losing the plot!' Harry yelled.

'Where must I look?' Phyllis asked.

'Goodreads,' Harry said, in a small voice. 'Search for my name.'

'Oh crap, Harry. Let me get my laptop,' Phyllis said.

Harry heard the muffled sounds of her putting the phone down, then opening her laptop, then he heard her booting it up and typing. After a minute or two, he heard her suck in her breath sharply.

'What? What? Phyllis? Is it bad? What? Oh my god. It *is* bad, isn't it? I knew it.'

'Oh Harry, buddy,' Phyllis's voice came through the phone, from what sounded like very far away. 'Oh shit.'

GOODREADS

1*

Matthew Pearson: Did not read, but it looks like shite!

1*

Dillon Wessels: This author wants to control what readers think of his book. So, from me, he gets a 1-star review.

1*

Brian Wilder: Suck eggs, Harry Shields!

1*

Newman Garamond: This author is ageist, he doesn't like old people. Well, the feeling is mutual.

1*

Claude Dougedispeville: How do I give it less than one star? This book made me actively angry, I'm still annoyed thinking about it now. I know sometimes a bad review might make some people more interested in reading it … more power to you. I hope you like it better than I did. Wholehearted and deserved DNF.

1*

Cormac Barnes: I only read one chapter, but I found it bland, to be honest. This book is full of clichés. The author says it took him three years to write – maybe he should have taken four.

1*

Lydia Dembe: I read this author's first book, Monday Never Comes, and it was okay, I suppose. And for all I know this one might be just okay, too. Don't plan on sticking around in his world long enough to find out.

1*

Guy Neidich: Even at one star, this book is completely overrated.

1*

Mickah Nelson: One star for this book, only because there's no option to leave no stars.

1*

Boris Burke: This author should have kept his mouth shut.

1*

Lynette Shore: This is one very Badly Behaved Author.

1*

Melanie Barry: Once on a Tuesday by Harry Shields was actually on my list of books to buy, but now I think it's not for me. He deserves this lonely star.

1*

Rhonda Reese: All white male authors are trash.

1*

Gerry Higginson: Weak genre fiction, dollied up to read like literary fiction by a narcissistic author with an ego the size of France. It's a big fat no from me.

1*

Byron Potter: One star. Would not recommend!

1*

1*

1*

1*

1*

1*

1*

1*

1*

1*

1*

1*

1*

1*

Harry

    9:05: Hi, you've reached Myra Berelowitz, I can't take your call right now, please leave a message. Beep.

Harry tutted and hung up as his call went to voice message. He knew Myra had told him not to call, but this was an emergency. And too nuanced a situation to explain in a voice message. He would wait ten minutes and try again.

    9:11: Hi, you've reached Myra Berelowitz, I can't take your call right now, please leave a message. Beep.

    9:15: Hi, you've reached Myra Berelowitz, I can't take your call right now, please leave a …

    9:37: Hi, you've reached Myra Berelowitz, I can't …

    9:39: Hi, you've reached Myra Berelowitz, I can't take your call right now, please leave a message. Beep.

    'Hi Myra, it's me, Harry. I've hit a spot of bother online. It's nothing too serious, I'm sure it will blow over. Call me when you get a moment so we can discuss. Thanks.'

    10:46: Hi, you've reached Myra Berelowitz, I can't take your call right now, please leave a message. Beep.

'Hi Myra, Harry again. I've been trying to reach you, but you haven't been answering. It keeps going to message. Perhaps you left your phone at home? Or maybe your battery is flat? These things happen. There's been a small kerfuffle in an online book club I belong to. I was hoping we could chat about a media strategy to manage it? I was also wondering whether you'd had a chance to look at my manuscript yet? Call me. Thanks.'

10:49: Hi, you've reached Myra Berelowitz, I can't take your call right now, please leave a message. Beep.

'Hi Myra, about that last message, I know you said you'd let me know about the manuscript once you'd had a chance to read it and for me not to ask about it again. Please forget I mentioned it. I would however be exceptionally grateful if you could call me back urgently regarding that other small issue of the teeny, tiny online spat. Chat soon, I hope.

Oh, it's Harry.'

10:52: Hi, you've reached Myra Berelowitz, I can't take your call right now, please leave a message. Beep.

'Hi Myra, Harry Shields … I thought I'd better clarify, just in case this is a new phone, and you've lost all your contacts. Or maybe you have another client named Harry?'

12:17: Hi, you've reached Myra Berelowitz …

12:49: Hi, you've reached Myra Berelowitz, I can't take your call right now, please leave a message. Beep.

'Myra, hi, it's me, Harry here again. Harry Shields. Harold. Still trying to reach you. I know you're busy but this is urgent.

Please call me. Or text, WhatsApp, iMessage, email, DM via Facebook, Twitter, X, LinkedIn, Instagram, Threads, Snapchat (I started a profile in case you use that platform), TikTok, Telegram? Whatever suits you. It won't take more than a minute for me to fill you in.'

12:51: Hi, you've reached Myra Berelowitz, I can't take your call right now, please leave a message. Beep.

'Me again. Harry that is. Okay maybe don't reach out to me on X, I've had to close that account down, just temporarily.'

14:16: Hi, you've reached Myra Berelowitz, I can't take your call right now, please leave a message. Beep.

'Myra, I could really do with some support here. Please call me urgently.'

14:59: Hi, you've reached Myra Berelowitz, I can't take your call right now, please leave a message. Beep.

15:36: Hi, you've reached Myra Berelowitz, I can't take your call right now, please leave a message. Beep.

16:52: Hi, you've reached Myra Berelowitz, I can't take your call right now, please leave a message.

'Hi, Myra, me again. Perhaps you're on an international flight, and unable to answer your phone? I feel like this situation might be getting out of control. I really need some support. And I was thinking, we might need to reach out to my publishers just to set them at ease that this is simply a blip on the radar, no big deal. These things happen. And as they say, all PR is good PR. This might even improve sales on the new one. We could frame it as a publicity stunt? Call me back. Please. It's urgent. Thanks.'

18:20: Hi, you've reached Myra Berelowitz, I can't take your call right now, please leave a message.

18:27: Hi, you've reached Myra Berelowitz …

18:39: Hi, you've …

18:57: Hi, yo—

20:23: Hi, you've reached Myra Berelowitz, I can't take your call right now, please leave a message. Beep.

RECORDED MESSAGE: This voicemail is full and cannot accept any more messages.

Norma

'I'm home,' Norma called out, her voice full of anxious fake cheer, as she put her bags down at the door.

Steve grunted from behind his laptop on the couch at Slacker HQ.

'How was your day?' Norma asked, sing-song-nervously.

Steve grunted again.

'Oh, a double grunt kind of day?' Norma hovered in the doorway, wondering if it was too soon to ask him what he thought of her book.

Steve grunted one more time.

'So, what did you think?' Norma asked. It was probably too soon, but she needed to know.

'Of ...?' Steve asked, looking up from his laptop, distracted.

'My manuscript ... that you were going to read today, while I was at work. Remember? In between job-hunting,' Norma said, sitting down beside him on the couch.

'I've been busy, Norma,' Steve said, turning up the volume on a football match.

'Oh,' Norma said, 'right.'

Steve turned up the volume another few notches, in what Norma recognised as the unsubtle-est hint ever.

'Odd that you've been so busy. Remember how this morning when I asked what you had going on today, you said, "Same-old, same-old, innit?" So I said, "Great, so you'll be able to take a look at my manuscript today then?" And you said, "Sounds like a plan." Ring any bells?'

'It's not my fault that I've been so busy, Norma,' he said, shifting a magazine on the coffee table with his slippered foot, to cover an ashtray full of joint butts. 'There's been the whole job-hunting thing and of course working on my *own* book.'

Norma caught his sarcastic inflection, and decided to ignore it. 'I can see that. You've been so busy you haven't even had time to shower or get dressed today. Poor thing, you must be knackered.'

'I'll read it tomorrow,' Steve said.

Norma glared at him and cleared her throat as she pressed the mute button on the remote, in her own unsubtle-est hint ever.

'I suppose I could have a quick flip through it tonight,' Steve said.

'You could? That would mean so much to me, thank you. I'll get dinner going while you make a start,' Norma said as she turned off the television, then slipped the remote control into her pocket and passed Steve the manuscript. 'Be honest, okay? I can take it. Like I would be about yours, if you ever showed me any of it.'

'What's that supposed to mean?' Steve snapped.

'Just what I said: that when you finish your manuscript, if you ask me to read it, I promise to be completely honest about it.'

'Are you insinuating that I'll never finish my manuscript?'

'No, I don't need to insinuate that, Steve, you're doing that all by yourself. Are you going to pick a stupid fight with me over nothing now, or are you going to read my novel?'

Steve rolled his eyes and made a big fuss of turning the first page.

As Norma went past him to go into the kitchen, she noticed that the front page of her manuscript had been folded down the middle so he could mull his weed on it. She muttered under her breath, and couldn't help hearing him muttering under his too.

Later, Norma was standing at the bedroom door hardly allowing herself to breathe, trying to detect any sounds coming from the other room, when her phone pinged, startling her.

BOOK PEOPLE

> THIS IS GETTING SERIOUS! I need you to do something about it urgently!

She hadn't had any more DMs from Shields since she'd warned him against commenting on reviews of his book. But she'd known she'd hear from him again sooner or later – things had turned into a shit-show for him out there, and no longer just contained within her Facebook group either. The toxicity had leaked out into Goodreads and then X. She felt sorry for him, but it was a kind of eye-roll-pity, strictly reserved for people who sealed their own fate.

Norma hummed 'Ironic,' by Alanis Morissette. She didn't need this right now. The sooner she got rid of Harry, the sooner she could focus her attention and ears back onto whether there were any noises coming from the lounge.

> Hi Harry, unfortunately every time I close down a thread or delete an awful comment to try stop the conversation, someone else starts a new thread. I'm not sure I can stem this tide. As I said before, I think it would help if you stopped responding. You're only stoking the fire.

Miss Jacobs, I need to warn you, if you don't take all those posts and comments down, I'll ...

> Are you threatening me?

No, I'm just saying ...

> That sounds a lot like a threat. And I think you should stop. You're in enough trouble already.

Norma's inbox paused. No bouncing dots, no messages, just silence. Then she heard a noise from the lounge. Was it a chuckle or just a fart? And did it come from Steve or the TV?

Norma attempted nonchalance as she walked into the kitchen to boil the kettle for another cup of tea. She'd made herself a cup when she last walked into the kitchen faux-nonchalantly half an hour ago. But she couldn't think of any other reason to walk past Steve now.

'Still busy, Norma,' he snapped.

'I thought maybe I heard you laugh?' Norma said timidly.

'Joe sent me and the boys a meme of a dog running into a wall. It's hilarious,' Steve said.

'Maybe I'll go have a bath while you read,' Norma said, her stomach knotting.

An hour later, she walked back through the lounge to boil the kettle again, humming, one towel wrapped around her body, another turbaned around her head.

'Still busy,' he said.

She could see he was just over half way. That was quick. Was it a good sign? She imagined the blurb she might get from some current bestselling author: 'Endlessly readable' or 'Unputdownable'. Or was it so terrible that he was skim-reading it?

When Norma came back into the lounge forty minutes later, Steve was reading and pacing.

'Norma. You have to stop bugging me. This takes time.'

Norma flushed. 'Maybe I'll go out,' she said.

'Leave the remote,' he barked.

Norma stood on the pavement and adjusted her spectacles. She looked up the street one way, and down the other way. She hadn't thought about where she was going to go, she just knew she couldn't stay in the flat a second longer. She was too anxious to read, too unfocused to watch Netflix on her laptop, too rattled by what was happening on the Facebook group to hang out there. It was too late for the shops, and she wasn't in the mood for a pub on her own. So she WhatsApped Marina.

                                        What you doing?

Shooting.

                                        A film?

A target.

                                        No, really, what are you up to? Steve's reading THE MANUSCRIPT and I need a distraction.

Really shooting, at the range.

                                        At ten o clock on a Tuesday night?

Why? When do you go to the range?

A second later, Marina pinged her a pin.

Come.

                                        I don't have anything to shoot anything with.

I thought you settler types had guns all over the show.

                                        You're confusing South Africans with Americans.

You can use my spare.

Norma pasted the address into Uber and wondered why her best friend had a spare. And a spare what? Gun? Crossbow? Shot-put seemed unlikely, although with Marina, anything was possible.

She'd met Marina in a kebab shop five years earlier – Marina's first and last night on the job. And since Norma had never been in that dive before or since, it had always felt to them both like fate that they'd found each other.

Despite their being best friends, the ins and outs of Marina's life remained a mystery to Norma. That was just how her friend rolled. She never kept the same job for more than a few months. In fact Norma had no clue where she was currently employed. The jobs she'd previously had (that Norma knew about) included school lunch lady, seamstress, large-scale outdoor mural painter, horse whisperer, carer in a mental institution, carer in an old-age home, carer in a kindergarten, hostess in a hookah bar, whatever it was she was doing in that kebab shop that night, and, possibly, a high-end dominatrix. But Norma often wondered if it wasn't all a front. For what? MI6? Or something even more secret?

Then, somewhere along the contour map of their friendship, Norma had met Steve through Marina, and the rest was history. Although not such great history anymore.

Harry

Harry poured himself a glass of milk. He didn't even like milk. But that's what people in the flicks did when they couldn't sleep, although unfortunately the movies never showed what people with lactose intolerance did.

This whole thing had turned into a nightmare. He'd thought that by commenting he could make the group come around, but his interactions had only made things worse. Exponentially.

There were now hordes of new comments on all The Good Book Appreciation Society posts relating to him or his books, or authors behaving badly, or reviewing culture. Far too many for him to respond to them all. And the situation on Goodreads was just as dire, if not worse. Seven new one-star reviews had popped up in just as many minutes. His posts and comments had been screen-shotted and shared widely across the internet and WhatsApp, so there was no point taking them down now. Going viral might be every author's wildest dream, but going viral for all the wrong reasons was every author's biggest nightmare.

Every negative review hurt more than the last one. As he scrolled through one of the latest ones on Goodreads he felt the sting of it. Someone named Dougal Flannery had given *Monday Never Comes* one star, together with a crushing single sentence review:

I wouldn't even recommend this novel to someone I detested.

Harry started composing responses in the Word document open on his screen. The one that was supposed to contain his award-winning award acceptance speech.

> Dear Dougal, I wouldn't recommend you to someone I detested either.

> Dear Dougal, you're a prick.

> Dear Dougal, when reviewing something a fellow human being has created out of thin air, surely kindness is, if not a prerequisite, then at least always a consideration?

> Dear Dougal, not all books are for all people, but some readers have the good manners not to trash other people's hard work.

Harry clicked back into Goodreads to leave his response to Dougal's review. He hadn't decided which one he would go with yet; they all felt appropriate, albeit some far too kind. As he clicked to comment, he came across a notice posted by Goodreads at the bottom of the page:

> Dear author, we really, really (really!) don't think you should comment on this review, even to thank the reviewer. If you think this review goes against our Review Guidelines, please flag it to bring it to our attention. Keep in mind that if this is a review of the book, even one including factual errors, we generally will not remove it. – Goodreads Admin

He sunk back in his Sayl. He probably shouldn't comment. Commenting was what had gotten him into this position in the first place.

There was no winning for authors. If you cared too much when you were reviewed, you looked like an over-sensitive narcissist, but what was he supposed to do? Just stand by and let thousands of strangers, who judging by his sales figures, were unlikely to have even read his book, slander him and his work? In his heart, Harry knew he should step away from it all and focus on something else – work on his speech or start a new book – but he was so hurt and furious that he couldn't focus on any one thought for more than a few seconds. Nobody could write in the midst of this kind of conflict.

He wondered if any of this would affect his chances at the upcoming awards ceremony. Although surely it had all been contained on Facebook, Goodreads and X? He still had that award in the bag, he was sure of it. And anyway, the judges would have already made their decision, and everybody knew from years of small print, that the judges' decision was always final.

Harry poured a shot of brandy into his milk to try make it more palatable, and had a thought; in the same way he believed people should have to pass a test before they were allowed to have children, perhaps readers should have to do the same before they were allowed to review a book? Take a test to ensure they were mentally fit for the task. Now that made sense. That would stop undereducated fools like this trashing important books like his. He drained his glass, and clicked on the Goodreads page. He'd leave a comment, sharing his brainwave with all those stupid, spiteful reviewers. They'd asked for it.

Norma

'It's after two in the morning! Where have you been?' Steve asked, as Norma traipsed into the flat.

'Shooting with your sister,' Norma said.

'You were what? Urgh, never mind.' Steve said.

'How'd it go?' Norma asked, holding her breath.

'I've been worried about you, Norma. I'm exhausted. We can talk about it tomorrow.'

'What? No, I'll never be able to sleep, Steve! You can't leave me hanging like that. Plus I'm completely hopped up on adrenaline. And you shouldn't mess with a woman who knows how to fire a pistol.'

'It's late, Norma ...' Steve started.

'It's not like you have a job to go to tomorrow. You can sleep in as late as you want.'

Steve blinked at her, and she knew she had him. 'I'll make us coffee and meet you on the couch in five,' she said, heading for the kitchen.

Norma carried two mugs back into the lounge, and sat down, running her sweaty palms along her thighs. 'I'm ready,' she said. 'No, wait!' She leapt up and grabbed a notebook and pen from the counter. 'Now I'm ready. Wait, wait,' she leapt up again and grabbed a packet of Hobnobs. 'Sustenance,' she explained, settling back on the couch, her knee bouncing with nervous energy. 'Okay, now I'm ready for reals.'

'Alright, so before anything else, I want to say, well done for making it this far,' Steve said, tapping her manuscript on his lap.

'Thank you,' Norma said, prickling with nervous energy.

Steve paused, then started again. 'Are you absolutely sure you want to hear this?'

Norma nodded, her throat thick. She didn't trust herself to speak.

'Because sometimes someone asks you to be honest, and then you are, but when they hear what you have to say, they wish they had rather asked you to tell a white lie,' Steve said. 'Like sometimes when you ask me if I like what you're wearing?'

'Steve.'

'Okay, okay. I'm going to be honest with you, Norma, because I care about you, and because you asked me to be. Shall we have a Hobnob?'

'Please stop stalling, Steve. Just put me out of misery already, I swear I can handle it,' Norma said. Not sure that she could.

'Okay,' Steve said, shaking his head slowly. 'I think it's a good thing you showed this to me before you showed anyone else.'

'Steve, please, I'm begging you, just pull off the plaster and tell me already.'

'Okay. But it's not good, Norma.'

Norma felt the ground shift beneath her. 'What's wrong with it?' she breathed.

'Granted, I only skim-read it, but from what I saw, it's just ... it's a bit immature.'

Norma flinched.

'It made me cringe. And not the good kind of cringe,' he continued.

'There's a good kind of cringe?'

'There are some bits that are okay-ish, I guess. And you might be able to turn it into something that resembles a novel, with a bit of elbow grease and some half-decent formatting. But right now, to be honest, Norma, it's more of a series of loosely strung-together paragraphs and tropes than an actual book.'

Norma tried to look unfazed, but felt hot tears welling up behind her eyes. She swallowed hard to push them back and dug a fingernail into the fleshy skin between her thumb and finger. *You will not cry in front of Steve*, she repeated to herself. She'd begged him to be honest: she couldn't be upset that he had taken her at her word.

Steve glanced at the notes he'd scribbled on the back of the manuscript in a blunt pencil. 'Want me to carry on?'

Norma swallowed and nodded.

'I think there are too many characters, and the plot feels a little, how can I put this gently? Too convoluted and derivative, with just so many clichés ...'

'Thank you for reading it,' Norma said quietly, wondering if humiliation was a terminal condition.

'What's your plan with it?'

'I was going to wait and see what you thought. Then I thought I might spin through another draft based on your feedback, and then who knows ... maybe put it out to some agents? Of course, I know this is just the dirty first draft,' Norma said, picking imaginary lint off her pants, which were streaked with oil and dirt from the range.

'I wouldn't send it out, bug,' Steve said gently. 'I don't think it's good enough to show anyone else.'

'I know it still needs tons of work. But are you sure you're not saying all of this because you're the one who was supposed to be writing a book, and I've stolen your thunder?' Norma asked, wiping the tiniest tear from the corner of her eye.

'Norma! You don't believe I would do anything quite so diabolical, do you? There's room for more than one author in any family. Just look at Jonathan Safran Foer and Nicole Krauss.'

'Didn't they get divorced?' Norma asked.

'You know what I mean. There are plenty of words to go around. And plus, this, this ... this thing you've written is nothing like anything I would write in a million years. I just don't want you to embarrass yourself by sending it off to anyone. What kind of boyfriend would I be if I didn't protect my girl from exposing herself? Come here,' he said, knocking her spectacles skew as he tried to wrap his arms around her.

'I know you only want what's best for me,' Norma said, nudging her glasses back in place.

'And with your book page and everything you do there, imagine if those people found out you wrote this – your reputation and the page's reputation would be shot,' Steve added, now twirling a strand of her hair in his fingers. Like he used to, before he quit his job and started smoking too much weed.

Norma nodded thoughtfully into his armpit.

'Also, you know all the experts say that writers should put their first manuscript away in a drawer and forget about it, then move straight on to the next one. They say the first one is like sweating out a fever. You need to purge it and move on.'

'*A Confederacy of Dunces* was John Kennedy Toole's first manuscript. And he won the Pulitzer Prize for it,' Norma said, her voice a whisper. Not mentioning the first manuscript Steve had been working on since she'd met him.

'Didn't he have to commit suicide before anyone would even consider looking at it? We don't want you to have to do anything foolish like that, do we?' Steve said.

'I don't think his book won the Pulitzer because he committed suicide, Steve; that was just an entirely unrelated and tragic arc in the story of his life.'

'Still, you asked for my advice, and this is coming from a place of literary experience. Honestly, I wouldn't show this to anyone, not if you want to maintain a shred of self-respect.'

'By literary experience, are you referring to the fact that you've been writing the same novel for years?' Norma asked.

'I know you're hurting, Norma, and we all lash out and try to hurt those closest to us when we're hurting, so I'm going to ignore that jab,' Steve said.

'It wasn't a jab, it was the truth,' Norma said.

'Now you're deflecting. Textbook response,' Steve said, shaking his head.

Norma had a sudden urge to smash Steve's face in. But he was probably right. There had been many, many moments while she'd been writing her book that she'd felt embarrassed, big tranches that made her want to bin the whole thing. But after that, there had been sentences, or a joke or sometimes even a paragraph that felt right, and those had propelled her forward. But maybe it's just that thing where you don't think your own kitchen smells. Steve's dad's kitchen always whiffed of stale chip oil and mildew, and nobody there ever seemed to notice it.

But she really didn't want to embarrass herself. Maybe she would take his advice and shove it in a drawer for a few weeks. Come back to it with some distance. She wondered if manuscript blindness was a thing? Like snow blindness.

'Why don't you stick with the numbers, and leave the word stuff to me, hey, bug?' It was the second time he'd used that old nickname for her. He hadn't called her that in months. 'Bed?' he asked, with a gentle smile. Then he dropped her manuscript on the coffee table and held his hand out to take hers.

That was also a foreign gesture. Things had once been pretty good between them, but ever since Steve had stopped working – stopped doing anything, in fact – their routine had been consistent. Norma would say goodnight and Steve would stay on the couch gaming or watching movies. Norma would get into bed and spend a couple of hours on her manuscript, and Steve would slip into bed, or more often than not, fall asleep on the couch sometime after three or four in the morning, and sleep through her leaving for work. They had fallen into a rut-sized rut.

Norma took his hand and they walked towards the bedroom.

'You know Norms, you can't just decide you're going to be a writer, and then wake up the next day and be one.'

'I don't know about that,' Norma countered. 'Surely if you plant your arse on a seat and get a book out, then you could be considered a writer?'

'Oh Norma, you're so silly,' Steve laughed.

Norma dropped his hand. 'So, you're saying that someone who has been working on a manuscript for years, but has barely advanced it by a single word in months is more of a writer than someone who's shown up on the page every day for just a few months?'

'Yes, that's exactly what I'm saying,' Steve said.

Harry

When Harry and Victoria arrived at The Local Grill, fifteen minutes late, Neil and Clive were already at the table with a bottle of wine.

The Shields had been friends with Neil and Clive Booth-Stewart longer than any of them cared to remember, and over the years, dinner had become a regular monthly fixture in their calendars, as well as evenings at the Philharmonic, weekend brunches, the occasional show. They were even planning a trip together.

Neil owned a logistics supply company and Clive was an anaesthesiologist who'd worked at the same hospital as Victoria during their specialty training.

'Sorry we're late,' Victoria said, bustling over to the table. 'I could not get Harry off his computer and out of the house. He would have brought it with him if I'd said he could – set himself up at our table like some kind of millennial digital nomad with a man bun who DJs in his spare time.'

'Victoria, darling, you look fabulous as always. Harry, you look like shit,' Neil said.

'Thank you, Neil. I'm afraid Harry hasn't been sleeping very much,' Victoria said.

'You won't believe what's happened, you guys,' Harry blurted.

'Crikey, you haven't even sat down yet, Harry,' Clive said. 'Somebody pour that man a bottle of wine.'

'I got the most disgusting, vindictive review you've ever seen,' Harry said as he took his seat.

'I'm afraid he's taken this one rather personally,' Victoria said, pushing her glass towards Neil with a nudge for him to fill it.

'Well, you would have too! It's slanderous, a vicious personal attack.'

'Where was this review?' Neil asked, filling Victoria's glass, then topping it up a little more when she nudged it an inch closer to him.

'I belong to this book club on Facebook – it's called The Good Book Appreciation Society. It's got thousands of followers. I've been thinking of leaving it for a while now, too many amateurs. But then this thing came out of nowhere, and now it's filtered into Goodreads and X too,' Harry wailed.

'He's gone viral,' Victoria said, sipping her wine and accepting a menu from the waiter.

'I've been considering engaging a lawyer,' Harry said.

'Please excuse me, just popping to the gents,' Neil said.

'Crikey, I'm sorry, that's terrible, Harry,' Clive said. 'Cancel culture has completely changed the digital landscape.'

'It's been such a personal attack, I feel entirely destabilised by the whole thing. And I've been unable to write.'

'What are you working on?' Clive asked.

'I just delivered my new novel to my agent and I've been working on my acceptance speech for that Golden Page Award I've been nominated for. I'm a cert to win it,' Harry added.

'That's brilliant, Harry. Congratulations. You see, it's not all doom and gloom,' Clive said, raising his glass.

'What's brilliant? What are we toasting?' Neil asked as he returned, placing his mobile on the table.

'Neil, did you just go to the bathroom to google his review?' Clive asked, snatching up the phone to examine the internet page open on it.

'Sorry. But I wanted to see if it was as bad as he said it was, and I couldn't exactly google it at the table in front of him.'

'Did you see it?' Harry asked.

'I did,' Neil said.

'And?' Clive asked.

'He's right. It's really bad. Sorry, Harry. Possibly even worse than bad.'

'Did you see the Goodreads ones too?'

'I did,' Neil said, grimacing. 'Why would you respond though, Harry, and like that? Hasn't anyone ever told you not to feed the trolls?'

'But ... but ... I couldn't not, Neil! It's like she had it in for me. I *had* to respond, I had to stand up for myself.'

'One *has* to order the tiramisu here; one doesn't *have* to respond to trolls on the internet, Harry,' Victoria said.

'Crikey, Harry! These Goodreads reviews are awful,' Clive said as he scrolled. 'One star, one star, one star ... Wait, why on earth would you say this stuff about needing to take a test before having children? Have you lost your mind?'

'Mmhmm,' Neil said.

'I've told him to shut down all his social media accounts, at least until things die down. These things always blow over eventually, don't you think?' Victoria said.

'I shut down my X account,' Harry said.

'No you didn't, X shut down your X account. He's been suspended from the platform temporarily for hate speech,' Victoria explained.

'The disgusting things these people have been saying. Surely it's slander? I have a right to defend myself, don't I?' Harry said, ignoring Victoria. 'This Edna Molton monster, I swear, if I ever find out where she lives ...'

'He's obsessing over it. Not eating, not sleeping, not writing,' Victoria said to them, as if Harry wasn't present. 'It's not healthy. I'm four seconds short of writing him a script for an antidepressant.'

'Vicky's right, Harry. I think it's best to sit this one out. Let the angry crowd subside,' Clive said.' That seems to be the only thing that works in these kinds of mob justice situations.'

'But it's not fair. Now no matter what happens, this is what will show up any time anyone googles my name, for all eternity,' Harry whined. 'It's like Richard Gere and that gerbil. My work is so much more than this. I'm sure most of them haven't even read the book. It's just all these angry book reviewers, bloggers and trolls jumping on the bandwagon, trying to take me down.'

'Trying and succeeding,' Victoria said pointedly.

'Shall we order? I'm famished,' Neil said, clapping his hands to get everyone's attention.

'I was looking at the bouillabaisse,' Victoria said, running her eye down her menu. 'It's very good here. Are we doing starters?'

'I can't help wondering why she's targeted me, though? It's been such a personal attack. And I've never even heard of this woman. Does her name sound familiar to any of you? Edna Molton,' Harry said, enunciating her name.

'The rump looks fantastic, but last time I had the garlic sauce it repeated on me for days,' Clive said. 'I think I'll do it with a mushroom sauce this time.'

'No garlic? Blessed relief,' Neil smiled, patting Clive's hand.

'She looks like she must be in her eighties. It doesn't make sense. It's Edna Molton, M.O.L.T.O.N. I can't help wondering if maybe we know each other from somewhere. Ring any bells?' Harry asked.

'Oh look, they've got mussels. Harry, you like mussels, don't you?' Clive said.

'I've got my eye on the moussaka. But I'm hungry, shall we order a salad for the table too? Maybe Greek?' Neil said.

'Good idea. Oh, speaking of, I had a thought about dinner the first night of our trip to Cheltenham. There's this Michelin-starred restaurant, but we probably need to book soon if we want to get in,' Clive said.

'Maybe I've met her before and offended her, and I didn't realise it. At a literary festival, or a book launch, or a signing or something,' Harry ploughed on.

Neil and Clive shot concerned looks at Harry over their menus, and

Victoria shook her head behind her own menu.

Oblivious, Harry went on: 'I've also reached out to Goodreads. It's preposterous that they allow people to review a book and give it one star when it's blindingly clear they've never read the book. Surely that goes against their community guidelines?'

'Can anyone see a waiter?' Victoria asked, raising a hand over her head. 'We need more bread sticks.'

'And probably more wine,' Clive said, glancing around.

Norma

When Norma got home from work, Steve was taking one of his increasingly rare showers. Her manuscript was lying on the coffee table, where he'd dropped it the night before. She picked it up and ran her palm over the cover page, mosaicked with mug rings and joint burns, a crease down the middle of the cover page speckled with flecks of tobacco and weed.

What to do with it now? Ignore Steve's feedback and see how far she could take it, at the risk of being humiliated when publishers and agents echoed Steve, only less gently? Could her confidence handle that? Or should she take his advice and put it away in a drawer? Although his advice leaned more towards setting it on fire than setting it aside.

Was he jealous, or was he legitimately trying to protect her? Norma paged through the manuscript and cringed as her eye caught a sentence in which her character was shouting something 'angrily'. A paragraph later, the same character was standing up and sitting down at the same time. She'd even used the word 'innit' more than once on the same page, in two different characters' dialogue, which suddenly felt wooden, clichéd and, as Steve had put it, 'immature' – despite the fact that when she'd read it a week earlier, it had felt sharp and nuanced.

She'd seen so many writers on The Good Book Appreciation Society who'd fallen in love with their own words and become blind to criticism, no matter how fair or even-handed. That Harry fool for one. She didn't want to be like that. What made her think she was a writer anyway? She was an accountant. Accountants didn't write books; they were just supposed to balance them.

And what about the club? As Steve pointed out, if she did manage to find a publisher and the members hated the book, that would be even more humiliating. Most of the members were into literary fiction. They talked about serious books, not the kind of fluff she'd written – they were bound to hate it. She wasn't sure she could handle the embarrassment.

One solution could be to pitch it to publishers under a pseudonym. That way nobody would ever know it was her. It was also a way to get a second opinion without exposing herself publicly. The thought of a publisher sniggering at her and her words made her flush with shame.

Norma carried the manuscript and her laptop into the spare room, clicked on the file containing the document. Then she deleted her name on the front cover, and replaced it simply with 'Jane', then stood at the printer, waiting for the new page to spit out.

'Finished writing another book already?' Steve asked, startling Norma. He stood in a towel, dripping as he peered over her shoulder.

'Who the hell is Jane?' he asked, snatching the page as it inched out of the printer.

'I thought maybe it could be me,' Norma said, feeling embarrassed.

'A pseudonym?' Steve asked.

'So I don't embarrass myself, or degrade the value of the club,' Norma said, prodding at her spectacles and humming 'Another One Bites The Dust' by Queen.

'As I said last night,' Steve said, leaning against the desk and handing her the page as if it were toxic, 'based purely on the quality of what I read, it's unlikely anyone would want to publish it. But if by some fluke someone did decide to pick it up, no publisher would ever let you publish under a pseudonym. It makes marketing a book impossible, unless you're a seasoned author with a huge fanbase, like

Robert Galbraith. And even then, nobody wanted to buy the Galbraith books in the beginning, not until the publishers leaked who the author really was. I think they thought it would be this big cult bestseller, but nobody gave a shit about the first book until they knew who wrote it.'

'Doesn't it add an element of intrigue? You don't think it can work?' Norma asked.

'No, how does a pseudonym attend a book festival, or a book signing, or run a social media account? Publishers want you to have more of a public face these days, not less of one.'

'I s'pose.'

'But maybe you're onto something with the club. How many members do you have now?' Steve asked.

'Sixteen thousand,' Norma said.

'Wow – wasn't it just at thirteen thousand the other day?'

'We've had a bit of a population explosion, with all the controversy around that author I told you about …'

Steve cut her off. 'There might be a chance for you to get published based on the size of the group. There are a million unethical publishers out there, and one might decide to publish you regardless of the quality of the manuscript, so they can tap into your club as a marketing tool. They don't care how stupid you look, or who's laughing at you behind your back, because if just one per cent of your members bought a copy, based on the fact that you wrote it, those would be good sales for a shitty debut.'

He was probably right. She'd seen plenty of unethical publishers taking advantage of people, publishing their misery memoirs, or influencers putting out shoddy manuscripts that you couldn't help feel were a bad idea on the author's part. There was the fifteen-year-old girl, a few years back, who'd been encouraged by an ambulance-chasing publisher to write a memoir naming and shaming people she knew, and that hadn't ended well. At least for the author. It went plenty well enough for the publisher, as the memoir went viral for all the wrong reasons, and the young girl had to be hospitalised after a failed suicide attempt – which boosted sales even more.

'You're right, this is a terrible idea,' Norma said, dropping the manuscript into the desk drawer. 'Let's get out of here, I've wasted enough time on this stupid thing. Captain Pow's, my treat?'

'I'll be ready in five,' Steve said.

As they walked down the street, Norma reached for Steve's hand. He stopped and looked at her hand in his. 'What?' he asked.

'What-what?' Norma asked, trying to keep her voice steady.

'This,' Steve said, indicating their entwined hands swinging between them. 'Since when are we a holding-hands-when-we-walk-to-Captain-Pow's kind of couple? You're acting strange, Norma. What's up?'

Norma took a deep breath. 'Okay, there is something I need to tell you … but I don't want you to get upset.'

'What?' Steve said, dropping her hand and taking a step back.

'Don't panic, it's nothing major.'

'What then? You'd better tell me.'

'Actually, it is something major, I don't know why I said it wasn't major. But nobody died or anything, if that's what you're thinking, so not that kind of major,' Norma stuttered, adjusting her spectacles and humming a bar from 'Trouble' by Pink.

'Norma!' Steve shouted. 'Stop humming and tell me. What?'

'Don't freak out, but I've done something.'

'What kind of something?'

'Come on, I'll tell you over a beer,' Norma said, taking his hand again.

'No way, Norma. You can't do that, you have to tell me what's going on right now!' Steve pulled his hand out of hers and crossed his arms over his chest.

Norma sighed. 'I couldn't tell you about this before because I didn't want you to try talk me out of it.'

'Norma, if you don't tell me what's happening right this minute, I am literally going to lose my shit right here on the pavement. And then some rando will film it on their cellphone and post it to the internet, and it will go viral, and someone else will call the police, and we'll both get arrested and we'll have to spend the night in jail while we're trending on X. Tell me.'

'Alright, so I had to quit my job.'

'Um, you did what now?' Steve asked, his eyes bulging.

'I quit my job. Just like you did,' Norma said. 'I know it sounds like a big deal, but don't panic, I have a plan.'

'Well I'm glad you have a plan, because you're the only breadwinner in the family in right now, so it is kind of a big deal. Shit, Norma, why didn't you talk to me about it first?'

'Because I knew you would try to talk me out of it. But you're not the only person on the planet who wants to quit their job and follow their dreams. I have dreams too.'

'Well, if your dreams are for us to live in a cardboard box under a bridge, then you're well on your way. Does this have anything to do with that ridiculous manuscript?' Steve asked.

'Ouch, Steve. No, it's not just about my "ridiculous manuscript",' Norma said, making air-quotes with her fingers. 'This is about my future, and how I want the rest of my life to go. But thanks for the encouragement.'

'I'm sorry, but it's just that now we're royally fucked.'

'I told you, I have a plan. I have a financial cushion,' Norma said.

'What the fuck is a financial cushion?' Steve shouted.

'I have this all figured out, Steve. I have enough money set aside to see us through for six months, then I'll get a promotion,' Norma said, glancing around at a couple of passers-by who were staring.

'A promotion? From what? Dumbass to idiot?'

'Listen Mr quit-your-job-without-anything-else-lined-up, who are you calling a dumbass? I didn't just resign without any backup. I sort of have another job lined up.'

'Thank god. Is it sort of at another accounting firm? Maybe that's not such a bad idea – there's nothing like starting a new job to increase your base salary. Did they headhunt you? That's even better, then you have some room to negotiate,' Steve said.

'No, it's sort of in a completely different industry. I can't do the accountancy thing anymore, Steve, it's killing me. Those people. That place. I'm dying there. You know that. You see me every day.'

'What new industry?' Steve asked.

'Publishing.'

'Publishing? What the hell do you know about publishing?' Steve said, his face twisting into an angry question mark.

'Um, I know you're not on social media, so you're out of the loop, but you do remember I run a book club on Facebook, don't you?' Norma said.

'And I run the remote control to the telly – that doesn't make me a movie studio head. What's the new position?' Steve asked.

'It's only temporary.'

'What is it?'

'I got a position as a publishing intern for six months.'

'You've got to be kidding me, Norma. You're forty-two. Do they even pay interns these days?'

'Yes, of course they do, nobody works for free anymore, this isn't the nineties. They're giving me twelve quid an hour …' Norma said.

'Wait, what's that? One thousand five hundred quid a month?'

'No. Thank god I'm the accountant in the family. It's £1950 a month,' Norma said.

'Norma, that doesn't even cover our council tax and the Doritos bill. How on earth are we going to afford to live on that?' Steve yelled.

'Please stop shouting, Steve. Like I said, I have a plan. I'm a quick learner, I've got more maturity under my belt than the average intern, plus previous office and financial experience, and I've got the book club. So, I reckon they'll promote me in no time at all, and I'll be back to earning a great salary before we know it. Plus, I'll have the inside track on getting both our books published, and I'll be a much happier person, because at last I'll be doing a job I actually like for the first time in my adult life. So I don't see all this as anything less than a win-win situation, for us both.'

'You have no idea what you've done, Norma,' Steve said.

'Thank you again for the vote of confidence,' Norma said. 'And anyway, maybe this is an opportunity for you to consider getting a job. I've been supporting you for the last nine months, ever since you quit to finish your book and get it published. And that clearly isn't happening, so perhaps it's your turn to support us, while I follow my dream?'

'Do you think it's too late to tell the firm that you've changed your mind?' Steve said, ignoring her.

'That's the thing, Steve, I haven't changed my mind. This opportunity is such a long-shot, it's highly unlikely it will ever come around again. Do you have any idea how rare it is for a company to take on a forty-two-year-old intern?'

'Yes, because what forty-two-year-old in their right mind, with any self-respect, would choose to go back to the bottom rung of the corporate ladder?'

'I'm not sure you should be quite so lippy. Why is it okay for you to torpedo your career to follow your heart, but if I do, it's a disaster and we're screwed? Also, you do realise that we're that clichéd couple standing on the pavement on a Friday night, having an argument?' People were really staring at them now.

'Norma, you need to go back in there on Monday morning first thing and apologise. Tell them you've made a terrible mistake, that it was hormones or you've got your period or menopause, or whatever. Tell them that you're unstable and you're sorry and you need your job back.'

'No, YOU don't understand, Steve, I resigned three weeks ago. I've almost finished working out my resignation period.'

'Fuck, fuck, fuck, fuck!' Steve yelled. 'Did they fill your position yet?'

'I don't know. Why?' Norma asked.

'Maybe I could take it?'

Norma stifled a laugh, 'What? As an accountant, with twenty years' experience?'

'Sure, why not? You never make it look that hard. Get up in the morning, go to work, use a calculator, spreadsheet some shit, come home again in the evening grumpy and frustrated. And repeat.'

'The only thing that makes sense about what you just said is the fact that you'd actually consider getting a job.'

'I don't think you understand quite how much shit we're in now,' Steve said.

'Melodramatic much? I don't know why you're being so negative about this, Steve. Ever since I made this decision, I've felt a massive weight lift off my shoulders. You should be happy for me.'

'Well the weight is off yours and on mine.'

'I know it's a lot to digest, and I'm sure you feel like the rug has been pulled out from under you. That's totally normal under the circumstances. But everything is going to be fine. Especially if you're willing to get a job. Writing a book is sexy on a first date, but it's not quite as hot when you've been together for years. And you've barely managed to write a page in the last year.'

'You don't know that I haven't written a page this year,' Steve squeaked.

'Have you written a page this year?'

'That's not the point! Intention counts too, you know?'

'Yes, except, nobody out there is lining up to publish your intentions. And you also intended to take out the bins last night, and that didn't happen either,' Norma said.

'Christ, I'm freezing my nuts off out here,' Steve said.

No longer hand in hand, Norma followed a stomping Steve under the sign that read, 'Capta n Pow's Chows' and into London's only Global-Asian restaurant with a missing 'i', run by a family from Essex.

Nothing had changed inside Capta n Pow's Chows in all the time they'd been going there. In fact, Norma suspected not much had changed in the last seventeen years the establishment had been there. Certainly not the décor or the tables and chairs, not even the table-cloths, and definitely not the stained, dog-eared menus, or the staff. It was a strange place, run by Brits, serving Eastern cuisine, or what a bunch of Brits who had never been further east than Dover imagined what Eastern cuisine might be.

'Table for two?' the host asked, squinting at them through one eye, the other covered by a patch.

'Hi Captain Pow,' Norma said.

'Yes two, just like every week. Preferably the table we always ask for by the window, but ultimately the one you always give us in that corner between the kitchen door and the toilets,' Steve said sarcastically, as Captain Pow shoved two menus too far under his armpit for Norma's liking, and guided them to the restaurant's worst table.

'Maybe since we didn't put up a fight about this table the first few times we came here, they assumed we like it and now it's "our" table. Maybe they think it's romantic?' Norma said.

'He can't not recognise us every single time we come here, can he? Or is that just his shtick?' Steve asked, as they settled.

'I always thought the patch was a prop, but now that I think about it, maybe he's legitimately visually challenged?' Norma said, adjusting her spectacles.

'Why would it be a prop? It's not a pirate restaurant, it's a fake Asian restaurant, run by a bunch of Brits who wouldn't know their Korean from their Japanese if someone was holding a samurai sword to their necks,' Steve said.

'We'll feel awful if we find out he's actually had some tragic accident and lost an eye along the way,' Norma said.

'Champagne cork?'

'Kamikaze pigeon?'

'Running with scissors?'

'Ex darts-champion?'

Norma giggled.

'Although, you know, I could swear sometimes he wears the patch on the right and sometimes it's on the left,' Steve added.

Norma glanced at the menu, not that there was much point. Captain Pow wasn't big on taking orders. Instead of 'London's only Global-Asian restaurant, run by a family from Essex', their pay-off line should have been 'You get what you get, and you don't get upset.'

As if to underline this, a waiter delivered a Chinese brand beer to Norma, and a Japanese brand whisky to Steve.

'Do you think this is what we would have ordered anyway?' Steve asked, handing Norma the whisky as she handed him the beer.

'I don't know, we've never been given the chance to find out,' Norma said, clinking the ice in her glass. 'I've learnt to like it. Shall we toast to new endeavours?'

'Norma, I know you're excited about this move, and both of us are pretending nothing big has just happened, but it's a massive problem. I need you to reconsider.'

'I know it's not ideal, Steve, but that job has been killing me. I can't live the rest of my life like this. I had to do something. And books have always been my escape, so publishing felt right. It's the first time I've been excited by the thought of work in years. If I were to wait for the right time to pivot, I'd never do it.'

'At any other point in our lives, we would have been fine, but there are extenuating circumstances right now that you don't understand, Norma.'

'Well, nothing sounds good about that.'

'I wasn't going to say anything about this yet, but since you decided to drop a bomb, you've changed my timeline,' Steve said, picking the label off his beer.

'That sounds terrifying. Can we pretend nothing bad has happened for a bit longer, so I can eat something before you put me off my meal? Plus, I'd like to continue being excited about my future for just a few more minutes.'

'Sure, I can pretend our lives aren't imploding for a little longer. Denial is a much more fun place to live than whatever this street of terror is called,' Steve said, glancing at the menu. 'Right, what do you feel like not ordering?'

'Too late,' Norma said, as the waiter placed two plates of food down in front of them.

'What do you think it is? And why do they even bother giving us menus?' Steve asked, handing them back to the waiter.

'Could be chicken? Hey, we may never know what we're eating here, but it always tastes good, and the price isn't bad,' Norma said, reaching for a set of chopsticks.

They ate a bit, then swapped plates and continued eating their new dishes in silence.

'Okay,' Norma said, putting her chopsticks together on the plate of whatever it was that she hadn't ordered. 'We'd better get this over with. I guess I'm ready for you to ruin my meal.'

'I don't think I'm ready,' Steve said, chasing a last mung bean around his plate.

'No point putting it off much longer – apparently the future is coming whether we like it or not.'

'Don't freak out, okay?'

'Steve, in the history of the world, has saying that ever actually stopped anyone freaking out?'

'I've done something a little stupid, by accident, and I'm in a bit of trouble,' Steve said.

'Police trouble?' Norma asked.

'What? No! What do you think I am?' Steve shouted.

'I'm not sure I know anymore,' Norma said. 'What kind of trouble?'

'Money trouble.'

'Okay, you're going to have to tell me, Steve. I can't drag this out of you syllable by syllable, it's too late, I'm too tired, and if we sit here much longer, they're going to start bringing us desserts we don't recognise and wouldn't have ordered, like last time,' Norma said.

'I've accidentally managed to get into an uncomfortable financial situation,' Steve said.

'I'm not surprised. You've been living off your savings since you *left* Amazon. Your money was never going to last forever,' Norma said.

'Why did you say "left" like that?' Steve asked.

'You can say you quit all you want, but I've been wondering if maybe you weren't asked to leave? Just quitting a job out the blue without any backup plans seems like an odd decision. But regardless of how you left, how long did you think your savings from being a middle-tier IT manager at Amazon were going to last?'

'There's more to it than that, Norma. I've lost more than my savings,' Steve mumbled.

'God, what have you done, Steve?' Norma asked, shifting her spectacles, leaning back and humming.

'It was for research for a book,' Steve said.

'You're researching debt?' Norma asked.

'No, one of the characters in my book gambles online,' Steve admitted.

'You gambled online?'

'That's how research works. I needed to know how online gambling works; what it feels like, what happens when you do it, how it feels when you win, how it feels when you lose. All that kind of thing.'

'And does your character fall into debt?' Norma asked.

'He does,' Steve said.

'So it's life imitating art. Does his girlfriend kill him in a global Asian restaurant when she finds out?' Norma said.

'I'm sorry, Norma.'

'I reckon you're less sorry you did it and more sorry that you've had to come clean to me about it,' Norma said. 'What was it, cards? Horses?'

'Does it really matter how? The point is we're going to have to work out how to pay it back.'

'Who's we? I don't see how any of this is my problem. You got yourself into this, and you're going to have to get yourself out of it. I have enough on my plate, especially now,' Norma said as Captain Pow plonked two bowls down in front of them. Both were filled with something brown and sticky, swimming in pools of melting ice cream. The Captain took two spoons out of the top pocket of his shirt, and dropped them onto the table.

'Norma ...'

'Steve, please stop. I can't do this with you anymore. The job, or rather the no job, the writing that isn't writing, and now debt. I have my own stuff going on. I'm only just getting my life figured out.' Then just in case anyone brought more unsolicited food to their table, Norma took out her credit card and waved it in the air to get Captain Pow's attention.

A moment later he appeared with the bill and a credit card machine.

'You couldn't just let me enjoy my pivot for one minute,' Norma said as she tapped her card on the machine.

'Card declined,' Captain Pow said.

'Try again,' Norma said to him.

'Wait, Norma, there's more,' Steve said quietly, swirling his spoon around in his ice-cream soup.

'I'm kind of in the middle of something here, Steve,' Norma said as she tapped her card on the machine again.

'Declined,' Captain Pow said.

'Yes, except, that's the thing, Norma,' Steve said.

'What? What's the thing, Steve?' Norma said, whipping her head around so fast her neck twinged.

'This kind of absolutely is your problem,' Steve said.

'How so? Hang on a minute, where did you get the money to gamble from?' Norma said, batting the spoon out of his hand, so it clattered onto the plastic-covered table, sending melting ice cream splattering.

Captain Pow stepped away, giving them a moment of privacy, even though everyone in the restaurant was listening in.

'What kind of idiot would extend a line of credit to someone like you?' Norma continued.

'It wasn't my credit,' Steve finally said.

Norma felt the vein pulsing in her neck shoot up into her forehead. 'Tell me it wasn't my credit, Steve.'

'Okay, it wasn't your credit, Norma.'

'I'm about to lose my shit, Steve, now is not the time to make a joke.

Was it my credit?' Norma asked through gritted teeth.

'It was your credit,' Steve said.

'But how? I don't understand.'

'Your card,' Steve mumbled, nodding at the card she was holding.

'But I get notifications on my phone whenever my credit card gets used. It always goes "ping".'

'I was surprised that you didn't notice when the notifications stopped. You're normally quite vigilant. I thought you'd miss them straight away and stop me.'

'I'm sorry, Steve, but I've been a bit busy with my mid-life career transformation, so sue me for not noticing that my phone stopped going ping.' Norma tapped the card on the machine one more time. It whirred to life and beeped loudly twice.

'How did you get them to stop notifying me?' she asked, her voice low.

'I'm an IT geek, that's what I do,' Steve said. 'I rerouted the ping.'

'You hacked into my credit card profile?' Norma said.

'Something like that.'

'This just gets better and better. And by better and better, I mean worse and worse.' Norma's voice was climbing again.

Steve looked around nervously.

'Oh, I see. You thought if you told me in a public place, I'd be less likely to make a scene? That's the oldest trick in the book, Steve.'

'Well, it's more that I thought you wouldn't try to murder me in front of so many witnesses,' Steve said, as a mum with four kids traipsed past their table to the bathroom. 'I'm sorry, Norma. I didn't mean for it to get this bad. I was up at first. Like really up. And I was going to stop at the top. I'm not an idiot, I know how these things go. I was going to surprise you with the profits, take us somewhere nice. We haven't been anywhere nice in ages. But then my luck turned, and before I knew it I was down. And then ... well, you shouldn't leave your credit card and stuff lying around.'

'What? I shouldn't leave my own credit card and my mobile phone lying around inside my own handbag, inside my own home? You're right, that was careless. But in retrospect, it seems there's quite a bit I shouldn't have done. Like staying with you this long. I don't know what I was thinking. Actually, it's not your fault: you're right, it's my fault. I should have known something like this would happen.'

'I was going to fix it before you found out, Norma, I swear. I've had tons of ideas about how to make the money back before your next statement comes, I was getting right on it, but then when you told me you'd given up your job and you're going to be earning less than minimum wage from next month, I panicked.'

'How much do you … do I owe?' Norma asked.

'A lot,' Steve said.

'How much?' Norma asked again, through gritted teeth.

'All of it,' Steve said.

'All of it? What, all of the money in the world? All of the money in the bank? All of the money in my account, in this card? What all of it?' Norma hissed.

'All of the money in your limit. That's why I'm telling you. I didn't want you to be taken by surprise.'

'Oh, you didn't want me to be taken by surprise, did you?' Norma said, tapping the card on the machine again so it beeped in denial. Then tapping it once more, eliciting more beeping. 'Epic fail, Steve, because believe it or not, I have now been taken completely by surprise.'

Steve stared into his bowl.

'What are we going to do now? I just quit my job and took on a barely paying internship, and in a few minutes, we're going to have to explain to a man who wears a patch over alternating eyes, that we don't know how we're going to pay for who the fuck knows what we ate. What's your plan?'

Steve looked around nervously and reached for his wallet.

Harry

Harry patted his pocket again, feeling for his speech. He'd finally scribbled a few thoughts on a handful of cue cards in the taxi on the way to the awards.

It didn't matter how long he'd taken to put it down, it was how long he'd been thinking about it that really counted, as he'd told Victoria when she'd rolled her eyes at him in the taxi while he frantically scrawled his speech with the driver's chewed pen. Which had then leaked, turning his fingers black and smudging the lapel of his dress shirt. He pretended to be bothered by the stains for Victoria's benefit, but privately he thought they lent him a more literary air. It was how he imagined Mark Twain would have shown up to the Golden Pages in 1905.

'I see you've been in a spot of bother online, old chum?' Dominic Zeal's rough, wet voice grazed Harry's ear.

Why Dominic Zeal had been put next to him at what Harry considered *his* table at The Golden Page Awards, was a mystery. Zeal was a hack, a D-lister at best. The fact that he'd even been nominated had been the talk of the industry when the shortlist had been announced. It was rumoured that since his father was titled, it was his family money the Golden Page people had their eye on, rather than his literary talents.

Zeal always spat when he talked, and Harry made a big performance of wiping his cheek with his handkerchief before responding,

'Oh that, it's nothing. All PR is good PR. In fact, it was my publicist's idea from the start. They planted that review,' Harry lied with a conspiratorial tone. 'You know, drum up some interest for the pending launch of my new novel.'

'What a tremendously odd idea,' Zeal sprayed. 'I think you may want to ask those publicists for your money back, old chap. I'm not sure getting a diabolically shit review and then getting cancelled is the best way to sell books.'

'Oh, I would hardly say I've been cancelled.'

'No, I'm sure you wouldn't. But it's certainly what everyone else is saying. Truth is, nobody thought you would have the balls to show up here tonight. You've been quite the topic of conversation, Shields.'

Harry followed Zeal's gaze, picking up furtive glances from the authors, publicists, publishers and editors at the surrounding tables. Many of whom were having whispered conversations behind their hands.

'Come on, Shields! What author in their right mind responds to bad reviews?' Zeal said with, Harry noted, rather too much gleeful zeal. 'It's media training 101.'

Harry turned his back on Zeal and said in Victoria's ear, 'Do you think I have time to pop to the bathroom before the announcement?'

'Again, Harry? That'll be the third time you've been,' Victoria said. 'Do we need to get your prostate checked?'

'You know my bowels get irritable when I'm nervous, and public speaking makes me nervous.'

'Oh my darling, I've been telling you for weeks, I really don't think you have anything to be nervous about tonight. And anyway, I don't think you have time, look, they're getting ready to announce the award,' Victoria said, pressing her palm down on his knee to still the bouncing.

The lights dimmed and a spotlight roamed the floor as music started to swell. Harry's stomach lurched as Priscilla Holmsworthy, host of the popular TV game show *Word Nerd*, walked on stage in a floor-length red ballgown, to billowing applause. This was it, he thought. His first big award. Fortunately, Richard Osman was in the under 100 000-word octogenarian crime category, so Harry was sure he had this one in the bag.

He scanned the crowd and spotted Osman at a table across the room, rather worryingly closer to the stage than they were. He took a deep breath, clenched his buttocks and patted his pocket, checking for his speech one last time. Then tried to focus on Priscilla, who was speaking about the pedigree of the awards and the challenges the brave judges had faced in selecting just one winner in this category from the sea of entries.

Priscilla's voice boomed as she got to the announcement: '... and the winner of this year's Golden Page award, for a second novel in the crime category written by a British author, is ...'

... the lights dimmed and the expectant music drum-rolled, as Priscilla made a big show of opening the envelope, then pausing for effect. Harry felt Victoria's nails digging into his thigh. He would have bruises later, but it would be so worth it. He sat up straighter and pasted his practiced, pleasantly surprised smile on his face, for when the cameras would land on him.

'... Harry ...' Priscilla Holmsworthy announced.

'I knew it, I knew it!' Harry whooped, bursting out of his seat, punching the air with his fist.

There was a smattering of surprised applause as he bent down to give Victoria a quick peck on the cheek, then bounded up to the stage, as the spotlight found him.

Which was when Priscilla Holmsworthy cleared her throat and continued: 'The winner is: Harri ... et Blumenthal! For her novel, *In the Darkest Hour*. Harriet, come up and get your Golden Page award.'

A sudden awkward silence fell before the crowd launched into smatterings of uncomfortable applause, drowned out by laughter and the hum of chatter.

Harry was frozen halfway up the stairs to the stage. Too far from his seat to scuttle back down quickly, and too close to Priscilla to be inconspicuous. He sensed the spotlight pausing then doing a confused loop away from him, searching for the right target. When the spotlight found Harriet Blumenthal, it followed her from her table, past Harry, still rooted to the spot, then up the stairs and onto the stage.

'What are you doing?' Victoria hissed, as he crept back to his seat, snickering and murmurs from the surrounding tables filling his ears, not quite drowned out by the sound of Harriet Blumenthal now delivering her acceptance speech, which he could barely hear through the rush of roaring in his ears. The snippets he did catch were beautifully written, perfectly timed, self-deprecating, funny and full of humility.

'I thought she said my name,' Harry hissed, his face burning with humiliation.

'But she said Harriet Blumenthal's name,' Victoria said.

'Obviously I know that now!' Harry whisper-shouted.

'Old chap, that was priceless!' Zeal spluttered as he slapped Harry hard on the back, sending him reeling forward onto his plate, his leftover beetroot hummus starter slapping onto his shirt front. Zeal was howling with laughter, tears rolling down his fat whiskered cheeks. 'Did you really think you'd won? I can't believe you'd ever think so. No wonder you're the laughing stock of the internet. This is more entertaining than the Cabinet playing musical chairs!' Zeal guffawed.

'OH WILL YOU JUST SHUT THE FUCK UP, YOU TALENTLESS, PATHETIC, SPITTING EXCUSE FOR A HACK! EVERYONE KNOWS YOU CAN'T GET IT UP SINCE YOU HAD COVID, EITHER IN YOUR BOOKS OR YOUR BEDROOM! AND EVERYBODY KNOWS YOU WERE ONLY NOMINATED TONIGHT BECAUSE YOUR OLD MAN HAS GOBS OF CASH, AND YOUR WIFE'S BLOWING THE AWARDS DIRECTOR, YOU UTTER CUNT!'

Harry realised he was shouting, and that he'd caught a perfectly timed gap to use completely unacceptable language just as Harriet Blumenthal had paused for dramatic effect in her acceptance speech, right after thanking her agent, her children and the Lord Jesus. There was a collective gasp of shock from the crowd. Every eye turned to him and the ballroom went church-quiet, until a show producer in a control booth somewhere instructed the sound guy to cue the music, and Priscilla Holmsworthy bustled Harriet Blumenthal off the stage, clutching her award and what was left of her undelivered speech, shooting a glare over her shoulder at Harry.

The second they cleared the stage, the room erupted.

'Victoria, can we go, please? I want this to be finished.'

'Oh, don't worry about that, darling, I suspect you are now nothing if not completely finished,' Victoria said, reaching for her pearl-encrusted clutch.

Harry

'How'd it go, bud?' Phyllis asked.

'I did the diametric opposite of win,' Harry said into the phone, his voice low.

'Oh no, Harry. You were so sure you had it in the bag.'

'I know, and instead I embarrassed myself in front of everyone, Phyllis. It was mortifying. I'll never be able to show my face in public again. It couldn't actually have gone any worse.'

'Oh Harry, I'm sure it wasn't that bad.'

'No, you're right, it wasn't that bad, it was worse.'

'What time is it over there? It's gotta be late.'

'Time doesn't mean very much to me anymore, Phyllis.'

'That's a good line, Harry, write it down and use it in your work. It's the only thing that makes these bad things that happen to us mean anything. Write your feelings while they're still fresh.'

'I can't seem to take my eyes off this car crash, Phyl.'

'You're not still feeding the trolls, are you? Harry, step away from your computer. You're in a career-destroying spiral. You need to listen to me here, buddy, and walk away. This is textbook. People are always baiting authors, trying to get them to react and cause a stink. You're falling into their trap,' Phyllis said.

'I think the internet might be driving me crazy.'

'Ultimately, it's driving us all bananas, Harry. It's the 5G implants.

In generations to come, I suspect they will look back on this as the Ground Zero of the downfall of humanity.'

'They are eviscerating me. Have you seen all the threads on The Good Book Appreciation Society on Facebook, Goodreads and X? There's even a Reddit thread now.'

'You do know that Facebook has been proven to radicalise its users, don't you? And it was absolutely, unequivocally the cause of the Covid pandemic. You know that, right? And don't even get me started on Bill Gates.'

'This is way scarier than any of those conspiracy theories, Phyllis. Here's the thing that nobody understands: from now on, every time anyone anywhere in the world googles my name or any of my books, this whole thing will be the first thing that comes up. Forever. Even if I die in a horrible accident, or save a child from a burning building, or win a Pulitzer. Even when I donate all my work, notes and research to the British Library, this will still be the defining moment in my career. They're taking me down, Phyl! It's like what happened to Richard Gere with that bloody gerbil.'

'That seems a bit extreme, Harry.'

'Extreme? From a woman who thinks JFK survived his assassination and still lives in Utah as a televangelical preacher?'

'I'm not wrong! There's no real proof that ...'

'I'm sorry, Phyl, I can't burrow into the JFK can of worms with you right now. My life has imploded, I haven't slept in days, Myra still hasn't gotten back to me about my manuscript, and probably never will now. Victoria isn't talking to me because she's so embarrassed about what happened tonight. I got a death threat by DM. An actual death threat. Did I tell you that? Someone might actually kill me. And worse, what if nobody ever publishes me ever again, Phyl? My career, my life, it's all over. O.V.E.R!' Harry cried.

'What happened there tonight, Harry?'

'I shouted at Dominic Zeal. I think I may have even shoved him. And I called him pathetic, and that wasn't even the worst of it,' Harry said.

'Oh puhleez, that's what everyone says behind his back anyway, that old blow-hard. You just had the balls to say it to his face. It's not such a big deal, Harry. Write a cute, instagrammable apology to Zeal, send him a set of fancy leather-bound books and a bottle of scotch, then photograph it all, and put it on X. Everyone will have forgotten about it before the next pandemic hits. You know it's going to be boils, right? Or frogs. And if we survive that, and still nobody forgives you, the world is going to be hit by a monster asteroid in two years anyway, so who cares? I wouldn't lose a second of sleep over any of this, Harry.'

'I can't believe I've gone viral,' Harry said.

'Harry, reframe your thinking, writers dream of going viral.'

'Not like this, Phyl. We want to go viral because our books resonate with people. But how can my books resonate with people if there are a bunch of trolls talking them out of even reading them in the first place?'

'You should view this whole debacle through the lens of that old adage that there's no such thing as bad publicity.'

'Not you too, Phyllis. The only people who say that are people who have never been caught up in bad publicity. I even have my own trending hashtag on X, did I tell you? It's #OneStarHarry.'

'You know that the X servers are all located in the White House, don't you?'

Harry groaned.

'Harry, the bottom line is that every story needs a villain. And this is your fifteen minutes to be the villain. I'm sure at some point we'll all get a go.'

'People have already given my third book one-star reviews and I don't even have a publishing deal for it yet.'

'You see, there's an upside to this whole nightmare. Even perfect strangers are already thinking about your next novel, Harry, it's pre-pub buzz. It's a sign.'

'A sign my career is over.'

'Harry, I've got to go, I've got a radio interview in half an hour. But I'm here for you whenever you need me. And we have the Book Festival of London to look forward to. We can hang out and catch up then.'

'Good luck with your interview. Do me a favour and don't mention your theories on 9-11 live on air,' Harry said. 'Or wait, on second thoughts, maybe you should – it might take the heat off me if you go and get cancelled.'

'Stop responding to the trolls, Harry.'

'I will,' Harry said, hanging up, then going back to check The Good Book Appreciation Society page one more time, before logging out as himself and logging back in as Gaill A. And shortly thereafter as Bernard Phillips. He'd told Phyllis he'd stop commenting, but he'd never said his other voices would stop. He might not get to have the last word, but one of his aliases always could.

THE GOOD BOOK APPRECIATION SOCIETY

MEMBERS: 20 827

Brian Wilder: Well, well, well, book friends. Take a look at who's gone viral for storming the Golden Page Awards stage when another author won the award he thought he deserved. Then verbally and physically assaulted a fellow nominated author. You guessed it, only everyone in this club's least favourite author: Harry Shields.

Check out this video from the awards show. It's only been on YouTube for a few hours and it's already gone viral. The video was taken by sixteen-year-old Jarred Blumenthal, who attended the black-tie event with his mother, Harriet Blumenthal, author of the crime thriller *In the Darkest Hour*, the novel that actually won the award. Blumenthal was hoping to film his mum's award acceptance speech for the family album, and ended up catching all the action on his mobile.

Harry Shields doesn't think it's okay just to abuse his readers, now he's abusing fellow authors too. If anyone deserves to be cancelled, it's this guy. Please join us all on Goodreads to offer him a one-star review of his books (even ones he hasn't published yet) and his personality.

COMMENTS:

Edna Molton: Can't say I'm surprised, this author is always going around being unprofessional. And I can't say I enjoyed his book very much. But don't let him hear me saying that, he'll just have another tantrum.

Dax Goby: Look @Lucille Cooper, this is that video I was telling you about.

Lucille Cooper: Thanks @Dax Goby, wow, he's really lost it, hasn't he? Looking forward to seeing you later for our book club dinner.

Norma

'Oh bugger,' Norma muttered, as she watched the video Brian Wilder had posted to the group.

It was grainy, hand-held footage taken on a mobile from across the ballroom, so the sound quality wasn't good either, but thanks to the closed captions she could still get a pretty good idea of what had gone down. It was clear that Harry Shields was deeply unstable.

Norma saw no relevance in the video for the group. It had nothing to do with books or reading, and neither did the few comments it had racked up in the minutes the post had been live. She smiled at the comments by Dax and Lucille – those two members needed to get a room, preferably a library. Then she deleted the post, and the few comments went with it. She was glad she'd caught and deleted it early, and hoped Harry Shields was sleeping off his shame and a probable monster hangover, and hadn't seen it. Although there was no way he'd be able to avoid the video online. It was being shared all over the world, and was already heading for seven hundred thousand views on YouTube. What was important was that he didn't see it on her page, though. She didn't want to be on the receiving end of another barrage of all-caps threatening hate mails from him.

After deleting the post, and doing her morning scan of the page, Norma lay back against her pillows and closed her eyes. She was exhausted after tossing and turning all night, listening to Steve snoring loudly on the couch.

'Sleep okay?' Steve asked, yawning, as she passed him on her way to the kitchen to make coffee.

'Steve, we need to talk.' Norma's fingers shook as she prepped the coffee machine – she wasn't sure whether it was because she needed caffeine, or because she was so furious. 'What's the plan? You said you had irons in the fire?'

'I have a couple of ideas.'

'Like?'

'You could sell the group?' Steve said, joining her at the coffee machine, reaching for his mug.

'The Good Book Appreciation Society?' Norma said. 'Who would want to buy a Facebook page? And anyway, that's my happy place, it's the only thing I've ever done that's been even vaguely successful. I don't think I could sell it, even if it was worth something.'

'Couldn't you monetise it somehow?'

'How?' Norma asked.

'I'm not on Facebook, so I don't know what goes on over there, but couldn't you ask the members for a monthly subscription fee or donation for running it, like Wikipedia does? They're all readers, I'm sure they've got tons of cash. A hundred quid each, every month, from however many thousand members you have – that would be a start,' Steve said.

'Why on earth would they pay such an exorbitant amount, or any amount, to be part of the group when there are hundreds, if not thousands, more groups out there just like it, and they're all free?' Norma snapped, adjusting her spectacles.

'No need to bite my head off. I have other ideas too.'

'Do any of them involve you getting a job?' Norma asked, shooting him a dirty look.

'Writing my book right now is my job,' Steve said.

'Can't you finish your book on the side, like everyone else does?' Norma said.

'What if you took money out of your company credit card to pay off some of the debt? Just as a short-term solution?' Steve suggested. 'We would pay it back.'

Norma gave him another filthy look. 'That's a great idea, Steve. Steal money from the company that as of one week from now, I will no longer officially be working for. Who would then have me arrested for fraud and theft. I was hoping for a leaving party, not a going-away-for-a-five-to-nine-year-stretch party.'

'We could borrow from a loan shark? Use the flat as collateral?'

'Or, unpopular opinion here, you could get a job, Steve, like everyone else in the world. And then we could use that salary to pay off the minimum payment due every month on that card until the day we die. How's that for a novel idea?'

'We could gamble? Take a chunk out of our savings and go big, put it all on red or black?'

'You mean my savings? I don't recall you having any savings left. So now you want to gamble what's left of my money? Have you learnt nothing from what happened to you?'

'Remortgage the flat and bet that?' he suggested.

'You couldn't just let me have my mid-life crisis pivot in peace, could you? You had to screw it up for me.'

'Norma, you're an accountant, you work with tons of money every day. There must be some way we could slice a little off the top so nobody would notice. You read stories in the news about people doing that all the time.'

'Yes, and they're in the news because they got caught.' Norma shook her head.

'How much do you think we could get for our air fryer?' Steve said, looking around the kitchen.

'So, that's the extent of your plans? Fraud, theft, gambling, or flogging all our stuff on Facebook Marketplace? If that's the case, I feel confident that I'm in good hands. And can I just flag that at no point did you suggest we sell your PlayStation, but my air fryer is fair game.'

'Norma, don't be like that. We're going to have to work together to figure something out.'

'Who's we?' Norma shouted. 'Why do WE have to figure this out together? You broke this on your own, you're going to have to fix it on your own. And you're going to have to do it soon: my next minimum payment, of who the hell knows how much, comes due on the twenty-fifth.'

'We could sell the flat?' Steve said.

'This isn't going to work, Steve. I think we need some space.'

'Yes, exactly. We could sell the flat, pay off the debt and rent something with more space.'

'You're delusional. That's not the kind of space I meant. I meant space away from each other. Like you all the way over there, and me very far away from you, over here. You need to move in with a mate, or Marina, or your dad or your mum for a while. Until we've figured out how to deal with this.'

'Not my dad! And you want me to move in with my mum? She's hours away, and we barely speak. Or Marina? I don't even know where she lives. Do you?'

Norma shook her head.

'And anyway, the two of you are closer than the two of us, so maybe you should move in with her?'

'After all this, you're still taking the piss, Steve. You have to go.'

'Don't do this, Norma,' Steve said, his voice barely audible.

'Steve, you're the one who's done this, not me. I can't trust you anymore. Do I have to lock my handbag away? Hide my jewellery? Chain the air fryer to the kitchen counter? I think this will be best for everyone.'

'It's obviously not best for me.'

Norma was about to respond when her phone started ringing. It was an unknown number, so it was probably a marketing cold-caller, but she answered it anyway, anything to end this conversation.

'Norma Jacobs?'

'Speaking,' Norma said.

'My name is Miles O' Hennessey, I write a blog called "The Writing Life", maybe you've heard of it?'

When Norma didn't respond he continued, 'I was wondering if I could chat to you about this author who's gone viral after responding to a review on your Facebook page?'

'How did you get my number?'

'The internet is a very useful place, Ms Jacobs. Anyway, I was hoping to chat to you briefly ...'

'No comment,' Norma said, and hit the disconnect button.

'Who was that?' Steve asked.

'For crying out loud, it's not even seven am,' Norma said, staring at her phone.

Steve sidled up to her. 'Bug, things are stressful right now, you shouldn't do anything rash. Please can we talk about this?'

'No, Steve, my mind's made up. I'm going to meet Marina later this morning, and when I get back, I need you to be out.'

'This is my home too. Why do I have to move out? You're the one who wants space. I'm quite happy with the space we have.'

'Because I'm the one paying the mortgage, Steve. You haven't put a cent into this flat since you quit your job. So sure, I can move out, but then I'll stop paying and I can't see you managing to keep up the mortgage payments by yourself.'

When Steve didn't respond, Norma took her coffee back into the bedroom and closed the door, so she could have a good cry in peace while she got ready to go meet Marina. Her mobile rang again, with another number she didn't recognise.

'Hello?'

'Norma Jacobs, this is Martina Halvorsen from *The Morning Show* on ...'

Norma hung up and turned off her phone.

Harry

'Hello Mr Shields, my name is Gemma Franks, I'm a reporter with *The Times* ...'

'Oh no ...' Harry said, and moved to red-button her. He'd been avoiding calls from numbers he didn't recognise the entire day, and he'd only answered the phone this time because it said 'unknown number' on his screen, and Myra's assistant had once called from their offices and it had shown up as an unknown number. It was also why he hadn't changed his number when the onslaught of press and bloggers trying to reach him for comment had started. It was hard to avoid calls when you were desperately waiting for one.

While the Author Behaving Badly stuff on Facebook and Goodreads had caught the press's attention, the video from the awards that had gone viral had really captured their imaginations. There had even been two journalists camped outside their townhouse that morning trying to get a comment out of them, or at the very least some snaps to sell to some grubby rag. Victoria reckoned it must have been a very slow news day.

'Wait, Harry. Mr Shields. Please don't hang up. I'm a huge fan, and I just want to help you tell your side of the story.'

None of the calls or emails he'd fielded so far had sounded like this one. If she really did want to tell his side of the story, and not just drag him back through the mud, this might be an opportunity to fix this whole situation. He wasn't the baddie everyone was making him out to be, people needed to know that.

'Are you still there, Mr Shields? Please, just give me a minute to explain myself. I've read both your books. The one twice, the other three times.'

Harry brought the phone back up to his ear. 'You have?'

'Oh yes, I first read *Monday Never Comes*, when it came out, my ex gave it to me for my birthday, only decent thing she ever did for me. I loved it. I put it into my book club, where it did the rounds. And then of course we picked up *Once on a Tuesday* the minute it was launched, and really loved that too. Couldn't put it down. I almost missed a deadline over it, so you owe me one,' she laughed. 'I just want to say that I'm sorry this has happened to you. I saw the video and I wondered if maybe there wasn't another side to the story? You're a smart, rational guy, and a great writer – I can't imagine you would just storm the stage like that for no reason. I truly believe in innocent until proven guilty, Mr Shields, it's the pillar of my work. Google me and you'll see. Someone just needs to give you the opportunity to tell your side of the story.'

'That's exactly what I think!' Harry said, feeling a lump form in his throat. He felt seen for the first time since this whole thing had started. Maybe he'd gotten it all wrong, and he'd just been looking in the wrong corner of the internet. Perhaps there was a whole neighbourhood of the net where people saw how wronged he'd been. And that he hadn't stormed the stage, that he'd legitimately thought he'd won. It was the kind of mistake anyone could make. And maybe there were also people out there who agreed with him that he'd HAD to respond to all those haters on social media to protect his integrity.

'I was hoping we could chat. I'd love to help set the record straight. Everyone is always so quick to cancel famous people these days, don't you think?'

'I wouldn't say I was famous, exactly,' Harry said, flushing.

'So, you'd consider talking to me?' Gemma asked.

'Well, I wouldn't want to disappoint a fan.'

Norma

'You kicked him out?' Marina asked.

'Yup. Your mobile will probably ring any second, with enquiries from your new housemate, eager to leave an indent of his arse on your couch, deposit his squeezed-out teabags on the edge of your sink, and spend freely on your credit card until he puts you in the poor house, too,' Norma said, as they settled in at the counter at Tonkotsu, their favourite Ramen spot.

Marina had strange eating habits. She followed a daily diet of Monster Munch, miso soup, McDonald's and Cadbury's Crème Eggs, punctuated by regular visits to Michelin-starred restaurants and some of the finest Ramen holes-in-the-wall you could find in London.

'Speaking of mobiles ringing. What's going on there, Grand Central?' Marina asked, nodding at Norma's phone, which was lighting up with a new call or message every few seconds.

'This idiot author went viral on my page for responding to a negative review of one of his books, and then he did some crazy shit at an awards show last night, so the press are trying to reach me for comment.'

'No ways,' Marina said. 'Cool, next stop *The Graham Norton Show*.'

'Being tossed off his red sofa, maybe. It couldn't have happened at a worse time, with all this Steve stuff. And just as I was getting my shit together, and about to start living my best life.'

'You've always had your shit together, Norma, that's one of the things I admire most about you. That, and that thing you do with the numbers.'

'Accountancy? Well, as you know, I quit my job. I'm going into publishing for minimum wage instead. Sorry, but there is now officially nothing left for you to admire most about me.'

'Not true. I admire all of it. It takes big balls to change your life. But I've got to say, when you told me what he'd done to you, it felt pretty good finally not to be the only member of the family into some weird shit or other.'

'Have you heard from him?' Norma asked.

'Not a peep. But he knows that if he's looking for sympathy, he'll have to look elsewhere. And anyway, there's no way the people where I live would let anyone else move in. You could say we're at capacity. He's unlikely to head deep into the countryside to find Mum, so he's probably going to have to hit up our old man.'

'I don't even know where you live, Marina. Would you tell me if I asked?'

'Probably not. But it's for your own good.'

'You're right, I'm sure he'll hit up your old man,' Norma said.

'I'm not sure which of them I feel sorrier for. Hey, did you cancel your credit card yet?'

'Do you think I need to? He's hit my limit. My card wouldn't go through at Captain Pow's last night, so there's nothing else to get at.'

'You should probably cancel it anyway, just in case. He's quite good at finding a way, my bruvva is. Couldn't you claim fraudulent activity on your account, open a case and try get some of the cash back?'

'What, and tell them the man I live with took my credit card and mobile phone out of my bag in our home, and used it to gamble online? It's highly unlikely they'll do anything other than wonder how I could have been so stupid as to let that happen. I honestly don't know what I'm going to do.'

'I don't see how this debt is your problem. He spent the money, surely he needs to get a job and pay it back?' Marina asked.

'In theory, sure. But who's going to hire him, Marina? Previously unemployed, middle-aged, middle-manager white guy wanna-be authors, who smoke too much weed and don't particularly want to work anymore, are hardly in demand.'

'He seems quite good at hacking into credit cards. Maybe someone can hire him to do that?'

'Got any contacts for him on that front?'

'Ha, nice try,' Marina said. 'I'm not a hacker. Well, not anymore.'

'If by some miracle, he managed to get a job, he might make enough to pay the monthly minimum payment due, but he's unlikely to be able to pay off the whole thing, I reckon.

'Ultimately, it's my card, my problem. I don't know what happened, Marina: one minute we were a normal, happy couple, jump forward a few years, and I barely recognise the guy and I'm discussing handing him over to the cops with his twin. How did we get here?'

'Things change. People change. Let me order for us, you go call the bank and cancel the card just in case, right? Then you'd better tell me where you're at with this quitting and publishing thing. Although if you use the word "pivot" again, you're buying lunch, even if you have to wash the dishes to pay for it.'

Harry

'A million and something hits, that's really something, Harry,' Neil said, holding out his mobile, playing the clip from the Golden Page Awards so everyone at the table could see.

'Crikey, that's a lot. And I read somewhere that the Zeal bloke is suing you,' Clive said. 'Ooh look, they have bottomless mimosas.'

'Guys, please don't get him started, he hasn't mentioned that video innnn ... all of twelve minutes,' Victoria said, looking at her watch. 'I was hoping we might make it to fifteen, and set a new world record.'

'But he's gone viral again, Vicks, we have to talk about it,' Neil said. 'Do you have any idea how many people that is? It's like the population of a whole country, or like fifty full O2 stadiums.'

'I'm in hell,' Harry said, 'and the press won't stop calling, and none of this would have happened if it wasn't for that revolting octogenarian and her disgusting review.'

'Now you've done it,' Victoria said. 'Here we go again.'

'I think I know what I'm going to do about her,' Harry said.

'Harry, please, it's Sunday morning, can we not just eat our brunch in peace?' Victoria pleaded. 'Did somebody say they have bottomless mimosas?'

'Victoria, you'll want to hear this too. I know you all think I've gone a bit overboard, but I've finally come up with a healthy way to channel my frustration.'

'Frustration? I'd call it more like rage,' Clive said.

'I'll own it,' Harry said. 'Yes, I have been pretty furious about the whole thing.'

'And distracted,' Victoria said.

'And unreasonable,' Neil added.

'Point taken, guys! I know this thing has consumed me and it's been a little unhealthy, but I think I've come up with an appropriate response.'

'Okay, I'll bite. What is it?' Clive asked.

'I'm going to write her into a new book, and then have terrible things happen to her, before ultimately killing her off very violently,' Harry said, with a smug smile.

'I had a feeling it was going to be gory,' Neil said.

'Crikey,' Clive said.

'It's classic Writer's Revenge,' Harry said.

'Are you going to use her real name in this book?' Victoria asked.

'Of course. What's the point of killing her if she doesn't know she's dead? Where's the revenge in that?'

'Isn't that defamation?' Victoria asked.

'They always put those disclaimers in the front of novels, any likeness to any person living or dead is entirely coincidental, blah, blah, blah, etcetera,' Harry said.

'She and her family aren't going to be happy. I think you need to think about this very seriously, Harry. Maybe consult a lawyer?' Victoria said.

'I can put you onto one of mine,' Neil suggested.

'You guys are missing the point. People pay thousands in auctions to have their names written into famous people's books. Stephen King and Marian Keyes do it all the time,' Harry said.

'I don't know if that's quite the same thing. Those fans are choosing to be written into the book. And I love you, my darling, but I'm not sure you're quite famous enough for that just yet,' Victoria said.

'Why don't you stick to laparoscopies and leave the writing to me?' Harry snapped.

Victoria's eyes narrowed, and Neil and Clive made cat-mewing sounds, as the waiter came to deliver their order.

'So how were you thinking of killing her?' Neil asked.

'Crikey, morbid much, Neil?' Clive said.

'Well, I thought for starters, her nemesis, in the book, who is a famous author …'

'Of course he is,' Victoria said.

Harry shot her a glare before continuing, '… first I'm going to have her nemesis, the famous author, play some pranks on her, like tracking down her email address and signing her up for dozens of sales newsletters every day, and spam for weird products, like sex toys and adult incontinence pants and Jehovah's Witness pamphlets. And then the famous author character is going to opt her telephone number in with as many call centres as possible. AND he's going to have a pizza delivered to her house every single day for six months. With blue cheese and anchovies on all of them,' Harry said, triumphantly.

'That's a good one,' Neil laughed.

'Please don't encourage him,' Victoria snapped.

'And then right at the end, maybe he'll kill her with a blunt machete,' Harry said, stabbing at and then forking scrambled eggs into his mouth.

'You really are angry about this, aren't you?' Neil said.

'You could say it's captured my imagination,' Harry said.

'A little therapy can go a long way, is all I'm saying,' Victoria said.

'So can a little arsenic in her tea,' Neil mumbled.

'Neil!' Clive scolded.

Norma

As Norma fired up the coffee machine, she fired up her mobile, and it lit up with WhatsApp notifications.

Fourteen of them. And it wasn't even six am.

One was from yet another book blogger asking to interview her, another from the producer of a popular podcast, inviting her to chat about 'the whole Harry Shields debacle', and the rest were from Steve.

Steve's first voice note had come in just after two in the morning, and then there had been a steady stream of them until ... ping, that one, right then. Clearly she'd been the only person in London to get any sleep.

Norma loaded a coffee pod and pressed play on the earliest voice note.

> Hey Norms, I was having a think and you know what we should do? Remortgage the flat, then take that capital and create an olive oil and wine business. It's a brilliant idea. It'd just be a small hole-in-the-wall shopfront on the high street, keeping overheads low, then we'd have these huge vats filled with either olive oil or wine. We could import them from South Africa, you're from there, you know people, and everybody knows they make great wine. Then customers bring their own empty bottles and fill them up, and pay by the gallon or the pint or whatever. We could even franchise it.

> Picture one on every street corner. Like an olive oil Costas. What do you think? Genius, right?

Norma could hear a pub in the background. She deleted the following two voice notes without listening to them, then clicked on one which had come in an hour after the first.

> No, hang on a minute, Norms, forget those last ideas. If we're going to remortgage the house, we should take that money and buy a racehorse. Have you seen how much money those guys make? They're practically printing it. And they always have nice cars, so they must be doing something right. We could call it something arsey and double-barrelled like, 'artisanal-sourdough-baker' or something silly for a laugh, like 'Pull-me-a-pint'. That would be brilliant. I can hear it now, 'And coming down the final stretch, Pull-me-a-pint's pulling ahead.' Please consider it, Norms, it's a winner of an idea, I reckon.

Steve's voice was getting progressively more slurred with each new voice note. She deleted three more, and clicked on an even later one.

> Me again. I've got it, Norma, the perfect plan. My mate Bald-Derek, you remember Bald-Derek, with the gammy hand? Say hello, Bald-Derek ...

Norma heard some guy slurring her name in the background.

> So Bald-Derek knows this guy, Money-Phil, whose cousin has a great 'in' on stock tips. We'll take your savings, or that remortgage money and play the stock exchange using his tips? Tons of people make a killing doing that. No reason that couldn't be us. And it's clever because it's passive income. You make money while you sleep. Bald-Derek says Money-Phil really knows what he's doing. We'll never have to work another day in our lives, Norms. Problem solved! Message

> me, alright? Are these messages even going through to you? Why aren't you checking your phone?

Norma sipped her coffee as a fresh voice note pinged into her phone.

> Aha, blue ticks. I see you've just listened to my voice notes. I knew you'd come around eventually. I think this is the opportunity we've been waiting for, Norms. We can make our money back and solve all our problems. Plus more exponentially down the line. Or what if we take your savings and play the lottery? With the amount of tickets we'd be able to buy, we'd definitely be guaranteed to win something, you know all about statistics, statistically there's no way we wouldn't win something. Then once we've won and sorted this mess out, we can focus on us again. I know things have kind of fallen apart, but we can fix this, I know we can. We were good together once.

Norma wasn't about to respond, and she had to get ready for work. Today was the first day of the rest of her pivot.

Harry

'You really are the life and soul of the party these days, Harry,' Victoria said in the cab home.

'But Vicks ...' Harry started.

'You quite put me off my shakshuka,' Victoria cut him off.

'I know I've been pre-occupied with this, but ...'

'I know, I know, I've heard it all already, Harry. It's the end of your career, it's slander, it's manslaughter. And here I thought you were distracted and off in the clouds when you're writing a book. Turns out you're more distracted when you're not writing one.'

'You could be a little more supportive, I'm going through a lot here, what with that shocking review, and being cancelled, and that whole awards ceremony nightmare. And then that hideous video going viral, Zeal likely to sue. My phone ringing off the hook with journalists who want a piece of my flesh. And Myra hasn't even read my manuscript.'

'I have been supportive, Harry. I was supportive when you almost got us kicked out of the theatre. I was supportive when you hogged the conversation at dinner the other night. I was supportive when you woke me up at three in the morning the night before I had to do a big hepatobiliary op, to read out a string of one-star reviews on Goodreads. I was supportive when you humiliated both of us at that ridiculous awards show. And I was supportive when you bored Neil and Clive so badly at breakfast this morning that Neil pretended the dog sitter had called to say the shih tzu was vomiting, so they had an excuse to leave early. I'm not sure how much more support I have left in me.'

'I'm not happy about this either, Vicks. It's not like I wanted my entire life to fall apart.'

'You could have fooled me, Harry. It's almost like you're enjoying it in some sick part of your brain. If you had just stepped away from it in the beginning like I told you to, like everyone told you to, instead of stoking it up all day, every day, the flames would have died down on their own. But you keep picking at the scab. No wonder it won't heal.'

'I don't think you understand how much damage this woman has done to me, my reputation and my career, Victoria.'

'No, I do actually. But I also understand that you're doing even more damage by not letting it go. And what about the damage all of this is doing to us and to me? I'm a respected surgeon, Harry. Imagine what people must think. When am I going to get my husband back, Harry? And when are you going to settle down and write your next bloody book? I can't help thinking that maybe all this fuss is actually procrastination,' Victoria said, as the taxi pulled up outside their home. She was out the door before the driver had even come to a full stop.

'She's right, your missus,' the taxi driver said, turning in his seat to look at Harry. 'Ignoring them all is the best thing you can do. I tell you, I wrote this novel, and …'

'Nobody asked you,' Harry snapped as he tapped his card on the machine, and passive-aggressively didn't leave a tip.

Inside, Harry skulked into his study and logged onto the book club page. He only had to scroll past a couple of posts to find the original bad review, the one that started it all. There was a pile of new comments, likes, angry faces, and one-star reviews. He'd hoped the post would drop further down the page with time as new threads were posted, but people kept on commenting, so it kept bobbing to the surface like a bloated body.

He scrolled down until he found his own response post, which also had new comments and angry-face emojis, and also refused to drop down the page. He'd come to think of these as The Posts Of His Downfall, and it felt like they would never stop dominating the top third of the page, despite JK Rowling having just posted more of her views on social media, which could usually be guaranteed to shoot everything else right down the page.

There was a time he'd dreamed of having a post about his books, by an actual reader, with lots of comments, dominating the top third of this page consistently for days. Now he just wished other posts would get traction so that his would start to lose steam.

Maybe, Harry thought, if he added a new post to the page, that would help move things along.

So, he logged in as his retired octogenarian orthodontist from Bridgeport, Connecticut: Bernard Phillips. He was a reasonable man, maybe he could help.

THE GOOD BOOK APPRECIATION SOCIETY

MEMBERS: 57 987

Bernard Phillips: I'm a big fan of crime thrillers. The really gory ones you can't put down. Where terrible things happen to people and you can't stop turning the pages until you know who did it and what happens next.

How do writers do it? They're always coming up with innovative ways of killing people off. If I were a writer, and I had a character to kill, I'd lure them into the dentist's chair (a small stone pushed into a bagel would do the job) and then put poison in the happy gas.

But I'm no monster; the victim would be an unkind, spiteful woman, who attacked other people without any provocation. So she'd need a fitting ending.

If you were to do away with a hideous character in the most violent, cruel way possible, how would you go about it?

COMMENTS:

Chris Colt: I would kill the old witch off in a terrible fire.

BOOK PEOPLE

[Freda Kruger has reported this comment.]

Shireen Worcestershire-Watts: I once read a novel where two strangers met on the Tube, got chatting and discovered they both had awful people in their lives, so they decided to murder the other person's person, thinking nobody would ever link them to each other, so they'd get away with it.

Simon Phillips-Farmer: That's the storyline for *Strangers on a Plane*, @Shireen Worcestershire-Watts, not on the Tube. And he can't very well do that in his book. As you've said, it's already been done, apparently now twice.

Karen Granger: @Shireen Worcestershire-Watts @Simon Phillips-Farmer, surely you're confusing things with the Patricia Highsmith novel?

Gus Higginson: What about a sniper?

Michelle Zanders: Violence is never the answer. Maybe a little nightshade in her tea. It's a peaceful death.

Linda Petal Dabb: You're right, violence is never the answer. Spreading peace and love. 🌸🌈

Gus Higginson: You could always get a sniper.

Avukile Chingwita: In movies, they often hit people over the head with something heavy, or get into a fight and push the person over and they hit their heads on the edge of a coffee table or fall down a flight of stairs and die. That's what I'd put in my book.

Gus Higginson: Sniper anyone?

[Freda Kruger has reported this comment.]

Dax Goby: What about a hit and run?

[Freda Kruger has reported this comment.]

Lucille Cooper: That's a good one, @Dax Goby.

Tammi Kentridge: A hit and run could work, but you'd have to make sure there were no cameras in the area. They film everywhere these days. In all the streets, inside our houses. I even saw this documentary where they showed how the government is secretly implanting cameras in babies as they're born. So they can track our actions throughout our lives.

Felicity Mauberger: That is the most ridiculous conspiracy theory I've ever heard. And here I thought readers were supposed to be erudite. How on earth would they have enough people in control rooms to monitor the actions of every single human being on the planet twenty-four hours a day over an entire generation? It would never work.

Sumaya Govender: If I was to ever kill anyone hypothetically, I would hypothetically push them in front of a hypothetical train when nobody was hypothetically watching.

Tammi Kentridge: They have cameras at all the train stations too. They would catch you for sure.

Gus Higginson: DM me if you need a sniper.

[Freda Kruger has reported this post.]

Harry

'I had some ideas on how to get back at her, wanna hear, Phyl?'

'It depends, Harry. Are we talking plot for a new book, or is this some real-life murder and mayhem you're plotting?' Phyllis said.

'It doesn't matter, either-or, whichever,' Harry said, his words tumbling out on top of each other. 'Also, the craziest thing, I think I can hear colours now.'

'Harry, when last did you get some sleep?'

'I don't think I need sleep anymore, Phyl. Did you know, there are studies that say after a certain point with no sleep, your body simply adjusts. Like if you stop using shampoo. Same thing. The less you get, the less you need. In fact, no sleep makes you more alert, more focused,' Harry babbled.

'I don't think there are any studies that say that at all, Harry. In fact, every study I've ever heard of says exactly the opposite, about sleep and shampoo. That's just what *they* want you to believe.'

'So, about that revenge. I could send a drum kit to one neighbour, a saxophone to another and a trombone to a third neighbour, and maybe an aviary of parrots to a fourth neighbour. Not just the singing ones, those ones that talk and squawk. You'd be amazed at what you can get delivered overnight off Amazon. I wonder if I could get one that swears?'

'Harry ...' Phyllis began.

'Scratch that one, you're right, too expensive,' Harry said, putting a line through the words on his notepad. 'I have plenty more. What about this one? So, you know how we don't think she's actually ever read either of my books? Because she clearly wrote all of that just to ruin my life. What if we kidnap her, tie her up and force her to read my books and the new manuscript?'

'What would that achieve, Harry?'

'I'm sure she'd change her mind about them if she actually read them. And then she could post new reviews, and give them five stars – maybe she'd even post an apology. Then everyone would rally round me, and help put a stop to this madness. They might even cancel her instead.'

'You need help, Harry,' Phyllis responded, after a long pause.

'You're right, I wouldn't be able to kidnap her on my own. I'd need someone to drive the car, and help me get her into and out of it. Especially if we have to drug her,' Harry said.

'Harry, that's not what I meant. I think you need real psychological help. Or at the very least you need a good night's sleep. Please promise you'll step away from the computer and try get some sleep? I'm going to phone you tomorrow to check in on you.'

'Okay, I'll try. Night, Phyl,' Harry said.

'Night, Harry. Don't do anything stupid, okay?'

Harry put down the phone, reached for his pen and scratched out all the ideas he'd bounced off Phyl. He'd come up with something more elaborate. Those were all far too tame.

Norma

Norma was the first intern to be shown into the boardroom on the ground floor of the publishing house, set in a rambling old building in the centre of London.

It was the most intimidating boardroom she'd ever been in. With her nerves jangling and three too many coffees roiling around in her stomach, she took the seat closest to the door, in case she needed to make a run for the bathroom. Norma wondered if any of her favourite authors had ever sat at the table. Was her bum where Hilary Mantel's had once been? Was she drinking from the same glass as Marian Keyes? It was all possible. That was the glamour of publishing.

Norma hadn't been waiting long when a young woman in her early twenties with pink hair was shown in. She took a seat across the table from Norma, they said an awkward hello, and the woman stared at her attentively.

Next a young man was shown in, his blond hair streaked with green. He took the seat beside the pink-haired woman and greeted her. Norma nodded and smiled at him, and he nodded and smiled back, tongue piercing glinting.

A third young woman with hair so black it appeared blue, was shown into the room. She also took a seat across the table from Norma, next to green hair and pink hair. They all acknowledged each other, then turned to look at Norma expectantly. They reminded her of tropical birds. She shifted in her seat and nudged her spectacles up her nose, actively forcing herself not to hum.

'Are you, like, our boss or what?' Pink broke the silence at last.

'God, no,' Norma sputtered.

'Work here?' Pink asked.

Norma shook her head.

'Dropping your kid off to intern?' Green hair asked, looking around.

'No,' Norma said again.

'My mom has that same blouse,' Green offered.

Just smile and wave, Norma thought, like royalty, and maybe if you're lucky you might die very suddenly, from some rare, pain-free illness. It was no fun being the diversity hire.

'OMG, I love your shoes, they're super-retro,' Pink continued.

'Thanks. I have had them for a long time,' Norma said.

'Proper retro,' Green exclaimed. 'Australian?'

'The shoes? No, they're from here, and I'm from South Africa.'

All three nodded in unison.

'And believe it or not, I'm also an intern, like you guys,' Norma said with a smile, hoping it would stop them staring and commenting on her wardrobe.

'Aren't you, like, too old to work?' Green hair asked.

'I think so, but my bank balance disagrees,' Norma joked. None of them laughed.

She was about to explain her situation when the boardroom door swung open and a man in his late fifties, wearing Levi jeans and large, black-rimmed spectacles swept into the room in a cloud of importance and Davidoff Cool Water, carrying a tablet in one hand and a coffee in the other.

'I don't have a lot of time, we're launching a new vampire cookbook this week and moving buildings in two months, so things are a bit of a circus. But I wanted to do a quick hello and orientation. I'm Daniel Piper, publisher here at Harbour Books, and I'll be overseeing your internship, for my sins.'

Norma nodded vigorously, wanting to seem enthusiastic because she felt enthusiastic – something she couldn't recall feeling in the workplace in decades.

'Before I send you off on your first assignment, have any of you heard of Jose Saramago?'

Norma was about to raise her hand, but Pink and Green were staring blankly at Daniel, and Blue appeared to be reading something on her mobile under the boardroom table, so she kept quiet. No need to make enemies on her first day.

Daniel continued: 'In 1953, Saramago submitted his first manuscript to a publisher in Portugal, but the publishers never got back to him. He was in his mid-thirties and it shattered his confidence, spiralling him into a deep depression. Thirty-six years later, when the publishing house moved, they contacted Saramago to say they'd discovered his manuscript at the bottom of a slush pile and wanted to publish it.'

'Talk about getting ghosted,' Pink muttered as she snapped her gum.

'Saramago turned down their offer, saying that since they hadn't had the decency to contact him when he'd submitted it all those years earlier, he didn't want it to be published while he was still alive. The memory of the pain he'd felt was too hard to bear. He said they could only publish the book after his death.'

'Drama queen much?' Green said.

'Ultimately,' Daniel continued, 'that novel, called *Skylight*, was published in Portugal in 2011, a year after the author died. But this story doesn't have an entirely unhappy ending. Before his death, Saramago published more than twenty books, and won the Nobel Prize for literature in 1998.'

'Shoddy work on the publisher's part,' Norma heard Blue say.

'So,' Daniel clapped his hands and stood, gathering his things. 'The moral of the story is, do not be fooled. This first job you're going to do here as interns may not appear glamorous, but that doesn't make it any less important. And it could, one day, even turn out to have historical significance. Follow me.'

Norma and the rainbow of interns grabbed their things and followed Daniel down a corridor. They passed big, bustling open-plan spaces, as well as a series of small quiet offices and meeting rooms. Books were piled everywhere. This was a company that had clearly grown out of its shell. They went down an old service lift to the bowels of the building, where Daniel unlocked a room at the end of a dark, dusty corridor.

Daniel felt for the light switch, and a bank of fluorescent lights flickered several times before half of them came on, revealing a large room with no windows, packed with mismatched office furniture. Tables with only three legs leaned up against walls, along with office and boardroom chairs with cracked pleather, or missing wheels, and sad-looking filing cabinets minus drawers.

Norma coughed as she took in the dusty scene. Just about every broken desk, chair, cabinet and square metre of floor was stacked with manuscripts. Piles of them, each one with an elastic band around its waist. Some yellowed with age. Whiter, newer stacks of pages closer to the tops of the piles. The room was so packed with furniture and manuscripts and fish moths that the five of them could barely get more than a few feet inside.

'Most publishers have slush piles, but I'm embarrassed to say we appear to have let ours get out of hand, and have subsequently found ourselves the proud owners of a slush-pile room. I wish I could say that it hasn't quite been thirty-six years since anyone looked at some of these, as in the case of Saramago, but looking at this, it feels like it might have been that long,' Daniel said. 'Much of it before my time here, so fortunately I can't shoulder all the blame.'

'You want us to read through your slush pile?' Norma asked, her heart quickening. Being paid to read was what she'd always dreamt of. This was why she'd tanked her stable career, two decades in the making.

'Oh god, I hope not,' Green said, a horrified look on his face.

'Oh no, no, no,' Daniel laughed, waving him off. 'There's no way you're equipped for that. As I mentioned, we're moving in a few months, after being here for forty-eight years. We outgrew this building a decade ago. Anyway, we stopped accepting unsolicited manuscripts around then too, and actively stopped requesting hard copies of manuscripts even longer ago, but you wouldn't say that to look at this lot. Old habits die hard out there, and they just kept coming in, so we stashed them in here, always planned on dealing with them, but never quite got there. So now with the move, and you lot, well ...'

Pink and Green groaned.

'So your job is to get this lot into a more, shall we say, manageable arrangement. Starting with a full clean,' Daniel said, running a finger over the top of a cabinet and pulling a face at the dust caking his finger. 'You're going to have to take all this furniture out. Leave the pieces that are broken beyond repair in the corridor and we'll arrange to get them turfed. Then you'll have to do something about this dust. It'll probably need a good vacuum, and the floor will need a wash just so you can get to the manuscripts without choking. You'll find everything you need over there,' Daniel said, pointing out a pile of cleaning supplies including a vacuum cleaner, mop and bucket in the corridor.

'Vacuum?' Green said. 'Sorry, but you'll see that doesn't appear as one of my core competencies on my CV.'

'Then,' Daniel continued, ignoring him, but not without the briefest eye roll, 'if I were you, I would rearrange whatever furniture is left in here, so it's a little less "dumping ground for dead furniture", and a little more "room where you can see the floorboards." Once you've done a good clean, we expect you to arrange the manuscripts chronologically, according to genre. They should all be dated on the cover page.

'The brief in a nutshell is: Create a space where we have an inkling of where to start sifting through these bad boys, so we can get them in some kind of order before we move. Half the members of the board thought we should just toss the lot of them, but imagine if we ended up chucking out the next Saramago? We'd never forgive ourselves, and I'd probably lose my job. So, onwards to sorting.'

It was Blue's turn to groan, at which Daniel shot her a hard stare, and she stopped mid-groan.

'How is cleaning a room learning about publishing?' Green said. 'I thought we would be arranging book launches, signing new authors, going to literary festivals.'

Norma's eyes widened. The privilege was strong with this one.

'All in good time, grasshopper,' Daniel said with a smile.

'Grasshopper?' Green said.

'It's a reference from *Karate Kid* ... the movie? Never mind!' Daniel said with the sigh of a Gen X being forced to communicate with a Gen Z. 'This may seem menial now, but you could be behind us finding a future Booker or Nobel winner. Do it for Saramago. Onwards!' He held his fist in the air in a power salute, spun on his heel, and left them coughing in a trail of dust.

'Cleaning? That's me gone then. Adios motherfuckers!' Green said, doing his own career pivot out the door.

Pink stood with her hands on her hips chewing gum with an open mouth, and Blue was already busy on her mobile, either pretending that she wasn't there, or that they weren't.

'And then there were three,' Norma said.

'Like Charlie's Angels. Like, the perfect amount for crime fighting,' Pink said.

'I'm Norma, by the way', Norma said with a small wave.

'I'm Britttennay,' Pink said.

'Britney, nice to meet you.'

'No, it's, like, Britttennay,' Britttennay corrected her. 'B.r.i.t.t.t.e.n.n.a.y, you spell it like you say it. It's phonetic, see.'

'You mean *you* spell it like *you* say it,' Norma said.

'Like, that's what I said,' Britttennay said.

'Three t's, that's quite something,' Norma said.

'It's my favourite letter,' she said. 'My second favourite letter is "n".'

Norma cleared her throat to get Blue's attention. 'Hey, I'm Norma, and that's Britttennay, with three t's and two n's.'

'I'm Bavinga,' Blue said, looking up from her phone.

'Britttennay, Bavinga, nice to meet you. Where should we start?' Norma asked, nudging her spectacles into place.

'I started by googling what interns in publishing do, and I've got to tell you, it's not this,' Britttennay with too many t's and n's said, then read off her phone: 'According to Wiki, a publishing intern may help with editorial, creative, and/or business tasks. For editorial tasks, the intern reports to the Managing Editor. For creative or graphic design tasks, the intern reports to the Creative Director. For business tasks, the intern reports to the Publisher.'

'I wonder who the intern reports to for cleaning tasks?' Norma said.

'So much to read, so little time,' blue-haired Bavinga said, reaching for the dusty manuscript on top of the pile closest to her.

Harry

Harry couldn't decide whether to read the article or not. Just about everyone he knew who was still talking to him had messaged to tell him he was in the paper, and they had all warned him against reading it.

He wouldn't read it, he decided. If that journalist had lied to him to get him to talk, he didn't want to know about it. It was just more toxic backlash that would set him even further back. WWHD: what would Hemingway do? He wouldn't give a rat's ass about public opinion, Harry thought, as he closed his laptop decisively and went for a brisk walk around the block to clear his head.

Back at his desk, Harry clicked through to *The Times* website and scrolled the front page. He would only read the headline and by-line, he told himself, to see if it had been written by that Gemma lady. That was all he needed to know. Then he would close his laptop and be done with it forever.

WRITER LOSES THE PLOT
By Gemma Franks

It *was* her. His so-called biggest fan.

If she was so unethical that she had no qualms about lying to a source to get a story, no surprise that she would lead with such an awful pun. It was an easy win for a sleazy, lazy, corrupt writer.

He would just scan the first line of the article, he thought, to see if he had grounds to sue her or the paper.

> British author Harry Shields was today years old when he realised that responding to a bad review of his novel with an equally bad attitude was not the way to win over readers, book bloggers, fellow authors or awards judges.
>
> The controversy started on The Good Book Appreciation Society, a book club on Facebook with around fifty-nine thousand members. The platform encourages readers to leave honest reviews of the books they've read. When one member did exactly that, this author did not take the criticism well.
>
> Ignoring age-old advice, Shields decided to respond to the review and other commenters with a slew of abuse. This turned what could have been a fleeting Facebook post, seen by a few hundred people, into a series of events that would see the group explode, the author get cancelled, and his career ruined.
>
> The moment Shields responded, the group turned on him. Then the angry Facebook mob became an angry mob on X, and everyone decamped to book platform Goodreads to leave one-star reviews of the author's books, Monday Never Comes (Victory Books), and Once on a Tuesday (Victory Books).
>
> Most of the one-star reviews are short, sharp and brutal. And many of the reviewers admit to never having read a Shields novel.
>
> Not satisfied with being cancelled online, the author caused a scene at the Golden Page Literary Awards event, held at the British Museum on Friday night. He stormed the stage in a rage when Harriet Blumenthal, author of In the Darkest Hour (Zone Publishing), was announced winner of the award and sought-after twenty-thousand-pound prize.

Following that, Shields got into an altercation with fellow nominated author, Dominic Zeal (62). As Blumenthal was delivering her acceptance speech, Shields verbally and physically assaulted Zeal (Bloody Sunday, Hachette), accusing his wife, British Museum patron Fanny Zeal (52), of having sex with an awards judge, then shouting obscenities at him. All of which was filmed by Harriet Blumenthal's son, Jarred Blumenthal (16), and posted on YouTube, where it has already surpassed a million views.

'That man ruined what should have been the highlight of my literary career and a proud family moment,' said Blumenthal, the Golden Page award-winning author.

Dominic Zeal said he'd been advised by legal counsel not to comment, as he is in the process of pressing charges of assault, and would be suing Shields for loss of income. 'I have been unable to write ever since the incident, which has also left me with severe post-traumatic-stress disorder and a broken marriage,' Zeal went on to comment.

Shields's most recent novel has an average rating of 1.02 stars on Goodreads, with nearly 16,000 one-star reviews.

'This is the lowest star rating of any book we've ever hosted on the site,' reports Amanda Milner, media liaison for Goodreads.

Harry stopped reading. Breathing heavily, and clutching his chest, he reached for his mobile phone.

'Harry, can I call you back in an hour? I'm at the park with Chemtrail,' Phyllis's breathless voice came down the line.

'Phyl, no, please wait. Did you see *The Times*?' Harry yelled down the phone.

'You do know that newspaper is owned by the Freemasons, don't you? Harry, I have to ... no, Chemtrail, don't eat that!'

'Wait, Phyllis, this journalist wrote an article about me, and I don't know what to do,' Harry said, with a sob.

'They're all writing about you right now, Harry. I told you, you just need to wait it out, it will blow over,' Phyllis said.

'She lied to me, and misquoted me. She told me she was going to tell my side of the story, that's why I talked to her.'

'You talked to a journalist, Harry? Is that ever a good idea?' Phyllis asked.

'She said she was a fan of my work and she could tell everything had been taken out of context, that she was on my side. She was going to set the record straight.'

'Chemtrail, put that down! Bad dog!' Phyllis shouted.

'Listen to this,' Harry spluttered. *'Shields leapt onto the stage and tried to grab Blumenthal's award ...'*

'Oh Harry, you didn't do that, did you? No, Chemtrail, drop that ball, it's not yours.'

'Of course I didn't do that, Phyllis. I told you, I didn't storm the stage. I thought they were saying my name, Harry, not her name, Harriet. It was an honest mistake, it could have happened to anyone. Well, anyone named Harry. I told that so-called journalist what really happened, but she just wrote whatever she wanted to make me look bad. But wait, it gets worse.'

'It does? There's worse? Shit Harry.'

'Listen to this,' Harry continued reading: *"'I'd do it all again and I'd say it all again," the disgraced author said earlier this week in a telephonic interview from his home in Ealing.'*

'Oh no, you didn't really say that, Harry?'

'Yes, I did, but that's not what I meant. She's twisted my words, taken them out of context,' Harry wailed. 'I meant that I don't regret defending my books against online comments from people who have never even shown the courtesy of reading them.'

'She's a journalist, Harry, lying is what they do. That's ninety-nine per cent of the reason half the world thinks JFK died on the grassy knoll that day. I thought you'd turned off your phone and you weren't taking calls from the press?'

'It was an unknown number, I had to answer it. What if it had been Myra?'

'So you just believed what this complete stranger told you? Because journalists have always proven themselves so trustworthy? Chemtrail, do not roll in that! No, bad dog!' Phyllis yelled.

'It goes on, Phyl, it gets even worse on the next page ...'

'There's a next page? In *The Times*? Harry, that's impressive.'

'... *Shields blames 82-year-old widower, Edna Molton, a retired Shropshire paediatric nurse, for everything that's happened. "She's a vindictive, evil monster, who doesn't deserve to be allowed to read books," Shields said, of the octogenarian who posted the initial negative review of his book on The Good Book Appreciation Society on Facebook.*

'At the time of printing, Molton was unreachable for comment ...'

'Oh Harry, she's an octogenarian, and a paediatric nurse! The optics on this are not in your favour. Chemtrail, I told you not to roll in that ...! Oh Chemtrail. Harry, I have to go. DO NOT go online again, okay? Turn off the internet, and don't answer the phone for at least two weeks. You HAVE to lay low and wait out this storm. I have to go, Chemtrail has ...'

The line went dead before Harry could hear what else Chemtrail had done.

Drunk, Harry thought. He needed to be very drunk, very urgently.

THE GOOD BOOK APPRECIATION SOCIETY

MEMBERS: 62 945

Dick Lewies: WOW, just wow, you guys. I literally just turned the last page of the classic novel, Breakfast at Tiffany's, by Truman Capote. I loved every second of it. I'm tempted to say it's the best book I've read this year. I'm on a classic novel reading kick right now. I believe they broaden one's horizons.

What a romantic ending, when Holly and the writer end up together! Woof. This is one novel I will keep on my shelves to read again and again.

What classic novel do you suggest I read next?

COMMENTS:

Ruth Burstein: Um spoiler alert!

Jessie Bert: Yes, thanks for ruining the ending for the rest of us.

Noel Coates: Do you mean which should you read next, or watch next @Dick Lewies?

Phillip Flanders: Are you sure you read the book @Dick Lewies?

Dick Lewies: Just finished it after three straight days reading it, @Phillip Flanders. Couldn't put it down.

Phillip Flanders: The reason I ask is because in the book, Breakfast at Tiffany's by Truman Capote, the writer never sees Holly again. But in the movie, Breakfast at Tiffany's, directed by Blake Edwards, it has a different ending. I thinks perhaps you might be lying to make friends?

Lauren Van Week: Awkies!

Noel Coates: You asked what book to read next, Dick Lewies. How about the classic bestseller by Pierre Bayard, How to Talk About Books You Haven't Read?

Geneva Fulverton: Well that's embarrassing. But it does lead to an interesting conversation. Anyone else on the group (other than high school students who have a setwork exam the next day on a book they haven't read) pretend they'd read a book when they hadn't, or when they'd only seen the movie, in a vain attempt to try sound intelligent?

[Dick Lewies has left the group.]

Norma

The interns huddled in the corridor, covered in dust, eating their lunch around the broken office furniture they'd spent the last two hours dragging out of the slush-pile room.

Pink was picking at a poke bowl with a pair of collapsible neon chopsticks she'd produced from her oversized neon money belt, and Blue had a tray of sushi picked up from a hip hole in the wall down the street. Feeling every year of her age and a few additional ones, Norma pulled out the ploughman's sandwich Meal Deal she'd picked up at Tesco's on her way in that morning.

'What led you to publishing, Britttennay?' Norma asked, emphasising all the t's and n's in her name, thinking it would be easier to carry on calling her 'Pink'.

'My dad knows the financial director here,' she said. 'They were at Harvard together in America, like a billion years ago.'

'Did you always want to be in publishing?' Norma asked.

'I hate books and reading, but my dad said if I didn't at least, like, try get a job, him and my stepmom were going to cut me off and take away my credit card. So I thought I'd better, like, give it a go. But I can't say this feels right for me,' Britttennay said, popping a chickpea into her mouth.

'I didn't realise there were people out there who actively hated books,' Norma said. 'I always thought that of all things, books were rather innocuous.'

'The way I see it, there's, like, a movie or series out there of just about all the books ever written, or at least all the good ones anyway, so what's the point of books? Plus, what about the damage books do to all those trees and the environment? They have, like, a monster ecological footprint, you know?'

'Because movies are so environmentally friendly,' Norma laughed. 'What about you?' she asked Blue, who still had her nose buried in her mobile while she ate.

'Are you, like, an influencer, B?' Britttennay asked, snapping her gum, which, Norma noted had been in her mouth the whole time she'd been eating.

'Why do you ask?' Bavinga said.

'You've been, like, glued to your mobile even more than me. So, I just figured ...' Britttennay trailed off.

'I'm not on social media,' Bavinga said.

'Chatting to hook-ups?' Britttennay asked.

'Actually, I'm reading,' Bavinga said.

'What are you reading?' Norma asked with a smile.

'I just finished the latest Sally Rooney. It was okay. And this one is *Flight Behaviour*, by Barbara Kingsolver. It's not new, but it's good.'

'Seen it, not seen it.' Britttennay said, ticking off the one with her finger in the air above her head, and crossing off the other one. 'Who's in that second one? And is it out as, like, a movie or a series?'

'I don't know,' Bavinga said, looking perplexed. 'It's a book. A classic.'

'I was going to ask you why you're working here, but I get it now,' Norma said.

'What about you?' Bavinga asked.

'You mean, why is an old lady like me interning at a publishing house?'

'That's not what I asked, but sure, it's not something you see every day.'

'I was an accountant, but I've fallen out of love with it, and I run this book club on Facebook, plus I love to read. Publishing seemed like the right move for me. So, I gave it all up to come and do … well, do this,' Norma said, dropping a manuscript on the table in a puff of dust that made her cough.

'When did you come here from South Africa?'

'About fifteen years ago. I have a British passport and came for a gap year after I finished my studies in Joburg, and just kind of never left,' Norma said.

'I've read Deon Meyer,' Bavinga said. 'He's really good.'

'He is, isn't he? We have a ton of great authors there.'

'Do you miss home?' Bavinga asked.

'This is home now. But sure, I miss it sometimes. The people, the weather, the space – those kinds of things. But once you've earned pounds, how do you go back to earning a broken currency?'

'Oh my god, you guys have to see this dog, it's singing the US national anthem,' Britttennay said, holding her phone out for them. When neither moved to look, she pulled it back. 'Sorry, I get distracted easily. ADHD. I'm happy to share my Ritalin. What series are you guys talking about?'

'It's not a show, it's just my life,' Norma admitted. 'But there have been a few plot twists I didn't see coming.'

'You know what we should do next?' Britttennay called out.

'What?' Norma asked.

'We should, like, totally make a TikTok.'

Harry

'What are you watching, Harry?'

'Oh nothing, Victoria, just my career going down the toilet.' Harry was slumped on the couch, staring at the television, computer also open on his lap.

'Oh Harry, don't be so melodramatic. I meant what show is that?' Victoria asked.

'Naked and Afraid.'

Victoria raised an eyebrow at him.

'A man and a woman are dropped into an unforgiving landscape in the middle of nowhere – the jungle or desert or a swamp or something, and they have to stay alive and find their way out,' Harry said.

'And let me guess, they're naked?'

'Very much so. And afraid.'

'What do they win?'

'Nothing. They just get to stay alive, if they can, and if they don't have to be airlifted to a hospital, or lose a toe, that's an added bonus.'

'Reality TV, Harry. Are those the depths into which we've descended?' Victoria asked.

'It's not reality TV, it's on the Discovery Channel,' Harry said.

'At least you've stopped doom-scrolling social media, so that's a start. It's the first time I've seen you do anything other than scroll and mutter to yourself in days.'

'This show is a metaphor for my life, Victoria. They've also been stripped of everything, like me, and they're ... they're ...' Harry stuttered.

'Yes, they're naked and afraid, I get it, Harry. Why don't you come to bed? It's late, and you haven't slept in days.'

'But the show's not finished. There are seven more seasons.'

'Oh my darling, I have a feeling this show is never going to be finished,' Victoria said, kissing him on the forehead and heading to bed.

When she came down to get a cup of coffee the next morning, he was still sprawled on the couch, eyes red but open, still watching television, with only three more seasons to go.

Norma

Norms, I've been worried about you. You haven't responded to any of my voice notes, so, I messaged my sister to see if you're okay. She told me to fuck off!

She always did like you more than she liked me. So much for blood being thicker than water. Anyway, she said your internship is going well. I'm happy for you, Norms, I really am. And she said you haven't changed your number, you just don't want to talk to me. But she didn't say you didn't want to hear from me ... so, here I am again, another day, another voice note. Please get back to me soon about the great investment ideas I've been sending you, okay? We've got to move on one of them fast if we want to rake it in and pay off our debt. Gotta go, I'm running out of data.

Me again. This is the last voice note I'm going to send you, Norms, so I hope you're listening carefully. I got a killer tip on a filly running in the eighth race today, from Fergal who works down the off-licence. But we have to act now, Norma. This is the last opportunity I'm going to give you. We need some cash to put down on the race, and Fergal won't front me again. Get back to me soon, okay? The race is in a few hours.

Hi Norma. So, I know I said that last voice note was the

last one, but Pony Soprano turned out to be a lame duck. I should know not to listen to that bloody Fergal. I hope his head ends up in a bed, Fergal, not Pony Soprano. He only has one ear, he lost the other in a pub brawl. Probably gave some geezer bad tips. Bullet dodged there, lucky us. Hey, maybe now is the time to buy a couple of lottery tickets? Call me.

Harry

'Matcha tea, please love,' Leon said to the waitress as he slid into the booth across from Harry and set his Ray-Bans on the table. 'Good to see you, Harry, mate.'

'I'm sure it is, you got PayPalled for it,' Harry said, sipping the black coffee the waitress had just put down in front of him, and swearing as he burnt his tongue. Restaurant coffee was always either arctic or volcanic – there was no happy medium.

'Can't pay the rent with book and film credits, can you? Even the ones that win at the BAFTAS,' Leon said.

'So you always say, Leon.'

'Oh, come on Harry, you know I'm the number one cop consultant in town,' Leon said. 'Worth every cent.'

'You should put that on the cover of your memoir, Leon.'

'You offering to ghostwrite it for me, mate? Imagine that! I consult on all your books, and you go on to consult on mine. What would you call that? Poetic justice?'

'You paying? I'll take two hundred quid an hour, not a word down without the PayPal confirmation,' Harry snarked, emptying two sachets of sweetener into his coffee.

'Touché, Harry, touché. So, I haven't heard from you since you finished your last novel, what was that – a year or so ago? So I reckon it's that time again. You got a new one on the go, mate?' Leon asked, as the waitress put his drink down in front of him.

Harry shrugged.

'It's taken you long enough. So, what's this one about, then? A cop? A politician who gets in tight with a cop? A cop on the take? A cop on the run?'

'Oh, you know ...' Harry trailed off.

'No, I don't know, and I can't read minds, that's why I'm asking, Harry. And you do know that shit will kill you, right?' Leon indicated the crumpled sweetener sachets. 'Aspartame. It's the serial killer of ingredients.'

'I know it's healthy, but I'd rather die than drink that shit,' Harry pointed at the green sludge in the cop's cup.

'This?' Leon said, holding it up. 'This is matcha tea. Educate yourself, son. It's full of antioxidants and is known to boost brain function. Speaking of, you look like shit, which leads me to believe that the book must be going well. You burning the midnight oil? Got some plot holes you need me to iron out? Did I ever tell you, I was the one who gave Baldacci the final twist in his second latest?'

'You've only told me twice,' Harry said.

'So, are you going to tell me about yours then, or are we going to sit here talking about my career and your aspartame addiction for the rest of your hour or part thereof?'

'I'm making a start on something.'

'Okay shoot, Harry. Get it, it's a pun. 'Cos I'm a cop. It's a good line. You'll want to get that down. You can use it in the book if you want. No extra charge.'

'Okay so, this character I'm writing about, let's call him, erm ... Har ... er Barry, is dealing with someone, let's call her ... Edna, and she wrote this disgusting, unforgivable stuff about him on a Facebook book club, which has caused his life to implode and everyone in the world to turn on him,' Harry said.

'Okay, I'm with you so far ...' Leon said.

'So, say, if my character wanted to find out where that person lives, the one who said all this outrageously bad propaganda about him online, how would he do that?' Harry asked, fiddling with another sachet, his knee bouncing, one eye twitching.

'Okay, well, let's see, is your character a cop?' Leon asked.

'No, he's a writer,' Harry said.

'What else does your character have to go on to find this Edna's address?' Leon asked.

'Just her name and Facebook profile, that's all. I was wondering, could you get an IP address or whatever it's called, and then find her physical address from that?' Harry asked.

'That depends on whether she uses a VPN,' Leon said.

'It looks like she may be in her eighties, so I doubt she knows what a VPN is,' Harry said.

Leon raised an eyebrow. '"Looks like?" "She may be?" You don't know how old your character is, Harry?'

'This stuff is always evolving,' Harry added quickly.

'Okay. So, as far as I know, with the right tech you can definitely get someone's IP address off their Facebook page, or from a messenger chat. But an IP address may not give you an exact physical address down to the precise building, not without a bit more information from the service provider who issued that IP address,' Leon said.

'So, could you help me find her address, then? Maybe subpoena the information from the service provider?'

'Harry, mate, I'm starting to get the feeling that this isn't as hypothetical a fictional situation as you've made out. Are you sure you're doing research for a new novel, and this isn't something a bit more ... personal?'

Harry looked at Leon who was watching him closely, first examining his face, then taking in his bouncing knee.

'You're not thinking of doing anything stupid, are you, Harry, mate?'

Harry held his gaze, his eye twitching.

'Because if you are, as a police officer, I have to advise you to step away from whatever this is, mate. You don't want to be a bad headline, alright, only a good headline, like winning a Booker.'

'So, Leon, what you're saying is that my character, erm ...'

'Barry, it was,' Leon said.

'That's it, Barry ... my character, Barry, could, if he needed to, find someone's location or at least general vicinity off their Facebook profile?'

'There's not going to be any credit for me in the back of a book for this one, is there, Harry?'

'The truth?' Harry said.

'That is my preferred mode of transport, yes.'

'No, probably not,' Harry admitted.

'No thanks in the acknowledgements?' Leon asked.

'Nope.'

'And no possibility of becoming the cop consultant on set when the book finally gets turned into a series or movie?'

'Highly, highly unlikely.'

'We wouldn't by any chance be doing anything illegal here, would we, Harry?'

'I just want to see what she looks like, Leon, that's all. Check her out. At most I might approach her. But all completely innocent and friendly, just a chat, nothing sinister, I swear – you have my word.' Harry said. 'I just need her address from you, urgently.'

'Harry, I'm a full-time cop who consults part-time on books and shows on the telly. I'm not a private detective.'

'I'll pay you as much as you want,' Harry said, his voice an octave higher.

'Alright, I'm calling it, mate. You should get help,' Leon said, gathering his keys and Ray-Bans off the table.

'I thought I was – from you,' Harry said.

'Not that kind of help, mate.' Leon stood. 'Harry, you know I'm here for you when you get going on the writing and are ready to talk about hypothetical cop procedures for your book.'

'On receipt of a PayPal confirmation,' Harry mumbled.

'That's it, you've got it. You know where to find me. Thanks for the matcha, mate,' Leon said, striding out of the restaurant.

Harry sighed. If Leon wasn't going to help him get the IP address, he would have to help himself. He'd written a private detective character before; surely being one in real life wasn't that different?

Harry drained his coffee, ordered another one, then logged into The Good Book Appreciation Society on his mobile. He searched for all posts and comments made by Edna Molton on the page, then started to pick through them, to see if he'd missed any clues.

She'd created very few posts over the years, mostly commenting on other people's posts, politely thanking them for their reviews and making note of titles that interested her or ones she'd already read and enjoyed. Harry carried on scrolling.

And then after about twenty minutes, there it was, in a post Edna Molton had commented on three years earlier, about people scribbling notes in the margins of library books. Maybe his luck was starting to turn.

THE GOOD BOOK APPRECIATION SOCIETY

MEMBERS: 4 237

Cathy Park: The Case of the Murder Mystery Marginalia … I was thrilled to discover Louise Penny's Inspector Gamache in the library, *The Brutal Telling*. But this is not the main point of this post. In the first few pages, I came across a few swear words in the novel that had been scratched out by a reader. Then another reader had rewritten the swear words back in, in cross black ink and capital letters.

Then the original 'Scratch Out' reader obviously became too much for 'Black-Ink-swear rewriting' reader, who went on to add their own mini-tirade in the margin alongside one of the cross-outs of the word 'Fuck'.

That note, transcribed word for word as follows:

'Please stop, you narrow-minded idiot. Sanctimonious prat imposing your views on the language used by the author.'

But funny how the 'Scratch Out' reader missed the French swear word in the next line. Almost as though they could only be outraged in one language. I was delighted by this bookish drama, and couldn't wait to share it here.

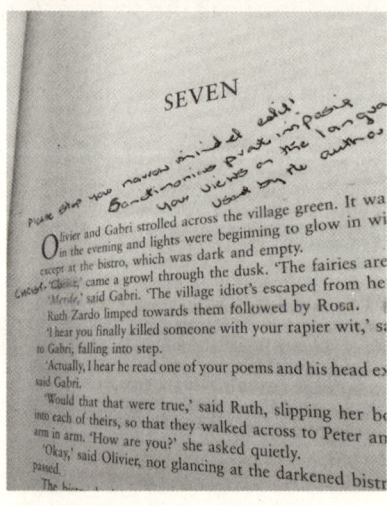

BOOK PEOPLE

COMMENTS:

Karen Granger: There is no excuse for errors. I always correct typos when I find them in books. #WordNerd #GrammarMatters

Cathy Park: @Karen Granger, yes, I'm often tempted to do that. But this is at a whole other level.

Kelly Vos: I'm a librarian and senior citizens are the worst vandals. They scratch out, obliterate and comment as they go. It's very funny.

Jenstrix: Who is unethical enough to write in a LIBRARY BOOK. Don't they understand that it doesn't belong to them??!

Patricia Balsdon: OMG – I am of the no damage to books ever school. Unless I am altering a trash book from the fourth-hand shop. Would never write in a book. Or for that matter turn down a corner – horrors!

Sandy Fisher: I use the Tunbridge Wells library. We have a very active scratch-out swear-words reader.

Bethany Culbert: I'll admit, I had a library book once that had one of the horse's names for a general, so I lightly corrected it in pencil, and wrote a pencil footnote: "*wrong name* is a horse".

Edna Molton: Nobody would ever dream of doing that type of thing at the Ludlow library. I'm a member of the Friends of the Library here and we keep a close eye on that kind of anti-social behaviour.

Sally Smith: The sanctimonious idiot doesn't understand French, apparently.

Cathy Park: Sally Smith Oui, merde.

Julia Fraser: Write your notes in your own books. Library books should not be defaced at all!

Harry picked up his cup and took a triumphant sip, only to find it cold and empty.

Searching back through all Edna Molton's posts and comments on The Good Book Appreciation Society page had been a stroke of genius. He finally had some answers. Edna Molton lived in Ludlow, and she'd been a Friend of the Library there for years. Surely she'd be easy to find now?

Paying Leon had been a waste of two hundred quid. The old adage was true; if you wanted something done you had to do it yourself. At least now he was one step closer to making Edna Molton pay.

Norma

'For crying out loud, Marina, your brother will not stop sending me these ridiculous voice notes. I honestly think he may have lost his mind. Listen to this one.'

> Me again, Norms. So you clearly weren't into the property investment idea I sent you in that last voice note. No worries, plenty more ideas where that came from. I'm feeling my creativity spiking through my veins. Here's another one. What if we start a business where we find people who are being overcharged for their electricity and we, no wait, that isn't right, hold on, okay this is it, we partner with a guy who works at the electricity company, who can hack into the system and deduct the electricity, no wait, that isn't it either. This idea seemed much clearer last night down the pub, I should have written it down. I have another idea I'm working on. I'll send it soon.

'Does it involve him getting a job, the lazy shite?' Marina asked.

'At what point do you think he's going to unPeter-Pan himself long enough to get his act together?' Norma asked.

'Probably never. Sorry, Norms, he's a shit.'

'Marina, I'm telling you, it's just endless voice notes, with these ridiculous ideas, but no real contribution yet. He's driving me mental.'

'Poor tosser. At this rate he'll spend all his time trying to come up with an easy way to make a quid until Pops either kicks the bucket or kicks him out, whichever happens first.'

'If only he spent half that time looking for a job. He was so motivated when we first started dating. I loved that about him,' Norma said.

'He was in IT. Maybe he didn't get enough natural sunlight,' Marina said.

'We live in London, nobody gets enough natural sunlight.'

'There are these crazies in California who think they don't need to eat food, because the sun will give them all the nutrition they need,' Marina said.

'Good thing they live in LA. They'd starve here.'

'They ultimately all end up in those fancy clinics on drips, anyway,' Marina said. 'I once worked at one of them in Milan, we used to sneak those drips on our breaks. They're incredible, especially when you've got a hangover. So, what are you going to do about Steve and your minimum payment due?'

'I'm definitely not going to respond to his voice notes. I don't want to encourage him.'

'He called me yesterday,' Marina said.

'Did he ask you to loan him money?'

'He wanted me to invest in that property-plan-timeshare-Ponzi-scheme thing. I told him to fuck off for like the twelfty dozenth time.'

'He's definitely lost the plot, Marina. Beers later? I've got to get back to my internship.'

'I want to hear all about that. I'm in for the beers. There's a new bar down past Soho, where the barmen are all jugglers. It gets really messy if you can convince them to have a couple of shots.'

'I'm in.'

Harry

'Harold, you've been a busy boy, haven't you?'

'Myra, thank god, I've been trying to reach you for days,' Harry said, trying to keep the desperation out of his voice.

'Harold, tell me something: are you trying to kill me?' Myra said.

'You saw Facebook?' Harry asked.

'Fuck Facebook, Harold. I saw Goodreads and *The Times*, and the video on YouTube that's had over a million fucking hits, and *The Booktrade* and twelve other news stories, as well as every one of the hundred or so what-the-actual-fuck-is-your-man-doing? messages that have slid into my email, DMs and WhatsApps over the last two weeks. You've literally rolled in petrol and set yourself on fire, haven't you?'

'I can explain …' Harry faltered. Although he wasn't sure that he could.

'You can? Really? Because to be honest, it's inexplicable to me that an author poised to hit the big time with his third novel, decides to tank his own career,' Myra barked down the phone.

'I didn't mean for this to happen, Myra,' Harry said.

'Then why did you respond to all that nonsense on that page, Harold? And what was all that at the Golden Pages? I was wondering if perhaps you'd had a head injury? Or are you on narcotics of some kind? That might at least help us get out of this. Or if you've lost your mind, I can spin that. Mania perhaps? A deep depression brought on by a mid-life crisis or a chemical imbalance? Yes? Even diabetes? Low blood sugar makes people do strange things. We can check you into rehab for a couple of months, everyone always understands that, darling. You could even get some work done while you're in there, added bonus. We'll be back in business six weeks from now.'

'You don't understand, Myra, I didn't have a choice, I had to respond. Protect myself, defend my work, speak my truth. They were eviscerating me on that page for no good reason.'

'And how did responding work out for you, Harold, hmm?'

'You know influential people in the literary world, Myra, can't one of them help?' Harry whined.

'You're right, I do know influential people, but ninety-nine-point-nine-nine per cent of them have already called, emailed or pinged me to ask what the hell you were thinking?'

'So, short of telling the world I'm certifiable, or on crack, there's nothing you can do?' Harry whimpered.

'It doesn't have to be just crack or crank anymore, we could also go with a good old-fashioned opioid addiction. Or what about psychedelics, Harold? Mushrooms are all the rage now. Perhaps you have an old injury that needed painkillers, and things got out of control? Everybody loves a rehab comeback story, darling. You could even write a misery memoir about your addiction while you're in there – now that I could sell.'

'I'm not an addict, Myra. Nobody who knows me would believe that. Isn't there anything else you can do?'

'Sure Harold, let me just hack into the Goodreads master servers and delete the thousands of one-star reviews for your books. Then I'll recall *The Booktrade* newsletter that goes out to three million subscribers in the publishing industry around the world. After that, darling, I'll buy one of those *Men In Black* memory wiper wands and go around to every major publisher in the country, and the million-plus people who've seen your video on YouTube, and wipe their memories clean, shall I?' Myra said, her voice rising. 'What did you have in mind, Harold?'

'I just thought ... you could ... I thought ...' Harry trailed off.

'Look Harold, forget about all of that. There is nothing we can do about this hellscape you've created. I called to talk to you about your manuscript.'

'You read it?' Harry said, sucking in a breath.

'I said I would.'

'I thought maybe you wouldn't ... given the current, um, er, situation ...' Harry trailed off again.

'You mean you being cancelled?'

'Yes, that,' Harry said.

'I read the first three chapters because I said I would.'

'What did you think?' Harry asked.

'It has some form of potential, Harold.' He heard her pulling on her vape and could picture her in her office in her oversized spectacles, smelling of cloves, surrounded by books, awards and furniture selected by an overpaid, over-hyped, over-caffeinated, over-dressed-in-black interior designer. 'But we need to talk about your POV,' she continued.

'What? First person?' Harry asked.

'Yeeees,' Myra said, dragging out the word, 'you know as well as I do, that a compelling first-person narrative is not easy to maintain in a novel. So I was surprised at your choice, darling.'

'I wanted it to be immediate, personal.'

'I understand that, Harold, but going with the first person POV of a woman of colour is an interesting choice. What with you being a white male and all.'

'My other two books explore the inner lives of men. I wanted to show my range, not feel constrained by the boundaries of genre, sex and stereotype. I'm a writer, Myra, I can't be put in a box.'

'Although, some kind of box is precisely what you might need at this point, Harold. I just wanted to check something with you – I didn't have time to read the whole thing, but am I right in understanding that the entire book is told from the perspective of Kalisha, a black woman?'

'Yes, as I explained, I wanted to explore the inner lives of women, through a political and racial lens,' Harry said.

'But Harold, you write crime thrillers.'

'Literary crime thrillers,' he said.

'If you say so. Look Harold, I'm going to cut to the chase here, I don't have time to waste. Do you really think it's wise for you to write an entire novel from the first-person perspective of a woman of colour?'

'Because I'm not a woman or of colour?' Harry asked.

'Precisely,' Myra said.

'Would you have said that if I hadn't been cancelled?'

'Yes, Harold, absolutely. The sex scenes in particular feel awkward,' Myra said.

'So what do you suggest?' Harry asked.

'Well, the core idea isn't terrible, but you need to change the point of view. You could write it from the cop's perspective, perhaps? What I read of him, I didn't hate. And he could give you potential for this to become a series. Or maybe from the point of view of the coroner; he was marginally interesting,' Myra said.

'So does this mean ... do you think somebody might actually publish me again, even after all of this ... um ... this attention?' Harry asked.

'Well, let's not get ahead of ourselves. Why don't you work on the draft, fix the point-of-view catastrophe, and by the time we get the manuscript where it needs to be, who knows, this might all have died down to a dull roar. Unless you're willing to consider the rehab idea? I wouldn't dismiss it outright, Harold. I could work with rehab.'

'I ... I don't know how I'd feel about that,' Harry said.

'Okay, so then you get back onto the draft, alright darling? Oh, and Harold?'

'Yes Myra?'

'Get off the fucking internet and stop fucking calling me.'

'Yes Myra,' Harry said quietly, but she'd already cut the call.

THE GOOD BOOK APPRECIATION SOCIETY

MEMBERS: 73 291

Bernard Phillips: Hello book friends, me again, Bernard Phillips, from Bridgeport, Connecticut. I was recently at a literary festival, at a panel where Gordon Mathieson was being interviewed about his bestselling new novel. One of the questions someone asked was whether he felt comfortable writing from a middle-aged woman's perspective, since he is, quite obviously, not in fact a middle-aged woman.

Mathieson answered, 'Does that mean I can't ever write a novel about a serial killer, since I'm not actually a serial killer?'

It got me thinking, has oversensitive woke culture pushed us to the point that writers are no longer allowed to write characters that are not in their lived experience?

COMMENTS:

Chris Colt: If you ask me, the world is taking all of this woke stuff too far. Women are always whining about everything. Write whatever you want, and if you don't like what's been written, or who has chosen to write it, there is a very simple solution, don't read it. Now go get me a beer.

[Freda Kruger has reported this comment.]

Chris Colt:

Thomas Dooley: I'm a published author of five novels (all available on Amazon) and in my view, the trick is research. If you do your research properly, really inhabit your characters and write them properly, then you can write from any perspective.

Zabitt123: I instantly got seven thousand new followers the second I followed this account. You too can have the same big influencer results.

[Freda Kruger has reported this comment.]

Karen Granger: Isn't that cultural appropriation, though? #WordsMatter

Ruth Burstein: I'm tired of white men's opinions. I've stopped buying books written by white men altogether. The world would be a better place if they took up less space and stayed in their lane. I'm instantly turned off when white men try to write outside of their lived experience.

Chris Colt: So white men can't write about women or black people, but women or people of colour can write about anyone and anything they want? How is that fair?

Brian Wilder: I agree, and it's not just what we're allowed to write about that's being policed. Face it, a middle-aged straight white guy just can't get a publishing deal these days, no matter how hard he tries, or how well he writes. It's very unfair.

Avukile Chingwita: There you go, from your place of patriarchal privilege, moaning that something isn't fair after being on the back foot for three and a half seconds. Please white guys, try being an enslaved minority for centuries, then you can have an opinion on what's actually unfair.

Bernard Phillips: *Madame Bovary* by Gustave Flaubert springs to mind. Male author. Female first person POV. A much read, much-lauded classic.

Shanti Khumar: @Bernard Phillips, that was written in 1856. Are we really using it as a benchmark in the twenty-first century? When it comes to current fiction, I start off suspicious and wary when a male author tries to pull off a female voice, particularly one outside of their race.

Michelle Zanders: Sex scenes written by men from a female perspective just about always creep me out.

Mikaela Pace: *Pulls up a chair, and makes popcorn*

Linda Petal Dabb: Just a reminder, we're all friends here. Love and light.

Ruth Burstein: Women seem more able to pull off writing sex than men, if you ask me.

Michelle Zanders: Have you ever seen that Bad Sex Writing award? If there was ever proof of your hypothesis @Ruth Burstein. Most of the winners-slash-losers are men, attempting the most awful and embarrassing purple prose, usually with a straight face. They don't even realise how bad it is.

Chris Colt: So when men write bad purple prose we get called out for it, but it's okay for millions of women to read that Fifty Shades stuff because it was written by a woman? That's a load of bollocks.

[Freda Kruger has reported this comment.]

Gerry Rawson: I don't think bollocks is the word. Lady garden seems to be the preferred term.

[Freda Kruger has reported this comment.]

Karen Granger: This conversation is being derailed! Plus it is dangerously close to vulgarity. #WordsMatter

Shanti Khumar: Vulgarity isn't the problem here. It's the heteronormative fabric of multiple patriarchies interlocking with rampant capitalism that constantly privileges the white male voice.

Chris Colt: You lost me there, love, unless 'rampant' was a pun.

Geneva Fulverton: Not funny @Chris Colt.

Felicity Mauberger: Sheesh @Chris Colt, learn to read a room.

Harry

Harry finally dragged himself away from his computer to get coffee, ragged after an all-nighter spent monitoring and responding to his Bernard Phillips post about men writing as women. Things had escalated fast again, and he had needed to protect his aliases' reputation, as well as his own right to write what he liked.

When he stepped into the kitchen, he started. Neil and Clive were sitting in the breakfast nook, nursing cappuccinos and serious expressions.

'What are you two doing here? Do we have plans? Who died?' Harry asked.

'We need to talk, Harry,' Victoria said, following him into the kitchen, then blocking the door, her arms crossed over her chest.

Harry looked from Victoria to Neil, then to Clive, who was now picking imaginary fluff off his slacks.

'We're all worried about you,' Neil said.

'We're worried this is going to ruin you, Harry,' Clive said.

'This isn't how I want to live for the rest of my life, my darling. This cancel business is all you think about, it's all you talk about. You're not eating or sleeping. Only watching endless episodes of that *Naked* rubbish, which is only going to make your brain deteriorate even further. You're not only ruining your own life, Harry; now you're ruining mine too, and I take exception to that,' Victoria said.

'Wait, is this, are you guys ...? Is this one of those tough-love intervention things?' Harry said, pointing at them.

'Harry, you've got a rewrite to get onto. You can't carry on obsessing over this one bad review by a total stranger, and the resulting fallout and that appalling awards show debacle,' Victoria said. 'I know you; you tend to fixate on things.'

'And get oversensitive,' Clive said.

'And procrastinate,' Neil added.

'Wait, is this an intervention or a roast?' Harry asked.

'We've decided that we can't spend time with you anymore if you're going to continue obsessing over this nonsense. It's exhausting, and to be honest, quite boring. You literally never stop talking about it,' Victoria said. 'Ever.'

'You really do never shut up about it,' Neil agreed.

'So what are you saying?' Harry said, looking around at them.

'We've decided we're going to have to pause our friendship,' Neil said. 'You can't come with us to Cheltenham next week.'

'We think you should stay here, focus on your rewrite, and on moving on from this chapter in your life. Exchange one chapter for another one, so to speak,' Clive said.

'But Victoria and I have been looking forward to this trip with you guys for months,' Harry said.

'I'm still looking forward to it,' Victoria said.

'You're going without me?' Harry gaped at her.

'Yes, of course. I'm not the one who has a rewrite to do. I booked time off work months ago and arranged cover for all my surgeries. It was like arranging the Normandy invasion. There's no way I'm not going,' Victoria said.

'So, you're abandoning me at my most vulnerable?' Harry said, knowing he sounded pathetic.

'It's no good me staying here and distracting you. We're actually giving you a gift, you should be grateful. No responsibilities, no distractions, just one whole week where you can sit down and do the important work you need to do to move through this terrible period of your life. We all think it's the perfect solution,' Victoria said, and both Neil and Clive nodded vigorously.

'Wow,' Harry said. 'Just wow.'

'Imagine how good you'll feel once you've gotten your rewrite done, darling?' Victoria said. 'I know you, Harry. Once you hit your stride, you'll be off and away, and then you won't want anyone around slowing you down. You never want me here when you're writing.'

'And doesn't everyone say that the best thing you can do to get through something like this is to stop reacting to it, stop responding, and simply move on. So that you don't let those fuckers get you down,' Neil said.

'If you fall off the horse, just get straight back on it,' Clive said.

'The best way to get over one person is to get underneath another,' Neil added, and both Victoria and Clive shot him a glare.

'We're doing this because we love you,' Clive said.

'I feel like you're doing this because you hate me, to be honest,' Harry sulked.

'Don't be ridiculous, we don't hate you,' Neil said. 'We just don't like you very much right now.'

'Harry. I'm not sure how much more of this I can take. And I don't know how many other ways I can say this: you need to move on, and I think this is one way we can help you do that,' Victoria said.

'Guys, I know you mean well, but I don't think you realise that there's something sinister going on here, something dark, even illegal ...' Harry started.

'There he goes again,' Neil said.

'Harry, who cares?' Victoria shouted.

'I care, Vicks, and you should too. First, it's just a bit of cyber-bullying. What's next? Global warming? Murder?' Harry yelled back.

'You're not even making sense anymore, Harry,' Victoria sighed. 'You're just rambling nonsense and spilling tea down your shirt half the time.'

'So, that's it, you're all going on my ... on our holiday without me? Can I just remind you that this trip was my idea?' Harry shouted, folding his arms to cover the tea stains down the front of his sweatshirt. 'It's a literary festival! I'm the author here!'

'Try to understand, Harry; it's not because we want to, it's because we have to,' Clive said.

'You've given us no other choice,' Victoria said.

Harry slumped into a chair and laid his head on the table. Just when he thought things couldn't possibly get any worse, it turned out that they always could. And generally did.

Norma

Norma was in the slush-pile room, paging through a nine-hundred-page crime thriller, set in a town in Alaska with a population of twenty-three. She wondered why it needed to be such a long book when there weren't that many possible suspects.

She was about to skip to the end, to find out whether it was the sheriff, the late-night DJ, the ice fisherman, or one of his three girlfriends who'd murdered the school teacher, when her phone buzzed with another voice note from Steve.

Norma set aside the manuscript, shored up her strength, plugged in her earphones and played the message.

> Norms, I know I fucked up. But I've finally figured out THE best way to pay back the money. This is a SURE THING, Norma. I tried to call earlier, but it always goes to voicemail. Is there something wrong with your phone? So, you know that retirement fund you have from the firm? What if you cashed it in and invested in crypto? There's a big wave coming, Norma. But now is the time to do it. We need to move on this fast, before everyone else cottons on.

Norma deleted the voice note.

'Audible?' Bavinga asked.

Norma laughed, 'You do know that most people use their mobiles for things other than reading or listening to novels, right?'

'God, you weren't making a TikTok were you?' Bavinga said, shooting a glance at Britttennay, who, no surprises, was doing just that.

'It's my ex – he keeps sending me these ridiculous voice notes,' Norma said.

'How long ago did you break up?' Bavinga asked.

'A few weeks, but it's taking longer to sink in for him than it has for me.'

'How long were you together?' Bavinga asked.

'Almost three years. And probably a year and a half too long.'

'I was still in high school when you started dating,' Bavinga said with a laugh.

'Please don't remind me,' Norma said.

'Sorry, ignore me, I'm not fully house-trained.'

'I'm not sure why we dragged it out this long,' Norma said.

'Lucky you aren't married, it's way easier and cheaper to break up with someone than it is to divorce them,' Bavinga said. 'My folks have been divorced four times, I should know.'

'They both got remarried to other people four times? That's a lot, and a coincidence,' Norma said.

'No, to each other. Married, divorced, married, divorced, married, divorced – and repeat,' Bavinga said. 'Actually, come to think of it, their last wedding was about the same year you and your ex first got together. So you guys lasted way longer than they did, even though you never got married.'

'Probably because we didn't get married. Are your folks together now?' Norma asked.

'Not officially. but you never know what kind of wedding they're planning next. I wasn't at the first one, obviously. Then there was a beach wedding when I was nine, an elopement to a Vegas Elvis chapel wedding when I was thirteen, and the most recent was a destination wedding in Thailand three years ago.'

'Are there any other kinds of weddings left?' Norma asked.

'You'd be surprised how many more ways there are for them to try again. We haven't had a forest wedding yet, or a big fat Greek wedding, and we could probably still manage a very religious wedding.'

'Or an underwater one? Cameras are waterproof nowadays,' Norma said.

'There's also outer space,' Bavinga added.

'I wonder if there are the same variety of divorces as there are weddings?' Norma asked.

'My parents are researching that for you as we speak. So far, they've had one hostile one in court, one amicable one out of court, and one mediated by a Brené Brown wannabe, and they're in the middle of the fourth one, so stay tuned.'

'Your parents' divorce lawyers must be smiling,' Norma said.

'Actually, my mum is a divorce lawyer, so maybe she knew what she was doing all along.'

'She must be good at her job,' Norma said.

'Practice makes perfect.'

'I know it's a very personal question, and you don't have to answer, but did they just keep changing their minds about each other?' Norma asked.

'I think they both have short memories. The saying only goes as far as trick me once, shame on you, trick me twice, shame on me. There's no advice for when you get tricked three or four or five times.'

'Well, I guess that's for when the next – maybe final – divorce happens?' Norma said.

'One can only hope, but I wouldn't bet my inheritance on it. Or should I say, her settlement.'

'It couldn't have been very easy for you, growing up like that,' Norma said.

'You mean, way to get a kid's hopes up over and over?' Bavinga laughed. 'It's okay, when it's all you know, it's all you know. And we have books, and those never leave.'

'Do you have brothers or sisters?' Norma asked.

'Nah, I'm the only one they screwed up, so that's a lucky break. You?'

'No kids myself. Never wanted any. And as far as siblings go, just my ex's sister, Marina. She's like a sister. I intend keeping her in the break-up.'

'Did one of you cheat?' Bavinga asked.

'Yes, he cheated the max out of my credit card.'

'Oh shit.'

'Such a shit! You have no idea.'

Harry

The constant doomscrolling of his own demise was giving Harry heartburn, so he clicked over to Google to research how long it would take to melt a body in a bathtub using lye.

If the solution was heated, he could dissolve an entire corpse in just three hours. Although he wasn't sure how he would heat the lye. He was about to google that when Phyllis rang.

'Harry, buddy, you're still alive? Or maybe I should ask: is your reviewer still alive?'

'Hi Phyl.'

'How are you getting along, bud? I saw a missed call from you when I woke up this morning, but it came through in the middle of the night, so my phone was off.'

'I wanted to tell you that Myra rang,' Harry said.

'What did she say?'

'She read the first three chapters of *The Wednesday Protocol*.'

'Great news. After everything that's happened, I wasn't sure she would.'

'You and me both,' Harry said.

'And?' Phyllis prodded.

'She liked the concept, but it's a total rewrite.'

'At least she didn't outright hate it.'

'No, she only hated my POV,' Harry said.

'What did you go with?' Phyllis asked.

'First person.'

'Ah, notoriously hard to pull off.'

'Of a black woman,' Harry added.

'Uh-huh. I see.'

'I had a thought, Phyllis,' Harry said. 'Victoria's going away with some friends, and I need to get to work on this rewrite. What if you popped over to London, super last-minute? You can stay here, we've got a spare room. We could have a little writers' retreat. Lock ourselves in and write all day, then hang out, compare word counts, plot, grab a bite, that kind of thing. It would be a working holiday for you in London – you love London.'

'I'd love to, Harry, but I have my lecturing schedule, and Celia, and then there's Chemtrail. She's on a course of de-worming tablets, and let's just say she does not take pills easily. Can't just shove 'em in a block of cheese like you can with other dogs, and Celia refuses to do it, after their last standoff ended in tears – and not Chemtrail's either.'

'I know you're busy, Phyl, but the truth is, I'm worried about what I'm going to do while Vicks is away. I'm having some crazy thoughts.'

'Channel them, Harry. Channel them into your rewrite, that's all you can do. That's what you HAVE to do.'

'I know,' Harry said, his voice small.

'Harry, I'll see you at the London Festival of Books soon. We've got that panel together and the signings. We can get dinner afterwards, a couple of drinks, catch up, bitch about the other writers, our agents and our publishers, and work through all this together in person, alright?'

When Harry didn't answer, her voice got stern: 'Say alright, Harry.'

'Alright, Harry,' Harry said quietly.

'Promise me you won't do anything stupid before then.'

Harry mumbled something.

'Harry, you're going through a rough patch, that's all. Put your head down, work on that rewrite. It sounds like Myra has handed you a lifeline. And you said she loved your core idea, I bet it's killer, if you'll pardon the pun. And this too shall pass,' Phyllis said gently.

'Yeah, yeah,' Harry said.

'I have to go, Chemtrail is glaring at me, it's past time for her walk. You've got this, Harry, just don't forget to breathe, let all the negativity pass you by, get rewriting, and don't do anything crazy. Oh, and stay off the internet!'

Phyllis was right, Harry thought, as he hung up. He needed to stay off the internet. And he would, just as soon as he'd logged into Facebook as Gaill A, and written a quick angry review. That always made him feel better.

Norma

'Marina, I just got my credit card statement. I'm in deep shit,' Norma said down the phone.

'My brother's a dickwad,' Marina replied.

Norma could hear a chainsaw in the background. It sounded like it was eating through something chunky and metallic.

'I'm so tired of thinking about this shit-show all the time. But mostly I'm angry. I want to murder that idiot,' Norma said. 'And we just broke up, I should be crying all over the place, shouldn't I? But I've barely shed a tear, what's that about? What if I'm a psychopath, with late-onset tendencies?'

'You are not a psychopath, Norma.'

'I don't even know what I'm feeling.'

'Wanna get a bottle of tequila?' Marina asked.

'It's eleven in the morning, and you sound like you're angle-grinding London Bridge.'

'Time is just a construct. Wait, I know what you need. I'm sending you a pin. Don't ask any questions, just meet me there in an hour. Wear trainers and clothes you don't mind getting fucked up,' Marina said.

'Why? Are we going to kill your brother, and bury his body?'

'We'll do that next time. My thing first. See you in an hour,' Marina said before hanging up.

Looking into her closet, Norma realised that she didn't mind any of her clothes getting messed up. There wasn't a single item that screamed 'big deal in the publishing' industry. If anything, her wardrobe was more suggestive of 'big deal in the living in your car' industry.

She threw on her oldest trainers and stuck Marina's pin into Uber, with forty-five minutes left to get to wherever 'there' was.

Norma scrolled through The Good Book Appreciation Society page while she waited for the car to arrive. That Edna Molton had added a new post. The image was a doctored photograph of Harry Shields's latest novel, *Once on a Tuesday*, except she had photoshopped the title to read *Never on a Tuesday*. And she'd also written a fake blurb for the book about how one shouldn't read it on a Tuesday, or a Wednesday or a Thursday, Friday or Saturday either. It was a spiteful post. The whole thing had gotten out of control. Norma deleted the post; it had only been up on the page for twenty minutes, and it only had a few hundred views, so she hoped she'd managed to delete it before Harry had seen it. If he hadn't already gone mad, this would definitely send him over the edge. Of course he had brought most of this on himself, and he was an arrogant piece of shit, but, she didn't think he deserved this kind of humiliation.

Harry

'What time is your train?'

'We leave just after nine tomorrow,' Victoria said, as she zipped up her toiletry bag and popped it into her suitcase.

'I still can't believe you're going without me.'

'We've talked about this a hundred times, darling, maybe even a thousand. It's starting to get tedious. You said yourself that you're struggling to focus. You're distracted, and from where I'm standing, it looks like you're coming apart at the seams. Neil, Clive and I think this is for the best.'

'What about what I think?' Harry whined.

'I think we can all agree that what you think right now is not to be trusted. This is the perfect opportunity for you to pull yourself towards yourself, and get your rewrite done for Myra. The fact that she hasn't fired you yet is some kind of miracle, so you need to honour the great kindness she and the universe have extended you. I can't imagine you would be able to replace her at this point,' Victoria said, setting her suitcase by their bedroom door.

'I hope you lot have a great time on my holiday, being all cultural, going to panel discussions, listening to live music and drinking cocktails without me,' Harry muttered.

'It will be tough, but I'll try have a good time despite your absence, my darling,' Victoria said as she dabbed night cream onto her face.

'Are you even going to miss me?' Harry asked.

'I'll try schedule it in between brunch and cocktails.'

Harry got out of bed and slipped his feet into his slippers.

'Where are you going, Harry? You know I was only teasing you. Of course I'm going to miss you, darling. Please don't sulk, you know I hate it when you sulk,' Victoria called after him.

'I'm not sulking, Vicks, I'm just not feeling very tired.'

'How can you not be tired? You haven't slept properly in weeks. For heaven's sake, Harry, you're a walking zombie.'

'Maybe it's adrenalin? I don't know. Honestly, I feel like I'll only toss and turn and keep you up. And you've got a train to catch in the morning.'

'Promise me you won't read or comment on any more of those toxic posts, or watch that Golden Page Awards attack video on YouTube on repeat all night again?'

Harry nodded as he headed for the stairs. It wasn't an attack, he thought; it was an assault, and he was the victim.

Norma

Norma turned three hundred and sixty degrees on the site of the dropped pin and hummed 'Where are we now' by David Bowie. She was in a nondescript industrial area of London, on a nondescript street. None of the shop fronts in the forest of grey cement buildings hinted at where Marina was taking her.

She was about to WhatsApp her friend when Marina wandered around the corner in a waft of Giorgio Armani for men, wearing black vintage denim jeans, folded into a deep cuff, long Doc Martens, and a fitted black shirt, her straight black hair tied back. Perennial fag between her fingers. She was the only person Norma knew who still smoked and made it look cool.

'Are we "there"?' Norma asked.

'We are in fact "there",' Marina said.

'And where is "there"?'

'Here,' Marina said. 'Come.'

Norma followed her down a dark side alley to a narrow door that had a small keypad, a buzzer and a camera eye staring down at them. Marina rang and they waited a moment before the door buzzed and she pushed it open. Norma followed her inside and the door shut with a heavy metallic clunk behind them.

'This isn't MI6, is it?' Norma whispered.

Marina shook her head, laughing, and carried on down the corridor.

Norma followed her down a flight of stairs. 'I'll never forgive you if this is one of those escape room games, Marina,' she hissed.

Marina indicated for Norma to keep following her as they stepped through another door and into a large basement space.

'Jesus, Marina. Like I'm not having a bad enough life already? You brought me to a gym?'

'Fuck off. Like I would ever take you to a gym. Come meet Felix. You'll thank me later.'

The warehouse was lit by fluorescent overhead bulbs, and smelled like sweat. Marina was right; it wasn't a gym, it was an old-fashioned boxing studio. Two shirtless guys were sparring in a ring in the middle of the room. Shafts of dusty light streamed in from pavement level through small windows high up on one wall. A handful of guys were lifting weights or pounding punching bags.

A big guy loped towards them. He was two parts Axl Rose from Guns N' Roses, one part the late, great Meatloaf, but neither in their glory days – more as the musicians might look today. Tall, not lean, but tough and pock-marked. As he got closer, Norma saw that he had one droopy eye, stringy, long, blond hair, and a bandana tied around his forehead. He wore stained, faded sweatpants and a vest with the words 'Old's Gym' in cracked, peeling lettering across his chest.

'Tammy,' his voice boomed as he bent down to give Marina a hug.

'Tammy?' Norma said, eyebrows raised.

'Thanks for fitting us in, Felix. This is my friend I told you about, Norma. She's the one my fuckhead brother screwed over. I thought you could help her out with a bit of therapy.'

Felix tossed a pair of boxing gloves at Norma, who made no move to catch them, so they bounced off her and fell to the floor as she stood humming 'I would do anything for love, but I won't do this', by Meatloaf.

'Thank you, but I'm not … I don't … I'm not … athletic,' Norma stuttered, picking them up and politely trying to hand them back.

'On,' Felix grunted. Then whistled at the guys in the ring, who stopped sparring and climbed out.

Marina took the gloves from Norma and held one open, so she could slip a hand into it. 'Give it a go. If you don't like it after five minutes, stop.'

Reluctantly, Norma slid one hand into one glove, then the other. Felix pulled the ropes open for her and she climbed in. Getting a foot hooked, she stumbled into the ring. The floor was spongy and she pulled herself up using the ropes, spectacles askew, a bead of sweat already sliding down the side of her face.

Marina hung over the edge of the ring, whooping encouragement.

'Hit,' Felix commanded, positioning himself in front of her.

'One moment,' Norma said, humming as she walked over to Marina. 'Spectacles,' she said. Marina reached forward and pulled them off her face.

Norma returned to where Felix was standing and launched her right fist at him, landing a soft punch in the middle of his padded glove.

'Hands up,' Felix grunted again, indicating the hand she wasn't hitting with. 'Fuckhead's name?' Felix asked Marina.

'Steve,' Marina shouted.

'This dot,' Felix said to Norma, indicating the yellow circle in the middle of the palm of his padded glove, 'is fuckhead Steve's face.'

Norma nodded.

'Right, left, right, left. One – two, one – two, one – two, one two. Hard,' Felix said. 'Got it?'

'Hard,' Norma repeated. Then she launched at him. One – two, one – two, one – two, one – two.

As she got in a rhythm, Norma felt her chest starting to burn, but she pushed through, punching harder and harder. After about fifteen minutes circling the ring following Felix's instructions, Norma dropped wheezing to the floor of the ring, a puddle of angry tears, sweat and quivering muscles.

Felix stepped back and nodded approval. Norma's heart was pounding so loudly in her ears, it was all she could hear. When Marina hovered over her, she squinted and raised her fists. Marina pulled off the gloves and handed her a towel. She wiped her face and when she put her glasses back on, they steamed up instantly.

'Better?' Marina asked, as they sat side by side in the ring. Norma caught her breath and tried to find an inch or two of her t-shirt that wasn't drenched in sweat, to wipe her spectacles with. Norma nodded, as a tear mixed with sweat rolled down her cheek.

'I'm so sorry, Norma,' Marina said, putting an arm around her.

'For bringing me here, or for Steve?' Norma asked.

'I'll never be sorry for bringing you here.'

'So, where do you know him from, "Tammy"?'

'Felix? London Arena, 1995. The Nigel Benn and Gerald McClellan fight. He was on the Benn team,' Marina said.

'And you were ...?'

'In the ring, between rounds, holding up the numbers in a tiny American-flag bikini.'

'Of course you were,' Norma laughed.

'What are you going to do?' Marina asked.

'The internship barely covers my property taxes, so the minimum payment due on my card will have to come out of my savings, and then side hustle, baby, cos a girl's got to eat,' Norma said.

'And drink,' Marina said. 'I could always rob a bank?'

'Thing is, I don't know if you're joking or if you would actually go out tomorrow night and rob a bank for me,' Norma said.

'It would have to be the night after, I've got this spray paint thing in Brixton tomorrow. But I'm not kidding, if you need help making these payments, I'm here.'

'I know you are, thank you. You're the better Watson by a mile. But I need to sort out my own shit.'

'But it's not your own shit, is it? You should tell Steve he has to pay, and let him figure it out.'

'You and I both know that telling him to pay is like telling a short person to grow taller,' Norma replied. 'So, side hustle it is, until something better comes along.'

'I thought you already had a side hustle with the book club?'

'I do, but book clubs on Facebook don't pay, even ones with over eighty thousand members, so, I suppose it'll be a side-side hustle.'

'Holy shit, your club has grown! Wasn't it at twenty thousand just the other day?'

'Yes, funny what a bit of controversy on social media, a narcissistic author, and a couple of column inches in *The Times* and *The Guardian* can do. That fool may have been cancelled, but in the process we've been discovered. I've been inundated by journalists and book bloggers, and while they're a bunch of vultures, all this press has given the club a huge boost.'

'I guess you could always go back to accountancy.'

'God, now you sound like Steve. I could, but I was supposed to be leaving that life in the rear view. I would hate myself if I went back to it so soon and didn't even give this exit plan a shot. I'd sooner go back to South Africa.'

'You wouldn't!' Marina said.

'Nah. I do miss it sometimes, but my life is here now.'

'So, what are you thinking?' Marina asked.

'I've got a couple of ideas,' Norma said.

'Now *you* sound like Steve,' Marina said, making Norma snort out a laugh. 'Seriously though, I've got contacts if you wanted to be, say, a clown at kids' parties, a snake charmer, a movie-set extra, a drug mule, a bartender, barista, llama wrangler, school lunch lady, club promoter, mural painter, train conductor, air stewardess, supermarket product promoter, Red Bull girl, back-up singer or a fluffer?' Marina offered.

'And don't forget boxing-ring bikini babe. Thanks, but I was thinking more along the lines of working nights and weekends in a book store,' Norma said.

'I can't help you there, love, I've never done anything as out there as that,' Marina said.

Harry

Harry was a writer, so he knew this was not how stakeouts were supposed to go. In books, the detective or PI rarely took a bus to the station, then a train to their stakeout, and then hardly ever just showed up at their stakeout's address, unsure if it was even their address, having found it on a voter's roll from twelve years earlier. And then they definitely hardly ever did their stakeout around town on foot, pulling their overnight bag behind them on wheels.

If Harry were the real deal, he'd be in a banged-up car, stuffed with takeaway food wrappers and used coffee cups. But Harry didn't have a car or a drivers licence; Victoria always drove if they went anywhere.

When Harry's train pulled into Ludlow station dangerously early that morning, he popped into a local cafe for coffee and a fry-up. He thought one should never commit illegal acts on an empty stomach – in case you got caught and imprisoned, and didn't see a decent meal for the next four to seven.

Once he'd eaten, he pulled out his notebook to make a start on his stakeout notes.

4:17: Unholy early start. Train ride mostly uneventful. Spilled coffee on trousers.

8:03: Arrived. Breakfast at local greasy spoon. Two eggs, bacon, toast, baked beans. Latte. Now running lat(t)e. (Ha!)

9:33: Google-mapped to get to target's potential address. Airbnb check-in only after three pm, so had to wheel case behind me. All town streets cobbled.

Note to self: write to Ludlow town council to complain about excessive cobbles. And next time bring backpack instead of wheelie-case.

9:56: Settled on wall just along from target's home. Hid suitcase behind neighbour's wall. Pretending to read bestseller, *For the Madness of Love* by Frank Dyson, so as not to draw attention.

10:14: Target's home: small, well-kept cottage, neat garden. Lights on indicate subject in residence. Dog turds in garden indicate small dog. Yapping confirms it.

10:46: Twenty-seven pages in, Dyson prop book quite good. Light rain has set in, which somewhat compromises cover.

11:58: Elderly woman exited house. Confirmed as Edna Molton, based on binocular profile picture. Pursuit complicated because of noise of wheels on cobbles. Fortunately target moves slowly and doesn't seem to notice. Note to self: Target hard of hearing?

12:16: Target entered police station.

12:17: Decamped to nearby coffee shop with view of police station.

Note to self: Why police station? Did Edna see me following her? Is she reporting me?

12:23: Sweating, pulse racing, heart rate elevated. Ordered latte and cream bun so as not to appear suspicious.

12:32: Formed alibi in case of police questioning: town has castle. Am famous writer, researching new novel: moving tale of sixteenth-century knight persecuted for being redhead, almost loses knighthood and red head.

12:33: No sign of Edna. Need bathroom. Can't risk losing sight of her. Heart rate remains elevated, palms sweaty. Rain ongoing. No longer just a light shower. Note to self: Next time bring umbrella.

12:48: Queasy. Uneasy.

12:50: Waiter cleared plate and cup, can't sit here much longer at empty table with full bladder. Target still inside police station.

Convinced they are now staking me out.

12:52: Feel like I'm being followed. And so the hunter becomes the hunted.

12:53: Full-blown panic attack.

12:54 – 1:07: Breathing exercises.

13:12: Target now inside building society. Waiting around corner with suitcase. Don't think I've been seen. Unless police are still following me, following her, to prove I'm following her. Pretending to read again to deflect suspicion. Book VERY good. But hard to concentrate with full bladder.

13:16: Desperate.

13:19: Relieved self in bushy municipal bed with awkward view of building society. Low point. Hope won't be nabbed for public urination in addition to stalking.

13:43: Target finally left bank.

14:15: Target eating prawn sandwich in cafe.

14:17: Six crème eggs for stakeout lunch.

Note to self: next time, pack umbrella *and* lunch.

15:04: Target in library. Watching exit.

15:27: Still no sign of target.

15:48: Got sucked in by Dyson novel, now on page 76. Potentially missed target's exit?

15:56: Entered Ludlow Library in search of target. Found Molton browsing latest crime fiction. Tried to leave inconspicuously. Knocked over returns cart. Target didn't notice.

16:42: Target checked out three books. Planning on destroying those authors' careers as well?

Note to self: Offing her a service to fellow authors? Possibility of knighthood?

16:47: Followed target home.

16:59: Exhaustion, dehydration, sore feet. Reflux from crème egg lunch. Muscular sensitivity in arms from dragging suitcase. Dyson novel still excellent.

17:36: Checked into Airbnb.

17:39 – 21:58: Siesta.

21:59: Room small but clean. Dinner from honesty mini bar: 4 bottles booze (mini). 2 packets cheese & onion crisps. 2 packets peanuts.

Note to self: This is stakeout diary, not *Bridget Jones' Diary*.

22:07 – 23:36: Doomscrolling, responding to new comments and death threats. YouTube video has now been viewed 1.4 million times.

23:39: NOTES:

1. Why police station?
2. Library visit thoughts: does this mean she didn't even buy my books before she slated them? Bad review AND lost sales.
3. Not fan of cheese and onion crisps. Gassy. Leaves thirst and persistent oniony taste.

04:46: Turned last page of the Dyson book. Brilliant. Will post disparaging review on GBAS as Gaill A.

THE GOOD BOOK APPRECIATION SOCIETY

MEMBERS: 73 682

Gaill A: It's just gone 5am as I turn the last page of *For the Madness of Love*, by Frank Dyson. If you think I stayed up all night reading this book because it's so excellent, you'd be wrong.

I only stayed up to finish it because I committed to reading it with my IRL book club which meets later today.

I wanted to like this novel. After all, judges of the world's most prestigious literary prize loved it and so did most of you. But I don't get the hype. I can't help but wonder if you aren't all just sheep, following popular opinion? Terrible books like this get great reviews, and brilliant books like *Once on a Tuesday* by Harry Shields get panned, and the author gets cancelled. How?

The story revolves around a small blind boy, a dog with three legs, and an adopted girl with alopecia. Emotional blackmail, much? If you want me to have empathy for your main character, giving them disabilities is the easy way out. Create a character I have empathy for without using their disabilities as a crutch, then we can talk.

No to Frank Dyson, no to the members of the GBAS who have claimed to love this book, and no to all those fancy literary award judges. Just no.

COMMENTS:

Linda Petal Dabb: Is all this negativity really necessary? Love and light.

Chris Colt: I once had a girlfriend with alopecia, at least she didn't clog up the shower drain.

[Freda Kruger has reported this comment.]

Bernard Phillips: I agree, the Shields is a very good read.

Norma

Norma stopped paging through a poetry manuscript and dropped it on a pile for one of the others to look at. She found poetry impenetrable. Poets never said what they really meant. Then she deleted two new voice notes from Steve without listening to them and scrolled through The Good Book Appreciation Society. What she'd come to think of as 'The Trouble With Harry' was still boiling over on the page.

Since Norma had last scrolled through the page, Edna Molton had posted another 'Authors Behaving Badly' diatribe. It felt like the woman was actively baiting the author by now, trying to get him to respond so the internet would continue devouring him whole. There was something cruel about it.

Norma also scrolled through a slew of angry comments in response to a disparaging new review from that Gaill A troll. Along with distressed comments from both the Association For The Blind, as well as the Alopecia Society. And she was also going to have to draft an apologetic response to a concerned DM that had come in from the RSPCA. It was astonishing how much damage one post could cause. Norma shook her head and returned to the list she'd been making on the back of one of the slush-pile-room manuscripts; a memoir about a crocodile wrangler who'd grown up in the Australian outback, then moved to London to make a go of it, despite the distinct lack of crocodiles in metropolitan London's natural habitat. Norma had briefly skim-read the book, just to make sure she wasn't making her list of side-side-hustle pros and cons on the back of a manuscript that might go on to win The Booker. 'See you later, alligator,' she said, returning to her list. She may not be a good judge of poetry, but she could tell a non-fiction train wreck from a mile away.

At the top of her list, she'd written, in all caps:

'PROS AND CONS OF WORKING IN A NEW BOOKSHOP
(VS SECOND-HAND ONE)'

Then she spent five minutes trying to word it better, but sticking with it in the end, opting for clarity over simplicity.

Then she'd drawn a line down the middle of the page to create a column for the pros and one for the cons.

She scanned what she'd written so far, wondering if she'd missed anything important.

PROS (of working in a new bookshop):
1. More money.
2. Seeing the new books as they come out, hot off the press. Legitimately thrilling.
3. Get to work at big-name book launches. Imagine who I might meet.
4. Room for promotion.

CONS (of working in a new bookshop):
1. ~~More expensive books, if I wanted to buy any.~~
Norma crossed that one out. Who was she kidding? Thanks to Steve, she could no longer afford to buy anything new or even second-hand ever again.
~~2~~
1. Would be the oldest employee for sure.
~~3~~
2. Would have to be much more polite and chatty working in a fancy

new book store. Emo grumpiness comes standard in the second-hand ones.

~~4~~
3. Uniform??

Four pros. Three cons. In her heart she knew she was more of a second-hand bookshop kind of person, but in the end the 'more money' pro won. She took a screenshot of her list and WhatsApped it to Marina, who sent back more cons within seconds.

CON 4: Still, not as much fun as being a clown at kids' parties, is it?
CON 5: No balloon animals!

Harry

Harry had only just arrived home from Ludlow when Victoria video-called him from Cheltenham. He answered, trying to make it appear as if he'd been working.

'Darling, how are you? I just popped back to my hotel to get a jumper, and I thought I'd call before we get busy for the evening.'

'Are you having a good time?' Harry asked, although he could see she was. She looked happy, tanned – or was she just flushed, maybe tipsy?

'Fantastic. You would have loved this trip, Harry.'

'You don't say. Rub some salt in, why don't you?' Harry said.

'Don't blame me, it's not my fault that you got obsessed with an octogenarian reviewer, got cancelled, tried to claim a prize that wasn't yours, shouted at a rich author in public, called him a cunt, and made your friends hold an intervention and go on a trip without you.'

Definitely tipsy, Harry thought. 'Please Vicks, don't remind me.'

'Sorry, darling. We'll just have to come back to celebrate when you've finished your rewrite. That will be fun, won't it?'

'I'm sure it will,' Harry said, drawing angry circles on his notepad.

'Speaking of, how's the rewriting going?'

'I got words down yesterday,' Harry said. Victoria didn't need to know that none of them were part of the rewrite.

'You see, I knew if we just gave you some space, you would pull yourself right out of that boring old slump.'

'Thanks, but I would rather the space you'd given me had been in the Comoros. It hasn't stopped raining here.'

'Oh don't be flip, Harry. Anyway, darling, if you were in the Comoros, you'd be spending your days and nights drinking cocktails and lying on the beach, and you wouldn't have gotten to any of this great rewriting you're doing. You should be thanking us, not sulking. Just think how happy Myra will be when you deliver that rewrite.'

'So happy,' Harry said, unhappily.

'Darling, I'd better go, the guys have arranged a hot-air balloon ride, if you can believe that. If you don't hear from me again, it's because we're out to dinner afterwards, and I don't want to wake you up if we only get back to the suite late,' Victoria said.

'You have a suite?' Harry said, recalling his mini room in Ludlow, with the mini bar and mini bed.

'Didn't I tell you? What a palaver. There was a piece of shell in one of Clive's oysters on our first night, and Neil had pretended to be that famous travel writer he looks like so we could get the booking, so they bumped us up to private suites, in exchange for signing non-disclosure agreements. It's a pity you don't look like anybody, Harry. Wait, maybe Woody Allen? But then didn't he get cancelled too?'

'Enjoy the hot air balloon and the suite,' Harry said, through gritted teeth.

'Will do, toodeloo,' Victoria trilled.

Harry logged onto The Good Book Appreciation Society as Gaill A, to drop a few more caustic comments on his-her earlier review which had been spectacularly successful in its wreaking of havoc.

He took ten minutes to craft and post the ugliest put-down he could come up with for Gaill A to add to the comments of the post. Although he'd sidestep that Chris Colt, that guy was radioactive.

Taking his frustrations out on everyone by doling out anonymous abuse didn't make him feel 100 per cent better, but it certainly helped.

THE GOOD BOOK APPRECIATION SOCIETY

MEMBERS: 82 450

Brian Wilder: I've become obsessed with reading famous authors whose first books were massive flops. It's become something of a hobby.

Did you know that Emily Bronte couldn't find a publisher for Wuthering Heights, so she ended up self-publishing it? Unpopular opinion loading; I thought it was fine, but not astonishing.

The White Peacock was D.H Lawrence's first novel. It got terrible reviews, and was considered a flop. I also thought it was hard going.

Ernest Hemingway's first book, Torrents of The Spring, was first published in 1926. Ever heard of it? No, neither had I. That should hint at how well it did.

Turning to more modern authors, Sebastian Faulks is one of my favourite bestselling authors, and he's won more than a dozen big awards for his work. But his first novel is rarely mentioned. Even though it was well-received at launch, they only printed 1 500 copies, and a lot of those were later pulped. Since then, Faulks has made a career out of snapping up as many of them as he can find, and has declined to have the book reprinted or republished. Which means finding a copy is as rare as hen's teeth, and they sell for thousands.

From my understanding, it's usually just luck and timing if a manuscript happens to make it through the gauntlet of slush piles and publishing gatekeepers. And then so often it's the publisher's marketing department that dictates which books get enough airtime to become hits. We don't even realise it, but we barely have a say in which books do well – it's all marketing!

Anyone got any other famous authors' floppy first novels to recommend to add to my collection?

COMMENTS:

Lucille Cooper: Of course, there's the old story of JK Rowling, whose original pitch for *Harry Potter* was rejected twelve times before she found a taker.

Dax Goby: And don't forget, not an author, but The Beatles were turned down by at least four respected record labels before they were discovered.

Ruth Burstein: The moral of the story is, if your first book is bad, write a few more, they're bound to get better at some point.

Saul Silverstein: I was a publisher for thirty years, and I could never have said this while I was in the industry, but I'm retired now, so I don't give a crap. I can honestly tell you this for free; some people can write a hundred more, a thousand more, a million more books: they will never ever get any better.

Thomas Dooley: No, the real moral of the story is, if you ever find a copy of the Faulks book in a second-hand bookshop, buy it.

Harry Shields: Maybe the real moral of the story is that not everybody who thinks they can write, can or should write!

[Freda Kruger reported this comment.]

Brian Wilder : [is typing]

Norma

The slush-pile room had started to take shape. It no longer looked like an underground bomb shelter housing sixteen frat boys during a zombie apocalypse, but it did still lean towards small town after a tornado.

They were supposed to be sorting through the poetry slush-pile, but Bavinga was in one corner reading a Margaret Atwood novel on her mobile, Britttennay was making a TikTok that involved dozens of selfies from different angles, and which she was going to stitch together to a soundtrack, and Norma was still managing the fallout from that hideous Gaill A's latest post. She wondered if she shouldn't block her from the group, despite the fact that she hadn't specifically contravened any of the rules, but why did she always have to be so unpleasant? Lately the group, much like the rest of the world, felt like it was on a slippery slope of extreme, unprecedented ugliness.

'Do you guys think we'll ever move on to a different job here?' Bavinga asked, looking up from her mobile.

'What, like painting a wall, or tidying the staff kitchen?' Norma asked.

'Imagine if we actually got to meet employees, find out what they do day-to-day, got to actually work in publishing? That would be interesting,' Bavinga said.

'Surely they *have* to offer us some kind of broad work experience beyond cleaning and slush-pile sorting? We can't only do this for six months, can we? If we want our careers in publishing to gain any traction at all, we're going to need skills other than just knowing whether a manuscript titled *A fish called Gill* should go on the fiction or non-fiction pile,' Norma said, holding up an ancient tea-stained manuscript.

'Reminds me of that movie with Kevin Kline, but that was *A Fish Called Wanda*. Anyway, speak for yourself, I'm happy down here left to our own devices. I do not want a career in publishing, thank you very much,' Britttennay said. 'I want to be an influencer.'

'Literally, left to your devices,' Norma muttered.

'Sorry, but I also couldn't think of anything worse than working here,' Bavinga said.

'I get Britttennay not wanting to work in publishing, she doesn't even like books. But you love publishing.'

'Correction,' Bavinga said. 'I do not love publishing. I love books. There's a huge, massive, enormous difference.'

It was the most animated Norma had ever seen her – her settings were generally on low.

'So what do you want to do, then?' Norma asked. 'What's your dream career?'

'I want to have my own independent bookshop, where I hand-select every book, so that my customers know they're getting something good, and not just something the publishers marketing departments have thrown money at, or hyped up unnecessarily. Publishers are ruining the industry.'

'I can see you doing that,' Norma said.

'Me too,' Britttennay said. 'You'd be great at that. You could host book launches and movie nights and stuff.'

'Maybe one day you'll even stock my book,' Norma said.

Britttennay and Bavinga whipped their heads around to stare at her.

'You have a book?' Bavinga asked.

'Yes. No. Yes ... umm,' Norma said, and started to hum 'Lyin' Eyes' by the Eagles.

'Well that's decisive,' Britttennay said. 'As long as you're sure.'

'Norma, you'd better stop humming some old-people music and tell us everything. Otherwise you're on your own with that poetry pile,' Bavinga threatened.

'I don't mean you'll stock this book,' Norma said, then closed her eyes for a moment before speaking again. 'Yes, I wrote a book. But you guys, it's a terrible, terrible, terrible book, and absolutely nobody should ever read it. Maybe I'll start another one one day, and if I ever write something half decent with any kind of publishing merit, THEN maybe you'll be able to stock it in your beautiful independent bookshop, is what I meant. But it was a silly thing to say, just a joke,' she stammered. 'Ignore me.'

'I bet it's fan-fucking-tastic,' Britttennay said. 'You have a way with words. I mean, writing them, not saying them. Saying them, you can get a bit rambly when cornered.'

'When can we read it?' Bavinga asked.

'I know you'll think I'm just fishing for compliments, so that you guys can tell me it's great, and then we bat back and forth with you stroking my ego and me denying it. But seriously, guys, believe me, and I mean this, sincerely and truthfully and without an inch of a lie, it's a pile of shit. But that's also okay. Did you know that the majority of first novels are terrible? It's the ones that come after that have merit. That's what all the writing experts say.'

'I still think you should let us at least read it – you can't be an impartial judge of your own work. All the writing experts say that too,' Bavinga said.

'You have enough to read – look at all these,' Norma said, waving a hand at the chaos around them.

'We're not supposed to be reading them, remember. Anyway, yours is different: we actually, like, know you,' Britttennay said, snapping her gum.

'And anyway, they can't honestly expect us to be surrounded by all these almost-books, and not read any of them, can they? That would be depriving us, and possibly the rest of the world, of real gems, like this one,' Bavinga said, reaching for a nearby manuscript and flipping it open, then reading aloud from the random page she'd landed on.

Pickled Fish

I love everything about pickled fish.

The way it smells.

The way it tastes.

The way it stains my fingers when I eat too much of it.

And in this poem, by the

way, you are the pickled fish.

They fell around the room laughing.

'I just want you to know, in my next poem, you are the stapler,' Norma howled.

'You are the Kindle paperweight in mine,' Bavinga giggled.

'You are both like my deviated septum in mine,' Britttennay added.

'You see, that's why we absolutely have to read as many of these manuscripts as possible while we're down here, yours included, Norma,' Bavinga said.

'Except this one, I'm not reading this,' Britttennay said, picking up a manuscript from a forgotten pile in a corner, and reading the title off the cover: *'The Complete History of Office Paper: From Papyrus to Perforation* – a 700-page exploration of every conceivable type of paper used in administrative work, complete with diagrams of filing systems and an exciting bonus chapter on the evolution of the paper clip.'

Norma

Keith handed Norma her employee uniform: a t-shirt with the franchise logo printed on the chest, and an embossed metal name badge, with a magnet on the back, which attached the badge to her shirt.

'That's even brighter than I remembered.' Norma said, sliding the luminous green t-shirt out of the plastic.

'So that customers can find you more easily among the stacks,' Keith said.

'What's this?' Norma asked.

'That's your name badge, dear,' Keith said as if she were an idiot.

'Ummm, but this says "NORMAL".'

Keith looked at the badge she was holding. 'So it does.'

'My name is Norma, not Normal.' The word was printed in bold uppercase letters in a clear, no-nonsense font. 'Who's called "Normal"?'

'We don't judge here. We employ people with all sorts of challenges, from all walks of life. You're a case in point,' Keith said. 'Anyway, how are we supposed to know that's not a popular name down under?'

'Firstly, "down under" is Australia. I'm from South Africa. And secondly, nobody anywhere is called "Normal". It's not even a name, it's a noun or an adjective, depending on the context.'

'You had to fill in your name on the form. And Head Office would have gotten the information straight from there. So you must have made an error on your form, that's the only context I can think of,' Keith concluded smugly.

'Are you suggesting that I spelled my own name wrong?'

'It's possible,' Keith shrugged.

'No, I don't actually think it is possible, Keith. In your experience as the manager here, in a book store, possibly the most literate place on earth, have there been many employees who have struggled to spell their own name?'

'There's nothing we can do about it now, so you should probably just build a bridge and get over it,' Keith snapped.

'I'm not wearing that,' Norma said.

'Suit yourself. But you should know that there's a ten quid fine if you forget your name badge for a shift.'

'I'm not giving you ten quid,' Norma said.

'Oh, don't worry,' Keith said, looking at his watch, 'we just lob it off your pay check. Shift starts in seven minutes, you'd better get a move on, Normal, it's a five quid fine if you're late.'

'I'm not Normal!' Norma called after him.

'No, you aren't,' he shouted back over his shoulder.

Norma went into the mall's bathroom and pulled on her new work t-shirt. It was very tight. She pulled at the label so she could read it in the bathroom mirror. Medium. She'd specifically filled in 'L' for large on the uniform requisition form.

All she could imagine was that at Head Office, some idiot must have taken the 'L' she filled in for a large t-shirt, and replaced it with an 'M' for medium. Then they must have taken that wayward 'L', and dumped it on the end of her name badge.

Norma attached the 'NORMAL' name tag over her breast, on her too-tight lumo-green book franchise t-shirt, and looked at herself in the mirror. She looked like a Tellytubby named Normal.

Working in a book store at forty-two, in between interning at a publishers, wearing a too-tight t-shirt: no, there was nothing normal about her life.

Harry

'It looks like you didn't wash a single plate or cup or open a window, let alone have a shower or shave the entire time I was away, Harry. You've gone practically feral.' Victoria scrunched up her nose as she clambered over a pile of pizza boxes to open the curtains and windows.

'I've been busy,' Harry said. 'You wanted me to get back to work, didn't you? That's why you abandoned me in the first place.'

'You've been rewriting?' Victoria asked, ignoring his abandonment issues.

'Sort of,' Harry said.

'Writing or sort of writing?' Victoria asked.

'Sort of writing,' Harry said, 'but everyone knows that's the precursor to actual writing.'

'Or is it the precursor to getting committed to a facility by your wife? Do I need to worry about you, Harry? I was hoping to come back and find you in better shape,' Victoria said, hands on her hips.

'No, of course not, Victoria. It's just that all of this stuff that's happened to me, it's all kind of …'

Victoria took a deep breath and closed her eyes. 'I had really, really hoped you would have put all of this behind you by the time I got back.'

'I have, Vicks, it's just …' Harry started again.

'It's just nothing, Harry. I can't engage on this anymore, I refuse to enable this slump. This is what's going to happen now. I'm going to unpack and shower, and while I'm doing that, you're going to clean up in here, so it doesn't look like a basement pillaged by baboons. And then I'm going to order some food, and we're going to sit down together like grown-ups and have a nice welcome-home meal, a glass of wine and a catch-up. And I swear to god, Harold Shields, if you mention that review or any of those articles, or that damn club, or that outrageous YouTube video, or Edna Molton even once, I'm going to bloody divorce you on the spot.' With a click she extended the handle of her carry-on and wheeled it behind her, thunking up the stairs to their bedroom.

Harry dropped his head onto his laptop until the escape button shouted at him in a burst of short, sharp, sweary beeps. Nobody understood how soul-destroyingly hard it was to be an author.

Norma

'Norma, is that you?'

Norma spun around with *Catcher in the Rye* in one hand and *The Great Gatsby* in the other, to find Bavinga standing in front of her holding a copy of Jim Crace's *Being Dead* in one hand and his *Gift of Stones* in the other.

'No,' Norma squeaked.

'It's not you? That's funny, looks a lot like you, sounds a lot like you, and squeaks a lot like you,' Bavinga said.

'Yes,' Norma said, panicking.

'Yes, it's not you?' Bavinga said.

'No, it is,' Norma said and they both burst out laughing. They'd been together at work just a few hours earlier, and since they'd started interning, they'd become easy and comfortable in each other's company. But this was out in the real world, and they hadn't seen each other in the wild before. It felt different without the safety and familiarity of the slush-pile room.

'Do you work here?' Bavinga asked, looking confused.

'No,' Norma said.

'So, you just come here in a slightly too small, store-branded t-shirt and name tag that says "Normal" on it for some bizarre reason, just to hang out? Cool hobby,' Bavinga smiled.

'Yes. I work here. I just started.' Norma said.

'Side hustle?' Bavinga said.

'Side-side hustle, actually.'

'You've pretty much got my dream side-side hustle job,' Bavinga said.

'You can have my shift if you want.'

'My parents won't let me. They think I should get an education and a "proper job". No offence, their words, not mine,' Bavinga said. 'I think they're worried that if I did this, I'd never move on from it, then one day I'll be a sixty-year-old bookshop sales assistant. And they're probably right.'

'No offence taken,' Norma said. 'Although I don't think it would still be your dream job if you actually had to do it. The books are a dream; the customers and Keith the manager, on the other hand, can be a little ... challenging.'

'How so?' Bavinga asked.

'You see that guy over there in the black hoodie? I just saw him slip *The Da Vinci Code* into his backpack.'

'Well, to be fair, I wouldn't be caught dead buying that either. Are you going to report him to security?'

'I don't think so. If he wants to read it that badly, who am I to stop him? It's hardly like he's stealing a loaded shotgun. How much damage can it do? And anyway, if he's lucky, there are sensors at the door that will set off an alarm when he tries to leave with it.'

'Why if he's lucky?'

'Well, if he's unlucky and he doesn't get caught, he'll take that book home and actually have to read it, poor thing.'

Bavinga laughed. 'Isn't it exhausting having two jobs?'

'Because I'm so old?'

'No, because you already have a day job, and yeah, also because you're kind of old,' Bavinga agreed.

'Well if my idiot ex hadn't left me in major debt just as I quit my fairly well-paid job, I wouldn't have had to get a second not-so-well-paid job, and deal with petty thieves and Keith the dickhead manager.'

'The universe loves a plot twist,' Bavinga said.

'That it does,' Norma said, noticing Keith eavesdropping from the Esoteric aisle. 'I'd better get back to it, these books aren't going to shelve themselves.'

'See you at work tomorrow?' Bavinga said.

'Only if I don't die of old age first.'

THE GOOD BOOK APPRECIATION SOCIETY

MEMBERS: 87 999

Friends of the Ludlow Library: We are devastated to inform the group that our good friend and club member, Edna Molton, was involved in a tragic hit-and-run accident late yesterday, as she was leaving our library.

Edna is currently in intensive care, and will be undergoing surgery later today. Please hold her in your thoughts and prayers.

Please reach out to us if you have any information that could help the police in their investigation.

COMMENTS:

Norma Jacobs: This is shocking and devastating news. Thank you for letting us know. On behalf of every member of this club, we wish Edna a speedy recovery, and hope the police are able to find whoever did this and bring them to book.

Chris Colt: If you'll pardon the pun.

Ruth Burstein: Who would do something like that? That's why I prefer books to people. They can't be rude or mean, they never talk back, and they can't run you over with their car and then drive off.

Chris Colt: Wanna get a drink some time, and talk books, @Ruth Burstein?

Ruth Burstein: I'd rather set my own head on fire, @Chris Colt.

Chris Colt: You can just come out and say if you're a lesbian. Nobody minds these days.

[Freda Kruger reported this comment.]

Felicity Mauberger: @Chris Colt! What is wrong with you? (that's rhetorical, please don't answer.) I'm sorry to hear about this accident. Will hold Edna Molton in my thoughts.

Geneva Fulverton: Hey hasn't Edna Molton been having a fight on this page with that Badly-Behaved Author over that negative review she wrote about his book? I'm not pointing fingers, just saying, maybe that's a good place for the cops to start looking. #BookDetective

Linda Petal Dabb: Health and healing light from all of us, @Edna Molton. 🌸🌈

Norma

WEST MERCIA POLICE INTERVIEW TRANSCRIPT (CONT.)

INTERVIEW resumes at 9:32

DS SNOPES: Okay, let's go back a bit. So you're saying that after arguing with Edna Molton publicly on the group, Harry Shields did not 'leave in a huff'?

NORMA JACOBS: No, he did not.

DS SNOPES: Ms Jacobs, are you aware that as a result of a hit-and-run incident that occurred on Tuesday, Edna Molton is currently in intensive care in critical condition?

NORMA JACOBS: Yes, a member of the Friends of the Ludlow Library posted about it on the page yesterday. It's a shocking crime. I hope she'll be okay.

DS SNOPES: Do you know Edna Molton?

NORMA JACOBS: Not personally. I only know her as a member of the club.

BOOK PEOPLE

DS SNOPES: And what can you tell me about the arguments Mrs Molton got into on the page with Harry Shields?

NORMA JACOBS: They disagreed on a book. She hated it, and as the author, he took offence.

DS SNOPES: Would you say their argument escalated quickly?

NORMA JACOBS: Yes, but it's a book club. As I said, members often get into heated debates over books, it's nothing out of the ordinary. And it certainly doesn't mean he tried to run her over.

DS SNOPES: Nobody is suggesting that, Ms Jacobs. Do you know Harry Shields personally?

NORMA JACOBS: No, not personally. He's been a member of the club for a few years.

DS SNOPES: Would you say Mr Shields seemed *unreasonably* upset about the review Mrs Molton did of his book?

NORMA JACOBS: In my experience most authors tend to be ultra-sensitive about their work.

DS SNOPES: At any point has Mr Shields led you to believe that he might try take revenge on Mrs Molton?

NORMA JACOBS: Authors do take things more personally than most. But from what I've seen in the group, they're more violent with their words than they are with their actions.

DS SNOPES: Has Mr Shields ever led you to believe that he might try contact Mrs Molton?

NORMA JACOBS: He did message me directly about her a few times, but I got the feeling he was just blowing off steam. He's had a rough time since that review went viral. Cancel culture is intense. It's not surprising he's gone a bit mental.

DS SNOPES: You think he's 'gone mental'?

NORMA JACOBS: No more than anyone in the same situation would, I imagine.

DS SNOPES: Would you be willing to show us your communications with Mr Shields, Ms Jacobs?

NORMA JACOBS: Of course, and you can call me Norma.

DS SNOPES: Ms Jacobs, do you mind if I ask you where you were on Tuesday evening?

NORMA JACOBS: You can't possibly think I had anything to do with this?

DS SNOPES: I didn't say that. Asking your whereabouts is standard investigation procedure.

NORMA JACOBS: Don't you think it would be a bit counterintuitive to create a group where your number-one priority is growing membership, and then try to get rid of one of them?

DS SNOPES: If you wouldn't mind answering the question, Ms Jacobs?

NORMA JACOBS: During office hours on Tuesday, I was at work. I'm an intern at Harbour Books. And after that, I was at work at my second job, at Chapters Book Store, on Oxford Street, till just after nine pm.

BOOK PEOPLE

DS SNOPES: I'm going to need the respective managers' contact details so we can confirm that with them.

NORMA JACOBS: Be my guest, but I'm a new intern, stuck down in the slush-pile room all day at Harbour Books, so Daniel Piper may not know my name. And just so you know, the manager at Chapters, Keith, is a massive tosser, and he thinks my name is Normal.

DS SNOPES: What?

NORMA JACOBS: Never mind, it would take ages to explain, and you have a case to solve.

Telephonic interview terminated at 9:52

Harry

WEST MERCIA POLICE INTERVIEW TRANSCRIPT

DS SNOPES: Mr Shields, my name is DS Snopes. I'm with the West Mercia Police Department. Thank you for agreeing to talk to me.

HARRY SHIELDS: Do I need a lawyer?

DS SNOPES: Not if you haven't done anything wrong, Mr Shields. Have you done anything wrong?

HARRY SHIELDS: Not that I'm aware of. What's this about?

DS SNOPES: Would you be willing to answer a couple of questions about your activity on the Good Book Appreciation Society?

HARRY SHIELDS: If I must.

DS SNOPES: Mr Shields, we're currently investigating a hit and run in Ludlow that took place on Tuesday evening, involving Edna Molton.

HARRY SHIELDS: I heard about it.

DS SNOPES: Have you ever met Mrs Molton, Mr Shields?

HARRY SHIELDS: We belong to the same online book club.

DS SNOPES: But you've never met her in real life?

HARRY SHIELDS: Detective, it's an online book club, with tens of thousands of members, are you going to interview all of them as well?

DS SNOPES: Why? Did all of them get into a violent online argument with Mrs Molton, just before she was a victim of a hit and run?

HARRY SHIELDS: I wouldn't go so far as to call it a violent argument.

DS SNOPES: What would you call it then?

HARRY SHIELDS: More of a disagreement.

DS SNOPES: What was it about, Mr Shields?

HARRY SHIELDS: She thought my novel was terrible, and I disagreed. Nothing to commit a crime over.

DS SNOPES: That's not what the admin of the club told us. She said you've been very upset about the whole thing. Threatening, even.

HARRY SHIELDS: Detective, I'm afraid you're wasting your time. I was at home on Tuesday night.

DS SNOPES: And was there anybody home with you who could corroborate your story?

HARRY SHIELDS: My wife was away in Cheltenham with friends.

DS SNOPES: How convenient. Have you ever visited Mrs Molton's home, Mr Shields?

HARRY SHIELDS: I told you, I've never met her.

DS SNOPES: That's not what I asked, Mr Shields. I asked if you'd ever visited Mrs Molton's home?

HARRY SHIELDS: ...

DS SNOPES: Mr Shields, Ludlow is a small community, filled with retirees who tend to have an awful lot of time on their hands. I just happened to look back over the police reports from the day of the hit and run, and I couldn't help but notice that a local resident had lodged a complaint about a man urinating in public that day. And I have to say, their description of the individual bears a remarkable resemblance to yourself. So if there's anything you'd like to tell me before we access video surveillance footage from cameras around town ...

HARRY SHIELDS: ... It was for research!

DS SNOPES: You urinated into a bed of municipal petunias for research purposes?

HARRY SHIELDS: No, no ... that was an emergency, I drank too much coffee and there are very few public toilets in Ludlow, just one of the issues I plan on writing to the local MP there about. The research was for my writer's revenge.

DS SNOPES: Writer's revenge?

HARRY SHIELDS: It's how writers get revenge. They write books, put their detractors into them, and then kill them off one by one in as violent a manner as possible.

DS SNOPES: So you admit you wanted to kill her?

HARRY SHIELDS: Hypothetically! Only hypothetically!

DS SNOPES: You admit you hypothetically wanted to kill her or that you wanted to kill her hypothetically?

HARRY SHIELDS: Forget I mentioned it.

DS SNOPES: I wish I could, Mr Shields. But we have an elderly woman in critical condition right now, and it's our job to figure out who committed this crime. We tend to take violence quite seriously out here in the Midlands. So, you were saying, you visited Mrs Molton's home, for the purpose of researching her so you could kill her off 'hypothetically'?

HARRY SHIELDS: Well, it sounds bad when you put it like that.

DS SNOPES: Did you perhaps also do a hit and run for research, Mr Shields? Is there a hit and run in your new book? Is that how you decided to kill her off 'hypothetically' in the end?

HARRY SHIELDS: That's preposterous! I think I want to call my lawyer now.

DS SNOPES: I'm sure you do, Mr Shields. Just think, after all this research, you'll also be able put getting convicted and going to jail for attempted murder in your next novel.

Interview terminated at 14:37

Harry

When Harry's phone rang, he was logged into X as @Lance_Tuft (an investment banker whose bio read 'A massive fan of Grisham, Baldacci, Follett, and Shields'), and he was in the middle of an argument with several book bloggers who were ganging up on him.

'I'm calling for Harry Shields,' said a woman with a clipped voice.

'Speaking,' Harry said.

'I'm Janet Lindeman, calling on behalf of the Director of the London Festival of Books.'

'Hello Janet,' Harry said. 'I'm glad you called. I've been waiting for information about my upcoming panel.'

'That's why I'm calling, Mr Shields. We wanted to let you know that we would understand if you decided to step down from your panel.'

'Step down?' Harry said.

'Yes, in light of ... of ... everything that's been going on,' Janet hesitated, then continued. 'We would of course understand if you were unable to honour your commitment to the festival.'

'I don't understand,' Harry said.

'The thing is, we aren't convinced we'd be able to protect you while on our panel. So should you wish to excuse yourself, that would be acceptable to us.'

'Are you talking about the bad review?' Harry asked, feeling the floor dipping away from him.

'Yes, and all that business on Facebook and X and Goodreads and all the press, and the awards ummm ... incident ... and the YouTube video,' Janet said. 'It's all been very ... unfortunate.'

'Tell me about it! And you don't think you'll be able to protect me from what, exactly?' Harry asked.

'From the crowd.'

'The crowd of readers?'

'Precisely,' Janet said. Harry detected relief in her voice.

'What are you worried they're going to do, Janet? Not buy my books? Well I can tell you, you're too late, they're already not doing that.'

'I think you underestimate the wrath and potential violence of readers, Mr Shields,' Janet said.

'So what, are they going to throw their books at me?' Harry snorted. 'Mine have soft covers, so I doubt they'll do much damage.'

'You never know,' Janet said. 'That is, if they come to the panel at all. There have been rumours of not only violence directed at you, but also a possible boycott of your panel and our festival. We do need to consider the well-being, comfort and safety of the other authors.'

'Janet, I know all the authors on our panel – they'll be fine.'

'Some of them have already threatened to pull out of the festival should you remain part of the line-up.'

Harry sucked in air. 'I'm sorry Janet, but I won't be excusing myself, pulling out, or stepping down from your festival. Once I've committed to doing something, that is precisely what I do. In addition, I would like it noted for the record that I've done nothing wrong. Everything has simply been taken out of context and it's all gotten completely out of control. The best we can do, Janet, is carry on as normal, and wait for this silly little storm in a teacup to pass.'

'For what "record", Mr Shields? I believe we've misunderstood each other, or rather, you have misunderstood me. We are going to have to insist that you step down from the panel,' Janet said tightly.

'Oh, I see. You're not asking me, Janet, you're telling me?'

'Precisely. Good day, Mr Shields,' Janet said and hung up.

And there it was. Dead air. Harry had never been fired before. One star. Would not recommend.

Harry

'Hey Phyl.'

'Harry, buddy, it must be close on three a.m. there. What are you doing up?' Phyllis asked.

'Phyl, I got bumped off the London Festival of Books line-up. I won't be seeing you there this year,' Harry said.

'I heard,' Phyllis said, gently.

'How did you hear? They only just told me. I suppose all the authors are talking about it?'

'Just a few – the ones on our panel mostly. Cowards. I'm sorry, Harry.'

'That's okay,' Harry said, forlornly.

'You know, it's probably for the best. You can lay low, work on your rewrite. I promise you, Harry, this will blow over eventually, and then you can get back to your life.'

'It may not, Phyllis. The police were questioning me. That woman who left that bad review of my book on Facebook got knocked over in a hit and run, and I think I may be a suspect.'

'Oh shit, Harry.'

'What if she doesn't make it, and they find me guilty of murder, and I have to go to prison for the rest of my life? I don't think I'm built for prison, Phyllis.'

'That's ridiculous, Harry. There's no way that will happen ... unless ... you didn't do anything crazy, did you?'

'No, of course not! I can't even drive.'

'Well, I don't know if that's an alibi in a hit-and-run case. Maybe you drove into her *because* you can't even drive.'

'I swear I didn't do it, Phyl.'

'Well then, you shouldn't be a suspect very long. Anyway, it's standard procedure to question everybody at the beginning of an investigation. The police have to turn over every stone – you're a crime writer, you know that.'

'Yes, but ... there's something I didn't tell you ...'

'What, Harry?'

'Well, there's all the revenge stuff I've been talking about to just about anyone who would listen. And I went to see the old lady on the day of the accident. I didn't talk to her or anything, and I didn't do anything, I swear. I was just watching her. A stakeout. Followed her around a bit. I needed to see who she was. But the cops know I was there. They have cameras everywhere these days.' He was too embarrassed to tell her about the peeing thing.

'Are you nuts? Why did you do that, Harry? You know what they do with all that footage, don't you?'

'Yes, they use it to put people in jail.'

'Beyond that. They're watching us, Harry. All the time. It's part of a complex and nefarious black light surveillance network ...'

'If I go to prison, it's all your fault, Phyllis,' Harry interrupted her. 'I asked you to come to London while Victoria was away, remember? I pleaded with you. I told you I was worried I was going to do something stupid. If you'd have come to London like I asked you to, then none of this would have happened.'

'Harry. You have to stop all of this crap and move on.'

'I'd better go. On the up side, I'm sure I'll get a lot of writing done in prison.'

Norma

'There's one here called *Roads and Bridges*, by Simone Winchester,' Bavinga said, holding up a fat manuscript. 'Fiction or non-fiction?'

'Wait, let me guess, it's literary fiction, one man's journey to find the love of his life, and all the roads and bridges he has to take to get there?' Norma asked.

'Throw in Timothée Chalamet and I'd totally watch that movie,' Britttennay said.

'Actually,' Bavinga said, flipping through it and stopping to skim-read random pages. 'I think it's quite literally a book about all the roads and bridges of the West Counties.'

'I would not watch that,' Britttennay said. 'Even with our Timmy.'

Norma took it from Bavinga and weighed it in her hands, 'I'm guessing that's about 100 000 words: a lot of roads and bridges.'

'At that length, it could make like a limited series, like six half-hour episodes for the wanky History Channel,' Britttennay said. 'Still wouldn't watch it, though. Unless ... Benedict Cumberbatch.'

'Who?' Bavinga asked, taking the manuscript back from Norma and dropping it on the non-fiction 'HELL NO' pile. 'What's that one?' She asked, nodding at the slim manuscript Norma was busy with.

'It's called *The Rising Hawk*. It's a novella.'

'It's been done before. Movie. Like, I want to say, 2019, or 2020,' Britttennay said, paging through a manuscript that looked like it had been home to a family of moths. 'Like, do you think this one is about Swiss cheese?' she asked, holding it up.

'Your movie knowledge is encyclopaedic, Britttennay,' Norma said. 'You even know what year that was released.'

'Covid times. Like, we were on lockdown all the time. I watched tons of movies,' Britttennay said.

'You should go into the film industry, Britttennay. That's if you don't end up falling in love with publishing after all this weirdness,' Norma said, indicating the stacks of dusty manuscripts.

'This room is a bit mad, isn't it? There must be a thousand manuscripts in here, right? Some dating as far back as …' Bavinga rifled through a pile nearby before answering her own question, 'the eighties.'

'God, that's practically another century,' Norma said, sarcastically. 'Statistically though, surely there are at least a few potential prize winners lurking in here? There has to be. Maybe even a Booker or a Nobel?'

'Even a possible Pulitzer,' Bavinga added.

'Or an Oscar,' Britttennay said.

They continued working in silence. Picking up each manuscript, figuring out its genre, then sub-categorising the fiction into literary fiction or genre fiction. And the non-fiction into biographies, autobiographies, and memoirs, or history, travel guides and travelogues, academic texts, philosophy, essays, self-help and how-to guides. They had set up a table for each category with a piece of paper stuck to the wall above the table with the category name scrawled on it in a marker they'd found lying around. And each table had its own 'YES', 'HELL NO' and 'OKAY, MAYBE' pile. Then Britttennay had started her own pile for those that wouldn't become very good books, but that she thought might make a good movie.

'All these writers spent months, years, decades working on these manuscripts, but here they sit, unloved and unacknowledged,' Bavinga said.

'Disrespectful that they've just been dumped here, don't you think?

Unsolicited, unwanted. It makes me sad, all these lonely words,' Norma said.

'I don't know, maybe it can be hopeful too,' Bavinga said. 'We're here now, putting them in some kind of order. We might even be able to pull out a few gems. There's life in them yet.'

'It's so subjective though. Who's to say what will make this book more successful than, say, this one?' Norma said, holding up two manuscripts side by side.

'I'm to say,' Britttennay said. 'That one on the right is about a dinosaur mafia. Like, literally, it's set during the Mesozoic Age, and it's about their mafia. So it will definitely not be more successful than that one on the right, which is a romance novel set in a Mormon community.'

'It doesn't matter. These days, publishers know what they're looking for. They have lists, AI research, processes, sales reports, KPIs and influencers to consider,' Bavinga said.

'Not to mention what's trending on Netflix or TikTok,' Britttennay added.

'Despite that, it still feels so random. Imagine if the publisher decided to go with one of any of these hundreds of manuscripts, but the author died soon after submitting it, and never knew that someone actually wanted to publish their work, and so they died thinking their work wasn't good enough. It feels so tragic,' Norma said, picking up the next manuscript.

'What's that one?' Bavinga asked Norma, who was clutching a slim manuscript.

'A book of essays written from a cat's perspective, called *The Cat's Pyjamas*, "written" by Tabby McGee, and billed as non-fiction.'

'Nooo,' Bavinga shouted.

Norma dropped it under the 'fiction – short stories' label, on the 'HELL NO' pile.

'It's my birthday,' Britttennay blurted out.

'That's actually quite a cool title for a book. Is it fiction or non-fiction?' Bavinga said.

'It's not a book, it's my life. Today is, like, totally my birthday,' Britttennay said, with a grin. 'That's why I've been on the phone more than usual.'

Norma thought she'd been on her phone the same amount as usual – basically every second of every minute, but she decided not to say that. 'Why didn't you say anything?' Norma said instead, leaping up to give her a hug.

'Happy birthday, our Brittt,' Bavinga said, queuing to give her a squeeze. 'Why didn't you say anything till now?'

'I didn't want to make a fuss,' Britttennay said. Norma caught Bavinga rolling her eyes, and they both laughed.

'But me and some friends are, like, going out for a couple of drinks after work to celebrate. Say you'll both come?' Britttennay said.

'Sweet of you to include me, but I don't think ...' Norma started.

'I'm not sure I ...' Bavinga began.

'Come up with whatever excuses you introverts want, but I'm not taking no for an answer from either of you. You both forgot my birthday, so you owe me. Both of you bitches are coming to my party.'

'Britttennay, I'll be the oldest person there by decades,' Norma said.

'Don't exaggerate, you're not that old,' Bavinga said. 'And you're not leaving me to go on my own.'

'Okay, it's settled. Having you both there will be like the bestest birthday present ever. Holy shit, you guys, between my birthday timeline and my BookToks, my socials are exploding, I've gotta go deal with this. So excited.' Britttennay twirled off to the corner of the slush-pile room she'd annexed and turned into a selfie booth, fully equipped with a ring light and green screen.

Norma

'Do you have coffee?' Norma asked.

'Coffee liqueur? Espresso martini?' the barman asked.

'Ja, not the same thing, but whatever, I'll take the martini one,' Norma said.

'You know this is a night club, right? Not a Starbucks.'

'Thanks for the clarity, I'm so old, I couldn't tell.'

'That's what I thought,' he snapped as he swanned off to the other end of the bar.

They were in one of those uber-trendy London bar-slash-nightclubs. Some of the tables were equipped with seats that had bicycle pedals, where patrons could cycle for free wifi. Others had swings hanging from the ceiling, instead of seats. There were also pink neon sayings splashed in faux cursive on every wall, offering the perfect backgrounds for Instagram musings. Things that sounded appropriately meme-ish, but at the same time, ridiculous or nonsensical. Like, 'There is only today. Until tomorrow.' The words 'Flame emoji', with another one reading, 'I be unicorn'.

Near the bar was a huge QR code mural that allowed patrons to swap background filtered Instagram posts and hashtags for Jägermeister shots. There were also four contraptions that another barman informed her were sex swings, hanging from the ceiling in a VIP room, guarded by a bulldog of a man in a suit one flex away from bursting at the seams.

The toilets hadn't been forgotten when it came to eclectic selfie-worthy design either. The one she and Bavinga had popped into before going to find Britttennay had shiny black tiles, black-and-gold marble counters and carnival mirrors. One reflected Norma as short and fat, another as grossly disfigured, and a third as tall and slim, with a neck like a giraffe.

'Oh, I get it, these mirrors are supposed to be like Snapchat or Instagram filters,' Norma said.

'See, you're not that old,' Bavinga said.

Britttennay shrieked and came running, or rather clomping towards them when she saw them at the bar. She was wearing a minute white dress and hulking white platform heels. Norma thought it had probably taken more fabric to make the shoes than it did the dress.

Settled at the bar, surrounded by Britttennay and her friends, someone slid two shots towards them. 'It's called a suitcase,' Britttennay had to yell at them to be heard over the music.

'Why?' Norma asked.

''Cos once you've had one, you need to pack your bags, baby,' Britttennay squealed, holding her shotglass up in a toast. 'Here's to my birthday, bitches.'

Norma and Bavinga toasted, then downed their shots, laughing at the faces they both pulled.

'That tastes like reading a John Grisham novel,' Bavinga shouted in her ear.

'Literary snob,' Norma joked. 'I think it tastes like a Margaret Atwood novel.'

'Apocalyptic and outrageous?' Bavinga asked.

'Yes, but also a predictive masterpiece. I somehow know I'm going to be hungover tomorrow.'

Norma and Bavinga perched at the end of the booth they had next to the dance floor. Britttennay had ordered an ice bucket that was filled with bottles of champagne and different coloured glow sticks.

'Imagine if they were also reading books, like you? That would be hilarious,' Norma yelled in Bavinga's ear, nudging her to look up from reading on her mobile. Britttennay and her crew were sardined in the booth and had their heads buried in their mobile phones. Some typing, others animatedly talking into screens. None of them talking to each other.

'Bloody influencers,' Bavinga said.

'So they spend their entire lives pretending they're living, at the expense of actually living?'

'That pretty much sums it up,' Bavinga said. 'Without the influenced, there is no influencer. They have to keep up with their audience.'

'That's so sad-emoji.' Norma said, and Bavinga pulled a sad face and laughed.

'What you reading?' Norma asked her.

'Jim Crace, *Being Dead*. It's a masterpiece. This is my fourth time reading it.'

'I'm not a re-reader, there are just too many books. Don't you worry you're missing out on new stuff when you reread old stuff?'

'Rereading is rarely a waste, I always find something new I never saw on the first or second or third read. I have books I reread annually,' Bavinga said.

'I don't know how you find the time,' Norma said.

'Well it helps that I only have one sort-of job. My reading life wouldn't feel right without the re-reads shoved in between the newbies. It's like hanging out with an old friend.'

'Have you ever noticed how much easier it is to talk to someone who also reads?' Norma asked.

'You mean because they tend to be more intelligent, or because they're more interesting?' Bavinga asked.

'Yes, that, but also because you've always got something to talk about. Take you and me, for example. We're from completely different generations. I'm a Millennial, stuck in the mind and body of a Gen X, and you're Gen Z ...'

'My generation doesn't go by those anymore,' Bavinga said. 'We don't believe in labels.'

'You see, I didn't even know that. We have so few life experiences, issues or challenges in common, and yet I feel like I could talk to you for hours.'

'Good, because nobody else here is talking to us,' Bavinga said.

'Or even each other,' Norma said.

'Bathroom run?' Bavinga shouted to be heard over the pumping music.

'Right behind you,' Norma yelled back.

'I didn't actually need to pee, I just needed a moment to hear myself think,' Bavinga said, after they'd pushed their way through the crowds jostling for mirror space, to find a quieter corner out of the way of the selfie mural and hand-dryer traffic.

Norma tried to make sense of her hair, then wiped the racoon smudges away from under her eyes. 'Enjoy your face while it's still where you left it,' she said to Bavinga. 'It's all downhill after forty.'

'You do look stressed and sleep-deprived. How's all your life, book-shop-job, first novel, break-up, book-club-craziness going?' Bavinga asked.

'You know that guy I told you about, that author behaving badly?' Norma said.

'The one on your group who got the bad review, and then he was in that awards video that went viral, and the lady he was arguing with got taken out by a car?' Bavinga asked.

'Yeah, him. The police questioned me. I think they suspect he had something to do with that hit and run,' Norma said.

'No way! For a club full of oldies you've got a lot going on over there. I might have to repeal my ban on Facebook and join. Do you think he did it?'

'I'm not sure. He's definitely come unhinged. But Bavinga, if he did it, and if the old lady doesn't make it, would that make me an accessory to murder?'

'How do you figure that?' Bavinga asked, scrunching up her face.

'Well, they met through my club. If I hadn't started it, none of this would have happened. Plus, when we were chatting online, he did threaten to hurt her, and me for that matter, and I never reported it to anyone. Did I murder her with my inaction, and if it was him, what if he tries to hurt me too?'

'I think you read too many books, Norma. And anyway, isn't she still alive?'

'Yes, she's in a coma.'

'Okay, so let's not jump to the last page before we've read the middle, shall we?' Bavinga said, giving Norma's arm a comforting squeeze.

'If I am somehow vaguely responsible and I go to prison, and they don't have a decent library, you have to promise to bring me books,' Norma said, following Bavinga back to their booth.

She spotted a message from a number she didn't recognise:

> Hi Norms, sending from a mate's phone coz I only went and dropped mine in the toilet, didn't I. And only just managed to get your number out of Marina. You don't have an old phone you can lend me, maybe?

Norma hit delete, and settled back in her seat. Bavinga leaned over to shout in her ear: 'Speaking of books, I was thinking about your manuscript. Surely any publisher would beg to publish you, because you run that whole club? I mean even you said it's exploded with all this controversy.'

'I don't want to get published because I run a big book group, though,' Norma said.

Britttennay joined them at the bar, abandoning her friends in the booth, where they were creating Instagram stories of their latest round of shots.

'Shots, bitches,' Britttennay slurred, sliding three more glasses in front of them.' What are we talking about?'

'Norma's manuscript,' Bavinga said.

Norma tried to ignore the three neon-green future hangovers.

'I thought we could stick her manuscript on top of one of the slush piles and pretend we've just come across it and think it's brilliant, put it on the 'HELL YES' pile, and punt it to the powers that be?' Bavinga said.

'Like the powers that be even know who we are, or give a shit what we think about the slush piles in that room,' Britttennay scoffed. 'Hey, I know, I could sleep with that Daniel, he's not that bad-looking for an old guy,' she went on.

'Wow, that's a sick but generous offer. I'd never want you to do that for me,' Norma laughed.

'Wait, let me rephrase that. I've, like, already slept with Daniel,' Britttennay said with a grin.

Norma laughed.

Bavinga shook her head. 'Gross.'

'You guys, you are super kind to give a shit, but it all seems dishonest. If, and it's a big if – if I ever have a manuscript that's good enough to show to a publisher, I would want to get published on the merit of the work, not my club or who Britttennay is willing to screw,' Norma said. 'Although she doesn't seem that discerning, no offence.'

'None taken,' Britttennay smiled proudly.

'I don't agree. The world is tough, publishing is even tougher. The industry has raised the walls around publishing exponentially. So I think you do whatever it takes to get your foot in the door, and then you step away and leave it to the powers that be, i.e. the readers, to decide if it's good enough, which I'm absolutely positive it is, by the way,' Bavinga said.

'I could like blackmail Daniel into buying it, by threatening to tell his wife he slept with me, or even telling the board he slept with me,' Britttennay said.

'He's a slime-ball, Brittt, chances are the wife and the board already know what he's up to,' Bavinga said.

'But what if I *wanted* to blackmail him?' she hiccupped.

Bavinga closed her eyes and shook her head. 'Seriously, what's wrong with you?'

'Probably bad modelling during early childhood development,' Britttennay shrugged. 'Either that or too many movies. Which is what happens when you're a latchkey kid, raised by a single mom who's never home. Don't blame me, blame my circumstances,' she sang before tearing back to the booth, shouting, 'Tequila me, influencer-bitches!' at her friends.

'I mean it, Norma. You should think about it,' Bavinga said.

'Thank you, B, but trust me, this one is a leave-it-at the-bottom-of-the-slush-pile kind of thing. Speaking of leaving, how soon till we can duck? I'm about ready to allow the average age in this place to return to its twenties.'

Norma

'Let's get her to the couch, it's closer than the bed,' Norma said. 'Wow, she weighs a ton for such a tiny person.'

'It must be the shoes, looks like they weigh the same as her,' Bavinga said.

Britttennay mumbled as Bavinga gently placed a cushion under her head.

'I'll get a just-in-case-bucket, you get the shoes off,' Norma said.

'They're more like hooves,' Bavinga said, unbuckling the now off-white platform clonkers.

Once they'd gotten Britttennay settled, they made cups of tea and Norma opened a packet of Garibaldis.

'That was fun.'

'Was it, though?' Bavinga asked.

Norma laughed. 'I was being polite. Fun-ish, fun-esque, somebody's version of fun.'

'Hers, by the looks of things.' Bavinga yawned as Britttennay drooled down the side of the couch.

'I can't remember the last time I stayed out till three a.m.,' Norma said.

'Same. Staying up reading, maybe. I'm going to regret this tomorrow.'

'I suspect so is Brittt. Come on, I'll show you to the spare room-slash-study, so you can get some sleep, slash-write a book.'

'I'll get to work, there are still a few more hours before we have to show up for the slush pile,' Bavinga said.

'I warn you, though, your first one will probably be shite,' Norma joked as she showed her where the bathroom was and then led her into the study.

'So, this is where the writing magic happens?' Bavinga said.

'Less magic, more tragic. Here, I'll give you the grand tour: desk, chair, lumpy old sofa bed, carpet that could use a hoovering. Sorry, it's hardly The Four Seasons. Unless all four are winter in Russia.'

'Hey, I still live with my parents, and in this financial climate-change hellscape, it's unlikely I'll be able to move out until I'm in my triple digits, so the fact that you own your own chair, let alone your own place, is like that mind-blowing emoji to me.'

'Yeah your generation, which shall remain unnamed, isn't going to have it as easy with the whole property thing. But maybe it's not such a bad thing.'

'Why's that?'

'You're freer than us, and right now, I'm not sure how much longer I'll be able to afford my mortgage anyway. Maybe it's better to live with your folks forever than to have to move back to South Africa and live with your mum as an unemployable forty-two-year-old intern.'

'You could knock your mum off so you could inherit her property sooner? Problem solved.' Bavinga suggested.

'Watch this space, I reckon that will become a growing trend.'

'Home-owner homicide? I suspect so.'

'I shall sleep with one eye open,' Norma said.

As Norma got ready for bed, she checked in on the club one last time. The hit-and-run thing had only fuelled the flame of Harry's demise, and Norma was still having to delete threatening and bullying posts and comments daily. This lovely group, that had once been her hobby and her happy place, had started to feel ugly and tedious. She was having to be more vigilant and was spending way more time on the page than she ever had before. She was going to have to add time to the lengthening list of things she could no longer afford. Although at least since the hit and run, Shields had stopped responding to every comment. Or perhaps that was simply a function of the sheer quantity of comments – he'd have to quit his day job to respond to all of them.

The thought struck her: what if he really had done it? What if he'd actually tried to murder Edna Molton? And what if she didn't make it, so he'd have succeeded?

Norma wasn't sure why she'd played down his behaviour to the detective. Harry had threatened her, after all, and he'd come across as unhinged on the page and in his messages. He could very well have taken his revenge to the next level. Stranger things often happened in fiction and non-fiction, Norma thought, as she scrolled through a new post about the bible. She stopped short and sucked in a breath as she read the reams of comments, ranging from outrageous to just plain outraged. What was wrong with the world? Was this how things were always going to be from now on – ugly and combative? Since we were at war in the world, we also had to be at war online, art following life? Or was it just a temporary phase, and the world would grow out of it and find some peace? For the first time in the decade she'd been running the group, she wondered if she shouldn't shut it all down and move along.

She deleted the comments on the bible post that she considered hate speech or bullying, then turned off commenting and closed the Facebook app on her phone, relieved that she wasn't going to have to deal with more madness again till morning. A thought that came a minute too soon, as four new voice notes pinged in from Steve. Not responding wasn't putting him off. He spoke to her more now than he had in the whole last year they'd been living together.

> Hi Norms, I never heard back from you about the phone?
> I found one of my dad's phones lying around, so I'm using that, but the battery dies every four seconds.

I miss you, Norms. Hey which is the green jelly I like that you always used to buy and make for us? I tried the Royal and the no-name one from Tesco, but neither of them taste quite right. Or is that the one but you use a different kind of water or do you put in some kind of seasoning? Also, think about the bank account idea I sent you, okay? I know you're a straight arrow, but nobody gets hurt here, it's a massive corporation, which means it's a victimless crime, in fact they insure themselves against this kind of thing because they expect it. It's essentially sticking it to the man, so it feels win-win. Voice note me back, okay? Or text even, I don't mind.

Hi Norms, me again. I get that you're angry. But if you think about it, I did it all for us. I needed to do the research so I could finish my book, so I could make some money again. I thought that was what you wanted? Sometimes I don't understand women.

Okay last voice note from me, for now. I totally get it if you don't want to talk to me, but can you just let me know about the jelly please, it's urgent.

Norma cursed Steve Senior for having a spare phone, then set hers to silent so she could get a couple of hours sleep before her hangover, her morning and the eternal slush pile kicked in.

THE GOOD BOOK APPRECIATION SOCIETY

MEMBERS: 89 771

Michelle Zanders: Since this is The Good Book Appreciation Society, I was wondering if anyone has reviewed the Bible yet. Surely that's the very definition of the Good Book?

COMMENTS:

[Freda Kruger has reported this post.]

Jacqui Ivan: The best book ever written.

Dax Goby: I don't know, is it better than, say, The Heart's Invisible Furies, by John Boyne? I think not.

Lucille Cooper: Hahaha, @Dax Goby.

Chris Colt: 50 Shades of Grey could be considered the bible for the horny.

[Freda Kruger has reported this comment.]

Chris Colt: It was just a bit of fun, @Freda Kruger, no need to get your knickers in a twist, love.

BOOK PEOPLE

Karen Granger: You're all disgusting! Don't be surprised if you find yourselves burning in hell, come Judgement Day. #TheBibleMatters

Geneva Fulverton: I tried to read it a couple of years ago, and I couldn't get past the first fifty pages. I don't think it's aged well.

[Freda Kruger has reported this comment.]

Chris Colt: @Geneva Fulverton, fifty shades of the bible?

[Freda Kruger has reported this comment.]

Calumn Coulson: Samuel 22:3-4. 3 My God is my rock, in whom I take refuge, my shield and the horn of my salvation. He is my stronghold, my refuge and my saviour – from violent people you save me.

Avukile Chingwita: Is it the bestselling book of all time yet?

Gerry Rawson: You're kidding, right @Calumn Coulson, you're an intelligent adult, you can't really believe that stuff, can you? You do know the bible is the greatest work of fiction ever written, don't you?

[Freda Kruger has reported this comment.]

[Fiona Smith has left the group.]

[Doreen Peters has left the group.]

[Franklin Fenster has left the group.]

Calumn Coulson: The Bible says in 2 Peter 3:15, 'Always be ready to give a defence of the faith that is in you.'

Chris Colt: Wonder if they'll turn it into a rebooted series? That seems to be what happens with all popular fiction.

Shireen Worcestershire-Watts: DNF. Thought it was boring and unbelievable.

[Admin has turned off commenting.]

Norma

'Is it still a walk of shame if, like, you didn't shag anyone?' Britttennay asked.

'Technically, since we haven't been home and we're walking to work wearing the same clothes we wore last night, I can confirm that this is an official W.O.S.,' Bavinga said.

'Not that anyone ever notices what we're wearing down in the slush-pile room anyway,' Norma said. 'Which works in my favour, as you know, since you've seen my wardrobe.'

'I don't know, this vintage dress you loaned me is super-cool,' Britttennay said.

'That's the t-shirt I wear for grouting the shower,' Norma said.

Bavinga laughed.

'How are you feeling?' Norma asked Britttennay.

'Do either of you like smell tequila and burning metal? I smell tequila and burning metal. Other than that, smashing. But how much further like to the Tube station? I don't know why, but my feet are killing me.'

Norma caught Bavinga's eye, and they smiled.

'What if today is the day we finally advance out of the slush-pile room?' Bavinga asked.

'Hmm, I wouldn't count your manuscripts before they've hatched,' Norma said.

'Say they did let us out for good behaviour, what do you think Daniel will make us do next?' Bavinga asked.

'I wouldn't say we'd *all* been well behaved,' Norma said, nodding at Britttennay.

'Urgh, why'd you have to remind me of that,' Bavinga said. 'Just as my nausea was subsiding.'

'I reckon if they did ever let us out, it would be to do some task that will have great historical significance in our future careers, like getting coffee for an editor,' Norma said.

'Or hand-copying manuscripts from one grammage of paper to a higher grammage of paper,' Bavinga said.

'I thought you liked the slush-pile room?' Norma asked Bavinga.

'I do. It's quiet, it's clean …'

'Well, it's clean now,' Britttennay pointed out.

'Nobody bothers us down there, and there's always something to read. It's kind of my idea of heaven,' Bavinga said.

'Mine too,' Norma added.

'Believe it or not, I also like it down there,' Britttennay said. 'Do you think any of those books we've sorted through might ever get published and turned into movies or series?'

'Most definitely,' Bavinga said, with a small smile.

THE GOOD BOOK APPRECIATION SOCIETY

MEMBERS: 91 593

Edna Molton: I know I said I was never going to read this author again after last time, when I dared to have an opinion on his second novel, despite not being by his definition a 'professional reviewer'. Which according to him also means I have no right to any opinion on any book ever. But I have to tell you that morbid curiosity got the better of me. Is it possible, I wondered, to write a worse book than *Once on a Tuesday*?

So off I went to a bookshop to see what else this so-called author had written, and there it was: *Monday Never Comes*, by Harry Shields.

All I can say is that it's puerile twaddle, masquerading as literary fiction. How any publishing house saw fit to print it is beyond me. A series of well-trodden tropes strung together with adverbs might just be the best way to describe it, without giving away any spoilers. Not that there's enough of a plot to allow for spoilers.

If you do one thing in this lifetime, avoid this book. In fact, I'd go so far as to say, avoid this author. Imagine my relief at discovering that Harry Shields has not published anything else, and my hope is that he never does, so that we are all released from the burden of having to read him or hear him banging on about his books ever again.

COMMENTS:

Geneva Fulverton: Edna, are you out of hospital? What a relief, we've been worried sick about you. Wishing you a speedy recovery.

Avukile Chingwita: Well that's a brutal review. I'm not sure if it's made me want to avoid it or read it to see if it lives up to the shade.

Michelle Zanders: That was a mean review, but I think we do have to practice empathy. By all accounts, Edna has had a rather traumatic bump to the head. Perhaps she's not feeling herself yet.

Linda Petal Dabb: Edna, I think I speak on behalf of the whole group, when I say welcome back, we were so worried about you. What an ordeal. Love and healing. 🌸🌈

Felicity Mauberger: Did they catch the driver who knocked you over yet, Edna, love?

Friends of the Ludlow Library: This is a surprising and unexpected post. I'm not sure how to tell you all this, but I spoke to the hospital earlier today, and Edna Molton is still in critical condition, in a coma and one of her arms is broken. So even if she were awake, she would not be able to turn the pages of a book, let alone type. Not sure who wrote this review!?!

Dax Goby: No ways ... shit just got real! Look at this @Lucille Cooper.

Michelle Zanders: Holy wow.

[Freda Kruger has reported this comment.]

Ruth Burstein: Who is this posting?

Shireen Worcestershire-Watts: I don't understand what's happening.

Shanti Khumar: What kind of sick joke is this?

Mikaela Pace: *Grabs popcorn*

Chris Colt: Dead woman posting?

[Freda Kruger has reported this comment.]

Harry

Harry lost a slipper as he burst out of his study and raced into the bedroom.

'Victoria!' he whispered. Although he wasn't sure why he was whispering when his clear intention was to wake her up.

Victoria's eyes shot open as she bolted upright. 'What happened?'

'I don't think Edna is Edna. It's a fake profile!'

Victoria closed her eyes and fell back against the pillow. Then she reached for one of the pillows on Harry's side of the bed, covered her face with it, and screamed into it. Once she'd finished, she spoke to him in a quiet steady voice: 'Harry, if you ever wake me up like that again, I swear on your life, I will write my own detailed one-star review of your book, along with one of our marriage, and post them both on Goodreads.'

'Goodreads!' Harry yelped, leaping off the bed. 'I wonder if she posted the new review on Goodreads?'

'What's going on, Harry?' Victoria asked.

'Edna Molton!' Harry said.

'Not this again,' Victoria wailed.

'Victoria, I mean it, she just reviewed *Monday Never Comes* on the book club page. Well, she didn't just review it, she defecated on it, then ripped it to shreds, poured petrol on it, and set it alight.'

'I thought Edna Molton was in a coma?'

'She is,' Harry said, his eyes wide. 'That's what I'm trying to tell you.'

'I know I'm a surgeon, and so I have a marginally better understanding of the inner workings of the human body than the average civilian. But you do know that it's not possible to write and post a review on Facebook while in a coma?' Victoria said.

'Could it have been a scheduled post?' Harry wondered aloud.

'Harry,' Victoria snapped, 'why do you even care about this? She's an octogenarian from Shropshire who didn't love your books as much as you would have liked her to, for crying out loud. This is going to kill you, Harry. Or me. Or I'm going to kill you. I'm not sure which yet.'

'No, you're right, an octogenarian couldn't possibly know how to schedule a post. You know what this means, don't you?' Harry asked.

'Yes, it means that you've lost your mind, and it means that this is never, ever going to end. And it means that we will be in our eighties and you'll still be banging on about Edna bloody Molton and this one time you got a bad review on Facebook. Which by then won't even exist as a platform anymore, and Zuckerberg will still be serving consecutive life sentences for crimes against humanity. Or do I mean that ghastly bloke who bought Twitter and ran it into the ground?'

'No. It means that the review couldn't have been written by Edna Molton.'

'Well, I'm up now. I'll never get back to sleep. I'm going to get some ice cream. Something about our marriage has given me a sudden craving for Rocky Road. You coming?' Victoria asked, as she got out of bed.

'Someone must have hacked into her account and posted the reviews from her profile,' Harry said, his eyes wide. 'Maybe even as far back as before the hit and run. It all makes sense now.'

'I'm putting on a pair of jeans now,' Victoria said.

'Those disgusting reviews could only have been written by someone who has it in for me.'

'I'm putting on my coat.'

'They are someone's revenge,' Harry continued.

'I'm walking out the door now,' Victoria said.

'Which means these reviews aren't even remotely based on the actual quality of my novels. In fact, whoever wrote them definitely hasn't read them, as I suspected. And it means they might *also* be a suspect in her hit and run. Which means I may not be going to prison after all. What do you make of that, Victoria? Victoria?' Harry looked around their room, surprised to find himself alone.

Norma

The second Norma logged into Facebook, she knew something was up. Seventy-nine people had already reported a post on the page. She also had at least a dozen new direct messages.

Her jaw dropped as she scrolled down the page and hummed a few bars from *Jesus Christ, Superstar*, the Jesus Christ bit.

Someone had to be posting from the old lady's account: it was the only explanation that made any sense. Somebody who clearly had not seen the post about the hit and run and Edna being in a coma. The logistics of it made her head spin: she might need to start an Excel spreadsheet or create one of those murder walls crime authors used to get their stories straight.

Her computer pinged as yet another direct message flew into her inbox. Another tirade from Harry, and the little dots were dancing, so there was more coming.

Now do you believe me?

This is sinister beyond belief!

Someone is out to get me. I told you and you didn't do anything about it. And now an old lady is in hospital fighting for her life.

This is all your fault.

Are you going to call the police?

Norma started typing back. How was she supposed to know how to deal with this? She was just an ex-accountant publishing intern.

> Hi Harry, this is shocking. I don't know what to say, I'm not quite sure what to make of it.

I told you to deal with this when it all started, and you ignored me, and now look.

> I don't think we should be pointing fingers right now.

Of course you don't. Typical! Are you going to call the police to tell them and clear my name, or not?

> I don't know what I'm going to do, I need a moment to think.

Don't bother, I'll call them.

Harry

'Leon, it's Harry.'

'Hi Harry, I know it's you, your name shows up on my caller ID. Listen mate, I'm working, I can't chat.'

'Leon, it's not her,' Harry yelled into the phone.

'What's not who, Harry?'

'Edna Molton is someone else, Leon. She's not Edna Molton. She's been hacked. And the hacker's been attacking me. As her!' Harry said.

'I'm not following, Harry. Who is what?'

'While Edna Molton's in hospital, in a coma, somebody else is posting from her account. They obviously didn't know she was in a coma when they posted as her – they haven't even read my books,' Harry explained. 'You need to put an APB out on the IP ASAP.'

'I'll get right on it.' Leon said.

'You will?'

'No Harry, I was being sarcastic. My professional advice remains the same as last time you contacted me. You need to step away from the vehicle, mate.'

'Speaking of, maybe this guy is the person who hit and run her?'

'Well, let's think about that, Harry. You said she's in a coma and this person allegedly posted as her, not knowing she's in a coma. So that would indicate to me, that he, or she, or they, weren't aware of the hit and run.'

'I see what you mean,' Harry said.

'Yup, I'm not a BAFTA-winning cop consultant to writers for nothing,' Leon said. 'Look Harry, I have to go, I'm on the actual crime scene of an actual crime, but I'll look into it, alright, mate?'

'Leon, I ...' But his cop had already hung up.

Norma

'Hi, I'm looking for DS Snopes,' Norma said, when a woman answered at the West Mercia Police Department.

'He's not in at the minute,' the woman said.

'Please can you tell him Norma Jacobs called, and it's urgent. It's about the Edna Molton case. Someone is posting as her on my online book club on Facebook, which is impossible, since she's in a coma,' Norma said.

'Posting as who?' the woman asked.

'It's complicated, can you just ask DS Snopes to contact me, please?' Norma said.

'Will do,' the woman said, taking down Norma's details before hanging up.

Norma didn't know what to do next. Fighting crime in the real world wasn't as satisfying as fighting crime in fiction. In fiction nobody ever had to pause and wait for the cops to call them back. If this was a book, Snopes would have taken the call and leapt into action, abandoning whatever he'd been busy with at the time. But in the real world, people weren't at their desks twenty-four-seven. Systems went down, police had more than one case to deal with, there was paperwork. Things took time.

Plus, in real life, characters had to eat, go to the bathroom, pop down to the shops for milk and tofu, stand in a queue to renew their driver's license, or take a day off to get their flu shot.

And that, Norma thought yet again, was why people like her and Bavinga preferred the fictional world to the non-fictional one.

Harry

'So, if it wasn't Edna Molton, which it absolutely couldn't possibly have been, then who on earth do you think could have written those disgusting, slanderous reviews of my books?' Harry asked.

'I couldn't tell you,' Willoughby said.

'They haven't even read my books!' Harry said, seething with outrage.

'You don't say,' Willoughby said.

'Look, I've made a list of possible suspects. I'm thinking it could be someone in publishing; maybe a fellow author, jealous of my success?' Harry pushed the napkin across the table so Willoughby could get a better look at it.

'Could be,' Willoughby nodded, leaning in for a closer look at the napkin scrawled corner to corner with notes.

'You think? Or … could it have been my agent? I know it sounds unlikely, but she has been avoiding my calls – maybe she's gone off me. Or maybe it was my publisher's marketing department? Everyone knows they'll do anything to drum up sales for a new novel.'

'You have a new book coming out? Congratulations.'

'Well, no, not precisely, but for when I do …' Harry trailed off as he took the napkin back and scribbled something else on top of one of the existing scribbles, and underlining it, his angry nib tearing through tissue. 'Could it have been Victoria? She seems to have gone right off me lately. Or Neil or Clive? But why? Maybe one of them is no longer gay and has fallen in love with Victoria, and wants me off the scene?'

'That sounds reasonable,' Willoughby said, shifting from one foot to the other.

'Does it?' Harry asked, hopefully.

'I don't know. I was just saying that to try wrap up the conversation,' Willoughby said.

'Or it could have been another one of my friends, or so-called friends? So many of them are writers, and I've always felt they were jealous. Writers can be like that, you know?'

'They can?' Willoughby said.

'They really can be,' Harry said, nodding gravely.

'I'm sure,' Willoughby agreed.

'Come to think of it, I was an idiot to ever think it was Edna, I should have known the second I saw her that day in Ludlow. If I've got multiple personalities online, it makes sense that other people do too. Maybe that's why she was at the police station that day? Maybe she was reporting being hacked. She did go into the bank straight afterwards, and she was in there for ages. Not just the regular length of time for a normal deposit or withdrawal,' Harry mused.

'You have multiple personalities online?' Willoughby asked.

'Why are you focusing on that, Willoughby? Of all the things I've been telling you, that's the thing you zero in on?'

'Well, it's just, to be honest, that does seem a little shady,' Willoughby said.

'Focus, Willoughby. We're trying to figure out who would want to hurt me.'

'Actually, sir. I think the people at the other tables waiting for me to serve them might want to hurt you. Are you going to order or not?' said the waiter, running his fingers over the name badge on his chest. 'And my name is actually Brett, but I left my badge at home and they fine you here if you don't have one, so my mate loaned me his when he went off shift.'

Norma

'Hey, Normal!' Keith called, beckoning her off the shop floor and into his office.

Norma rolled her eyes and followed him into the three-by-three crevice in the back of the shop, which had no windows and no ventilation, and smelt like acne.

'It's Norma, and you know it,' Norma growled, standing in front of his desk.

Keith smirked. 'Normal, I thought I asked you to stack that new Devin Froman novel in a pyramid on the table front of house?'

'Yes, but you also think my name is "Normal" when it's actually Norma, so can we really rely on anything you say?' Norma said.

Keith ignored her. 'So, why then, I ask you, is there a display of independently published novels in the exact spot I told you to put the hot new release?'

'I figured that the big, shiny, new release is going to sell billions of copies anyway, with or without our front table display. Also, I skim-read it. It doesn't seem deserving, if you ask me.'

'That's the thing, nobody asked you, Normal,' Keith slotted in.

'I thought, who else could rather use the airtime on the table right where readers enter the shop? Well, what about these incredibly well-written, brave, independently published novels? Each of which has been devoured, loved and recommended on The Good Book

Appreciation Society page. Which, as I mentioned to you in my interview for this job, is the book club I run on Facebook, with almost a hundred thousand very astute readers.'

'Normal, I don't care about the readers, the publishers pay big money for that spot on the front table. I would go so far as to say that they pay both our salaries to be there.'

'That doesn't make it right, does it?' Norma said. 'And surely that's also an indictment of how little they pay us? That's the table that shouts about what we as a bookshop recommend for our customers. There's even a huge sign above it that says, "OUR RECOMMENDED READS". So shouldn't it be something that we do actually think they should read, and not something we're being paid to tell them they should read?'

'That's not how this industry works,' Keith said.

'I might be okay with it, if it was an even vaguely well-written book, but come on, we both know it's awful. The hero is a white man in his thirties, who every woman wants to sleep with and every man wants to be. And I'm not exaggerating, that's literally on the back cover. He even wears a panama hat. It couldn't be more insulting. Don't we owe it to our customers to do better?'

'Listen Normal, I can't spend hours debating this with you, because I don't want to. I'm your boss, you're supposed to just do what I tell you to do.'

'Even though what you told me to do is devoid of soul and insight?'

'You know what, we gave it a good bash, but I don't think this is going to work out.'

'You're firing me?' Norma asked.

'We don't like to use the term "fired". We've found that it can cause problems with HR.'

'What do you like to call it?' Norma asked.

'Let's think of it more as a conscious uncoupling.'

'You mean like Chris Martin and Gwyneth Paltrow?'

'Who?'

'Never mind,' Norma said. 'What are your official reasons for "consciously uncoupling" me?'

'Let's see. One, we're not a great match. Two, you're too old to work here. Three, you don't take direction very well, do you? Four, you yawn and hum a lot, and the customers don't like that. And five, what kind of person is named "Normal"? Shall I go on?'

Norma just glared at him.

'Don't forget to return the t-shirt before you leave the store at the end of your shift.'

'I'm wearing it – can't I just drop it off another time?' Norma asked.

'People always say they will, but they never do. So, there's a fifteen quid fine if you don't leave it here when you go. You're lucky we don't charge you to have it laundered, Normal.'

'I arrived in it today. I didn't bring anything else to wear.'

'There's a lost property box in the break room. I'm sure you'll find something suitable in there.'

'What about the name badge?' Norma asked, plucking it off her t-shirt.

'You can keep that.'

'Are you sure? No fine for not returning a name badge?' Norma asked.

'There is, but I seriously doubt we'll ever hire anyone named "Normal" again. I mean, what kind of name is that? So long, Normal, it's been real.'

Norma rifled through the lost property box, and found a pair of false teeth and an orthodontic plate, a walking stick, four bunches of keys, a soft toy some child must have been sad to lose, and a grubby, well-worn pack of playing cards. She should have taken the job at the second-hand bookshop, she thought as she first sniffed at, then put on the only piece of clothing in the box that might fit; it was a large child, or small man's flannel pyjama top, with a pattern of toy ducks across the front. It barely fit and it smelled of sick, but it was either that or a purple leotard.

Harry

'Phyllis, there's been a new development on the group.'

'Harry, I really hope you're going to tell me that you're talking about some kind of group therapy?'

'No, Phyl. The Facebook Group …' Harry said, as Phyllis groaned. 'Wait, Phyllis, hear me out. Edna Molton is not Edna Molton. Someone has been logging into her Facebook account as her. Someone who clearly has it in for me.'

'Identity theft? No way! You do know that ninety per cent of all identity theft is linked to Al Qaeda and terrorism?'

'What are you talking about?' Harry asked.

'It's pretty obvious, they need fake identities to buy their guns and all the things they need to make their bombs, and where do you think those fake identities come from? Groups like your Good Book Appreciation Society. If someone pretending to be an eighty-something-year-old retired whatever, named Edna Molton, from some small town nowhere, buys a gun with her ID, nobody asks any questions.'

'That doesn't make any sense, Phyllis. Why would a terrorist want to slander me in a book review? More importantly, you know what this means, right? It means that I can't be the main suspect anymore. I'm not going to prison.'

'That's a relief. You know they routinely do experiments on prisoners without their knowledge or assent?' Phyllis said, lowering her voice.

'Who do you think it is, and why, though?'

'Well, Harry, obviously it's the government, and it's obviously because another government is paying them for the prisoner experiments, Russia more than likely. Or maybe China.'

'No, not who's doing the experiments, I meant who's out there impersonating Edna, and why are they after me?'

'I wonder if the Bilderberg Group have anything to do with it? It smacks of their off-the-record agenda.'

'Speaking of the Russians, remember that literary festival we went to in Berlin? There was that writer, what was his name again, the insecure one?' Harry clicked his fingers, trying to remember.

'The Russian crime writer? Boris something or other like a gun?'

'Yes, that's the one. Boris Kalashnikov,' Harry said. 'What an awful pen name. Don't you remember, he asked me to write a shout for his new novel, and I said yes, but then his publisher sent me the proofs, and it was terrible, beyond dire.'

'Was that the crime thriller set in the Kremlin?' Phyllis asked.

'Yes, in the far future.'

'You're right, it wasn't very good.'

'Of course, I didn't want to do the shout for his cover, because, terrible book. So I told the publisher that I didn't want to do it, but by the time I'd read it and gotten back to them a couple of weeks late, they said I'd already agreed to do it and they had run out of time to get someone else, so I did one in the end, but it was one of those nebulous shouts, where the reader can pick up my heart wasn't in it. Along the lines of "You'll like this book if you're a fan of his work." And they put that on the cover of his book, and the book totally tanked. I mean it wasn't because of my shout obviously,' Harry rambled on.

'Obviously,' Phyllis agreed, 'although maybe ...'

'But maybe he thought it was. And maybe THAT'S who got Edna's log-in details, and wrote those reviews.'

'It's possible, buddy. But also highly unlikely,' Phyllis said. 'For an author to put in all that effort just to haze you, all the way from Russia, after all this time? Unless he's part of the Russian mafia? They also use fake identities to buy their guns, you know? But if it was him, and he is part of the Russian mafia, I'm sure his revenge would have been a little less ... well, vanilla.'

'Could be, could be,' Harry said.

'Harry, I'm worried that your obsession with all this is only getting worse. If you don't want to see someone to talk about it, maybe you should go get shit-faced, or buy a Porsche, or screw a twenty-six-year-old, or do whatever it is you middle-aged straight white guys in Britain do to get this kind of thing out of your system? Here we buy guns and shoot up public spaces.'

'I'm not really a gun kind of guy.'

'Probably for the best.'

'In Britain we mostly drink tea and feel repressed. How am I going to figure out who's doing this to me, Phyl?'

'I feel like you're listening to my voice, but you aren't hearing what I'm saying,' Phyllis said.

'Could it have been a reader who didn't like the ending of *Once on a Tuesday*, maybe? It did leave things on a hell of a cliffhanger.'

Harry heard Phyllis sigh. No, she was right, the ending of that book was perfect. As they said their goodbyes, he crossed 'Boris' off the list of possible suspects he'd scrawled in his notebook and went to pour himself another single-malt on the rocks.

Norma

'Fired! Just for trying to sell better books.' Norma finished telling Bavinga about promo-book-gate at Chapters.

'You were too good for them. You should try a second-hand bookshop or an indie bookshop instead, they have way better taste in books.'

'I'm not sure I'm cut out for retail, Bavinga.'

'So now what?'

'My friend Marina said I could make good money selling my eggs or blood plasma on the dark web. But I'm forty-two – I'm not sure how much egg my eggs have left in them.'

'What about your book?'

'What about it?'

'Writers who get published make money, don't they? Especially if they can sell it on to movie people. Oh no, now I sound like Brittt.'

'I think I'd have to pay someone to publish that. And anyway, I also think I'm going to need a more lucrative and immediate solution.'

'Wow, fired AND broke, plus there's that whole prospective prison thing, 'cos of the attempted murder hit and run. You, my friend, are having a particularly apocalyptic week.'

'Oh, I've been meaning to tell you, that may not be a thing anymore. It looks like someone hacked her account, so Harry – and me by association – aren't the only suspects in that hit-and-run case anymore.'

'Things are looking up.'

'That they are, if you ignore the whole no job, no boyfriend, no money, deep crippling debt and shit novel situation,' Norma said.

'You win some, you lose some,' Bavinga said as she dropped a manuscript she'd been skim-reading onto one of their non-fiction piles.

'Any good?' Norma asked.

'It's about neurodivergent aliens who take over X, and, surprisingly, yes, it is.'

Norma

DIRECT MESSAGE:

KATHY SPACER: To the group admin for The Good Book Appreciation Society, I'm writing to inform you that one of your club members, Michael Kerman, picked up my name from a comment I made on your page. He has been bothering me with messages, asking if I'm married and interested in a boyfriend. His English is poor and I'm certain he has an ulterior motive. He may also be preying on other innocent club members?

NORMA JACOBS: Thank you for letting me know, Kathy. I will remove him from the club immediately and report him to Facebook. I'm so sorry that you had to experience this. And good thing you didn't engage with this person.

KATHY SPACER: 👍

NORMA JACOBS: Hi Kathy, me again. I checked on the site's back end. As an admin, I can see all activity on the page, and it appears you added this Michael Kerman to the group yesterday. Is he a friend of yours?

[No response.]

NORMA JACOBS: I've blocked him, Kathy. Perhaps unfriend him and change your password, in case he has been stalking you and has ill intent. The internet is full of con artists.

Harry

'DS Snopes, thank you for calling me back. Albeit forty-seven hours later. Good thing I wasn't being held at gun point,' Harry said.

'Mr Shields, how can I help you?' DS Snopes asked.

'Snopes, I have great news for you, Edna Molton isn't Edna Molton! It's all been a con. So there is another suspect out there. I TOLD you I was innocent.'

'We know who knocked over Edna Molton, Mr Shields.'

'You ... wait, you know who knocked her over?'

'Yes, Mr Shields, it was the local sandwich-shop owner, doing a delivery to the library in his van.'

'What?' Harry's brain scrambled to put all the pieces into place.

'It was an accident, Mr Shields. The driver didn't even realise he'd bumped into her. He saw the dent in his van the following morning when he got to work. Ironically, he thought someone had driven into him, since the van was parked on the street overnight. So he came into the station to report that he'd been the victim of a hit and run,' DS Snopes said with a chuckle. 'Technically, he unknowingly turned himself in.'

'It can't be ...' Harry's voice trailed off.

'We've got it all on CCTV, captured by cameras at the store across the road from the library, Mr Shields, the number plate as clear as day, as is the signage on the side of the van. From the footage, it appears

Mrs Molton simply looked the wrong way before she crossed, and she stepped right into the path of the reversing van. She'd just the evening before come back from a birding trip in America, so we suspect she got confused about which side of the road we drive on here, poor dear, plus the jetlag had her discombobulated.'

'Why would a sandwich-shop owner in Ludlow knock her over and steal her online identity in order to write scathing reviews of my novels online?'

'Mr Shields, there's something else I wanted to share with you. Two weeks ago, Mrs Molton came into the station to open a police report, claiming that someone had attempted to defraud her online. The fraudulent online activity is completely unrelated to the hit and run.'

'But then why did …'

'Mr Shields, it's our understanding that someone, posing as a suitor, managed to con Mrs Molton into giving him her Facebook account details, and was then able to log into her Facebook account. Mrs Molton subsequently went overseas on her birding trip and was offline for a number of weeks while the con artist had their way with her social media identity. They also attempted to use her personal details to hack into her bank accounts, but were unsuccessful. When Mrs Molton returned to the United Kingdom, she discovered she'd been hacked and reported the fraud to the police and to her bank, and they were able to put additional safety measures in place to protect her accounts. It appears she hadn't gotten around to changing the password on her Facebook account and reporting the hack before she was run over.'

'Someone was posing as a suitor? But she's in her eighties!'

'The heart wants what the heart wants, Mr Shields. I'm afraid this kind of thing happens all the time online; people prey on the elderly, who are lonely and don't always have a very strong grasp of the dangers of the digital world.'

'Will you be able to trace the hacker, DS Snopes?'

'The hacker wasn't successful, Mr Shields. There was nothing stolen from Mrs Molton. In the end, no real crime was committed.'

'He stole her identity, her password, and caused me grievous bodily damage, Detective. That's a crime. I want to press charges. This needs to go to court!' Harry yelled into the phone.

'Mr Shields, it was an attempted hacking and Mrs Molton all but handed him her personal information on a silver platter. She's lucky he didn't get any further than abusing you. You're welcome to come in and press charges if you want to open a civil case.'

'Snopes, you're saying you're not going to do ANYTHING about it, and this criminal will be free to roam the streets and continue ruining people's lives and reputations?'

'Mr Shields, I'm sure you understand that if we were to put police resources into tracking every single person who attempted to scam old ladies out of their banking details online, we'd never have time to track down the people who successfully attempt murder or violent hit and runs, or commit felonies, or breaking and entering.'

'So that's it then? A heinous criminal walks free. And his victims get no justice?'

'I can assure you, Mr Shields, we are looking into it. Now if that's all you wanted to discuss, I have actual homicides to investigate.'

'Wait, I …' but DS Snopes had already moved on to his next case.

Norma

> Norms, I'm racing to an appointment. Come meet me there, we can chat and go for a drink afterwards. I'll send you a pin.

Seconds later Marina sent the pin. It was another random street address, with no hint on Google Maps as to her destination. Nameless and faceless. Norma grabbed her coat, hoping she wasn't headed to another boxing ring.

> I'm here, it's a random street corner. Now what?

> Go through the door with the signage for Bradley & Associates Law Firm, take a left at the reception desk and you'll find a flight of stairs. Go up five flights (sorry no lift) then all the way to the end of the passage. It's the door with the bullseye painted on it.

Let yourself in.

When Norma got to the bullseye, she took a moment to catch her breath, hum, and give her spectacles a nudge. Hand on the door handle, she paused and listened closely, wondering what she was walking into? Juggling school? Band practice? A meth lab where everyone worked naked?

She stepped cautiously into a small room with windows looking out onto the fire escape of the building next door. Marina lay on a red leather reclining chair in the middle of the room, with her arm extended, getting a tattoo.

'Hey,' Marina called out, 'This is Iris. Irie, this is my mate, Norma, she's also my shit-hole brother's ex. Irie, Norma. Norma, Irie.'

Iris was blonde, minute, and in her early thirties. She wore a pair of dirty, particularly short dungaree shorts, over a tiny white crop top, and a pair of oversized construction boots. There was something unusual about her, Norma thought, and then realised that her skin was milky white and she didn't have a single freckle, fleck or tattoo. But it was more than that; other than her head, she didn't have a single strand of hair on her face or arms. Not an eyelash or an eyebrow.

'Nice to meet you,' Norma said.

'Make yourself at home,' Iris said, in a thick Welsh accent.

'What are you getting?' Norma asked.

Marina tossed a crumpled piece of paper at her.

Norma took a seat on a battered couch and ironed out the piece of paper on her lap with the palm of her hand. The page had been torn roughly from a lined exercise book, and looked like it had been crumpled and uncrumpled dozens of times. On it was a long, complicated mathematical formula, scribbled in small, neat pencil strokes.

'Wow. What is this?' Norma asked.

'A formula,' Marina said.

'Thanks Einstein, I gathered as much. What for?'

'Work stuff,' Marina said.

'Got it!' Norma said. Not that she did, but she'd learnt it was futile asking.

'What about you?' Marina asked. 'What you getting?'

'No ... I'm not ... I don't ...' But maybe, Norma thought.

'You're considering it now, aren't you?' Iris said.

'I'm not really that kind of ... I haven't ever thought ... I don't know if I ... I mean maybe,' Norma stuttered, then hummed a few notes of 'Bad Decisions' by The Strokes and nudged her spectacles.

'It's on me, if you do want one – no pressure,' Marina said. 'So, how's everything going?'

'I'm not working at the bookshop anymore,' Norma said.

'Brilliant. Fired or quit?' Marina asked.

'Fired.'

'Cunts,' Marina said. 'I told you to rather do the clown for kids' parties thing.'

'Not practical though, is it, being a clown? Well, more of a clown than I already am. I doubt it pays more than minimum wage, especially when you're just starting out, and it's unlikely to come with perks or a pension,' Norma said.

'The cake is a perk,' Marina said. 'And the shoes are fun.'

'Hey, I have something for you,' Norma said, holding out her closed hand.

Marina stretched her free hand out and Norma dropped her bookshop name-badge into her friend's palm.

'I freaking absolutely love it, thank you,' Marina said, holding it to her heart.

'I thought you might.'

'I'm impressed, I thought you'd last longer,' Marina said.

'Three and a half shifts,' Norma said.

'I once lost a job the day before I'd even started it,' Marina said.

'Doesn't surprise me,' Norma said.

'Nor me,' Iris chimed in.

'So now what?' Marina asked.

'No idea.'

'That's the tattoo you should get,' Marina said. 'No idea.'

Norma raised an eyebrow and started humming again. That wasn't such a bad idea.

Norma

Heya, Norma, Remember back
when we first started dating,
you asked me if I'd ever thought
about marriage? Well I've been
thinking about it. I changed my
mind.

Yes, I will marry you.

What do you say?

Norma? I saw the blue tick, I
know you've seen my message.
What do you think? Is it a yes?

Hello?

Okay, take a day or two to think
about it.

Harry

'Stop talking about whatever you're talking about! You guys are not going to believe this. Those disgusting reviews weren't even written by Edna Molton!' Harry yelled as he and Victoria took their seats at brunch.

'We heard! Pass the mimosa jug, Clive,' Neil said.

'You ... what?'

'Sorry, love, it just slipped out,' Victoria said, holding her empty champagne flute out for Neil to fill.

'You told them?' Harry said, his mouth agape.

'On the group,' Clive nodded.

'On our group? I didn't see that,' Harry said.

'No, our holiday group,' Clive said, and Harry spotted Neil kicking him under the table.

'You have a WhatsApp group without me?' Harry sputtered.

'It's not a big deal, Harry. We needed somewhere to make holiday arrangements and send details and chat while we were away. We didn't want to interrupt you while you were working,' Victoria said.

'And you're still chatting on it now, without me, even though you're not away together anymore? That doesn't feel like "Not a big deal".'

'It's nothing. We just share holiday pictures and in-jokes. You wouldn't like it, Harry,' Victoria said.

'You're right, I don't like it,' Harry said, outraged.

'We didn't want you to feel left out while we were away,' Clive added.

'Yes, except now I feel even more left out. And I can't believe you told them my news, Victoria. After all your indifference, now suddenly you're interested.'

'Well, it suddenly got interesting,' Victoria said.

'Forget about the stupid group, Harry. Tell us about Edna,' Neil said.

'Okay, so, Edna is not Edna. I spoke to the policeman at the West Mercia Police Department, and it turns out someone hacked into her account to try and scam her out of her credit card details. In the process, they must have seen the club and written the reviews.'

'Wait, why would an online scammer want to write a bad review of your book on a Facebook book club?' Clive asked.

'I haven't figured that out yet,' Harry said. 'AND there's more: the police know who knocked Edna Molton over.'

'Victoria told us,' Clive said.

Harry shot Victoria another dirty look. 'You told them that too?'

'Sorry,' she said with a shrug.

'Just an unfortunate accident, completely unrelated to the identity theft. She was just back from America. She must have gotten confused, looked the wrong way before crossing the road, and boom,' Harry finished.

'Victoria said so. Which means they still don't know who hacked her account?' Neil asked.

'No. And because he didn't technically steal anything, they're unlikely to investigate it.'

'Do you have any idea who it is?' Clive asked.

'Not a clue,' Harry said. 'All I've got to go on is an IP address. What do you guys think I should do next?'

'I think the Caesar salad looks good,' Victoria said.

'No, I mean about who's been attacking me,' Harry said.

'Honestly Harry? At this point I'm so bored of this whole business, and I don't think you actually do want to know what I think about this,' Victoria said.

'What about you guys?' Harry turned to Neil and Clive.
'I agree,' Clive said, 'The Caesar salad does look good.'

Harry

Harry was in Waitrose, trying to decide which brand of puff pastry to buy, when his phone buzzed with a text from an unknown number.

> +44 7795 967826: I can tell you who wrote those reviews of your books on GBAS.

Harry moved away from Victoria. If she found out he was engaging with anyone on this, she would slice out his liver. He headed into the dairy aisle; she was lactose-intolerant, so unlikely to wander past.

Harry tapped out a response.

> What do you want?

> +44 7795 967826: Fifty thousand

> Quid?

> +44 7795 967826: No, fifty thousand Mars Bars. Of course quid.

That's preposterous.

> +44 7795 967826:
> 40 thousand?

Mate, you're having a laugh!

Harry typed back, channelling his inner Leon.

> +44 7795 967826:
> 30 thousand, that's my final offer.

'Do we need any coriander?' Victoria came up behind him, giving Harry a near heart attack.

Harry slid his phone into his pocket and mumbled an answer. He needed to think about this. The bribe, not the coriander. They definitely needed coriander.

An hour later Harry was back at his desk, staring at his phone, puff pastry in the oven.

He wondered how they got his number? Although privacy these days was an illusion. At the height of Covid, everybody was filling in track and trace forms at every restaurant, theatre and doctors' rooms. Between that and social media listening in on everything, it would be strange if anybody didn't have your number. Phyllis was wrong: it wasn't the Russians or the government or the aliens we needed to worry about stealing our private information, it was the telemarketers who would rather die than take you off a cold-call and email spam list, despite being told a thousand times that you weren't interested in their electricity and gas survey, or better cellphone prices, or two-drawer air fryer. Although maybe the two-drawer air fryer. You could at least cook your chicken and chips at the same time. Damn, he thought, they had plenty of coriander, but they'd forgotten to buy chips.

Harry's phone buzzed.

+44 7795 967826: So what's the information worth to your?

+44 7795 967826: *You*. Bloody autocorrect!

You know I can just track your cellphone to find out who you are?

+44 7795 967826: It's a burner. I'm tossing it after these messages.

Then how will I be able to reach you once I've got the money together?

+44 7795 967826: You let me worry about thank.

Thank?

+44 7795 967826: *that*! Autocorrect!

How do I know you really know?

+44 7795 967826: Because if I didn't know, how would I know to message you?

+44 7795 967826: And I'm asking the questions here. What's the information

>worth to you?

Fifty quid.

>+44 7795 967826: I'm not telling you for a penny less than five thousand pounds.

A thousand pounds is my final offer.

>+44 7795 967826: Four thousand.

Two thousand pounds is absolutely the highest I can go. But I'll need a couple of days to get it together, my ATM limit is a thousand a day.

>+44 7795 967826: I'll message you with meet-up details. Come alone or lose everything.

Everything, Harry thought. Wasn't much of a threat to someone with so little left to lose.

Norma

Norma was skim-reading a tatty manuscript from the bottom of the slush pile, about a time-travelling pigeon whisperer, inventively called *The Time-Travelling Pigeon Whisperer*. About a down-on-his-luck homeless man living in a park, who accidentally discovers he can communicate with pigeons and is transported across timelines by a Wood Pigeon he calls Hugh. Together, they must stop a secret society of time-travellers from altering key moments in history. Along the way, the homeless man finds out about love, friendship, and the shocking truth about the real builders of Stonehenge. She was only on page fifty-seven, but Norma thought it was shaping up to be entertaining enough to make it onto the Maybe pile.

'Interns, are you in here?'

The woman's voice startled Norma; it was the first time anyone had come down to the slush-pile room the entire time they'd been there. She was tall, and wore bracelets up and down both wrists and a colourful floor-length boho dress.

'Wow, look at what you've done! I thought nothing short of a Molotov cocktail could fix this disaster. I hear you've even been reading and rating them too?' she said, hovering over one of their 'HELL YES' piles, paging through the manuscript on top.

'We thought we'd make a start,' Bavinga said.

'I'm Talita, I'm from PR. Daniel wants to see you lot, stat – he says to bring your things.'

'Maybe they're moving us out of the slush-pile room?' Bavinga whispered to Norma, as she packed her mobile into her bag.

They trailed Talita, jangling from the wrists, up in the lift, through the building and into a large corner office.

Daniel looked up as they entered. A man wearing a funereal suit and a stern expression stood in the back corner of the room with his arms crossed. Nobody introduced him.

Britttennay took a seat in one of the two chairs in front of Daniel's desk, snapping her gum, while Norma and Bavinga hovered. Norma thought she'd never seen Bavinga look more uncomfortable. Not even when they'd been at the bar-cum-nightclub-come-influencer-factory, and one of Britttennay's friends had taken a selfie with her.

'Well, you lot have been busy, haven't you?' Daniel said.

Norma couldn't pinpoint the note of congratulations she'd been expecting. When nobody else spoke, Norma cleared her throat, and said, 'Thank you. It's been a big job, but we feel we're making good headway.'

'I hear you've even been reading and sorting the manuscripts, despite the fact that all we asked you to do was clean up and put the manuscripts in chronological order?' Daniel said, his voice steely.

'It's been a pleasure,' Britttennay said.

'I wasn't thanking you,' Daniel snapped.

Norma glanced at Bavinga, who looked like she might be sick on the carpet, while Britttennay carried on chewing and popping her gum.

'We think we've managed to pull out a few gems,' Norma said nervously.

'Apparently that's not all you've pulled out,' Daniel said. 'What about the BookToks?'

'BookToks?' Norma said.

'Yes, the BookToks you three have been posting about the manuscripts you've been reading: what about those?' Daniel said, as the man in the suit shook his head.

'We didn't do anything like tha—' Norma started, and then noticed Britttennay grinning.

'Aren't they fab?' she squealed, clutching her mobile phone. 'I had no idea they were going to be so popular. Like, who knew people were *that* curious about the kind of stuff you find in a slush pile in a London publishing house?'

'And am I right in saying that you've created a promo announcing that the manuscript featured in the BookTok that gets the most likes by the time your internship finishes, would go on to get a publishing deal?' Daniel said.

'COULD! I said it COULD *possibly* go on to get a publishing deal,' Britttennay corrected him. 'Asterisk, terms and conditions apply.'

Norma swung her head to look at Bavinga, who looked as surprised as she did.

'We seem to have run into a number of issues, team,' Daniel said. 'In terms of rights and permissions and that kind of thing, you could say we're royally fucked. What made you think we could simply put other people's work on the internet without their permission or any form of contract or remuneration?'

He paused, and when nobody answered, he continued.

'... So now we're in the fortunate position of having a horde of angry unpublished writers on our case. And yes, I'm being sarcastic. Not to mention the truckload of authors who've subsequently been published, who together with their agents and lawyers are super pissed-off at us, threatening legal action, demanding withdrawal, remuneration and apology. Everyone is ready to have our bollocks for breakfast, thanks to you lot.'

'Oh shit,' Britttennay said, legitimately surprised. 'I didn't think about that.'

'Of course you didn't. Over and above which, you have unleashed the kraken. We have unsolicited hard copy manuscripts pouring in from every corner of the planet from writers desperate to have their manuscript included in one of your BookToks,' Daniel said, indicating a corner of his office, where boxes were stacked on top of each other, printed manuscripts spilling out of them. 'We were supposed to be getting rid of the fucking things, not having more delivered to the office daily.'

Norma opened her mouth to defend herself, but Daniel cut her off.

'And you, Bavinga! I'm really disappointed in you. Of all people, you should know better.'

Bavinga was still looking at her feet as if they contained the secrets of the universe. Norma had to wonder why he had called her out like that.

'We're consulting lawyers and our rights department to try figure a way out of this nightmare that won't see us declaring bankruptcy. In the meantime, you need to shut down that bloody account,' Daniel said.

A bubble of laughter burst out of Britttennay. 'I'm not shutting it down, I've gained more new followers this week than I have in like the last six months. And anyway, it's my own personal account, it has nothing to do with this publishing house.'

Daniel glanced at the man in the suit, who shook his head again.

'Since we don't officially employ you full-time, we obviously can't force you to shut it down. But I strongly suggest that it's in your best interests to shut it the fuck down.'

'If you'd just made them sign the NDAs like you were supposed to ...' the man in the suit started.

'Shut up, Frank,' Daniel snapped. 'We need to keep you lot out of the slush-pile room until we can clean up the mess you've left behind. Talita, keep them out of trouble until legal figures out this shit-show. And don't let them out of your sight, or onto TikTok, Instagram, Facebook, LinkedIn, Threads, Reddit, Snapchat, X or even Be Real. Especially not that one,' he said, pointing at Britttennay.

'Bavinga, why did he say that to you? Do you know him personally?' Norma whispered as they followed Talita out of Daniel's office.

'Daniel? He's the publisher here,' Bavinga said, not making eye contact.

'You know what I mean. He knows you.'

'Well, I do work for him,' Bavinga hissed. 'Britttennay, why didn't you tell us what you were doing?'

'I did! I asked you to make TikToks with me a dozen times. You were never interested, always too busy reading.'

'You need to take that shit down,' Bavinga said.

'Not a chance, I know my rights. I've watched all nine seasons of *Suits*.'

'I don't know that you do. I think we're in deep shit,' Norma said.

'It's okay – if we get fired, you guys can just come work for me,' Britttennay said. 'My channel is blowing up. If it carries on like this, I'll need assistants.'

They followed Talita into an open-plan work space, cluttered with marketing paraphernalia, banners, posters, stacks of books, flyers, bookmarks and pull-up banners lying everywhere.

'Welcome to the marketing department,' Talita said. 'Drop your phones on my desk, I'll keep an eye on them for you for the moment. And then, since you did such a great job cleaning up down in the slush-pile room, let's get you started on tidying up in here, okay? We need you to put all those puzzle pieces together, so we can make sure nothing's missing before we send it to print.'

'Ahh, the glamorous world of publishing,' Norma said as they started assembling a two-thousand-piece jigsaw puzzle headshot of a mid-range cosy murder mystery author and his book cover, set against a thousand pieces of clear blue sky.

THE GOOD BOOK APPRECIATION SOCIETY

MEMBERS: 99 281

Megan Paulson: Writing and reading friends, maybe you can weigh in. I don't know whether to be ecstatic or furious. About a year ago, I submitted my first manuscript to a UK publisher. Among others.

It's a book of essays, all written from a cat's perspective, and it's called *The Cat's Pyjamas*. I know, fun, right?

At the time I sent it to seven different publishers. After about six months, I had gotten back five rejection letters. And I didn't hear back from two of the publishing houses at all.

Soon after that, Covid eased up, and we had to go back into the office, so I decided to shelve my literary career for the minute (if you'll pardon the pun).

So imagine my surprise when my son told me there was a very popular TikTok, or rather what they call a BookTok doing the rounds – ABOUT MY BOOK!!!! And not a very flattering one, I can tell you. It laughs at the idea of a cat writing a book, because they don't know how to use computers.

When I contacted the publisher associated with the BookTok (one of the ones who had never even bothered to get back to me), they said an intern at the publishing house was going through the slush pile, came across my book, and decided to make a BookTok about it.

I have such mixed feelings. I feel sad that the publisher couldn't be bothered to respond to my submission in the first place. I feel angry that they didn't ask my permission to post about it.

I feel peed-off at this young TikTokker for making fun of my book. But I also feel hopeful that a publisher might hear about it and want to pick it up. And excited that so many people have been exposed to my work and have loved it, despite the sharp commentary.

I also feel worried that another author might hear about the idea, steal it, write the same book and get famous from it. As I said, a myriad of feelings.

So, do I sue? Do I thank them? Or do I dust off the manuscript and try to flog it elsewhere, now that it has some acclaim?

COMMENTS:

Gerry Rawson: All publicity is good publicity, isn't that what they always say?

Karen Granger: Not to be pedantic, it's just myriad, not myriad of. You don't need the 'of'. #Wordnerd #GrammarMatters

Troy Phillips: I wish someone would do a BookTok of my unpublished manuscript.

Thomas Dooley: Yeah, I'd pay good money for that to happen to me too.

BOOK PEOPLE

Geneva Fulverton: I went to look at your BookTok and some of the others she's posted, and I have to say, as a reader, they kind of made me want to read all those books out of curiosity. Especially the ridiculous ones, like the one about bridges, and yours with the cat as the author.

Felicity Mauberger: You should sue. Those publishing companies have shallow consciences and deep pockets. That is your intellectual property, and they have no right benefitting from it. I bet it was the publisher's idea and they got the intern to execute it, so they could deny everything if it went badly for them in the end. It's all about plausible deniability these days.

Thomas Dooley: @Felicity Mauberger, if you think publishers have deep pockets, you clearly don't know a single thing about the industry. You know what they say, if you want to make a million, start with a billion and go into publishing.

Chris Colt: Don't be an idiot, Thomas Dooley. That's exactly what they want you to think! Meanwhile the chairman and board members are eating caviar for breakfast, lunch and dinner.

Thomas Dooley: @Chris Colt, you're delusional.

Linda Petal Dabb: Guys, guys, we're all readers and friends here. There's no need for this kind of hostility. Use your words to find resolution. Peace and light. 🌸🌈

Chris Colt: Oh please, @Thomas Dooley, what do you know?

Thomas Dooley: I'm in publishing, you fool!

Chris Colt: Douchebag!

Thomas Dooley: Bonehead!

Chris Colt: Jackass!

[Freda Kruger has reported these comments.]

[Admin has turned off commenting.]

Harry

'Alright, Harry, mate, I got your call and your proof of payment, so you're finally ready to get to work on our new novel? I knew you'd come around,' Leon said, sliding into the booth across from Harry. 'What's it about?'

'Leon, we need to talk about Edna Molton.'

'Harry. I'm going to thump you. You called, you said you were ready with book questions, you made the payment. I wouldn't have come if I'd known it was to talk about this nonsense again, mate!'

'I need you to listen to me, Leon. Trust me, this will interest you,' Harry said.

Leon sighed and called over a waitress. 'I'll have a kale, cucumber and ginger juice, please, love. Anything for you, Harry, or just more of this rubbish?'

'More coffee,' Harry said, his knee already bouncing under the table.

'Okay, I'll bite,' Leon said once the waitress had left. 'But word to the wise, maybe you should ease up on the caffeine.'

'Someone's trying to bribe me on WhatsApp.'

'Show me,' Leon said, taking a pair of spectacles from his pocket.

Harry handed his phone over to Leon.

'It must be the same person who wrote the reviews,' Leon said, peering at the screen.

'I thought that too,' Harry whispered.

'Fifty thousand pounds! He's having a laugh,' Leon chuckled. 'If he was giving you the whereabouts of a terrorist cell, maybe? But just to tell you who wrote a bad review of your book on a book club on Facebook?'

'May I remind you, it wasn't just a bad review, it was two scathing, acid, potentially life-threatening reviews and a ton of comments, and it spawned the downfall of my career.'

'Either way, this is delusional,' Leon said.

'Even criminal.'

'People are pretty desperate these days, Harry, especially these small-time online scammers. We see this all the time.'

'Could you guys trace the phone?' Harry asked, as the waitress delivered their drinks.

'I'm sure we could, I just doubt we ever would. And it's likely a burner, anyway. I can't say I see that much of a crime being committed here, other than a ridiculous bit of attempted extortion. I know I sound like a broken record, but you should ignore it and walk away, son.'

'Those reviews were a crime!' Harry yelled.

'I know this guy has hurt your feelings, Harry, but …'

'More than that, Leon, he's ruined my career and my reputation. No one will ever publish me again, which is going to seriously impact my ability to generate an income. What am I supposed to do now, work at a McDonald's?'

'That's a little dramatic, mate.'

'I swear, when I find out who this guy is, I'm going to sue the pants off him, if I don't kill him first.'

'That's smart, Harry, why don't you just confess premeditated murder to a cop? Look, I know this has been tough on you, mate, but, from what I've seen, you've been the one responsible for a lot of this fallout. If you and me just write something good, then a year from now, when all this chaos has died down, someone will publish us. Believe me, this is just a for now problem, not a forever problem.'

'Leon, you don't understand, the digital world leaves a footprint that lasts forever. I'll never be rid of those reviews and every time anyone googles my name from now to all eternity, this scandal will show up first on the search. All those articles. That video. And nobody will believe they were embellished and inaccurate, or taken out of context. It's a stain I'll never be able to get rid of. Because nobody ever clicks on the story of the author who wrote great novels, if they can rather click on the link to the story about the author who told his readers to eff off.'

'And stormed the stage at the awards we were nominated for, and called a fellow author the c-word.'

'Oh my god, even you've seen the clip.' Harry covered his face with his hands. 'You see, that's my point. And can I just add for the record, that, first of all, you *consulted* on *some* of the police procedures *I* put in *my* book, we did not write it together. And so no, *we* were not nominated for an award, *I* was nominated for an award. And anyway, you're missing the point. That blackmailing reviewer may not have robbed a bank or knifed anyone – that we know of – but that doesn't mean they aren't a rat-faced criminal who has done some very real damage.'

'Harry, if I was your therapist, I would tell you to try find a more constructive way to move forward. Focus on a new manuscript or write a short story – hell, write a shopping list, write anything. Then I would charge you a hundred and fifty quid for the hour, thank you very much.'

'Well you're not my therapist, Leon, you're my fucking cop. So instead of giving me dime-store, Christmas-cracker useless fucking advice, why don't you get off your lazy arse and help me catch this piece-of-shit criminal and put him behind bars?'

'I like you, Harry, so I'm not going to take any of that personally. The fact that this half-witted, small-time con artist is asking so much for such ridiculous, trivial information is probably the most criminal thing about this entire situation. And this is absolutely the last time I'm going to say this, because I'm getting sick of it coming out of my mouth, but I suggest you ignore him, get on with your life, and give this social media shit-storm an opportunity to die down to the dull roar of memory. Actually, that's a fine line, you should put that in our next book. Want to borrow my pen?

I won't even make you credit me, but I will send you a bill.'

'You can blow this off all you want, Leon, but the fact remains that there is something very sinister going on over here, it might even be a whole crime syndicate,' Harry said, spittle flying out of his mouth.

'I know I'm going to regret asking this, but clearly it's never going to just go away. What's your plan here, Harry? What do you imagine I'll do?' Leon asked, leaning back in the booth, extending both arms along the top of the red vinyl seat.

'Oh thank god, you're finally on board,' Harry said.

'Whoa. Let's not buy the wedding ring quite yet, mate.'

'Okay, I have two possible plans. The first is a classic bait and switch. When I go to hand over the blackmail money, you hide, then ambush him, pull off his balaclava, so we can see who he is, arrest him, and let the law take its course.'

'So the perp is a he, and he's wearing a balaclava in your imagination?' Leon said.

'Yeah, one of those black woollen ones.'

'Itchy. And your second plan?'

'In that one, we use his IP address off the reviews to figure out his physical address, then we do a classic stakeout to find out who he is. Once we have a suspect, motive will follow, then you arrest him, and we let the law take its course.'

'The world watches too much TV.'

'So you'll help me find him?'

'Harry, I want you to listen to me very carefully, okay? I'm a cop, and in the real world, cops don't help civilians commit crimes. I could lose my job. So what's going to happen here is that I'm going to enjoy the rest of my nice healthy juice, say goodbye to you, then I'm going to go back to my real life, and my real job, and for the last time, I'm going to suggest you do the same.'

'So that's a no?'

'See, you don't need me after all – your powers of detection are astonishing,' Leon said, draining the remainder of his juice in one sip.

Picking up his glasses and his keys, and squeezing Harry's shoulder hard enough to make him wince, he left the restaurant.

Harry slumped down on the table and groaned. Back to square one.

Norma

The lawyer was still there, looking even more funereal, when the three of them were led back into Daniel's office a few hours later.

Britttennay took her previous seat, still snapping her gum, and Norma and Bavinga hovered behind her in their earlier positions. Norma noticed Bavinga studying her feet again with professional intent.

'On the one hand,' Daniel picked up where he left off, 'what you three have done is deeply unethical, and has caused us immense reputational and legal damage, not to mention the financial consequences, which we're unlikely to have full sight of for months. But, I have to admit, on the other hand, publicity in this industry is bloody hard to come by, and you three have single-handedly managed to make slush piles sexy property. Which has taken us all by surprise.'

Britttennay pumped her fist, and Daniel shot her a glare.

'So, while I'm tempted to offer you all permanent positions in our publicity department, I'd also like to murder all three of you and throw your lifeless bodies out that window.'

The lawyer cleared his throat and looked uncomfortable.

'I'd be happier with the first option,' Britttennay said.

Daniel shot her another glare that actually managed to shut her up. 'You don't even ...' he started, but the lawyer cleared his throat even louder. Daniel closed his eyes and rubbed the bridge of his nose for a second, then took a deep breath, raised himself to his full height, then clenched both fists and placed them on his desk. 'Ultimately, we're going to need to be seen to take some responsibility for your actions, and distance ourselves from you as much as possible.'

'Told you. There's always got to be a fall guy,' Bavinga muttered.

'Bavinga, I swear ...' Daniel said.

'So, are we going with the promotion, then?' Britttennay asked.

'HR and legal have said that if we have any chance of plausible deniability, we're going to have to get rid of all three of you, with immediate effect.'

'But you can't fire them, they had nothing to do with it! I did it all on my own,' Britttennay protested.

'Makes no difference, it's all optics in the end. All three of you are to leave this building, and you can never, ever come back, physically or digitally, do you understand? I don't ever want to see you within a hundred feet of this building.'

They sat in stunned silence.

'Didn't you hear me? That's it, that's all. Get out,' Daniel barked.

The three interns traipsed out of his office, heads bowed, speechless, although Norma thought she heard Bavinga mutter something under her breath.

Ten minutes later they were huddled on the pavement, around the corner from the Harbour Books offices, unsure what to do next.

'I'm so sorry, you guys, they should have like just turfed me. Neither of you had anything to do with any of this,' Britttennay said.

'It's okay.' Norma hummed 'Live is Life,' by Opus.

'Meanwhile, I'm not even kidding, my TikTok is blowing up. My fans want more BookTok slush-pile reviews. Where am I going to get shitty manuscripts if we aren't working there anymore?'

'I reckon just about any publishing company in London and beyond would be delighted to pay you a fat salary after all this PR you've drummed up,' Norma said.

'The irony. Norma and I, who are actually interested in publishing are unlikely to ever get hired again, and you, with no interest in it at all, turn out to the be the most employable of the three of us,' Bavinga said.

'What are you going to do next?' Britttennay asked Norma.

'No clue. Maybe I'll look around in publishing a bit more, and if nothing crops up, then I suppose I'll have to shove my tail between my legs and go back to accounting.'

'I'm really, seriously sorry, I didn't mean for …' Britttennay said.

'It's okay. Maybe I'll start work on a new manuscript in the meantime,' Norma said. 'Who knows, in the end this might be the best thing that ever happened to all of us.'

'Hey, you think you have it bad? I just got fired from my first job, by my dad. How do you think that's going to look on my CV? And dinner at home tonight is going to be interesting,' Bavinga said.

Britttennay and Norma both whipped their heads round to stare at her.

'How do you think I got the job in the first place?' Bavinga said, shrugging.

'It clearly wasn't by shagging the boss. Unlike some people,' Norma said, bursting out laughing.

'Sorry I shagged your dad, Bavinga, I swear if I'd known, I possibly wouldn't have done it. And I definitely wouldn't have done it twice,' Britttennay said, trying to stifle a laugh.

'First of all, ewww, gross. And secondly, it's okay, it's not the first time this has happened with one of my friends, and it likely won't be the last. Why do you think my parents have been married and divorced four times and counting? Just whatever happens, don't marry him. I don't think I could cope if you became my step-mom.'

Harry

'1 star, dude's a dickhead.' Harry read out loud, in the thickest American accent he could muster. He'd tried reading this new 1-star review in as many different accents he could think of, but had decided American fit it best.

He was just contemplating his response to the review when the doorbell rang. And when he opened up, Neil and Clive burst in.

'I have the address,' Neil yelled, holding up a slip of paper in triumph.

'What's going on?' Victoria said, appearing in slippers, a book in her hands. 'Are we doing another intervention? You should have WhatsApped in our group.'

'Neil has someone's address,' Harry said, giving Victoria a withering stare.

'The scammer, the reviewer who started this whole thing – we've got an address,' Clive shouted.

'But how?' Harry asked.

'You do know that I own a massive logistics company, don't you? I got my IT team to track the IP address off that bad review,' Neil said.

'See, he's not just a pretty face,' Clive said, proudly.

'Give it to me,' Harry said, hopping up and down, trying to snatch the paper out of Neil's hand.

'What are you going to do with it?' Neil asked, holding it high above his head, out of Harry's reach.

'I don't know yet. Maybe just go see who's there, try figure out why they'd want to ruin my life? See if it's someone I know,' Harry said.

'We're coming with you,' Neil said.

'We can't all just show up on a stranger's doorstep,' Harry said.

'Why not? Safety in numbers,' Clive said. 'He can't shoot all three of us and get away with it.'

'Four,' Victoria added. She'd already changed her shoes and was reaching for her coat.

Harry's phone buzzed, 'It's Phyllis, I have to take this, I'll just be a minute,' he said, stepping away from his friends, one finger in his ear. 'Hi, Phyl, isn't it the middle of the night there?'

'I'm in London, for the festival, remember? I got here last night.'

'I completely forgot. I've been so wrapped up in all of this.'

'I just finished our … er … the panel. Do you want to grab a bite?'

'You're not going to believe this, Phyllis. My friend Neil managed to get an address for the reviewer, off the IP.'

'You see, I told you, they're always listening, Harry. If your friend can find an address off a post, just imagine what the Russians are getting on us?'

'I have to go, Phyl,' Harry said.

'Wait, Harry, what are you going to do with the address?'

'I think we're going to go and see who lives there.'

'Send me the address, I'll meet you there,' Phyllis said.

Norma

> I was fired AGAIN, Marina. Twice in one week. Can you even believe it? I thought you'd approve. Anyway, I just got home. Call me when you get a second and I'll fill you in.

Norma had gone from holding a high-paying job to having an internship for minimum wage and a side-side hustle bookshop job, then back to just the internship, and now she was fully full-time unemployed, with the minimum payment on her credit card due in days. She sighed as she dropped her keys and bag on the table at the front door, then stood there for a moment. The peace of the flat without Steve was still a novelty. She had yet to turn on the TV since he'd left. And she felt like royalty with the whole couch all to herself.

Her stomach rumbled. In all the commotion, she hadn't eaten. She opened the fridge, but without Steve, she hadn't seen the point in grocery shopping, so there was just some hairy cheese, a few beers, and two shelves of condiments to work with, so she grabbed her bag and headed straight back out the door.

'Menu,' Captain Pow said, shoving the dog-eared laminated sheet at her, tapping his ballpoint pen on the counter as he waited for her order.

This was the first time she'd ever been given the opportunity to choose what she wanted to eat at Captain Pow's. She scanned the menu, but the decision felt beyond her. 'You decide,' she said, handing it back to him.

Fifteen minutes later, mystery takeaway in hand, Norma headed back down the street to her flat. The hairs stood up on the back of her neck as she looked around before heading inside. She had the strangest sensation that she was being watched.

Harry

'What do you think she got?' Clive whispered.

'I bet it's the Chow Mein. Places like that make a great Chow Mein,' Neil whispered back, as they hovered behind a minivan outside a restaurant called Capta n Pow's Chows.

'Shhh, here she comes,' Victoria hissed, and they all tried to act casual as a woman walked past them, takeaway bag in her hand. They'd seen her go into the address Neil's IT manager had claimed the review had come from, and while they were bickering over what to do next, she'd re-emerged, after which they'd followed her to the restaurant.

'Who do you think she is?' Harry said.

'I must be honest, sexist as it sounds, I was not expecting a woman,' Victoria said.

'We don't know it's her – maybe she lives with someone?' Clive said.

'Now what?' Victoria asked.

'I vote we grab something to eat, since we're here already. Now that somebody said Chow Mein, it's made me really want Chow Mein,' Neil said.

'You're the one who said Chow Mein, Neil. Anyway, we're on a stakeout. How can you think about food at a time like this? We're supposed to be following the target, not stopping for a late lunch and a glass of chianti,' Harry grumbled.

'Well she's got takeaways, and she's heading back in the direction of that flat, so smart bet is she's going back home to eat. And anyway, what's our next move? We may as well grab a bite while we figure it out. We can even see her building from here in case she leaves again, or anyone else goes in. And anyway, aren't we supposed to be waiting for your American friend? I'm sure she'd like something to eat too. All in favour?' Neil said.

Neil, Clive and Victoria all raised their hands. Harry glared at them.

'Now that someone said Chianti ...' Clive said.

'FINE,' Harry grumped. 'But mains only, we're not staying long.'

'Ooh, they've got sweet and sour pork,' Clive said, as Neil pushed the door open and an eye-patched Maître d' led them to a table for five.

'I hope they've also got a half-decent Chardonnay,' Victoria said.

Norma

Norma was half way through taking off her make-up when the doorbell rang.

It was probably Marina, she thought as she looked at herself in the mirror. One half of her mouth Matte Ruby Woo, the other half Norma Naked. One eye fully made up, the other natural.

The doorbell rang again twice, with more urgency. And at the same time, her mobile phone started ringing. 'Unknown number' flashed on the screen. She let the call go to message as she put on her spectacles.

When she opened the door, there was a short, hollowed-out-looking man on the doorstep. The deep blue-black shadows under his eyes were magnified by his spectacles. Balding, but not quite all the way there. And while his face wasn't half-made up like hers, he looked half-scared, half-angry.

Behind him stood two women. One had very chic short hair and a Gucci handbag, the other had long straight unbrushed hair, and was carrying a canvas tote full of books. Two well-dressed men brought up the rear, both also bespectacled. The smaller, more ferrety one wore a striped jersey, the tall, more hirsute one was in a suit.

'Yes?' Norma said, wondering if they were Jehovah's Witnesses, but also thinking that Jehovah's Witnesses didn't usually carry Gucci. Her phone rang again, the same 'Unknown number' showing up on the screen.

'Sorry, can you give me one moment, please? I need to get rid of this, it's probably a journalist,' Norma said, stepping away from the door and swiping to accept the call.

'Hello,' she answered.

'Is this Norma Jacobs?' a woman said.

Norma's jaw dropped as out the corner of her eye, she saw the gang of strangers traipsing into her flat and settling around the living room as if they owned the place, chatting amongst themselves. Norma waved her hands at them wildly, indicating the door, but they took no notice.

'You have the wrong number,' Norma said bluntly, and hung up. There was suddenly a bunch of strangers in her flat, and she was not in the mood to deal with another nosy journalist.

'Sorry, who are you all? Let yourself in, why don't you!' Norma shouted, striding into the lounge as the doorbell chimed again. She shook her head – what the hell was going on?

'Who's that?' asked the ferrety man in the striped jersey.

'I have no idea. More importantly, who the hell are you?' Norma said, exasperated, pulling the door open.

'Marina! Thank god it's you,' Norma said, throwing her arms around her friend.

'I got your voice note, I bring the ceremonial ...' Marina stopped mid-sentence as she stepped inside, carrying a tub of rum-and-raisin ice cream. 'Shit, sorry, I didn't know you had people over.'

'Neither did I.'

'I know you,' the tall hairy man said, pointing a finger at Marina. 'Martina ... no wait, Marina something ... Marina Watson. You work at my logistics supply chain company.'

'You work at a logistics supply chain company?' Norma said to Marina, mouth agape.

'Best damn forklift driver I've ever seen.'

Norma's mobile rang, and she saw it was 'Unknown number' again.

'Christ, it's busier than Paddington Station round here,' the Gucci woman said.

Norma stepped out of the living room to answer, indicating to Marina to keep an eye on her surprise guests.

'What?' she answered the phone, more sharply this time.

'I'm looking for Norma Jacobs,' the same woman said.

'Okay, look whoever you are and whatever you're selling, I can't help you right now. I lost my job and I have a bit of a ... a situation, I think I may be being held up, I have to go,' Norma said, before hanging up. When she went back through to the open-plan living room and kitchen, the Gucci lady and the tote woman were sitting at the counter, Marina was on the couch and the short, haggard-looking balding man in spectacles was standing glaring at Norma, hands on hips while the ferrety guy in the striped jersey was in her kitchen, dishing up bowls of ice cream, which Marina's boss, the hairy guy in the suit, was handing around.

Marina's boss held a bowl of ice cream out for Norma. When she shook her head, he shrugged and settled next to Marina on the couch, keeping the bowl for himself.

'Anyone for tea?' the ferrety guy in the kitchen yelled, and Norma heard the kettle being switched on.

'You don't have any chilled Chardonnay, do you?' asked the Gucci woman.

'Will somebody please tell me who you are and what the hell you're doing in my flat?' Norma shouted.

'You don't know who they are?' Marina said.

'I don't have the foggiest. They got here right before you arrived. I stepped aside to answer my phone, which was ringing off the hook, and they just let themselves in,' Norma said, throwing her hands up.

'I'm Neil, and that's my husband Clive,' the hairy one said, indicating the ferrety one. 'We're the friends. That's Phyllis, she's an author from America, here for the London Festival of Books. We've never met her before. And those are our friends – Victoria, she's a surgeon, and that's her husband, Harry, who is an author too.'

'Harry,' Norma said, whipping her head round to take a look at the harrowed-looking man. 'You're not Harry, the author from The Good Book Appreciation Society, are you?'

'So you know that man?' Phyllis said accusingly, pointing at Harry.

'How did you get my address? I thought I told you not to contact me again,' Norma said.

'You're Norma Jacobs!' Harry said, his voice so high-pitched it was practically a yodel.

Norma's mobile rang. She swore as she saw 'unknown number' again, and red-buttoned the call.

'Harry, what are you doing here? If you don't all leave right now, I'm calling the police.'

'It was all you!' Harry roared, pointing a finger at her.

'What are you talking about?' Norma said.

'Norma, what's going on?' Marina said, moving to her side protectively.

'The reviews, the stinking, disgusting, toxic, poisonous reviews on The Good Book Appreciation Society. You wrote them. You've ruined my life! You've been trying to kill me.'

'What are you talking about, you lunatic?' Norma yelled back.

'You run the club, and according to the IP address we pulled, that disgusting, stinking review that started this whole nightmare was written right here at this address. It was you!' Harry shrieked.

'What possible benefit could there be for me to post mean reviews of members' books on my own page?' Norma yelled back. 'Why on earth would I do something so destructive to my own cause?'

'To cause controversy? Keep people coming back? Grow the group?' Phyllis offered.

'All publicity *is* good publicity,' Victoria added.

'And then you had the audacity to try blackmail me,' Harry shouted. 'Maybe that's why you did it, for the money?'

'Blackmail?' Victoria said.

'You're an extortionist,' Harry yelled.

'Wait, I'm lost, she can bend into a pretzel? What does that have to do with this?' Neil asked.

'That's a contortionist, you fool,' Clive said.

'Wait, you're saying that whoever posted that awful review of your book on the page, wrote it right here in this flat, and then they tried to blackmail you?' Norma asked.

'Don't pretend you don't know!' Harry said, his voice cracking.

Norma and Marina both snapped their heads to look at each other, eyes wide. 'Steve!' they shouted, in unison.

'That fucking idiot!' Marina said.

'Who's Steve?' Victoria asked.

'He's my ex. Her twin brother,' Norma said, pointing at Marina. 'He used to live here. We split up.'

'Steve?' Harry said, spitting the name out in disgust.

'There's something strange about your face ...' he drew a circle in the air with his finger.

'I was taking off my make-up when you arrived, but as you can see, I was interrupted,' Norma said icily.

'Wait, I don't get it,' Phyllis said, standing up. 'Why would her ex-boyfriend hack into an octogenarian's account on Facebook to slander Harry? Do you know this Steve person, Harry?'

Harry shrugged. 'I don't think so. Maybe? Do I?' he asked Norma.

'Didn't the police detective from Ludlow say someone had also tried to hack into her credit card?' Victoria asked.

Norma sighed. 'I think I know what's happened. Steve, my ex, he got himself into financial trouble, and he's been having some crazy ideas about how to get money. He may have done something really stupid.'

'Wouldn't surprise me,' Marina said. 'What a knob!'

'Okay, so I get the identity theft and the attempt to defraud old ladies online thing, but why the disgusting reviews? Why target Harry's writing?' Phyllis asked.

'You should ask him,' Norma said. 'I'm beyond understanding why Steve does anything he does.'

'Where is he?' Victoria asked.

'That fuckwit? He's staying with our dad in Croydon,' Marina offered.

'Shall I call him?' Norma asked.

'No,' Victoria said. 'I think we should pay him a visit.'

Harry

'How big would you say your brother is?' Harry asked Marina on the Tube.

'Bigger than you, but you're angry, I reckon you could take him,' Marina said.

'Are you sure he'll be home?' Clive asked, as they followed Marina down a knot of streets.

'If he's not, I doubt he would have gone very far,' Norma said.

Harry was suddenly glad he didn't have to face Steve alone. The closer they got, the more he realised that he didn't know what he was going to do when he met the man who'd ruined his life. He hadn't ever realistically thought that far ahead. He'd only wanted to hurt the guy, maybe even kill him. He'd fantasised about pummelling into his face with his fists, karate-chopping him in the neck, kicking him when he was down. Which was ridiculous; he wasn't the fighting type. But Marina was right: he was angry. Actually something beyond angry. He was outraged, he was incensed, and even more dangerously, he felt like he had very little left to lose.

A Tube journey and an Uber later, they crowded around the front door and Norma rang the bell. Harry peered over her shoulder, his heart pounding in his chest.

A man in his late seventies, his face worn and rumpled, opened the door, barefoot, wearing tracksuit pants and a grubby vest that strained around his belly. He was holding a can of lager in one hand and a lit cigarette in the other.

'Hi Steve,' Norma said.

'Norma,' he said, a surprised look on his face.

'That's your ex?' Neil asked.

'Hey, Dad,' Marina said, stepping forward.

'Hey kiddo,' Steve Senior said. 'This is quite a day for visitors. First that other bloke, now you and Norma and your entourage. Are we having a party?'

'Steve home?' Norma asked.

'What's that idiot done now?' Steve Senior asked.

'That's what we're here to find out,' Norma said.

'He's in the lounge, with some other bloke,' Steve Senior said, stepping aside to let them in.

The door opened into the kitchen. The flat was compact and grubby, infused with the smell of decades of baked beans, fryer oil and cigarette smoke. Harry followed Norma and Marina, his adrenalin spiking, his fists and his jaw clenched. They filed through into the small living room, which was stuffed just about wall-to-wall with a worn brown corduroy couch, matching arm chairs, and a large-screen TV.

Perched on a chair facing them was a man who looked remarkably like a younger, thinner version of Steve Senior. He even wore a similar tracksuit with trainers and he'd solved the problem of his receding hairline by shaving his head bald. The other man in the room was seated on the couch, his back to them.

Harry felt numb. He'd spent weeks behind the anonymity of a screen, imagining all the things he would do to get his revenge on the person who'd ruined his life. But things were different in person. He'd never hit anybody before – he didn't think he knew how. Plus he wouldn't want to break his fingers – getting words down was hard enough already. But he wanted this man to suffer, and he also needed answers: he had to find out why he'd done what he'd done. Harry's body trembled with fury and adrenalin. As they all piled into the room, jostling for space, the man on the couch turned and Harry's jaw dropped.

'Leon!' Harry shouted.

'Harry!' Leon exclaimed.

'You know him?' Victoria asked Harry, helping herself to one of the other chairs, as Phyllis perched on the arm next to her.

'He's my cop,' Harry said. 'I consult with him on my books.'

'What's your cop doing here?' Victoria asked.

'I don't know. What are you doing here, Leon?' Harry asked.

'I was about to ask you the same question,' Leon said.

'You're Harry?' Steve said, standing up and taking a step backwards.

Harry pointed at Steve and yelled, 'Leon, that's the bad reviewer. He's the one who's ruined my life. Arrest him, before he runs away!'

'Okay everybody, calm down. Steve's not going anywhere, are you Steve? Even if he wanted to, he wouldn't be able to get past you lot. Talk about bringing backup. Who are all these people, Harry?' Leon asked.

'I'm Neil, that's my husband Clive, we're the friends. That's Phyllis, she's an author from America, here for the book festival, we'd never met her before today. That's Norma, she's Steve's ex, that's Marina, she's Steve's twin sister. And that's Harry's wife, Victoria. And apparently that's Steve's dad, Steve Senior, but I suspect you've already met him,' Neil explained to Leon.

'What are you doing here, Leon?' Harry said again.

'After we met the other day I was curious, I had some questions. And I did tell you I'd follow up, and I'm a man of my word. So I made a call and the West Mercia Police Department gave me the IP address from the latest post on the page. I did a little digging and discovered your friend Steve here has been up to some dodgy dealings online, haven't you mate? So we were just having a friendly chat,' Leon said.

'Allegedly,' Steve muttered.

'From what I can gather, he's been trying to scam little old ladies out of their life savings, haven't you, our Steve?'

'Steve!' Norma yelled.

'Allegedly,' Steve said, a little louder.

'I think we'd better get you down to the station to figure this all out, mate, before this angry mob turns on you. You should be paying me protection money,' Leon said, getting to his feet. 'I accept Revolut and PayPal, don't I Harry?'

'Wait, before you cuff him and take him away, Leon, I need to know! Why have you done this?' Harry shouted at Steve.

'Allegedly,' Steve whispered.

'Why? Why slander me? Why write those disgusting, untrue reviews on Facebook? Why destroy a complete stranger?' Harry asked, his voice cracking. 'What have I ever done to you?'

'I thought you weren't on Facebook?' Norma cut in.

'I created a fake profile a while ago under some stupid name. I didn't want you to know I was in the group. I just wanted to see what the club was all about, bug. It kept growing and you were always talking about it, so I was curious. But then when he was so bloody annoying and obnoxious, I couldn't help commenting, and then we got into an argument, and the whole thing snowballed.'

'What about the blackmail?' Harry shouted.

'I don't know what you're talking about, I was just lurking, being a troll. I didn't do anything illegal,' Steve yelled back.

'Are we telling porky pies, mate?' Leon said. 'Here's what I think. I don't think it was innocent at all. I think you were on the group under a fake profile because you were trying to scam some poor unsuspecting old ladies out of their life savings. And then you got into it with old Harry here, and saw the opportunity to hustle *him* out of some cash too.'

'Allegedly,' Steve said again.

'Just saying allegedly all the time doesn't mean you didn't do it,' Leon said.

'You can't prove any of this,' Steve said.

'That's where you're wrong, mate. Once our digital forensics team logs into your computer, I bet we'll see all of it.'

'Did you even bother to read any of my books before you reviewed them?' Harry shouted, his voice cracking.

'Ahem, our books,' Leon said.

'Ahem, my books that you consulted on,' Harry corrected him.

'I read *Monday Never Comes*. Honestly, my manuscript is better,' Steve said.

'You have a manuscript?' Phyllis asked.

'Your manuscript?' Norma echoed.

'I didn't quit Amazon to finish my book, Norma. I'd already finished it and sent it off to a bunch of publishers and agents.'

'Why didn't you tell me?' Norma said.

'I was expecting them to call and offer me the book deal of a lifetime, Norms. That's why I quit. I was so sure it was happening. I was going to surprise you, but of course, that's not how it went down. I was so naïve. The rejection letters started pouring in. So I sent the manuscript off to even more agents and publishers, and then I got even more rejection letters. I tried to start another book, the one about gambling. But my confidence ... I was struggling to write. Seventy-two rejection letters,' Steve said.

Phyllis whistled.

'Why does this narcissistic wanker get to have his mediocre books published, but nobody will even look at mine? It's not fair. I put years into that book, quit my job over it and nobody else will hire me now. And then you go and shit a book out in a heartbeat, like it's no big deal, Norma ...'

'I knew my manuscript was going to upend you, that's why I never told you about it,' Norma said.

'I was a dick, Norms. The truth is, your manuscript isn't as bad as I said it was. You shouldn't listen to me. It needs work, obviously, but it's solid.'

'When are you going to arrest him, Leon? He's clearly guilty,' Harry shouted.

'Your brother doesn't seem to be a very good person,' Clive said to Marina.

'He's a total douche,' Marina sighed. Come on, bruv, I'll come with you to the station, I've got a lawyer on speed dial. Boss, I may be late for work tomorrow,' Marina said to Neil.

'Take all the time you need,' Neil said.

Norma

'How's your gourmet dog?' Marina asked, looking down on a busy lunch-time London from the forty-seventh floor rooftop.

'Pretty average, thanks. Your gourmet nachos?' Norma asked.

'Cardboard-esque.'

'How did you find this place?' Norma asked.

'I dated this woman who works for the PR company who handles the food truck's business. I heard they had to take the truck apart bolt by bolt, send all the parts up in the service lift, then reassemble the whole thing up here.'

'Seems counterintuitive to come up with such an epic plan and such a monumental location, and then serve un-cheesy nachos and average hot dogs.'

Marina pointed at a frame hanging on the side of the truck. 'See that? When they'd finished rebuilding the truck, those were the parts they were left with. They weren't about to unbuild it and rebuild it again, and it doesn't need to drive, so they just stuck 'em in there.'

'Screw loose,' Norma said.

'They say it's the highest food truck in the world.'

'Speaking of high, how's Steve?' Norma asked.

'I bailed that dickwad out. It was my turn, I guess, after all the times he's done it for me.'

'Family tax,' Norma said, and Marina nodded. 'Every time I start to feel sorry for him, or second-guess our break-up, my next credit card bill arrives and gives me thousands of fresh reasons not to.'

'Wonder what they'll do to him?' Marina asked.

'Fool sent me another voice note,' Norma said, reaching for her phone, scrolling to find it, then pressing play.

> Norms, it was great seeing you at my dad's, although I'll be the first to admit that the circumstances weren't ideal. I swear, I was just trying to figure out how to pay off our debt, but then things got complicated. But I did it all for us, for our future. I hope you can see that.

'There's another one, listen to this,' Norma said.

> Me again. They say the case will be wrapped up in the court system for months, but they take online fraud seriously here. So Marina's lawyer says they'll probably try make an example of me. She reckons I might get a little jail time. Or if I'm lucky, a suspended sentence with community service. I was hoping they'd send me to teach people how to use computers, so I can put my IT skills to work, but in light of my history, it's unlikely to involve anything digital. I'll probably have to pick up trash or serve in a soup kitchen. Whatever happens, I'm hoping we can try figure us out on the other side of all of this, Norms. I miss you. I'm sorry about everything. By the way, my proposal still stands. We get conjugal visits if we're married. And maybe I'll try my hand at another book, plenty of time and no PlayStation in there.

'What a twat!' Marina said.

'Your brother makes a terrible criminal.'

'How's the hit-and-run lady?' Marina asked.

'Edna? Back on her feet, doing physio, coming right slowly. She'll be okay, if she can remember to look the right way before crossing the street.'

'Steve never got a penny out of her, hey?' Marina asked.

'Not for want of trying,' Norma said.

'You've got to give him an A-plus for effort.'

'Or for arsehole.'

Norma's phone rang. She glanced at the screen: 'Unknown number again!' she said as she flashed her screen at Marina.

'Journos?' Marina asked.

'Probably.'

'Will they never give up?'

'They're relentless. This one hasn't stopped calling today. Let me get rid of her once and for all,' Norma said, answering the call with an unfriendly, abrupt hello.

'Ms Jacobs, please don't hang up again,' a woman said.

'What do you want?' Norma asked, her voice sharp.

'I know I've been calling you like a crazy person. I just need thirty seconds of your time. My name is Laetitia Pope and I'm a literary agent at Fabian & Co. I thought I'd give your number one last try.'

'You're a literary agent? I thought you were a journalist.'

'What made you think that? I'm calling about *Train Smash*. We spoke briefly yesterday, but you keep hanging up on me. I've been desperately trying to get hold of you.'

'My manuscript? Um, that's a working title.' Hearing her title said out loud made her cringe.

'I'm not sure if any other agents have gotten hold of you yet? I saw the BookTok about your manuscript, and I got excited when I saw the post, and how popular it's been.'

'There's a BookTok about *Train Smash*?'

'You didn't know? It has well over fifty-five thousand likes.'

'Bavinga and Britttennay!' Norma said.

'I beg your pardon?' Laetitia said.

'I'm ... I ...' Norma had no words.

'BookTok is desperate to have it published, you should see the comments. So I wondered if you'd be keen to meet to see if we can't find you a publisher to make BookTok's dreams a reality?'

'Is this some kind of joke?' Norma asked.

'Not even for half a second,' the woman said.

'I would love that,' Norma said, trying to keep her voice from wobbling.

'Fantastic. I'll message you so we can set it up. Just please don't block my number,' Laetitia laughed.

'I'm so sorry,' Norma said, 'honestly, if I'd known ...'

'Chat soon, I hope,' Laetitia said, laughing again before hanging up.

'That did not sound like an annoying journalist,' Marina said.

'I might actually get published,' Norma said to her, eyes wide.

'You didn't tell me you'd submitted your manuscript.'

'I hadn't. All I can think is that Bavinga must have taken the manuscript out of my desk drawer after Britttennay's birthday party, and gotten Britttennay to make a BookTok about it.'

'Ace! That means I've just eaten an average lunch from the world's tallest rooftop food truck with a published author.'

'Shortly after bailing your brother out of jail. You're living the life.'

'My CV is overflowing. We'll have to celebrate with some day-drinking. I'll go get us a couple of average, over-priced food-truck cocktails. Hey Norms, does this mean you're going to be rich and famous, and your money troubles will be over?'

'You're joking, right? Nobody makes any money in publishing. It looks like it's going to have to be accounting again for a bit. Unless you want to teach me how to drive a forklift? I could be your intern next?'

'Nah, I'm done with that, I quit this morning.'

'Neil will be devastated. Please tell me you didn't quit so you could write a book?'

'God no! Writing is for mugs and AI, innit. I'm thinking of going to pick dates in Turkey.'

'Wait, is that a euphemism?'

'I couldn't say,' Marina said.

TWO YEARS LATER

THE GOOD BOOK APPRECIATION SOCIETY

MEMBERS: 326 703

Michelle Zanders: I picked this book up at book club last week. I had to fight two other members to get it first, but I would have fought to the death. I was so curious about it, as I remember all that hullaballoo here on the page a few years ago.

Cancelled, by Harry Shields. A no-holds-barred account of his experience as an author who behaved so badly that he found himself cancelled across social media. He then fell out with the press, embarrassed himself in a video that went viral on social media, lost his friends, destroyed his marriage, and was suspected of attempted murder.

As a school teacher, I'm fascinated by how social media has changed the way we interact with each other. I see an increase in stupidity and a decrease in kindness, and this book is a case study in that, as social media becomes more toxic and narcissistic, with long-ranging social consequences.

I enjoyed this book in as much as one can enjoy a book that highlights how the world is falling apart around our ears. I despair.

COMMENTS:

Lucille Goby: Look at this, @Dax Goby, we should definitely get this book. Remember him?

Geneva Fulverton: You enjoyed it? I hated it. In fact I marked it as DNF* (did not finish) and gave it one star on Goodreads. I found it indulgent, and having witnessed the author's behaviour on this page back then, it smacked to me of a (still) vain and hollow attempt at redemption, without enough ownership of his part in what happened. It's easy to blame everything from cancel culture, to a reviewer, to mob justice, to society, the economy and social media, when this kind of thing happens to you. The real hard work comes in doing enough inward exploration to understand your own role and culpability in it. And I don't feel this author has done enough of that.

Bernard Phillips: ...

Harry

Life was a funny old thing, Harry thought, as he watched the English countryside fly past out the train window. He was on his way back from giving a guest lecture on cancel culture at a Welsh university, followed by panels and a book signing at a literary festival in Wales.

The London Festival of Books had never invited him back, and probably never would, and it was unlikely he'd ever be nominated for another Golden Page Award, or be represented by Myra Berelowitz again, but he'd come to terms with the shift his literary career had taken. And slowly but surely, as his book had gained traction, and he'd started making the rounds on the motivational speaking circuit, the literary world had begun to invite him back in.

It turned out that Victoria, Neil and Clive, Phyllis, Norma and even Leon had all been right: he'd just needed to wait for the dust to settle, then get busy with a new project.

Sure, he still had plenty of haters, and regularly had to answer for his actions during Q and A sessions at any talk or panel, but as his therapist said, the only way out was through. Plus controversy did draw a crowd and was good for book sales.

Harry returned his attention to his tablet and continued scrolling The Good Book Appreciation Society Facebook Page. His stomach lurched as his eye snagged on a post about his new book. He scanned it quickly, then made his way through the comments.

That Geneva Fulverton had a cheek, Harry thought. She'd always had it in for him. Who did she think she was? What did she even know about being cancelled or what he'd been through? What it does to you, how it changes everything. How he'd almost lost everything. Victoria had only moved back in with him a year later. Harry logged out of Facebook, then logged back in as Bernard Phillips, the retired octogenarian orthodontist from Bridgeport, Connecticut. The members always listened to him. He started typing out his response.

'I got you a coffee,' Norma said, handing him a lukewarm cup as she slipped past and settled into the window seat beside him.

'That's kind, thank you,' Harry said.

'No worries, after the stuff they were serving in the green room at the festival I thought this might not be so bad,' she said, taking a sip, then pulling a face. 'I was wrong.'

'How was your panel?' Harry asked.

'Incredible. I still find it hard to believe that I wrote one book, let alone two. And it feels surreal that anyone wants to read them or hear me bang on about them.'

'I know what you mean.'

'You weren't planning on responding to that comment, were you?' Norma asked, pointing at the Good Book Appreciation Society post open on his tablet.

'Of course not,' Harry said, quickly turning his tablet off. 'I was just having a look to see what people were saying.'

THE GOOD BOOK APPRECIATION SOCIETY

MEMBERS: 347 489

Avukile Chingwita: Is anyone else here a big fan of the acknowledgements in books? Especially when the author has a little fun or makes a personal note or in-joke.

I always read them. I like the insight into the author's inner workings or what went into the project. And I always read every name, which is weird because it's not like I'll know any of them. I've never met the author's husband or cousin, or even heard of their beta reader, editor or agent. But I love it when they thank their junior school English teacher, or include a list of all the people in the world who were of use, or of absolutely no use at all in their publishing journey. I like it when they call people by their nicknames, tell us what they ate on their toast while they were writing. That kind of thing. Share your Spotify playlist and your underwear size, if you want. If you ask me, the more in-jokes the better.

COMMENTS:

Michelle Zanders: I agree, I also read all of them. I once read a book where the author named his wife and children, and went on to say that without them, the book would have been finished two years earlier. I love that kind of stuff.

Geneva Fulverton: I'm going to start looking more closely at acknowledgements. I never thought to read them before.

Karen Granger: Sometimes the Kindle and Audible versions of books don't have them. That's why I prefer real paper books. #BooksMatter

Ruth Burstein: One of my favourite parts of a book. I also stay in the cinema until all the credits have finished rolling. I feel like everyone who worked on a creative project deserves credit, and as the reader or viewer, we owe them an extra minute of our time.

Helen Moffett: My favourite too! I always read them closely.

Chris Colt: Hell yes.

[Freda Kruger has reported this comment.]

ACKNOWLEDGEMENTS

I too love the acknowledgements in books, so I'll try not screw this one up, or forget anyone, I hear that's practically cause for divorce in LA.

Thanks to every member of The Good Book Appreciation Society, even the ones who've stormed out in a huff over the years. It's my happy place online and as you can see, great inspiration.

So much appreciation to the members who gave permission to use their posts and comments in this book; Cathy Park Kelly, Kelly Vos, Patricia Balsdon, Sandy Fisher, Bethany Culbert, Jennifer Strickland, Sally Smith, Julia Fraser. And S. It's very generous of you. Clearly the saying is true, you could not make this shit up – your words are better than anything I could have come up with.

Also apologies if any other comments or fragments of comments have slipped through that I haven't asked permission to use. It was unintentional. Please do let me know in case we sell enough to go to reprint, so I can correct my error. Also please tell your friends to buy this book, so we can sell enough to go to reprint, so I can correct my errors.

Thanks to Andrea Nattrass, my publisher at Pan Macmillan, I've been waiting patiently to have you publish me since that time in 2013 when you handed me the unpublished manuscript I left behind on stage at an event, because I am a loskop. It was worth the wait.

Thank you, Shakti, Nkanyezi, Zodwa, Jane and the entirely brilliant Pan publishing team, you were behind this book from day one, when not many other people were. I'm grateful for you.

Thank you Caitlin for the best cover ever.

Chryssa, you're never far from me. I thought of you and your wine and book clubs a lot writing this. I think you would have enjoyed this one. I miss you, my pel.

Thank you, Megan, for listening to me bang on above and below water, about how hard it was to write this when it was hard, and how fun it was when it was fun. Just kidding, it was only ever hard. And thank you for starting and naming our little IRL book club, which has since taken over a lot of my life. (Also thanks to our other original members, Mel, Mark, Gareth, Laurel, Nicky and Karin. Also Iain, although you were never actually a real member, and you know it!)

Thank you, Edyth for being an exceptional beta reader, friend, silent-invisible-GBAS-admin-partner and social media lurker.

Thank you Rahla, just thank you, for the friendship and the beta read of this and that other novel that cannot not be mentioned.

Vanessa, thank you for your read and your support and friendship.

Big thanks to Oli Munson, the best agent, and his team at A.M. Heath.

Thank you, Helen Moffett, an incredible editor and great friend, I know, I know, I'm supposed to just pick one, but I can't, you are equally both.

Thank you Sarah, my book person. So much encouragement, support, love and advice, so many conversations and so much plotting, weeding and crying, plus a cameo. There's no way in any cold dark hell I could do this without you and Mrs H.

And thank you to my Cloud, for giving me the time and support to do this ridiculously time-consuming thing.

To join the real-life Good Book Appreciation Society,
an online book club with over 23 000 members, simply search
for The Good Book Appreciation Society on Facebook.